Praise for

MY NOT SO PERFECT LIFE

"A sparkling, witty novel about social media and the stories we tell ourselves." —*People* (Book of the Week)

"You'll relate hard and root harder for Londoner Katie, whose quarterlife crisis feels even worse thanks to the Insta-perfect people all around her." —*Cosmopolitan*

"Something else separates this comic novel from the usual fare. . . . The soul of this book concerns female friendship and its dynamics. . . . [It] has a touch of real wisdom in its slapstick hand that will satisfy Kinsella die-hards as well as new readers." —*The Washington Post*

"With both warm-hearted and laugh-out-loud moments, Sophie Kinsella's *My Not So Perfect Life* was a joy to read. . . . Katie is relatable, bright and quirky—you'll find yourself cheering for her from the start, even as she learns that a perfect life isn't always what it seems, or what it's cracked up to be. Themes of friendship, love and living your true life rise to the top in this must-read stand-alone romantic comedy."
—"Happy Ever After," *USA Today*

"The book is fun, as Kinsella's books are, but it delivers a strong positive message, as well. . . . Kinsella creates a solid, likable character—one that I got to know and root for throughout the book." —Fairfield *Daily Republic*

"This one is [not only] a comic romance, but a family novel and even a business novel. . . . You'd be silly to bet against [our heroine], obviously, but the happy ending is well earned, not forced." —*Sullivan County Democrat*

"This is a really funny and relatable story about working women, women's relationships with each other and one plucky heroine's journey. . . . A perfect pick-me-up."
—*The Parkersburg News and Sentinel*

"Many laugh-out-loud hilarious moments in this feel-good novel about social media and personal branding, and the hectic realities behind our perfect online lives." —*Bustle*

"Pure escapist fun." —*PopSugar*

"Katie is a winning heroine. . . . Kinsella creates characters that are well-rounded, quirky, and a complete joy to read."
—*Kirkus Reviews* (starred review)

"With her signature humor, bestselling author Kinsella explores the frequent disconnect between perception and reality in modern life. . . . Driven by Katie's witty observations and numerous missteps as she attempts to reconcile various aspects of her identity, this novel is smartly satirical and entertaining." —*Publishers Weekly*

"Sophie Kinsella keeps her finger on the cultural pulse, while leaving me giddy with laughter. I loved it." —JOJO MOYES

"This latest stand-alone from best-selling author Kinsella is top-notch, thanks to a lovable, slightly flawed leading lady, many true-life situations, and loads of giggle-inducing humor. As Bridget Jones would say, 'Well done!' " *—Library Journal*

"Kinsella delivers yet another outstanding novel full of the wit and charm that her fans expect and adore. . . . A perfect combination of fun, laughable moments rounded out with some deep-seated family and relationship issues." *—Booklist*

"Sophie Kinsella's latest book about a young woman facing unexpected and unplanned-for career challenges introduces us to charming heroine Cat/Katie. Katie's pluck and perseverance, as well as her unfailing sense of humor and hope for the future, take her back and forth from her country home to her beloved London. There just might be a fabulous job and an amazing future (not to mention a new love interest) for her there . . . if she can just endure her horrible boss!"

—Bookreporter

By Sophie Kinsella

Confessions of a Shopaholic
Shopaholic Takes Manhattan
Shopaholic Ties the Knot
Can You Keep a Secret?
Shopaholic & Sister
The Undomestic Goddess
Shopaholic & Baby
Remember Me?
Twenties Girl
Mini Shopaholic
I've Got Your Number
Wedding Night
Shopaholic to the Stars
Finding Audrey
Shopaholic to the Rescue
My Not So Perfect Life

MY NOT SO PERFECT LIFE

Sophie Kinsella

MY NOT SO PERFECT LIFE

A Novel

THE DIAL PRESS
NEW YORK

My Not So Perfect Life is a work of fiction. Names, characters, places, and incidents are the products of the author's imagination or are used fictitiously. Any resemblance to actual events, locales, or persons, living or dead, is entirely coincidental.

2018 Dial Press Trade Paperback Edition

Published in the United States by The Dial Press, an imprint of Random House, a division of Penguin Random House LLC, New York.

THE DIAL PRESS and the HOUSE colophon are registered trademarks of Penguin Random House LLC.

Originally published in hardcover in the United States by The Dial Press, an imprint of Random House, a division of Penguin Random House LLC, in 2017.

Published in the United Kingdom by Bantam Press, an imprint of Transworld Publishers, a Penguin Random House UK company.

LIBRARY OF CONGRESS CATALOGING-IN-PUBLICATION DATA
Names: Kinsella, Sophie, author.
Title: My not so perfect life : a novel / Sophie Kinsella.
Description: New York : Dial Press, [2017]
Identifiers: LCCN 2016025629 | ISBN 9780812987713 (trade paperback) | ISBN 9780812998276 (ebook)
Subjects: LCSH: Man-woman relationships—Fiction. | BISAC: FICTION / Humorous. | FICTION / Romance / Contemporary. | FICTION / Contemporary Women. | GSAFD: Love stories.
Classification: LCC PR6073.I246 M9 2017 | DDC 823/.914—dc23
LC record available at https://lccn.loc.gov/2016025629

Printed in the United States of America on acid-free paper

randomhousebooks.com

4 6 8 9 7 5

Book design by Dana Leigh Blanchette
Title-page and page 1 illustration: © iStockphoto.com
Illustration on page 177 adapted from iStockphoto.com images

To Nicki Kennedy

PART ONE

CHAPTER ONE

First: It could be worse. As commutes go, it could be a lot worse, and I must keep remembering this. Second: It's worth it. I *want* to live in London; I *want* to do this; and commuting is part of the deal. It's part of the London experience, like Tate Modern.

(Actually, it's not much like Tate Modern. Bad example.)

My dad always says: If you can't run with the big dogs, stay under the porch. And I want to run with the big dogs. That's why I'm here.

Anyway, my twenty-minute walk to the station is fine. Enjoyable, even. The gray December air is like iron in my chest, but I feel good. The day's begun. I'm on my way.

My coat's pretty warm, even though it cost £9.99 and came from the flea market. It had a label in it, CHRISTIN BIOR, but I cut it out as soon as I got home. You can't work where I work and have CHRISTIN BIOR in your coat. You could have a genuine vintage Christian Dior label. Or something Japanese. Or maybe no label because you make your clothes yourself out of retro fabrics that you source at Alfies Antiques.

But *not* CHRISTIN BIOR.

As I get near Catford Bridge, I start to feel a knot of tension. I *really* don't want to be late today. My boss has started throwing all sorts of hissy fits about people "swanning in at all times," so I left an extra twenty minutes early, in case it was a bad day.

I can already see: It's a god-awful day.

They've been having a lot of problems on our line recently and keep canceling trains with no warning. Trouble is, in London rush hour, you can't just *cancel trains*. What are all the people who were planning to get on that train supposed to do? Evaporate?

As I pass through the ticket barrier I can already see the answer. They're crowded on the platform, squinting up at the information screen, jostling for position, peering down the line, scowling at one another and ignoring one another, all at the same time.

Oh *God*. They must have canceled at least two trains, because this looks like three trainloads of people, all waiting for the next one, clustered near the edge of the platform at strategic points. It's mid-December, but there's no Christmas spirit here. Everyone's too tense and cold and Monday-morning-ish. The only festive touch consists of a few miserable-looking fairy lights and a series of warning announcements about holiday transport.

Screwing up my nerve, I join the throng and exhale in relief as a train pulls into the station. Not that I'll *get on* this train (Get on the first train? That would be ridiculous). There are people squashed up against the steamy windows, and as the doors slide open, only one woman gets off, looking pretty crumpled as she tries to extricate herself.

But even so, the crowd surges forward, and somehow a load of people insert themselves inside the train and it pulls away, and I'm that much farther forward on the platform. Now I just have to keep my place and *not* let that scrawny guy with gelled hair edge in front of me. I've taken out my earbuds so I can listen for announcements and stay poised and vigilant.

Commuting in London is basically warfare. It's a constant campaign of claiming territory; inching forward; never relaxing for a moment. Because if you do, someone will step past you. Or step *on* you.

Exactly eleven minutes later, the next train pulls in. I head forward with the crowd, trying to block out the soundtrack of angry exclamations: "Can you move down?" "There's room inside!" "They just need to move *down*!"

I've noticed that people inside trains have completely different expressions from people on platforms—especially the ones who have managed to get a seat. They're the ones who got over the mountains to Switzerland. They won't even look up. They maintain this guilty, defiant refusal to engage: *I know you're out there; I know it's awful and I'm safe inside, but I suffered too, so let me just read my Kindle without bloody guilt-tripping me, OK?*

People are pushing and pushing, and someone's actually shoving me—I can feel fingers on my back—and suddenly I'm stepping onto the train floor. Now I need to grab onto a pole or a handle—anything—and use it as leverage. Once your foot's on the train, you're in.

A man way behind me seems very angry—I can hear extra-loud shouting and cursing. And suddenly there's a groundswell behind me, like a tsunami of people. I've only experienced this a couple of times, and it's terrifying. I'm being pushed forward without even touching the ground, and as the train doors close I end up squeezed between two guys—one in a suit and one in a tracksuit—and a girl eating a panini.

We're so tightly wedged that she's holding her panini about three inches away from my face. Every time she takes a bite, I get a waft of pesto. But I studiously ignore it. And the girl. And the men. Even though I can feel the tracksuit guy's warm thigh against mine and count the stubbly hairs on his neck. As the train starts moving we're constantly bumped against one another, but no one even makes eye contact. I think if you make eye contact on the tube, they call the police or something.

To distract myself, I try to plan the rest of my journey. When I get to Waterloo East, I'll check out which tube line is running best. I can do Jubilee-District (takes ages) or Jubilee-Central (longer walk at the other end) or Overground (even longer walk at the other end).

And, yes, if I'd *known* I was going to end up working in Chiswick, I wouldn't have chosen to rent in Catford. But when I first came to London, it was to do an internship in east London. (They called it "Shoreditch" in the ad. It *so* wasn't Shoreditch.) Catford was cheap and it wasn't too far, and now I just can't face west London prices, and the commute's not *that* bad—

"Aargh!" I shriek as the train jolts and I'm thrown violently forward. The girl has been thrown too, and her hand shoots up toward my face and before I know it, my open mouth has landed on the end of her panini.

Wh—*What*?

I'm so shocked, I can't react. My mouth is full of warm, doughy bread and melted mozzarella. How did this even *happen*?

Instinctively my teeth clench shut, a move I immediately regret. Although . . . what else was I supposed to do? Nervously, I raise my eyes to hers, my mouth still full.

"Sorry," I mumble, but it comes out "Obble."

"What the *fuck*?" The girl addresses the carriage incredulously. "She's stealing my breakfast!"

My head's sweating with stress. This is bad. *Bad*. What do I do now? Bite off the panini? (Not good.) Just let it fall out of my mouth? (Even worse. Urgh.) There's no good way out of this situation, none.

At last, I bite fully through the panini, my face burning with embarrassment. Now I have to chew my way through a mouthful of someone else's claggy bread, with everyone watching.

"I'm really sorry," I say awkwardly to the girl, as soon as I've managed to swallow. "I hope you enjoy the rest."

"I don't want it *now*." She glares at me. "It's got your germs on it."

"Well, I don't want your germs either! It wasn't my fault; I fell on it."

"You *fell* on it," she echoes, so skeptically that I stare at her.

"Yes! Of course! I mean, what do you think—that I did that on *purpose*?"

"Who knows?" She puts a protective hand around the rest of her panini, as though I might launch myself at her and bite another chunk off. "All kinds of weird people in London."

"I'm not weird!"

"You can 'fall' on me anytime, love," puts in the guy in the tracksuit with a smirk. "Only don't chew," he adds, and laughter comes from all around the carriage.

My face flames even redder, but I'm *not* going to react. In fact, this conversation is over.

For the next fifteen minutes I gaze sternly ahead, trying to exist in my own little bubble. At Waterloo East, we all disgorge from the train, and I breathe in the cold, fumey air with relief. I stride as quickly as I can to the Underground, opt for Jubilee-District, and join the crowd round the door. As I do so, I glance at my watch and quell a sigh. I've been traveling for forty-five minutes already, and I'm not even *nearly* there.

As someone steps on my foot with a stiletto, I have a sudden flashback to Dad pushing open our kitchen door, stepping outside, spreading his arms wide to take in the view of fields and endless sky, and saying, "Shortest commute in the world, darling. Shortest commute in the world." When I was little, I had no idea what he meant, but now—

"Move down! Will you move *down*?" A man beside me on the platform is yelling so loudly, I flinch. The Underground train has arrived and there's the usual battle between the people inside the carriage, who think it's totally crammed, and the people outside, who are measuring the empty spaces with forensic, practiced eyes and reckon you could fit another twenty people in, easy.

Finally I get on the tube, and fight my way off at Westminster, and wait for the District line, then chug along to Turnham Green. As I get out of the tube station, I glance at my watch and start running. Shit. I barely have ten minutes.

Our office is a large pale building called Phillimore House.

As I get near, I slow to a walk, my heart still pounding. My left heel has a massive blister on it, but the main thing is, I've made it. I'm on time. Magically, there's a lift waiting, and I step in, trying to smooth down my hair, which flew in all directions as I was pegging it down Chiswick High Road. The whole commute took an hour and twenty minutes in all, which actually could be worse—

"Wait!" An imperious voice makes me freeze. Across the lobby is striding a familiar figure. She has long legs, high-heeled boots, expensive highlights, a biker jacket, and a short skirt in an orange textured fabric which makes every other garment in the lift look suddenly old and obvious. Especially my £8.99 black jersey skirt.

She has amazing eyebrows. Some people are just granted amazing eyebrows, and she's one of them.

"Horrendous journey," she says as she gets into the lift. Her voice is husky, coppery, grown-up sounding. It's a voice that knows stuff, that doesn't have time for fools. She jabs the floor number with a manicured finger and we start to rise. "Absolutely horrendous," she reiterates. "The lights would *not* change at the Chiswick Lane junction. It took me twenty-five minutes to get here from home. Twenty-five minutes!"

She gives me one of her swooping, eagle-like gazes, and I realize she's waiting for a response.

"Oh," I say feebly. "Poor you."

The lift doors open and she strides out. A moment later I follow, watching her haircut fall perfectly back into shape with every step and breathing in that distinctive scent she wears (bespoke, created for her at Annick Goutal in Paris on her fifth-wedding-anniversary trip).

This is my boss. This is Demeter. The woman with the perfect life.

I'm not exaggerating. When I say Demeter has the perfect life, believe me, it's true. *Everything you could want out of life, she has*. Job, family, general coolness. Tick, tick, tick. Even her name. It's so distinctive, she doesn't need to bother with her surname (Farlowe). She's just *Demeter*. Like *Madonna*. "Hi," I'll hear her saying on the phone, in that confident, louder-than-average voice of hers. "It's De-*meeee*-ter."

She's forty-five and she's been executive creative director at Cooper Clemmow for just over a year. Cooper Clemmow is a branding and strategy agency, and we have some pretty big clients—therefore Demeter's a pretty big deal. Her office is full of awards, and framed photos of her with illustrious people, and displays of products she's helped to brand.

She's tall and slim and has shiny brunette hair and, as I already mentioned, amazing eyebrows. I don't know what she earns, but she lives in Shepherd's Bush in this stunning house which apparently she paid over two million for—my friend Flora told me.

Flora also told me that Demeter had her sitting-room floor imported from France and it's reclaimed oak parquet and cost a *fortune*. Flora's the closest in rank to me—she's a creative associate—and she's a constant source of gossip about Demeter.

I even went to look at Demeter's house once, not because I'm a sad stalker, but because I happened to be in the area and I knew the address, and, you know, why *not* check out your boss's house if you get the chance? (OK, full disclosure: I only knew the street name. I googled the number of the house when I got there.)

Of course, it's heart-achingly tasteful. It looks like a house in a magazine. It *is* a house in a magazine. It's been profiled in *Livingetc,* with Demeter standing in her all-white kitchen, looking elegant and creative in a retro-print top.

I stood and stared at it for a while. Not exactly lusting—it was more wistful than that. *Wisting*. The front door is a gorgeous gray-green—Farrow & Ball or Little Greene, I'm sure—with an old-looking lion's-head knocker and elegant pale-gray stone steps leading up to it. The rest of the house is pretty impressive too—all painted window frames and slatted blinds and a glimpse of a wooden tree house in the back garden—but it was the front door that mesmerized me. And the steps. Imagine having a set of beautiful stone steps to descend every day, like a princess in a fairy tale. You'd start every morning off feeling fabulous.

Two cars on the front forecourt. A gray Audi and a black Volvo SUV, all shiny and new. Everything Demeter has is either shiny and new and on-trend (designer juicing machine) or old and authentic and on-trend (huge antique wooden necklace that she got in South Africa). I think "authentic" might be Demeter's favorite word in the whole world; she uses it about thirty times a day.

Demeter is married, *of course,* and she has two children, *of course:* a boy called Hal and a girl called Coco. She has zillions of friends she's known "forever" and is always going to parties and events and design awards. Sometimes she'll sigh and say it's her third night out that week and exclaim, "Glutton for punishment!" as she changes into her Miu Miu shoes. (I take quite a lot of her Net-A-Porter packaging to recycling for her, so I know what labels she wears. Miu Miu. Marni in the sale. Dries van Noten. Also quite a lot of Zara.) But then, as she's heading out, her eyes will start sparkling and the next thing, the photos are all over Cooper Clemmow's Facebook page and Twitter account and everywhere: Demeter in a cool black top (probably Helmut Lang; she likes him too), holding a wineglass and beaming with famous designer types and being perfect.

And, here's the thing: I'm not *envious*. Not exactly. I don't want to be Demeter. I don't want her things. I mean, I'm only twenty-six; what would I do with a Volvo SUV?

But when I look at her, I feel this pinprick of . . . something, and I think: Could that be me? Could that ever be me? When I've earned it, could I have Demeter's life? It's not just the things but the confidence. The style. The sophistication. The connections. If it took me twenty years I wouldn't mind—in fact, I'd be ecstatic! If you told me: *Guess what, if you work hard, in twenty years' time you'll be leading that life,* I'd put my head down right now and get to it.

It's impossible, though. It could never happen. People talk about "ladders" and "career structures" and "rising through the ranks," but I can't see any ladder leading me to Demeter's life, however hard I work.

I mean, two million pounds for a house?

Two *million*?

I worked it out once. Just suppose a bank ever lent me that kind of money—which they wouldn't—on my current salary, it would take me 193.4 years to pay it off (and, you know, live).

When that number appeared on my calculator screen I actually laughed out loud a bit hysterically. People talk about the generation gap. Generation chasm, more like. Generation Grand Canyon. There isn't any ladder big enough to stretch from my place in life to Demeter's place in life, not without something extraordinary happening, like the lottery, or rich parents, or some genius website idea that makes my fortune. (Don't think I'm not trying. I spend every night attempting to invent a new kind of bra, or low-calorie caramel. No joy yet.)

So anyway. I can't aim for Demeter's life, not exactly. But I can aim for some of it. The achievable bits. I can watch her, study her. I can learn how to be like her.

And also, crucially, I can learn how to be *not* like her.

Because, didn't I mention? She's a nightmare. She's perfect *and* she's a nightmare. Both.

I'm just powering up my computer when Demeter comes striding into our open-plan office, sipping her soy latte. "People," she says. "People, listen up."

This is another of Demeter's favorite words: "people." She comes into our space and says, "People," in that drama-school voice, and we all have to stop what we're doing, as though there's going to be an important group announcement. When, *in fact,* what she wants is something very specific that only one person knows, but since she can barely remember which of us does what, or even what our names are, she has to ask everyone.

All right, this is a slight exaggeration. But not much. I've never met anyone as terrible at remembering names as Demeter. Flora told me once that Demeter actually has a real visual problem, some facial-recognition thing, but she won't admit it, because she reckons it doesn't affect her ability to do her job.

Well, news flash: It does.

And second news flash: What does facial recognition have to do with remembering a name properly? I've been here seven months, and I swear she's still not sure whether I'm Cath or Cat.

I'm Cat, in fact. Cat short for Catherine. Because . . . well. It's a cool nickname. It's short and punchy. It's modern. It's London. It's me. Cat. Cat Brenner.

Hi, I'm Cat.

Hi, I'm Catherine, but call me Cat.

OK, full disclosure: It's not *absolutely* me. Not yet. I'm still part-Katie. I've been calling myself "Cat" since I started this job, but for some reason it hasn't fully taken. Sometimes I don't respond as quickly as I should when people call out "Cat." I hesitate before I sign it, and one hideous time I had to scrub out a "K" I'd started writing on one of those big office birthday cards. Luckily no one saw. I mean, who doesn't know their own *name*?

But I'm determined to be Cat. I *will* be Cat. It's my all-new London name. I've had three jobs in my life (OK, two were internships), and at each new step I've reinvented myself a bit more. Changing from Katie to Cat is just the latest stage.

Katie is the home me. The Somerset me. A rosy-cheeked, curly-haired country girl who lives in jeans and wellies and a fleece which came free with a delivery of sheep food. A girl whose entire social life is the local pub or maybe the Ritzy in Warreton. A girl I've left behind.

As long as I can remember, I've wanted out of Somerset. I've wanted London. I never had boy bands on my bedroom wall; I had the tube map. Posters of the London Eye and the Gherkin.

The first internship I managed to scrape was in Birmingham, and that's a big city too. It's got the shops, the glamour, the buzz . . . but it's not *London*. It doesn't have that *Londonness* that makes my heart soar. The skyline. The history. Walking past Big Ben and hearing it chime, in real life. Standing in the same tube stations that you've seen in a million films about the Blitz. Feeling that you're in one of the best cities in the world, no question, hands down. Living in London is like living in a movie set, from the Dickensian backstreets to the glinting tower blocks to the secret garden squares. You can be anyone you want to be.

There's not much in my life that would score in the top ten of any global survey. I don't have a top-ten job or wardrobe or flat. But I live in a top-ten city. Living in London is something that people all over the world would love to do, and now I'm here. And that's why I don't care if my commute is the journey from hell and I don't care if my bedroom is about three foot square. *I'm here*.

I couldn't get here straightaway. The only offer I had after uni was in a tiny marketing firm in Birmingham. So I moved up there and immediately started creating a new personality. I had bangs cut. I started straightening my hair every day and putting it in a smart knot. I bought myself a pair of black glasses with clear lenses. I looked different. I felt different. I even started doing my makeup differently, with super-defined lip liner every day and black liquid eyeliner in flicky curves.

(It took me a whole weekend to learn how to do that flicky eyeliner. It's an actual skill, like trigonometry—so what I wonder is, why don't they teach *that* at school? If I ran the country there'd be courses in things that you'd actually use your whole life. Like: How To Do Eyeliner. How To Fill In A Tax Return. What To Do When Your Loo Blocks And Your Dad Isn't Answering The Phone And You're About To Have A Party.)

It was in Birmingham that I decided to lose my West Country accent. I was in the loo, minding my own business, when I heard a couple of girls taking the piss out of me. *Farrrmer Katie,* they were calling me. And, yes, I was shocked, and, yes, it stung. I could have burst out of my cubicle and exclaimed, *Well, I don't think your Brummie accent's any better!*

But I didn't. I just sat there and thought hard. It was a reality check. By the time I got my second internship—the one in east London—I was a different person. I'd wised up. I didn't look *or* sound like Katie Brenner from Ansters Farm.

And now I'm totally Cat Brenner from London. Cat Brenner who works in a cool office with distressed-brick walls and white shiny desks and funky chairs and a coat stand in the shape of a naked man. (It gives everyone a real shock, the first time they come to visit.)

I mean, I *am* Cat. I will be. I just have to nail the not-signing-the-wrong-name thing.

"People," Demeter says for a third time, and the office becomes quiet. There are ten of us in here, all with different titles and job descriptions. On the next floor up, there's an events team, and a digital team, and the planning lot. There's also some other group of creatives called the "vision team," who work directly with Adrian, the CEO. Plus other offices for talent management and finance or whatever. But this floor is my world, and I'm at the bottom of the pile. I earn by far the least and my desk is the smallest, but you have to start somewhere. This is my first-ever paid job, and I thank my lucky stars for it every day. And, you know, my work *is* interesting. In a way.

Kind of.

I mean, I suppose it depends how you define "interesting." I'm currently working on this really exciting project to launch a new self-foaming "cappuccino-style" creamer from Coffeewite. I'm on the research side. And what that *actually* comes down to, in terms of my day-to-day work, is . . .

Well. Here's the thing. You have to be realistic. You can't go straight in at the fun, glam stuff. Dad just doesn't get that. He's always asking: Do I come up with all the ideas? Or: Have I met lots of important people? Or: Do I go for swanky business lunches every day? Which is ridiculous.

And, yes, I'm probably defensive, but he doesn't understand, and it *really* doesn't help when he starts wincing and shaking his head and saying, "And you're really happy in the Big Smoke, Katie my love?" I *am* happy. But that doesn't mean it's not hard. Dad doesn't know anything about jobs, or London, or the economy, or, I don't know, the price of a glass of wine in a London bar. I haven't even told him exactly how much my rent is, because I know what he'd say; he'd say—

Oh God. Deep breath. Sorry. I didn't mean to launch into some off-topic rant about my dad. Things haven't been great between us, ever since I moved away after uni. He doesn't understand why I moved here, and he never will. And I can try to explain it all I like, but if you can't *feel* London, all you see are traffic and fumes and expense and your daughter choosing to move more than a hundred miles away.

I had a choice: Follow my heart or don't break his. I think in the end I broke a bit of both our hearts. Which the rest of the world doesn't understand, because they think it's normal to move out and away from home. But they aren't my dad and me, who lived together, just us, for all those years.

Anyway. Back to my work. People at my level don't meet the clients—Demeter does that. And Rosa. They go out for the lunches and come back with pink cheeks and free samples and excitement. Then they put together a pitch, which usually involves Mark and Liz too, and someone from the digital team, and sometimes Adrian. He's not just CEO but also the co-founder of Cooper Clemmow, and he has an office downstairs. (There was another co-founder, called Max, but he retired early to the south of France.)

Adrian's quite amazing, actually. He's about fifty and has a shock of iron-gray wavy hair and wears a lot of denim shirts and looks like he comes from the seventies. Which I suppose, in a way, he does. He's also properly famous. Like, there's a display of alumni outside King's College, London, on the Strand, and Adrian's picture is up there.

Anyway, so that's all the main players. But I'm not at that level, nothing like. As I said, I'm involved in the research side, which means what I'm *actually* doing this week is . . .

And, listen, before I say it, it doesn't *sound* glamorous, OK? But it's not as bad as it sounds, really.

I'm inputting data. To be specific, the results of this big customer survey we did for Coffeewite about coffee, creamers, cappuccinos, and, well, everything. Two thousand handwritten surveys, each eight pages long. I know, right? Paper? *No one* does paper surveys anymore. But Demeter wanted to go "old school" because she read some research that said people are 25 percent more honest when they're writing with a pen than they are online. Or something.

So here we are. Or, rather, here I am, with five boxfuls of questionnaires still to go.

It can get a *bit* tiring, because it's the same old questions and the participants all scribbled their answers in Biro and they aren't always clear. But on the plus side, this research will shape the whole project! Flora was all "My God, poor you, Cat, what a bloody nightmare!"—but actually it's fascinating.

Well. I mean, you have to *make* it fascinating. I've taken to guessing people's income brackets based on what they said in the question about *foam density.* And you know what? I'm usually right. It's like mind reading. The more I'm inputting these answers, the more I'm learning about consumers; at least I hope so—

"People. What the *fuck* is up with Trekbix?"

Demeter's voice breaks into my thoughts again. She's standing in her spiky heels, thrusting a hand through her hair, with that impatient, frustrated, what-is-*wrong*-with-the-world expression she gets.

"I wrote myself a set of notes about this." She's scrolling through her phone, ignoring us all again. "I know I did."

"I haven't seen any notes," says Sarah from behind her desk, using her customary low, discreet voice. *Saint Sarah*, as Flora calls her. Sarah is Demeter's assistant. She has luscious red hair which she ties into a ponytail and very white, pretty teeth. She's the one who makes her own clothes: gorgeous retro fifties-style outfits with circular skirts. And how she keeps sane, I have no idea.

Demeter has got to be the scattiest person in the universe. Every day, it seems, she misplaces a document or gets the time of an appointment wrong. Sarah is always very patient and polite to Demeter, but you can see her frustration in her mouth. It goes all tight and one corner disappears into her cheek. She's apparently the master of sending emails out from Demeter's account, in Demeter's voice, saving the situation, apologizing and generally smoothing things over.

I know it's a big job that Demeter does. Plus she has her family to think about, and school concerts or whatever. But how can you be *this* flaky?

"Right. Found it. Why was it in my *personal* folder?" Demeter looks up from her phone with that confused, eye-darty look she sometimes gets, like the entire world confounds her.

"You just need to save it under—" Sarah tries to take Demeter's phone, but she swipes it away.

"I know how to use my phone. *That's* not the point. The point is—" She stops dead, and we all wait breathlessly. This is another Demeter habit: She starts a really arresting sentence and then stops halfway through, as though her batteries have been turned off. I glance at Flora and she does a little eye roll to the ceiling.

"Yes. *Yes.*" Demeter resumes: "What's going on with Trekbix? Because I thought Liz was going to write a response to their email, but I've just had a further email from Rob Kincaid asking why he's heard nothing. So?" She swivels round to Liz, finally focusing on the person she needs to, finally coming alive. "Liz? Where is it? You promised me a draft by this morning." She taps her phone. "It's in my notes from last Monday's meeting. *Liz to write draft.* First rule of client care, Liz?"

Hold the client's hand, I think to myself, although I don't say it out loud. That would be too geeky.

"Hold the client's hand," declaims Demeter. "Hold it *throughout*. Make them feel secure every minute of the process. *Then* you'll have a happy customer. You're not holding Rob Kincaid's hand, Liz. His hand's dangling and he's not a happy bunny."

Liz colors. "I'm still working on it."

"Still?"

"There's a lot to put in."

"Well, work faster." Demeter frowns at her. "And send it to me for approval first. Don't just ping it off to Rob. By lunchtime, OK?"

"OK," mumbles Liz, looking pissed off. She doesn't often put a foot wrong, Liz. She's project manager and has a very tidy desk and straight fair hair which she washes every day with apple-scented shampoo. She eats a lot of apples too. Actually I've never connected those two facts before. Weird.

"Where *is* that email from Rob Kincaid?" Demeter is scrolling back and forth, peering at her phone. "It's disappeared from my in-box."

"Have you deleted it by mistake?" says Sarah patiently. "I'll forward it to you again."

This is Sarah's other pet annoyance: Demeter is always carelessly deleting emails and then needing them urgently and getting in a tizz. Sarah says she spends half her life forwarding emails to Demeter, and thank God *one* of them has an efficient filing system.

"There you are." Sarah clicks briskly. "I've forwarded Rob's email to you. In fact, I've forwarded all his emails to you, just in case."

"Thanks, Sarah." Demeter subsides. "I don't know *where* that email went. . . ." She's peering at her phone, but Sarah doesn't seem interested.

"So, Demeter, I'm going off to my first-aid training now," she says, reaching for her bag. "I told you about it? Because I'm the first-aid officer?"

"Right." Demeter looks bemused, and it's clear she'd totally forgotten. "Great! Well done you. So, Sarah, before you go, let's touch base. . . ." She scrolls through her phone. "It's the London Food Awards tonight. . . . I need to get to the hairdressers this afternoon. . . ."

"You can't," Sarah interrupts. "This afternoon is solid."

"*What?*" Demeter looks up from her phone. "But I booked the hairdressers."

"For tomorrow."

"*Tomorrow?*" Demeter sounds aghast and her eyes are swiveling again. "No. I booked it for Monday."

"Look at your calendar." Sarah sounds barely able to control her patience. "It was Tuesday, Demeter, always *Tuesday*."

"But I need my roots done, urgently. Can I cancel anyone this afternoon?"

"It's those polenta people. And then it's the team from Green Teen."

"Shit." Demeter screws up her face in agony. *"Shit."*

"And you've got a conference call in fifteen minutes. Can I go?" says Sarah in long-suffering tones.

"Yes. Yes. You go." Demeter waves a hand. "Thanks, Sarah." She heads back into her glass-walled office, exhaling sharply. "Shit, *shit*. Oh." She reappears. "Rosa. The Sensiquo logo? We should try it in a bigger point size. It came to me on my way in. And try the roundel in aquamarine. Can you talk to Mark? Where *is* Mark?" She glances querulously at his desk.

"Working from home today," says Jon, a junior creative.

"Oh," says Demeter mistrustfully. "OK."

Demeter doesn't really believe in working from home. She says you lose the flow with people disappearing the whole time. But Mark had it negotiated into his contract before Demeter arrived, so there's nothing she can do about it.

"Don't worry, I'll tell him," says Rosa, scribbling furiously on her notepad. "Point size, aquamarine."

"Great. Oh, and Rosa." She pops her head out yet again. "I want to discuss Python training. Everyone in this office should be able to code."

"What?"

"Coding!" says Demeter impatiently. "I read a piece about it in *The Huffington Post*. Put it on the agenda for the next group meeting."

"OK." Rosa looks baffled. "Coding. Fine."

As Demeter closes her door, everyone breathes out. This is Demeter. Totally random. Keeping up with her is exhausting.

Rosa is tapping frantically at her phone, and I know she's sending a bitchy text about Demeter to Liz. Sure enough, a moment later Liz's phone pings, and she nods vociferously at Rosa.

I haven't totally fathomed the office politics of this place—it's like trying to catch up on a TV soap opera mid-flow. But I do know that Rosa applied for Demeter's job and didn't get it. I also know that they had a massive row, just before I arrived. Rosa wanted to get on some big one-off special project that the mayor of London spearheaded. It was branding some new London athletics event, and he put together a team seconded from creative agencies all over London. The *Evening Standard* called it *a showcase for London's best and brightest*. But Demeter wouldn't let Rosa do it. She said she needed Rosa on her team 24/7, which was bullshit. Since then, Rosa has hated Demeter with a passion.

Flora's theory is that Demeter's so paranoid about being overtaken by her young staff that she won't help anyone. If you even *try* to climb the ladder, she stamps on your fingers with her Miu Miu shoes. Apparently Rosa's desperate to leave Cooper Clemmow now—but there's not a lot out there in this market. So here poor Rosa stays, stuck with a boss she hates, basically loathing every moment of her work. You can see it in her hunched shoulders and frowning brow.

Mark also loathes Demeter, and I know the story there too. Demeter's supposed to oversee the design team. *Oversee*, not do it all herself. But she can't stop herself. Design is Demeter's thing—design and packaging. She knows the names of more typefaces than you can imagine, and sometimes she interrupts a meeting just to show us all some packaging design that she thinks really works. Which is, you know, great. But it's also a problem, because she's always wading in.

So last year Cooper Clemmow refreshed the branding of a big moisturizer called Drench, and it was Demeter's idea to go pale orange with white type. Well, it's been this massive hit, and we've won all sorts of prizes. All good—except for Mark, who's head of design. Apparently he'd already created this whole *other* design package. But Demeter came up with the orange idea, mocked it up herself, and flung it out there at a client meeting. And apparently Mark felt totally belittled.

The worst thing is, Demeter didn't even notice that Mark was pissed off. She doesn't pick up on things like that. She's all *high five, great work team, move on, next project*. And then it was such a huge hit that Mark could hardly complain. I mean, in some ways, he's lucky: He got a load of credit for that redesign. He can put it on his CV and everything. But still. He's all bristly and has this sarcastic way of talking to Demeter which makes me wince.

The sad thing is, everyone else in the office knows Mark is really talented. Like, he's just won the Stylesign Award for Innovation. (Apparently it's some really prestigious thing.) But it's as if Demeter doesn't even *realize* what a great head of design she has.

Liz isn't that happy here either, but she puts up with it. Flora, on the other hand, bitches about Demeter all the time, but I think that's because she loves bitching. I'm not sure about the others.

As for me, I'm still the new girl. I've only been here seven months and I keep my head down and don't venture my opinion too much. But I do have ambition; I do have ideas. I'm all about design too, especially typography—in fact, that's what Demeter and I talked about in my interview.

Whenever a new project comes into the office, my brain fires up. I've put together *so* many bits of spec work in my spare time on my laptop. Logos, design concepts, strategy documents . . . I keep emailing them to Demeter, for feedback, and she keeps promising she *will* look at them, when she has a moment.

Everyone says you mustn't chivvy Demeter or she flies off the handle. So I'm biding my time, like a surfer waiting for a wave. I'm pretty good at surfing, as it happens, and I know the wave will come. When the moment is right, I'll get Demeter's attention. She'll look at my stuff, everything will click, and I'll start riding my life. Not paddling, paddling, paddling, like I am right now.

I'm just picking up my next survey from the pile when Hannah, another of our designers, enters the office. There's a general gasp and Flora turns to raise her eyebrows at me. Poor Hannah had to go home on Friday. She really wasn't well. She's had about five miscarriages over the last two years, and it's left her a bit vulnerable, and occasionally she has a panic attack. It happened Friday, so Rosa told her to go home and have a rest. The truth is, Hannah works probably the hardest in the office. I've seen emails from her at 2:00 A.M. She deserves a bit of a break.

"Hannah!" Rosa exclaims. "Are you OK? Take it really easy today."

"I'm fine," says Hannah, slipping into her seat, avoiding everyone's eye. "I'm fine." She instantly opens up a document and starts work, sipping from a bottle of filtered tap water. (Cooper Clemmow launched the brand, so we all have these freebie neon bottles on our desks.)

"Hannah!" Demeter appears at the door of her office. "You're back. Well done."

"I'm fine," says Hannah yet again. I can tell she doesn't want any fuss made, but Demeter comes right over to her desk.

"Now, please don't worry, Hannah," she says in her ringing, authoritative tones. "*No one* thinks you're a drama queen or anything like that. So don't worry about it at all."

She gives Hannah a friendly nod, then strides back into her office and shuts her door. The rest of us are watching, dumbstruck, and poor Hannah looks absolutely stricken. As soon as Demeter is back in her office, she turns to Rosa.

"Do you all think I'm a drama queen?" she gulps.

"No!" exclaims Rosa at once, and I can hear Liz muttering, "*Bloody* Demeter."

"Listen, Hannah," Rosa continues, heading to Hannah's desk, crouching down, and looking her straight in the eye. "You've just been Demetered."

"That's right," agrees Liz. "You've been Demetered."

"It happens to us all. She's an insensitive cow and she says stupid stuff and you just have to *not listen,* OK? You've done really well coming in today, and we all really appreciate the effort you've made. Don't we?" She looks around and a spatter of applause breaks out, whereupon Hannah's cheeks flush with pleasure.

"Fuck Demeter," ends Rosa succinctly, and she heads back to her desk, amid even more applause.

From the corner of my eye, I can see Demeter glancing out of her glass-walled office, as though wondering what's going on. And I almost feel sorry for her. She really has no idea.

CHAPTER TWO

For the next hour or so, everyone works peacefully. Demeter is on her conference call in her office, and I get through a stack of surveys and Rosa passes round a bottle of retro sweets. And I'm just wondering what time I'll break for lunch when Demeter sticks her head out of her door again.

"I need . . ." Her eyes roam around the office and eventually land on me. "You. What are you doing right now?"

"Me?" I feel a jolt of surprise. "Nothing. I mean, I'm working. I mean—"

"Could you bear to come and help me out with something a bit"—she gives one of her Demeter pauses—"*different*?"

"Yes!" I say, trying not to sound flustered. "Sure! Of course!"

"In five minutes, OK?"

"Five minutes." I nod. "Absolutely."

I turn back to my work, but the words are blurring in front of my eyes. My head is spinning in excitement. *Something a bit different*. That could be anything. It could be a new client . . . a website . . . a revolutionary branding concept that

Demeter wants to pioneer . . . Whatever it is, it's my chance. This is my wave!

There's a joyful swell in my chest. All those emails I've been sending her *weren't* for nothing! She must have been looking at my ideas all along, and she thinks I've got potential and she's been waiting for the most perfect, special project. . . .

My hands are actually trembling as I get out my laptop, plus a few printouts in a portfolio that I keep in my drawer. There's no harm in showing her my most recent work, is there? I reapply my lipstick and spray on some perfume. I need to look sharp and together. I need to nail this.

After exactly four and a half minutes, I push back my chair, feeling self-conscious. Here we go. The wave's cresting. My heart's thudding, and everything around me feels a bit brighter than usual—but as I thread my way through all the desks to Demeter's door, I try to appear nonchalant. Cool. Like, *Yeah, Demeter and I are just having a one-to-one. We're going to bounce some ideas around.*

Oh my God, *what* if it's something huge? I have a sudden image of Demeter and me staying late in the office; eating Chinese takeout; working on some amazing, groundbreaking project; perhaps I'd do a presentation. . . .

I can tell Dad about this. Maybe I'll call him tonight.

"Um, hi?" I tap at Demeter's door and push it ajar.

"Cath!" she exclaims.

"Actually, it's Cat," I venture.

"Of course! Cat. Marvelous. Come in. Now, I *hope* you don't mind me asking you this—"

"Of course not!" I say quickly. "Whatever it is, I'm up for it. Obviously my background's design, but I'm really interested in corporate identity, strategy, digital opportunities . . . whatever. . . ."

Now I'm rambling. Stop it, Katie.

Shit. I mean: Stop it, *Cat*. I'm *Cat*.

"Right," says Demeter absently, typing the end of an email. She sends it off, then turns and eyes my laptop and portfolio with surprise. "What's all that for?"

"Oh." I color, and shift the portfolio awkwardly. "I just . . . I brought a few things . . . some ideas. . . ."

"Well, put it down somewhere," says Demeter without interest, and starts rootling in her desk drawer. "Now, I hate to ask you this, but I'm *absolutely* desperate. My diary is a nightmare and I've got these wretched awards this evening. I mean, I can get myself to a blow-dry bar, but my roots are a different matter, so . . ."

I'm not quite following what she's saying—but the next minute she brandishes a box expectantly at me. It's a Clairol box, and just for one heady white-hot moment, I think: *We're rebranding Clairol? I'm going to help REBRAND CLAIROL? Oh my God, this is MASSIVE—*

Until reality hits. Demeter doesn't look excited, like someone about to redesign an international brand. She looks bored and a bit impatient. And now her words are impinging properly on my brain: . . . *my roots are a different matter. . . .*

I look more closely at the box. *Clairol Nice 'n Easy Root Touch-Up. Dark Brown. Restores roots' color in ten minutes!*

"You want me to . . ."

"You're *such* an angel." Demeter flashes me one of her magical smiles. "This is my only window in the whole day. You don't mind if I send some emails while you do it? You'd better put on some protective gloves. Oh, and don't get any stuff on the carpet. Maybe find an old towel or something?"

Her roots. The special, perfect project is doing her *roots*.

I feel like the wave has dumped on me. I'm soaked, bedraggled, seaweed-strewn, a total loser. Let's face it, she didn't even come out of her office looking especially for me. Does she actually, properly know who I am?

As I head back out, wondering where on earth I'm going to find an old towel, Liz looks up from her screen with interest.

"What was that about?"

"Oh," I say, and rub my nose, playing for time. I can't bear to give away my disappointment. I feel so dumb. How could I have ever thought she'd ask me to rebrand Clairol? "She wants me to do her roots." I try to sound casual.

"Do her roots?" echoes Liz. "What, *dye* them? Are you *serious*?"

"That's outrageous!" chimes in Rosa. "That is *not* in your job description!"

Heads are popping up all round the office and I can feel a wave of general sympathy. Pity, even.

I shrug. "It's OK."

"This is worse than the corset dress," says Liz significantly.

I've heard about the whole team once trying to zip Demeter into a corset dress that was too small but she wouldn't admit it. (In the end they had to use a coat hanger and brute strength.) But clearly roots are a step down even from that.

"You can refuse, you know," says Rosa, who is the most militant person in the office. But even she doesn't sound convinced. The truth is, when you're the most junior member of staff in a competitive industry like this, you basically do anything. She knows it and I know it.

"It's no problem!" I say, as brightly as I can. "I've always thought I'd be a good hairdresser, actually. It's my backup career."

For that I earn a big office laugh, and Rosa offers me one of her super-expensive cookies from the baker on the corner. So it's not *all* bad. And as I grab some paper towels from the ladies', I decide: I'll turn this into an opportunity. It's not exactly the one-to-one meeting I was after, but it's still a one-to-one, isn't it? Maybe this can be my wave, after all.

But, oh God. Bleargh.

I now know hairdressing is not my backup career. Other people's scalps are *vile*. Even Demeter's.

As I start to paint on the gooey dye stuff, I'm trying to avert my gaze as much as possible. I don't *want* to see her pale, scalpy skin or her little flecks of dandruff, or realize just how long it's been since she last did her roots.

Which, actually, must be no time at all. There's hardly any gray there: She's clearly paranoid. Which makes sense. Demeter is super-aware of her age and how we're all younger than her. But then, she totally overcompensates by knowing every Internet joke before anyone else, every bit of celeb gossip, every new band, and every . . . *everything*.

Demeter is the most on-the-case, earliest adopter known to mankind. She has gadgets before anyone else. She has that must-have H&M designer item before anyone else. Other people camp outside all night to get it—Demeter just somehow *has* it.

Or take restaurants. She's worked on some very big restaurant names in her time, so she has zillions of connections. As a result, she never goes to a restaurant except when it first opens. Or, even better, when it's not open yet except to special, important people like her. Then as soon as the general public is allowed in, or it gets a good review in *The Times,* she goes off it and says, "Well, it *used* to be all right, till it was *ruined,*" and moves on to the next thing.

So she's intimidating. She can't be easily impressed. She always had a better weekend than anyone else; she always has a better holiday story than anyone else; if someone spots a celebrity in the street, she always went to school with them or has a godchild going out with their brother, or something.

But today I'm *not* going to be intimidated. I'm going to make intelligent conversation and then, when the time is right, I'll make my strategic move. I just have to decide exactly what that strategic move should be—

"OK?" says Demeter, who is typing away at her monitor, totally ignoring me.

"Fine!" I say, dipping the brush again.

"If I have one piece of advice for you girls, it's don't go gray. *Such* a bore. Although"—she swivels briefly to face me—"your hair's so mousy, you wouldn't notice."

"Oh," I say, nonplussed. "Um . . . good?"

"How's Hannah doing, by the way? Poor thing. I hope I reassured her before." Demeter nods complacently and takes a sip of coffee, while I gape dumbly at the back of her head. That was an attempt to *reassure* Hannah?

"Well . . ." I don't know what to say. "Yes. I think she's all right."

"Excellent!" Demeter resumes typing with even more energy, while I lecture myself silently. *Come on, Katie.*

I mean, come on, Cat. *Cat.*

Here I am. In Demeter's office. Just her and me. It's my chance.

I'll show her the designs I've done for Wash-Blu, I decide in a rush. Only I won't just plonk them on her desk, I'll be more subtle. Make conversation first. *Bond* with her.

I glance for inspiration at Demeter's massive pinboard. I've only been in this office a few times, but I always look at the pinboard to see what's new. It's like Demeter's entire fabulous life, summed up in a collage of images and souvenirs and even fabric swatches. There are printed-out designs for brands she's created. Examples of unusual typefaces. Photos of ceramics and mid-century modern furniture classics.

There are press cuttings and photos of her at events. There are pictures of her family skiing and sailing and standing on picturesque beaches, all in photogenic clothes. They couldn't look more perfect. Her husband is apparently some super-brainy head of a think tank, and there he is in black tie, standing next to her on a red carpet somewhere. He's holding her arm affectionately, looking appropriately gorgeous and intelligent. Demeter wouldn't settle for anything less.

Should I ask about the children? No, too personal. As my eyes roam around, they take in all the piles of papers everywhere. This is yet another thing that drives Sarah mad: when Demeter asks her to print out emails. I often hear her muttering at her desk: "Read them on the fucking *screen*."

On the shelf beside Demeter is a row of books on branding, marketing, and design. They're mostly standard titles, but there's one I haven't read—an old paperback entitled *Our Vision*—and I look at it more closely.

"Is that book *Our Vision* good?" I ask.

"Brilliant," replies Demeter, pausing briefly in her typing. "It's a series of conversations between designers from the eighties. Very inspiring."

"Could I maybe . . . borrow it?" I venture.

"Sure." Demeter turns her head briefly, looking surprised. "Be my guest. Enjoy."

As I take down the book, I notice a little box on the same shelf. It's one of Demeter's most famous triumphs, the Redfern Raisin box, with its dinky little red string handles. Everyone takes those string handles for granted now, but at the time, no one had ever thought of such a thing.

"I've always wondered about Redfern Raisins," I say impulsively. "How did you get those string handles through? They must be expensive."

"Oh, they're expensive." Demeter nods, still typing. "It was a *nightmare* persuading the client. But then it all worked out."

"Worked out" is an understatement. It was a sensation, and the sales of Redfern Raisins rocketed. I've read articles about it.

"So, how did you do it?" I persist. "How *did* you persuade the client?"

I'm not just asking to make conversation; I really want to know. Because maybe one day *I'll* work on a project and want to push through some super-expensive feature, and the client will be all stroppy, but I'll remember Demeter's wise advice and win the day. I'll be Kung Fu Panda to her Master Shifu, only with less kung fu. (Probably.)

Demeter has stopped typing and she turns round as though she's actually quite interested in the question herself.

"What we do in our job," she says thoughtfully, "it's a balance. On the one hand it's about listening to the client. Interpreting. Responding. But on the other, it's about having the courage to go with big ideas. It's about standing up for your convictions. You need a bit of tenacity. Yes?"

"Definitely," I say, trying to look as tenacious as possible. I lower my brows and hold the hair dye wand firmly. Altogether, I hope I'm giving off the vibe: *Tenacious. Alert. A Surprisingly Interesting Junior Member Of Staff Whose Name It's Worth Remembering.*

But Demeter doesn't seem to have noticed my tenacious, alert demeanor. She's turned back to her computer. Quick, what else can we talk about? Before she can start typing again, I say hastily, "So, um, have you been to that new restaurant in Marylebone? The Nepalese–British fusion place?"

It's like catnip. I've mentioned the hottest restaurant of the moment, and Demeter stops dead.

"I have, actually," she says, sounding surprised that I've asked. "I went a couple of weeks ago. Have you?"

Have I?

What does she think, that I can afford to spend £25 on a plate of dumplings?

But I can't bear to say, *No, I just read about it on a blog, because that's all I can afford to do, because London is the sixth-most-expensive city in the world, hadn't you noticed?*

(On the plus side, it's not as expensive as Singapore. Which makes you wonder: What on earth does everything cost in Singapore?)

"I'm planning to," I say after a pause. "What did you think?"

"I was impressed." Demeter nods. "You know that the tables are handmade in Kathmandu? And the food is challenging but earthy. Very authentic. All organic, of *course*."

"Of *course*." I match her serious, this-is-no-joking-matter tone. I think, if Demeter had to put her religion down on a form, she'd put *Organic*.

"Isn't the chef the same guy who was at Sit, Eat?" I say, dabbing the brush into more gloopy dye. "He's not Nepalese."

"No, but he's got a Nepalese adviser and he spent two years out there. . . ." Demeter swivels round and looks at me more appraisingly. "You know your restaurants, don't you?"

"I like food."

Which is true. I read restaurant reviews like some people read horoscopes. I even keep a list in my bag of all the top restaurants I'd like to go to sometime. I wrote it out as a jokey thing with my friend Fi one day, and it's just kind of stuck around, like a talisman.

"What do you think of Salt Block?" Demeter demands, as though testing me.

"I think the dish to have is the sea urchin," I say without missing a beat.

I've read that everywhere. Every review, every blog. It's all about the sea urchin.

"The sea urchin." Demeter nods, frowning. "Yes, I've heard about that. I should have ordered it."

I can tell she's fretting now. She's missed out on the must-eat dish. She'll have to go back and have it.

Demeter turns and gives me a short, penetrating look—then swivels back to her computer. "Next time we get a food project, I'm putting you on it."

I feel a flicker of disbelieving delight. Was that a vote of approval from Demeter? Am I actually *getting somewhere*?

"I worked on the re-launch of the Awesome Pizza Place in Birmingham," I quickly remind her. It was on my CV, but she'll have forgotten that.

"Birmingham," echoes Demeter absently. "That's right." She types furiously for a few moments, then adds, "You don't sound Brummie."

Oh *God*. I'm not going into the whole ditching-the-West-Country-accent story. It's too embarrassing. And who cares where I'm originally from, anyway? I'm a Londoner now.

"I guess I'm just not an accent person," I say, closing the subject. I don't want to talk about where I'm from; I want to press on toward my goal. "So, um, Demeter? You know the Wash-Blu rebrand we're pitching for? Well, I've done some mock-ups of my own for the new logo and packaging. In my spare time. And I wondered, could I show them to you?"

"Absolutely." Demeter nods encouragingly. "Good for you! Email them to me."

This is how she always reacts. She says, "Email them to me!" with great enthusiasm, and you do, and then you don't hear anything back, ever.

"Right." I nod. "Perfect. Or I can show you right now?"

"Now?" says Demeter vaguely, reaching for a plastic folder.

She wanted tenacious, didn't she? I carefully put down the hair dye on a shelf and hurry to get my designs.

"So, this is the front of the box. . . ." I put a printout in front of her. "You'll see how I've treated the lettering, while keeping the very recognizable blue tone. . . ."

Demeter's mobile phone buzzes and she grabs it.

"Hello, Roy? Yes, I got your message." She nods intently. "Let me just write that down. . . ." She seizes my printout, turns it over, and scribbles a number on the back of it. "Six o'clock. Yes, absolutely."

She puts the phone down, absently folds the paper up into quarters, and puts it in her bag. Then she looks up at me and comes to. "Oh! Sorry. That's your paper, isn't it? Do you mind if I keep it? Rather an important number."

I stare back, blood pulsing in my ears. I don't know how to respond. That was my design. My *design*. That I was *showing* her. Not some piece of crappy scrap paper. Should I say something? Should I stand up for myself?

My spirits have plummeted. I feel so *stupid*. There I was, believing—hoping—that we were bonding, that she was noticing me. . . .

"Shit." Demeter interrupts my thoughts, staring at her computer in consternation. "Shit. Oh *God*."

She pushes her chair back with no warning and bashes my legs. I cry, "Ow!" but I'm not sure she hears: She's too agitated. She peers out of her glass office wall, then ducks down.

"What is it?" I gulp. "What's happened?"

"Alex is on his way!" she says, as though this is self-explanatory.

"Alex?" I echo stupidly. Who's Alex?

"He just emailed. He *can't* see me like this." She gestures at her head, which is all messy with dye and needs to be left for at least another five minutes. "Go and meet the lift," she says urgently. "Intercept him."

"I don't know who he is!"

"You'll know him!" Demeter says impatiently. "Tell him to come back in half an hour. Or email. But *don't* let him come in here." Her hands rise to her head as though to shield it.

"But what about your hair dye?"

"It's fine. You're done. All I do now is wait and wash it off. Go! *Go!*"

Oh God. Demeter's panic is contagious, and as I scurry down the corridor I feel hyper-vigilant. But what if I don't catch this Alex? What if I don't recognize him? Who is he, anyway?

I take up a position right outside the lift doors and wait. The first lift disgorges Liz and Rosa, who give me a slightly odd look as they pass by. The second lift whizzes straight past to the ground floor. Then the first lift arrives at our floor again and . . . *Ping.* The doors open and out steps a tall, slim guy I haven't seen before. And Demeter's right: I instantly know this must be him.

He has brown hair, not mousy brown but proper dark chestnut, springing up from his brow. He looks about thirty and has one of those wide-open, appealing faces that you get when you have good cheekbones and a broad smile. (He's not smiling, but you can tell: When he does smile it'll be broad, and I bet he's got good teeth too.) He's wearing jeans and a pale-purple shirt, and his arms are full of boxes covered in Chinese characters.

"Alex?" I say.

"Guilty." He turns to look at me, his face interested. "Who are you?"

"Um . . . Cat. I'm Cat."

"Hi, Cat."

His brown eyes are surveying me as though to extract the most information about me possible in the smallest amount of time. I'd feel uncomfortable, except I'm preoccupied by fulfilling my task.

"I have a message from Demeter," I announce. "She says, could you possibly come and see her in about half an hour? Or maybe email instead? She's just a bit . . . um . . . tied up."

Dyed up crosses my mind, and I almost give a little snort of laughter.

He picks up on it at once. "What's funny?"

"Nothing."

"Yes, it is. You nearly laughed." His eyes spark at mine. "Tell me the joke."

"No joke," I say, flustered. "So, anyway, that's the message."

"Wait half an hour, or email."

"Yes."

"Hmm." He appears to think for a moment. "Trouble is, I don't want to wait for half an hour. Or email. What's she doing?" To my horror, he starts striding down the corridor, toward our office. In panic I run after him, dodge right past, and plant myself in his way.

"No! She can't . . . You mustn't . . ." As he moves to get past me, I take a quick step to obstruct him. He dodges the other way, and I block him again, lifting my hands into a defensive martial-arts pose before I can stop myself.

"We're seriously doing this?" Alex looks like he might burst into laughter. "What are you, Special Forces?"

My cheeks flame red, but I hold my ground. "My boss doesn't want to be disturbed."

"You're a fierce guard dog, aren't you?" He surveys me with even more interest. "You're not her assistant, though, are you?"

"No. I'm a research associate." I say the title with care. *Associate*. Not intern, *associate*.

"Good for you." He nods, as though impressed, and I wonder if he's an intern.

No. Too old. And, anyway, Demeter wouldn't get bothered about seeing an intern, would she?

"So, who are you?" I ask.

"Well . . ." He looks vague. "I do a bit of everything. I've been working in the New York office." He makes a sudden move to get past me, but I'm there, blocking him again.

"You're good." He grins, and I feel a dart of anger. This guy is starting to piss me off.

"Look, I don't know who you are or what you need Demeter for," I say stonily. "But I told you, she doesn't want to be disturbed. *Got* it?"

He's silent for a moment, regarding me, then a smile

spreads over his face—and I was right, it's broad and white and dazzling. He's actually extremely handsome, I realize, and this belated recognition makes me blush.

"I'm crazy," he says suddenly, and steps aside with almost a courtly bow. "I don't need Demeter, and I apologize for being so rude. If it's any consolation, you win."

"That's OK," I say, a little stiffly.

"I don't need Demeter," he continues cheerfully, "because I have you. I want to do some research; you're a research associate. It's a perfect fit."

I blink uncertainly at him. "What?"

"We have work to do." He brandishes the boxes with Chinese writing at me.

"*What?*"

"Twenty minutes, max. Luckily, Demeter is obviously so tied up, she won't even notice you're gone. Come on."

"Where?"

"To the roof."

CHAPTER THREE

I shouldn't be here. Simple as that. There are a million reasons I should *not* have come up to the roof with a strange man called Alex about whom I know nothing. Especially when I've got a stack of surveys still to input. But there are three good reasons that I *am* here, standing on the top of the building, shivering and gazing around at the rooftops of Chiswick.

1. I reckon I could take him in a fight. You know, if he turned out to be a psychopath.

2. I want to know what these Chinese boxes are all about.

3. The idea of doing something that *isn't* coffee surveys or hair dye is so overwhelmingly alluring, I can't resist. It's as if someone's opened the door of my solitary-confinement cell and shone a light in and said, *Psst, want to come out for a bit?*

And by out, I mean *out*. There's no shelter up here, only an iron railing running round the edge and a few low concrete walls here and there. The December air is bitter and gusty, lifting my hair up and freezing my neck. The air seems almost gray-blue with cold. Or maybe it's just the contrast between the chilly, gloomy midwinter sky and the cozy warm buildings around us, all lit up.

From where I'm standing, I can see right into the office block next to ours, and it's fascinating. It's not a modern block like ours; it's more old-fashioned, with cornices and proper windows. A girl in a navy jacket is painting her nails at her desk but keeps stopping to pretend she's typing, and a guy in a gray suit has fallen asleep in his chair.

In the next room along, a rather intense meeting is happening around a grand, shiny table. A woman in a frilly uniform is handing round tea while an elderly man sounds off at everyone and another man is opening a large window, as though things are getting so heated, they need air. I find myself wondering what kind of company it is. Something more stuffy than ours. The Royal Institution Of Something?

A ripping sound makes me turn, and I see Alex crouching down, tearing into one of the boxes with a Stanley knife.

"So, what's the work?" I say. "Unpacking?"

"Toys," he says, holding the Stanley knife in his mouth as he wrenches the box open. "Adult toys."

Adult toys?

Oh my God, this was a mistake. This is *Fifty Shades of the Roof*. He'll be tying me up to the railings any minute. I need to escape—

"Not that kind of adult toys," he adds with a grin. "Proper toys for playing with—except for grown-ups." He lifts out something made of bright green rope and plastic. "This is a diabolo, I think. You know? The things you spin? And these are . . ." From another box he pulls out some steel tubes that look like telescopes. "I think they expand . . . yes. Stilts."

"Stilts?"

"Look!" He pulls one out to its full length and snaps down a foot piece. "Grown-up stilts. Want to have a go?"

"What *is* all this?" I take the stilts from him, climb on, instantly wobble, and fall off.

"Like I said, toys for grown-ups. They're huge in Asia. They're supposed to be an antidote to modern stress. Now they want to expand globally. They've hired the Sidney Smith Agency . . . you know Sidney Smith?"

I nod. I mean, I don't *know* the Sidney Smith Agency, but I know they're our rival.

"Anyway, now they've asked us to come in on it too. I've been tasked with looking at the products. What do you think so far?"

"Tricky," I say, falling off my stilts for the third time. "It's harder than it looks."

"I agree." He comes over to me on a second pair of stilts, both of us constantly stepping back and forth as we try to keep balance.

"But I like being taller. That's quite cool."

"Useful for seeing over crowds," he agrees. "Party stilts? That might work." He tries to stand on one stilt, sways, and loses his balance. "Shit. You could *not* do this after a few beers. Can you dance on them?" He lifts a leg, wobbles, and falls down. "Nope. Also, where do you put your beer? Where's the drink holder? This is a massive defect."

"They didn't think it through," I agree.

"They have *not* seen the full potential." He telescopes them back up. "OK, next toy."

"How come they got *you* to do this?" I ask, as I fold my own stilts up.

"Oh, you know." He flashes me a grin. "I was the most immature." He opens another box. "Hey. A drone."

The drone is a kind of military-looking helicopter, with a remote control the size of a small iPad. It must have demonstration batteries in it, because soon Alex has got it to float up in the air. As it comes flying toward me, I dodge with a yelp.

"Sorry." He lifts a hand. "Just getting the hang of it . . ." He presses a button on the remote, and the drone lights up like a spaceship. "Oh, this is great! And it's got a camera. Look at the screen."

He sends up the drone, high in the air, and we both watch the picture of the rooftops of Chiswick, getting more and more distant.

"You could see everything in the world with one of these," enthuses Alex, swooping the drone down and up. "Think how many experiences you could have. You could see every church in Italy, every tree in the rain forest. . . ."

"Virtual experiences," I correct. "You wouldn't be there. You wouldn't feel the places or smell them. . . ."

"I didn't say you could have perfect experiences, I said you could have experiences."

"But that's not an *experience,* just floating by from a distance. Is it?"

Alex doesn't answer. He brings the helicopter downward, switches off its lights, and sends it toward the neighboring building.

"No one's even noticed it!" he exclaims, as he gets it to

hover outside the window of the big meeting round the table. "Look, we can spy on them." He taps at a control on the touch screen, and the camera tilts to film the table. "Focus in . . ." He taps again, and the camera zooms in on some papers.

"You shouldn't do that," I protest. "It's sneaky. Stop it."

Alex turns to look at me, and something flickers across his face—as if he's chastened and amused, all at the same time.

"You're right." He nods. "Let's not be sneaky. Let's be up front."

He switches all the helicopter's lights back on and sets them to flash red and white. Then he carefully maneuvers the drone toward the open window.

"Stop it!" I say, clapping a hand over my mouth. "You're not going to—"

But he's already sending the flashing drone through the window, into the formal meeting room.

Just for a moment no one notices. Then a man in a navy suit looks up, followed by a gray-haired woman—and soon everyone's pointing. On the screen, we can see their astonished faces up close, and I stifle a giggle. Two people are peering out of the open window down to street level, but no one has even looked in our direction.

"There," says Alex. "They all looked stressed out. Now they're distracted. We're doing them a favor."

"What if their meeting's really important?" I object.

"Of course it's not important. No meeting is important. Hey, look, a microphone function. We can listen to them." He touches a button and suddenly we can hear the voices of the people in the room, coming through a speaker on the remote.

"Is it *filming* us?" a woman is asking in panicked tones.

"It's Chinese." A man is jabbing his finger at the drone. "Look at the writing. That's Chinese."

"Everyone cover your faces," another woman says urgently. "Cover your faces."

"It's too late!" says a girl shrilly. "It's seen our faces!"

"We shouldn't cover our *faces*!" a man exclaims. "We should cover the minutes of the *meeting*!"

"They're only draft minutes," puts in a blond woman, looking anxious and putting both arms over her printed sheets.

A man in shirtsleeves has stood up on his chair and is trying to hit the drone with a rolled-up piece of paper.

"No, you don't!" retorts Alex, and he presses an icon on the remote control. The next moment, the drone starts shooting spurts of water at the man, and I clap a hand over my mouth to muffle my laughter.

"Ah," says Alex. "So *that's* what that is. How about this one?" He presses another icon, and bubbles start streaming out of the drone.

"Argh!" The man jumps down off his chair as though under attack and starts batting at the bubbles. I'm laughing so hard, my nose has started to hurt. There are bubbles floating everywhere in the room, and people are shrinking away from them.

"OK," says Alex. "I think we've tortured these good people enough." From the side of the remote, he pulls out a tiny microphone on a wire. He holds it to his mouth, flips a switch, and makes a "quiet" gesture at me. "Attention," he says in clipped tones, like a World War II RAF pilot. "I repeat, attention, attention."

His voice rings out of the drone, and the effect on the people in the room is instantaneous. They all freeze as though in fright and stare up at the drone.

"Apologies for the inconvenience," Alex announces, in the same clipped voice. "Normal service will be resumed shortly. *God Save Our Gracious Queen . . .*"

I don't believe it. He's singing the national anthem. "Stand up!" he suddenly barks into the microphone, and a couple of the people at the table half-rise to their feet before sitting back down again and looking embarrassed.

"Thank you," Alex concludes. "Thank you so much." Deftly, he flies the drone out of the room and swoops it down, out of view. The people in the room are all crowding to the window to see where it's gone, pointing in different directions, and Alex pulls me out of sight, behind a low concrete wall. A few moments later the drone quietly descends behind us, all its lights off. It's obvious that none of the people in the room has the faintest idea where it disappeared to, and after a minute or two they head back to the table. I meet Alex's eye and shake my head.

"I can't believe you did that." A final giggle ripples through me.

"That made their day," he says. "Now they all have a dinner-party anecdote." He picks up the drone, places it between us, and surveys it. "So, what do we think?"

"Awesome," I say.

"I agree." He nods. "Awesome." He drags over another box and cuts the tape. "Look at this! Special jumping boots with springs!"

"Oh my God!" I gape at them. "Is that *safe*?"

"And in here we have . . ." He prizes open another box. "Neon light-up tennis rackets. That's hilarious."

"This is going to be the *best* project," I say with enthusiasm.

"Well, maybe." He frowns. "Only it's not that simple. We worked with Sidney Smith before. Didn't go well. So we have to think carefully before we commit." He taps his fingers distantly, then comes to. "They *are* great products, though, aren't they?" His eyes flash as he pulls out the light-up tennis racket, presses a button, and watches it glow neon-yellow. "I think I'm in love with this."

"So it's heart over head." I can't help smiling at his enthusiasm.

"Exactly. Bloody heads and hearts, never match up, do they?"

He starts wandering around the roof, tossing the racket up and down. Surreptitiously I glance at my watch. Shit. I've been here nearly twenty-five minutes and I'm so cold I can't feel my hands.

"Actually, I ought to go," I say awkwardly. "I've got loads of work—"

"Of course. I've kept you. Apologies. I'll stay up here a few more minutes, check out the rest of these boxes." He shoots me that dazzling white smile again. "I'm so sorry, I'm an idiot—I can't remember your name. Mine's Alex."

"I'm Katie—" I stop. "*Cat,*" I correct myself with a flush.

"Right." He looks a bit puzzled. "Well, nice to hang out with you, Katie-Cat. Thanks for your help."

"Sorry, it's Cat," I say, in an agony of embarrassment. "Just Cat."

"Got it. See you around, Just Cat. Say hi to Demeter."

"OK. I will. See you." And I'm about to head toward the door back into the stair shaft, when I hesitate. This guy's so easy to talk to, and I'm longing to pick someone's brains. . . .

"You said you'd done a bit of everything," I say in a rush. "So . . . have you ever worked with Demeter? Has she ever been your boss?"

Alex stills the racket and gives me a long, interested look.

"Yes," he says. "She has, as it happens."

"Only I'm trying to show her my ideas, and she won't ever focus on them, and . . ."

"Ideas?"

"Just some speculative stuff. Mock-ups. Rough concepts," I explain, feeling a bit embarrassed. "You know, stuff I've done in my spare time, whatever . . ."

"Right. Yes. I get it." He thinks for a minute. "My advice is: Don't show Demeter random ideas at random times. Pitch her *exactly* the right idea, *exactly* when she needs it. When you're brainstorming at a meeting, speak up. Make your voice heard."

"But . . ." My cheeks flame. "I don't get to go to those meetings. I'm too junior."

"Ah." He gives me a kind look. "Then get yourself into one."

"I can't! Demeter will *never* let me—"

"Of course she will!" He laughs. "If there's one thing Demeter's good at, it's championing junior members of her team and bringing them on."

Is he nuts? I have a sudden image of Demeter stamping on Rosa's fingers with her Miu Miu shoes. But I won't contradict him when he's helping me.

"Just ask," he reiterates—and his confidence is infectious.

"OK." I nod. "I will. Thanks!"

"No problem. See you, Cat. Or Katie. I think Katie suits you better," he adds, tossing the racket into the air again. "For what it's worth."

I don't know what to say to that—so I give a kind of awkward nod and push my way into the stair shaft. I'm late enough as it is.

By the time I get back to Demeter's office, she's rinsed out the hair dye and is typing furiously at her computer.

"Sorry, I got delayed," I say at her office door. "I'll just get my laptop. . . ."

She nods absently. "OK."

I creep in, grab my laptop and printouts—then pause. Here goes.

"Demeter, can I come to the group meeting tomorrow?" I say, as forcefully as I can manage. "I think it would help my development. I'll make up my work," I add quickly. "I'll only stay for an hour or whatever."

Demeter lifts her head and surveys me for a nanosecond, then nods. "Fine." She resumes typing. "Good idea."

I stand there in stupefaction, wondering what I've missed. Good idea? Just like that? Good idea?

"Is there anything else?" She raises her head, and now she's frowning faintly.

"No." I come to. "I mean . . . thanks! Oh, and I got rid of that . . . Alex guy," I add, feeling a faint flush come to my cheek. "At least, I don't mean *got rid of him.* I didn't throw him off the roof!" I give a high-pitched laugh, which makes me instantly wince and turn it into a fake-sounding cough.

(Note to self: Do not laugh in the vicinity of Demeter. Demeter never laughs. *Can* Demeter laugh?)

"Yes, I gathered," says Demeter. "Thanks." And now her expression so clearly says, *Go away please, random junior person,* that I back quickly out of her office before she can change her mind about the meeting. Or indeed about hiring me in the first place.

As I make my way back to my desk, I want to whoop. I'm in! I'm on a wave! I don't mind doing a million surveys if I can start feeling that I'm *getting* somewhere.

I click on my emails—not that they're ever very exciting—and blink in surprise. There's a new one with the subject heading *Hi from Alex.*

Hi, great to meet you. Are you free tomorrow lunchtime? Want to meet again to talk branding/meaning of life/whatever?

Alex

A glow spreads over me. This day just gets better and better.

Sure! Would love to. Where? BTW, Demeter said yes re meeting!

Cat

I send off the email—and a moment later a reply arrives.

Well done you! Quick work!

Let's meet at that Pop-up Christmas Cheer thing at Turnham Green. Say 1:00 p.m. and get a bite to eat?

Alex

A bite to eat. Get a bite to eat.

As I read the words over and over, my mind is skittering around in a cautious, hopeful way. *A bite to eat.* That means . . .

OK, it doesn't *mean* anything exactly, but . . .

He could have said, *I'll book Old Kent Road.* (All the meeting rooms at Cooper Clemmow are named after London Monopoly squares, because Monopoly was the first brand Adrian ever worked on.) That would have been the normal thing. But he's suggested a bite to eat. So this is kind of a date. At least, it's date-ish. It's a date-like thing.

He's asked me out! A really cool, good-looking guy has asked me out!

My heart surges with joy. I'm remembering his sharp eyes, his restless bony hands, his infectious laugh. His dazzling smile. His thrusting hair, disheveled by the breeze on the roof. I really like him, I admit to myself. And he must like me, or why else did he email me so quickly?

Except . . .

My joyous train of thought stops. What if he's invited lots of other people too? I suddenly picture them, all sprawling round a table with drinks and laughter and in-jokes.

Well, I won't know till I turn up, will I?

"What's up?" asks Flora as she comes by with her mug of tea, and I realize there's a massive, foolish beam on my face.

"Nothing," I say at once. I like Flora, but she's the last person I'm sharing this little nugget with. She'd tell everyone and tease me and it would all somehow get spoiled. "Hey, I'm coming to the group meeting tomorrow," I say instead. "Demeter said I could. It'll be really interesting."

"Cool!" Flora glances at my desk. "How's that awful inputting going? I still can't believe Demeter asked you to do it. She's such a cow."

"Oh, it's fine." Nothing can dent my joy right now, not even a boxful of surveys.

"Well, see you," says Flora. And she's two steps away when I add, as casually as I can, "Oh, I met this guy called Alex just now, and I couldn't work out what he does. Do you know him?"

"Alex?" She turns to me with narrowed brows. "Alex Astalis?"

I didn't even *look* at his surname on the email, I realize.

"Maybe. He's tall, dark hair. . . ."

"Alex Astalis." She gives a sudden snort of laughter. "You met Alex Astalis and you 'couldn't work out what he does'? Try, 'He's a partner.' "

"He— *What*?" I'm gobsmacked.

"Alex Astalis?" she repeats, as though to prompt my memory. "*You* know."

"I've never heard of him," I say defensively. "No one's mentioned him."

"Oh. Well, he's been working abroad, so I suppose—" She gives me a closer look. "But you must have heard of the name Astalis."

"As in . . ." I hesitate.

"Yup. Aaron Astalis is his father."

"I see." I'm in slight shock here. Because "Astalis" is one of those names like "Hoover" or "Biro." It means something. It means: *one of the most powerful advertising agencies in the world.* In particular, "Aaron Astalis" means: *supremely rich guy who changed the face of advertising in the 1980s and last year dated that supermodel.* "Wow," I say feebly. "What was her name again?"

"Olenka."

"That's right."

I love that Flora instantly knew I was talking about the supermodel.

"So Alex is his son and our boss. Well, one of them. He's, like, Adrian's level."

I pick up my bottle of water and take a swig, trying to stay calm. But inside I feel like squealing, *Whooooo!* Has this actually happened? Am I really going out to lunch with a cool, good-looking guy who's also the *boss*? I feel surreal. It's as if Life has come along and looked at my boxes of surveys and said, *Oh, my mistake. Didn't mean to land you with all that shit: Here's a consolation prize.*

"But he's so *young*." I blurt out the words before I can stop them.

"Oh, that." Flora nods, almost disparagingly. "Well, you know. He's some genius type. Never even bothered with university. He worked for Demeter years ago at JPH, when he was, like, twenty. But after about five minutes he went and set up on his own. You know he created Whenty? The logo, everything."

"Really?" My jaw sags slightly. Whenty is that credit card

that came out of nowhere and dominated the market. It's renowned as one of the most successful brand launches ever. It gets used in marketing lectures and everything.

"Then Adrian got him to join Cooper Clemmow. But he goes off abroad a lot. He's quite . . . you know." She wrinkles her nose derisively. "One of those."

"One of what?"

"Thinks he's cleverer than everyone else, so, you know, why bother about other people?"

"Oh," I say in surprise. That doesn't sound like the Alex I met.

"He came to a drinks party at my parents' house once," Flora says in the same tone. "He hardly even *talked* to me."

"Oh." I try to look outraged on her behalf. "That's . . . dreadful!"

"He ended up talking to some old man all night. About *astrophysics* or something." She wrinkles her nose again.

"Awful!" I say hastily.

"Why do you want to know about him, anyway?" Flora's eyes focus on me with more interest.

"No reason!" I say hastily. "Didn't know who he was. That's all."

CHAPTER FOUR

Nothing can crush my mood as I head home that evening. Not even the rain, which began halfway through the afternoon and has got steadily heavier. Not even a bus driving through a puddle and drenching me. Not even a gang of boys sniggering at me as I wring out my skirt.

As I open the door to my flat, I'm practically singing to myself. I'm going on a date! I'm going to the group meeting! It's all good—

"Ow!" I come to as my shin barks against something. There's a row of brown cardboard boxes lining one side of our hall. I can barely squeeze past them. It looks like an Amazon warehouse. What *is* all this? I lean down, read a label addressed to Alan Rossiter, and heave a sigh. Typical.

Alan is one of my flatmates. He's a website designer/fitness vlogger, and he's always telling me "fascinating" facts I don't want to know about muscle definition and bone density and once even bowel function. I mean, *urkk*.

"Alan!" I rap on his door. "What's all this in the hall?"

A moment later Alan's door swings open and he gazes down at me. (He's quite tall, Alan. But he also has a very big head, so somehow he doesn't *look* very tall. He actually looks weird.) He's wearing a black singlet and shorts and has an earpiece in, which will be some inspirational app like *Master Your Body, Master the World*, which he once tried to get me into.

"What?" he says blankly.

"These boxes!" I gesture at the crammed hall. "Are they yours? This is a fire hazard!"

"It's my way," he says, and I peer back, confused. His way? His way is to fill our flat with boxes?

"What do you mean, your way?"

"My way." He reaches into an open box and thrusts a plastic pouch at me, which has ORGANIC WHEY: VANILLA printed on it.

"Oh, *whey*. Right." I squint at the cardboard boxes. "But why do you need so much of it?"

"Business model. Gotta buy in bulk. Profit margins. It's a fierce business." He pounds a fist into his hand, and I flinch. Alan has this aggressive way of talking which I think he reckons is "motivational." I sometimes hear him exclaiming to himself while he's doing weights, saying, "Fucking *do* it, Alan. Fucking *do* it, you knobhead."

I mean, really? Knobhead? Is that motivational?

"What business?" I inquire. "You're a web designer."

"And whey distributor. It's my sideline right now, but it's going to be big."

It's going to be big. How many times have I heard my dad say that? His cider business was going to be big, for about six months. Then there were the hand-carved walking sticks—but they took so long to make, he was never going to turn a profit. Then he was going to make a fortune from selling a job lot of some new kind of mousetrap, which he'd got cheap off his friend Dave Yarnett. (They were *gross*. I'll take cider over mousetraps anytime.)

By now I have an instinct about these things. And my instinct about Alan's whey is not good.

"So, are you moving these boxes somewhere else?" I press Alan. "Like, soon?"

Maybe I shouldn't be so cynical, I tell myself. Maybe he has lots of buyers lined up and all this will be gone by tomorrow.

"I'll be selling them." He gives me a shifty look. "Making contacts."

I *knew* it.

"Alan, you can't keep it all here!" I wave my arms at the boxes.

"No space in my room," he says with a shrug. "I've got my weight bench. See you."

And before I can say anything else, he's disappeared back into his room. I want to scream. But, instead, I head to Anita's room and knock cautiously on the door.

Anita is quite an über-person. She's slim, composed, and works very hard at an investment bank. She's exactly my age, and when I moved into the flat, I got quite excited. I thought: *Yes! My new best friend! This will be so cool!* That first night, I hung around in the little kitchen, reorganizing my packets of food and glancing at the door, waiting for her to come in so we could start bonding.

Only when she did come in, to make some mint tea, she

fixed me with a cool gaze and said, "No offense, but I've decided I'm not really *doing* friends till I'm thirty, OK?"

I was so flummoxed, I didn't know what to reply. And, sure enough, I've never really had a proper conversation with her since. All she does is work or talk on the phone to her family in Coventry. She's polite, and she sometimes sends Alan and me emails about rubbish collection—but nothing more. I once asked her why she lived in such a cheap place when she could surely afford something better, and she just shrugged and said, "I'm getting my deposit together. I'm on thirty-one grand," as though it was obvious.

Now she opens the door and I see she's on the phone.

"Oh, hi!" I say. "Sorry to disturb you, only . . . have you seen all these boxes? Have you said anything to Alan?"

Anita puts her hand over the phone and says, in that impassive way of hers: "I'm being sent to Paris for three months."

"Oh."

"So."

There's silence, and I belatedly realize that what she means is: *I don't give a shit about the boxes. I'm off to Paris.*

"Right," I say after a pause. "OK. Well, have fun."

She nods and closes the door, and I look at it silently for a moment. London flat life hasn't been what I expected. I thought it would be all riotous laughter and quirky friends and hilarious stories involving pubs and iconic London landmarks and costume parties or traffic cones. But it hasn't panned out like that. I can't even *imagine* Anita in a costume.

To be fair, I did have some good nights out with the girls at my previous job. But all we *really* did was drink prosecco and bitch, and after then I had such a scare with my overdraft, I swore off going out for a bit. And at Cooper Clemmow, no one seems to socialize at all. Unless you count working late as "socializing."

Anyway, I think as I turn away, *who cares? Because I'm having lunch with Alex Astalis!* Already my spirits are lifting again. It's all good. I'll have some supper and then go on Instagram—

What?

I'm standing, aghast, at the door to the kitchen. It's a sea of boxes. The whole floor is covered, two deep. Boxes are blocking the bottom cupboards. And the freezer. And the oven.

"Alan!" I yell furiously, head back to his door, and pound on it. "What's going on in the kitchen!"

"What?" As Alan opens the door, he has a belligerent look. "I couldn't fit it all in the hall. It's only temporary, till I sell it."

"But—"

"This is my *business,* OK? Could you try *supporting* it?" He shuts the door, and I glare at it. But there's no point trying again. And I'm starving.

I return to the kitchen and cautiously step onto the top layer of boxes. They're so high, my head is nearly brushing the ceiling. I feel like Alice in bloody Wonderland. Surely this is a fire hazard? An *everything* hazard?

Perilously teetering on the cardboard, I just about manage to open the fridge, get out two eggs, and put them on the hob, which is around the level of my knees. At that moment, I get an Instagram private message from Fi, my best friend from uni. I only talk to Fi on Instagram these days; I think she's forgotten there's any other way to communicate.

Hi! How's it going? Sun's shining in Washington Sq Park, God, I love this place. It's great even in winter. Having soy lattes with Dane and Jonah, I told you about them? They are HILARIOUS! You have to come visit!

She's attached a selfie in what I assume is Washington Square Park (I've never been to New York). The sky is vivid blue and her nose is pink, and she's laughing at something out of shot. And I can't help feeling a small wrench inside.

Living in New York was always Fi's aim, just like mine was to live in London. It became a running joke between us at uni—trying to persuade each other to switch allegiance. One Christmas I bought her a Big Ben snow globe and Fi got me an inflatable Statue of Liberty. It was a game.

But now it's real. After graduation, I headed toward London in my roundabout way, while Fi moved to New York to do an internship. And she's never come back. She's totally in love with the city, and she really *has* got a crew of quirky friends, who live in the West Village and rollerblade and go antiquing at flea markets every weekend. She posts pictures all the time and she's even started writing in American spelling.

I mean, I'm glad for her. Really, I am. But sometimes I imagine how it would have been if she'd come to London instead. We could have shared a flat . . . everything would have felt different . . . anyway. There's no point feeling wistful. I quickly message back:

All good here! Was just hanging out with Alan and Anita, we have such a laugh!!! London life is crazy fun!!!

I bend down to stir my eggs, nearly cricking my back. And I'm about to add some cayenne pepper when—

"Aaargh!"

I hear myself cry out before I realize what's happened. The box beneath me has given way. I'm knee-deep in pouches of whey. And some of them must have burst, because white powder is floating up in the most revolting vanilla fug.

"What's happened?" Alan must have heard my scream, because he's already at the door of the kitchen, glowering. "Are you damaging my whey?"

"No, your whey's damaging *me*!" I yell.

One of my ankles does actually feel a bit twisted. And the cloud of whey powder is coating my eggs, I suddenly notice. Which is vile. But I can't make anything else—all my other food is trapped in the freezer. And I'm so *hungry*.

I try to scrabble out of the box, but I feel my shoe heel catching on another pouch and bursting it. (Oops. Maybe won't mention that to Alan.) More powder is floating up from the box, but this isn't white, it's beige. And it smells different. More savory.

"Alan," I say. "Is all this stuff supposed to be vanilla whey?"

"It *is* vanilla whey."

"Well, this isn't." I reach into the box and haul out the pouch I've just broken. "This is . . ." I consult the label. "Powdered chicken stock."

"What?" I pass the pouch over to him, and Alan stares at it in disbelief. "Nooo. What the *fuck*?" With sudden animation he rips open another box and delves inside. He pulls out two plastic pouches and surveys them in consternation. "*Chicken stock?*" And now, in a frenzy, he's pulling pouches out of the boxes and reading the labels. "Whey . . . stock . . . *more* stock . . . Jesus." He covers his face with his hands. "No!" He sounds like a gorilla in torment. "Nooooo!"

Honestly. It's only whey. Or not-whey. Whatever.

"They must have had a mix-up," I say. "Just get them to come and exchange the wrong ones."

"It's not as simple as that!" he practically bellows. "I got them from—from—"

He stops mid-sentence, and I keep very quiet. I'm not going to pursue this, because: 1. Clearly it's something a bit dodgy. 2. This is not my problem. And 3. I don't *want* it to be my problem.

Again, Alan's reminding me of my dad—and I know my dad. He brings you into his problems. He makes you feel like you can't walk away. And next thing you know, you're on the phone trying to sell pouches of unwanted chicken stock.

"Well, I hope you can sort it," I say. "Excuse me."

Somehow I manage to retrieve my foot and crawl cautiously back over the boxes to the kitchen door, with my plate of eggs balanced in one hand. I feel like I'm in some stupid endurance game show and, next minute, spiders will be descending from the ceiling.

"D'you want some chicken stock?" says Alan abruptly. "I'll sell it to you. It's top stuff, excellent quality. . . ."

Is he serious?

"No, thanks. I don't use that much chicken stock."

"Right." Alan subsides. He rips open another box, looks inside, and groans. He looks so distraught that I pat his shoulder.

"Don't worry," I say. "You'll work it out."

"Hey." He looks up, his face glimmering with hope. "Cat."

"Yes?"

"What about a pity shag?"

"What?" I peer at him in total incomprehension. "What do you mean?"

Alan gestures down at himself, as though it's obvious. "You feel sorry for me right now, yes?"

"Er . . . a bit," I say cautiously.

"So you should want to shag me."

OK, am I missing something here?

"Alan . . ." I can't believe I'm asking this question out loud. "Why should I want to shag you?"

"Because that's what a pity shag *is*. That's what it *is*." He reaches toward my bum and I move away. (OK, I leap away.)

"No!"

"No what?"

"Just . . . no! To everything! No pity shag. Nada. Never. Sorry," I add as an afterthought.

Alan gives me a reproachful look and slumps onto one of the boxes. "So basically you're heartless."

"I'm not heartless because I don't want to shag you!" I say furiously. "Just . . . shut up!"

I head to my room, shut the door, and plonk myself on my single bed. My room is so small, there isn't any room for a closet, so I keep all my stuff in a kind of hammock thing slung above my bed. (That's why I wear a lot of non-iron clothes. Plus they're cheap.) I sit cross-legged on the bed, put a forkful of scrambled eggs in my mouth, and shudder at the hideous synthetic vanilla flavor. I need to stop seething. I need to calm down and be Zen. I will therefore distract myself.

I find my Instagram account, consider for a moment, then post a picture of the Shard, with the caption: *Another amazing day, balancing work, play, and not much rest!!* Then I find a gorgeous photo of a hot chocolate with marshmallows, which I took the other day. It wasn't actually my hot chocolate, it was on an outside table at a café in Marylebone. The girl had gone to the ladies' and I swooped in for a picture.

OK, full disclosure: I stalk expensive cafés for Instagrammable pictures. Is there anything wrong with that? I'm not saying I *drank* the hot chocolate. I'm saying, *Look: hot chocolate!* If people assume it was mine . . . well, that's up to them.

I post it up with a simple caption: *Yum!!!* and a few moments later, a new message comes in from Fi:

Life in London sounds a blast!

I shoot back a reply:

It totally is!!!

Then, for good measure, I add:

Guess what, I have a date tomorrow . . . !

I know that'll get her attention, and sure enough her reply comes ten seconds later:

A DATE?? Spill!!!

Simply seeing her reaction makes me glow. Meeting Alex today—laughing with him up on that roof—I felt like a door was opening. A door to something different. Some sort of . . . I don't know. A new existence, maybe. And I know it's just lunch. But still. Every relationship starts off with *just* something, doesn't it? Like, Romeo and Juliet started off with *just* falling madly in love with each other at first sight.

OK. Bad example.

Nothing to spill yet, I'll keep you posted.

I add emojis of a cocktail glass and a smiley face and then—just for fun—I add a love heart.

I send the message, sit back, and take another bite of the horrible eggs. Then, on impulse, I scroll back through my previous Instagram posts, looking at the photos of London cafés, sights, drinks, and smiling faces (mostly strangers). The whole thing is like a feel-good movie, and what's wrong with that? Loads of people use colored filters or whatever on Instagram. Well, my filter is the "this is how I'd like it to be" filter.

It's not that I *lie*. I *was* in those places, even if I couldn't afford a hot chocolate. It's just I don't dwell on any of the not-so-great stuff in my life, like the commute or the prices or having to keep all my stuff in a hammock. Let alone vanilla-whey-coated eggs and obnoxious lechy flatmates. And the point is, it's something to aspire to, something to hope for. One day my life *will* match my Instagram posts. One day.

CHAPTER FIVE

Park Lane has always been my Holy Grail. It's the biggest meeting room at Cooper Clemmow, with a massive red lacquer table and funky chairs in mismatching colors. I've always imagined that sitting round this table would feel like sitting in the Cabinet or something. I've always believed this is the creative heart of the agency, where people come alive and ideas fizz across the table, where the path of branding is changed and history made.

But now I'm here . . . it's just a meeting. No one's changed the path of anything. All people have talked about so far is whether the limited-edition Orange Craze Bar was a mistake. (Craze Bar is our client, so we designed the packaging for the limited edition. But now they've given us ten boxfuls and they're making everyone feel sick.)

"Damn." Demeter interrupts proceedings with her usual dramatic air and gestures at her phone. "Adrian wants a word. I'll be two ticks." As she pushes back her chair, she glances at Rosa. "Can you carry on? Fill everyone in on CCY?"

"Of course." Rosa nods, and Demeter heads out. She's

wearing this amazing fringed suede skirt today, which I can't help gazing at as she leaves.

"OK." Rosa addresses the room. "So Demeter wanted me to tell you about this new potential client, CCY, or Contented Cow Yogurt. It's a range of organic yogurt from some farm in Gloucestershire." Rosa passes round a pile of cheaply printed brochures depicting yogurt pots with a plain Helvetica logo and blurry photo of a cow. "Their riff is how dairy farming is a threatened occupation but they're really great and . . . er . . ." She peers at her notes. "They eat organic grass, something like that?" She looks up. "Does anyone know anything at all about dairy farming?"

Before I can even draw breath, there's a burst of laughter round the table.

"*Dairy* farming?"

"I am so scared of cows," says Flora. "Like, seriously."

"She is," affirms Liz. "We saw some cows at Glastonbury and Flora freaked out. She thought they were bulls." Liz snuffles with laughter.

"They were!" wails Flora. "They were dangerous! And the *smell*. I don't know how anyone can go near them!"

"So who's going down to the farm to meet the Contented Cows?" Rosa is grinning with amusement.

"Oh my God." Flora raises her eyebrows high. "Can you *imagine*?"

"Ooh aaarh . . ." says Mark in a country accent. "The cows need milking, Flora. You'd best get to it, lass."

I've already opened my mouth and closed it twice. Do I know anything about cows? I grew up on a dairy farm. But something's stopping me from speaking. The memory of those girls in Birmingham calling me "Farrrmer Katie" flashes into my brain, making me wince. Maybe I'll just see how the conversation goes for a few moments.

"Demeter wants us to come up with ideas." Rosa looks around the table. "If I say 'countryside,' what do you think?" She stands up and reaches for a marker. "Let's do a bit of word association. 'Countryside' . . ."

" 'Smelly,' " says Flora promptly. " 'Scary.' "

"I'm not writing 'smelly' and 'scary,' " says Rosa impatiently.

"You have to," points out Liz. Which is true. The big thing at Cooper Clemmow is: *Everyone's voice is heard.* It's in the mission statement. So even if you put forward some really stupid idea, everyone has to treat it with respect, because it might lead to something brilliant.

"Fine." Rosa scrawls *smelly* and *scary* on the board, then glares at Flora. "But that's hardly going to sell yogurt. Would you buy smelly, scary yogurt?"

"Actually, I'm dairy-free," says Flora, a bit superciliously. "Do they have any, like, almond milk yogurt?"

"Of course they don't!" Rosa knocks a fist to her head. "They're a bloody dairy farm, not an almond farm."

"Wait." Flora looks at her with wide eyes. "Does almond milk seriously *come from almonds*? I thought it was just like . . . I dunno. A name or something."

Rosa gives a bark of incredulous laughter. "Flora, are you for real?"

"Well, how do they make it, then?" Flora challenges her. "How do they get the milk out of the almonds? Like . . . *milk* them? Squeeze them?"

"That's almond oil," volunteers Mark.

"Well, what do they do, then?"

For a moment Rosa looks caught out—then she snaps, "I don't know! And we're not talking about almond milk; we're talking about cattle milk. Cow milk. Whatever."

Enough sitting back. I *have* to get into this conversation.

"Actually . . ." I begin, raising my hand. "I *do* know a bit about—"

"So, how's it going?" Demeter cuts me off as she sweeps back into the room, holding a sheaf of papers.

"Hopeless!" replies Rosa. "This is all we've got." She gestures at *smelly* and *scary*.

"We don't know anything about cows," says Flora bluntly. "Or the country."

"Or almonds," puts in Mark.

"OK, people." Demeter takes charge in her usual way. She dumps the papers on the table and grabs a marker pen. "Thankfully, *I* know about the country, unlike all you poor urban creatures."

"Really?" Flora looks taken aback, and I sit up. I'm looking at Demeter with a new eye. She knows about the country?

"Absolutely. I go to Babington House at least four times a year, so I *do* have an inside track on this." She eyes us all as though daring us to disagree. "And the truth is, the country is very cool. It's absolutely the new town." Demeter scribbles out *smelly* and *scary* and begins writing. "These are our watchwords: *Organic. Authentic. Artisan. Values. Honest. Mother Earth*. The look we want is . . ." She considers for a moment. "Brown recycled paper. Organic hemp. Twine. Handmade. Rustic but fresh. And a story." She holds up one of the brochures. "So we don't just say, 'This yogurt comes from a cow.' " She taps the photo. "We say, 'This yogurt comes from an English Longhorn named Molly.' We run a competition: 'Bring your children to milk Molly.' "

I'm biting my lip. That cow in the photo isn't an English Longhorn; it's a Guernsey. But I'm not sure correcting Demeter on cow breeds in public is a very bright idea.

"That's good!" says Rosa. "I didn't realize you were so into the country, Demeter."

"The name Demeter actually means 'goddess of the harvest,' " Demeter replies, looking smug. "There's a very rural, down-to-earth side to me. I mean, I *always* shop in farmers' markets when I can."

"Oh, I *love* farmers' markets," chimes in Flora. "Like those eggs you get in straw? So cute."

"Exactly! Straw." Demeter nods and writes down *straw*.

"OK, I can see this now," says Mark, nodding and scribbling on his design pad. "All-natural. This yogurt isn't mass-produced, it's *crafted*."

"Exactly. Crafted. Very good." Demeter scribbles *crafted* on the board.

"So . . ." He pauses. "A *wooden* yogurt pot, maybe?"

"Oh my God!" exclaims Flora. "That is *genius*. Wooden yogurt pots! You could collect them and like . . . put stuff in them! Like pencils, makeup . . ."

"Very expensive," says Demeter thoughtfully. "But if we turned this into an ultra-ultra high-end brand . . ." She taps the marker on her hand thoughtfully.

"Prestige pricing," says Rosa, nodding.

I know about prestige pricing—it's where you charge more

money and consumers think, *Ooh, that must be good,* and buy a whole heap more.

"I think people would pay a lot of money for a wooden pot with artisan yogurt in it," says Mark seriously. "And the name of the cow printed on the pot."

"We'll brainstorm names," agrees Rosa. "The cow's name is crucial. It's everything, in fact."

"Daisy," suggests Flora.

"*Not* Daisy," counters Liz firmly.

"Anything else?" Demeter addresses the table, and I raise a hand. I fought to get into this meeting; I *have* to contribute.

"You could talk about whether they look after their cows properly?" I volunteer. "I mean, they're called 'Contented Cow Yogurt,' so they must be happy cows or whatever? And we could use this idea in the image?"

"Yes!" Demeter seizes on this. "Animal welfare, *huge*. Happy animals, *huge*." She writes *happy shiny cows* on the board and underlines it. "Well done." She gives me a nod, and I feel myself blossom. I contributed something in the meeting! OK, it was just a small something—but it's a start.

After the meeting ends, I send a batch of survey results to Demeter. Then she sends back a message saying: Actually, could she have them all in a different format? Which on the one hand is a pain. But on the other hand means that at least I don't sit there all morning doing nothing but getting nervous about my date-or-whatever-it-is. I'm occupied; I'm focused; I'm barely even thinking about lunchtime. . . .

OK, full disclosure: This is a lie. I'm *totally* getting nervous. How could I not? This is Alex Astalis. He's huge! As I now realize, having googled him for two solid hours last night.

I can't believe I thought he was some random guy. I can't believe I thought he might be an *intern*. This is the trouble with meeting people in real life: They don't come with profiles attached. Or maybe it's a good thing. If I'd known he was so important, I never would have messed around on stilts with him.

Anyway, time to go. I pull my hair behind my ears, then forward. Then back again. Argh, I don't know. At least my bangs look OK. I hadn't realized how high-maintenance bangs were before I got them. They're so bloody *needy*. If I don't smooth mine down with hair straighteners every day, they pop up all morning, like, *Hi! We're your bangs! We thought we'd spend all day at a forty-five-degree angle; that OK by you?*

Anyway. It really *is* time to go.

I stand up so self-consciously that I'm sure everyone will turn from their screens and say, *And where are* you *going?* But of course they don't. No one even notices as I leave.

The pop-up Christmas Cheer place is a bit of a walk from the office, and as I arrive I feel rosy-cheeked and out of breath. Apparently it "pops up" every December but no one knows quite how to describe it. It's a kind of market-cum-café-cum-fairground, with a "gingerbread house" for children and mulled wine for grown-ups and carols blaring through a sound system.

I see Alex at once, standing by the mulled-wine stand. He's wearing a slim-fit coat, a purple scarf, and a gray hipster cap and holding two plastic glasses of mulled wine. He grins as soon as he sees me and says, as though we're mid-conversation, "You see, *this* is the problem. They have a merry-go-round but no one to go on it." He gestures at the merry-go-round—and he's right. There are only a couple of toddlers sitting on horses, both looking fairly terrified. "All the children are in school," he adds. "Or they've gone home for lunch. I've been watching them disappear. Mulled wine?" He hands me a glass.

"Thanks!"

We clink the plastic and I feel a little exhilarated swoop inside. This is fun. Whatever "this" is. I mean, I can't quite work out if it's business or . . . not-business. . . . Whatever. It's fun.

"So. To work." Alex drains his drink. "And the question is: Can we rebrand this?"

"What?" I echo, puzzled.

"This. This pop-up."

"What, *this*?" I look round. "You mean the . . . fair? Market thing?"

"Exactly." His eyes gleam. "It doesn't even know what to call itself. But they want to roll out all over London. Cash in on seasonal cheer. And go large. Bigger venues. Advertising. Tie-ins."

"Right. Wow." I look around the stalls and fairy lights with new eyes. "Well, people do love Christmas. And people do love a pop-up."

"But a pop-up *what*?" counters Alex. "Is it a gourmet-food destination or is it fun for the kiddies or a craft fair or what?" He brandishes his empty glass at me. "What do we think of the mulled wine?"

"Very good," I say truthfully.

"Whereas the merry-go-round . . ." He wrinkles his nose. "A little tragic, no?"

"Maybe they need to focus on the food." I nod. "Food is a huge deal. Do they need the other stuff?"

"Good question." Alex starts toward the merry-go-round. "Let's try it out."

"*What?*"

"We can't assess the merry-go-round unless we go on the merry-go-round," he says gravely. "After you." He gestures toward the horses, and I grin back.

"Well, OK!"

I clamber up onto a horse and fumble for my purse, but Alex holds up a hand.

"On me. Or, rather, on the company. This is essential research." He climbs up onto the horse next to mine and pays the attendant, who is a grumpy-looking guy in a parka. "Now I expect we'll have to wait for the hordes to join us," Alex observes, and I can't help giggling. It's us and the two toddlers—no one else is even nearby. "In your own time!" Alex cheerfully calls to the guy in the parka, who ignores us.

I can feel my bangs blowing about in the wind and curse them silently. Why can't they stay put? This is quite bizarre, sitting on a wooden horse, at eye level with a guy who in theory is my boss but doesn't *feel* like my boss. Demeter feels like my boss. Even Rosa feels a bit like my boss. But this guy feels like . . . My stomach squeezes with yearning before I can stop it.

He feels like fun. He feels like cleverness and irreverence

and wit and charm, all packaged up in a long, lean frame. He feels like the man I've been waiting to meet ever since I moved to London, ever since I *wanted* to move to London.

I surreptitiously run my eyes over him and a fresh wave of longing overcomes me. That knowing flash in his eye. Those cheekbones. That *smile*.

"So what's happening with the products from Asia?" I ask. "The stilts and stuff?"

"Oh, those." A frown crosses his face. "We're not taking the project on. We don't think it'll work, teaming up with Sidney Smith."

I feel a tweak of disappointment. I suppose I'd half-imagined working on the project with him. (OK, full disclosure: I'd *totally* imagined working on the project with him, maybe late into the night, maybe ending up in some passionate clinch on the shiny lacquer table in Park Lane.)

"So, head won over heart."

"That's right."

"Shame," I venture, and an odd, lopsided smile passes over Alex's face.

"Heads. Hearts. Same old, same old."

"Although *actually*," I say after a moment's thought, "maybe it was heart over head. Maybe you don't *want* to work with Sidney Smith. So you've made out like it was a rational business decision but it was instinct all along."

I don't know what's giving me the confidence to speak out so openly. Maybe it's the fact we're both sitting on fairground horses.

"You're bright, aren't you?" Alex gives me a sharp look. "I

think you're right. Truth is, we just don't like those Sidney Smith guys."

"There you go."

"*Is* there a difference between heads and hearts, anyway?" Alex seems fascinated by the topic.

"People talk about 'head over heart,'" I say, thinking aloud. "But they mean 'one part of their head over another part of their head.' It's not really 'head over heart,' it's 'head over head.'"

"Or 'heart over heart'?" Alex's eyes glint at me.

There's a strange little silence between us, and I wonder where on earth I can segue naturally from here. I'm not sure if it's the way he's looking at me or the way he said "heart" like that—but either way, my own heart's feeling a bit fluttery right now.

Then Alex leans over, breaking the mood. "Hey. Your hair's gone mad."

Abruptly I forget all about the Asian products, heads, *and* hearts. My bloody, *bloody* bangs.

"It always does that," I say flushing. "It's awful."

He laughs. "It's not awful."

"It is. I should never have got bangs cut, but—" I stop dead. I can't exactly say, *But I wanted to look like a different person.*

"It's just a bit . . . the breeze . . ." He leans over from his wooden horse toward mine. "May I?"

"Sure." I swallow. "No problem."

Now he's gently tweaking my bangs. I'm fairly sure this is against company policy. Bosses aren't supposed to adjust hair, are they?

His face is only inches away from mine now and my skin tingles under his gaze. His brown eyes are surveying my face in that frank, interested way he has. As they meet mine they seem to have a question in them. Or . . . do they?

Oh God, am I *inventing* all this? My thoughts are lurching wildly back and forth. I can feel a spark here, I really can. But can he? I mean, I only met this guy yesterday. Now I'm on what might be a date—*feels* like a date—except he's my superior, and I don't know for sure what's going on. . . .

Without warning, the merry-go-round starts up, and Alex, who's still leaning toward me, falls half off his horse.

"Shit!" He grabs at my horse's neck.

"Oh God!" I cry out. "Hold on!"

The horses are farther apart from each other than you'd think, and Alex is now suspended between the two, almost horizontally. He looks like some action hero between two cars. (Well, not *exactly* like an action hero, since this is a merry-go-round, and jingly music has started playing, and a little kid is pointing at him and yelling, "The man fell off his horsey!")

His hands are gripping my horse's neck, and I can't help staring at them. He's got bony fingers. Strong wrists. His sleeve has ridden up to reveal a tiny tattoo on one: an anchor. I wonder what that's all about.

"I should have had horse-riding lessons first." Alex is panting as he tries to right himself.

I nod, trying not to laugh. "Merry-go-round horses *are* pretty dangerous. I mean, you're not even wearing a riding hat. It's foolhardy."

"Reckless," he agrees.

"Oy! You!" The man in the parka has noticed Alex. "Stop mucking around!"

"OK!" With an almighty heave, Alex gets himself back in his saddle. The horses are swooping up and down as we spin around, and I grin madly at Alex.

"I take it back!" he shouts over the music. "This is great!"

"Yes!" I call back. "I love it!"

I want to freeze-frame this moment in my mind. Whirling around on a merry-go-round, with a gorgeous, funny guy . . . at Christmas . . . I mean, all I need is for a few snowflakes to fall and the scene will be perfect.

"Rosa!" Alex suddenly calls to someone on the ground, and my scene splinters. Rosa? As in . . . *Rosa*? "We're up here!" Alex waves his arms. "Gerard! Rosa!"

There's Rosa, in her dark-green peacoat, staring up at us blankly. Beside her, a gray-haired guy I don't recognize is tapping at his iPhone. As the merry-go-round comes to a halt, I feel my happy glow fade away. Right. So whatever this is, it's not a date.

I mean, I never thought it was a date. I *didn't*. I only ever thought it was date-*ish*.

Was it date-ish? Just for a few minutes?

We both slither down from our horses, with Rosa watching unsmilingly, and I suddenly feel stupid that we were up there in the first place. Alex heads straight to Rosa and the gray-haired man.

"Hi, there! Rosa, you know Cat."

"Gerard," says the man, and we shake hands.

"What are you doing here, Cat?" Rosa frowns. "I didn't know you were on this project."

"I brought her into the group," says Alex easily. "Another pair of eyes. Where are the others?"

"On their way," says Rosa. "And I really think, Alex, that this is all about *specifics*. I spoke to Dan Harrison today and he's incredibly vague. . . ." As she talks, she heads toward the market stalls. Alex seems absorbed in what she's saying, and Gerard—whoever Gerard is—is sending a text.

As I trail along behind, I feel totally mixed up. So this was always a work thing. It was always a group thing. Am I all wrong about everything? Did I fabricate that spark between us? Am I a deluded loon, crushing on my boss?

But then, as we're walking along, Alex turns and gives me a little wink. A little flash of camaraderie. *You and me,* he seems to say. And although I don't react beyond smiling politely back, I clutch it to my heart like a hug. I *didn't* invent that. That was something. I'm not sure what—but something.

I don't stay at the pop-up for as long as the others, because Alex gets caught up in some long phone call from New York, during which Rosa makes it quite plain she thinks I should go back and carry on with the surveys.

"It was great that you gave your input, Cat," she says briskly. "We love hearing from junior staff. I mean, it was very cool that Alex asked you along. But you've really got to crack on with that research, yeah?"

And there's something quite steely about her tone. So, without even saying goodbye to Alex, I head back. But I don't feel dispirited—quite the opposite. When I reach the office, I run up the stairs and hum the merry-go-round tune as I make my way to my desk.

Flora looks up. "Hey, Cat. I was looking for you. So, listen, do you fancy going to Portobello on Saturday?"

"Wow!" I say in delight. "Definitely! I'd love to! Thanks!"

Don't sound so overexcited, I chide myself. It's only going to Portobello market. It's no big deal. People do this all the time.

But the truth is, I don't. Weekends can be a bit lonely for me, not that I'd ever admit it.

"Great!" Flora beams. "Well, come to my house first—we're just round the corner—and then we'll go Christmas shopping. . . ."

As Flora babbles on, I sit at my desk, suffused with happiness. Life's turning around! First of all, an interesting man is . . . well. What is he? He's on the horizon. And now I'm going to Portobello with Flora, and I can post loads of cool stuff on Instagram . . . and it'll be true. For once, for *once*, it'll be true.

CHAPTER SIX

The next morning is a proper crisp winter's sunny day. In fact, it's so bright, I almost need sunglasses as I step out of the house. I pause on the doorstep to get some lip balm and see Alan at the front gate, engaged in some kind of argument with a stunning teenage girl as he unfolds his bike.

She has glowing latte-colored skin, bright blue-green eyes, super-short hair—almost shaved—and long teenage legs poking out of a school-uniform skirt. She's holding a stack of flyers, and it's these at which Alan seems to be directing his ire.

"Charities are all corrupt," I hear him saying in disapproving tones. "I'm not doing it anymore. It's all middle-management bollocks and tube ads. I'm not paying money for a tube ad. You want to help someone, help a *real* person."

"I am a real person," objects the teenage girl. "I'm called Sadiqua."

"Well, I don't know that, do I?" says Alan. "How do I know you're not a con artist?"

"OK, *don't* give me any money," says the girl, sounding exasperated. "Just sign the petition."

"Yes, and what will you do with my signature?" Alan raises his eyebrows as though to say, *I win*, and gets on his bike. "And this path is private property," he adds, gesturing to our crumbling, crappy path. "So don't get any ideas."

"Ideas?" The girl stares at him. "What ideas?"

"I couldn't say. But I'm telling you: private property."

"You think I'm planning to occupy your front path or something?" says the girl incredulously.

"I'm just saying, private property," Alan repeats impassively. He cycles off and the girl makes a furious sound, like the whinny of a horse.

"Tosser!" she exclaims—and I have to agree.

"Hiya," I say as I approach her, wanting to make up for Alan's rudeness. "Are you collecting for something?"

"Petition for the community center," she says, in such a garbled way it comes out "Psh'ncommucenter." She hands me a flyer reading *Save Our Community Center,* and I glance over it. It's all about cuts and children's prospects and it seems like a really genuine thing, so I put a couple of pound coins in her tin and scrawl my name on the petition.

"Good luck!" I say, and start striding off down the road.

A moment later I'm aware of a presence at my shoulder, and I turn to see that Sadiqua is following me.

"Hi," I say. "Did you want something?"

"What do you do?" she asks chattily. "Like your job and that."

"Oh! Well, I'm in branding. Creating images and logos for products. It's really interesting," I add, in case this is my chance to provide Inspiration To The Younger Generation. "It's hard work but rewarding."

"D'you know anyone in the music industry?" Sadiqua continues, as though I haven't spoken. "Because me and my mate Layla, we've got a band and we made a demo." She produces a CD from her pocket. "Layla's uncle made these. We just need to get them out there."

"That sounds great!" I say encouragingly. "Well done."

"So can you take one?" She thrusts it at me. "Get it heard?"

Get it *heard*? By whom?

"I'm not in the music industry," I explain. "Sorry—"

"But branding, that's music, innit?"

"Well, not really—"

"But music in ads?" she persists. "Who does the music in ads? Someone does all that and they need sounds, don't they?" She blinks at me with her blue-green eyes. "They're looking for new sounds?"

You have to admire her persistence. And she's right, someone does do the music in ads, even if I have no idea who it is.

"OK. Look. I'll see what I can do." I take the CD from her and put it in my bag. "So, good luck with it all—"

"D'you know any model agents?" she carries on without missing a beat. "My auntie says I should be a model, only I'm not tall enough, but why does that matter in a photo? Like, they got Photoshop, so why does it matter? Why d'you need to be tall and thin? They've got Photoshop. Just use Photoshop, know what I mean? Photoshop." She looks at me expectantly.

"Right," I say warily. "Actually, I don't know much about modeling either. Sorry, I *do* really need to keep walking. . . ."

Sadiqua nods with resigned disappointment, as though it's only what she expected of me. Then, easily keeping pace with my stride, she reaches into her pocket.

"You want some jewelry? I make jewelry." She pulls out a tangle of beaded bracelets and thrusts them at me. "Fiver each. You buy them for your mates and that."

I can't help bursting into laughter.

"Not today," I say. "But maybe another day. Aren't you supposed to be collecting for your community center?"

"Oh, that." She gives a philosophical shrug. "That's gonna close, anyway. I'm just collecting because, like, we're all collecting, but we won't save it or nothing."

"You might!" I say. "What does it do, exactly?"

"All sorts. Like, they give kids breakfast and that. I always used to have my breakfast there, 'cos my mum never—" Sadiqua stops dead, and her bouncy veneer falters for an instant. "They give you Corn Flakes and that. But it costs money. Corn Flakes every day costs money, dunnit?"

I look at her silently for a moment. I like this girl. She's funny and energetic and actually very beautiful, even without Photoshop.

"Give me a few more flyers," I say, and take them from her. "Maybe I can help you raise some money."

At the office I find an old CD drive in the cupboard, so I plug it into my computer and listen to Sadiqua's CD. Obviously I'm hoping that it'll blow me away and that I've discovered a star. Sadly, it's just two girls singing a Rihanna song and then dissolving into giggles. But I decide I'll still do what I can with it, and I'll *definitely* try to raise money for her community center.

I don't have any specific plans, or even ideas really, and I'm certainly not planning to bring it up with anyone. But then, on my way out that evening, when I see Alex waiting for the same lift as me, I find myself panicking for things to say. It's gone 9:00 P.M.—I had a stack of stuff to catch up on—and I didn't expect to see anyone. Let alone him.

I haven't seen him since the carousel yesterday, but of course he's crossed my mind about ninety-five thousand times. As I approach, I can feel the blood moving to my face and a horrible awkwardness rising up my throat. How *are* you supposed to talk to an attractive man you think you might have a thing for, anyway? I've lost every natural instinct I ever had. My face feels frozen. My hands feel flappy. As for eye contact, forget it. I have *no* idea what the appropriate level of eye contact is right now.

"Hi," he says, smiling, as I reach the lift doors. "You're working late."

"Hi." I smile back. "I had some stuff to do." And I know the onus isn't on me to continue the conversation, but as I mentioned, I'm panicking. So before I can stop myself, I blurt out: "I've got a really great cause I'd like to put forward as the company charity."

This isn't strictly true. I don't *know* it's a great cause—I only have Sadiqua's word for it. But right now I need a topic of conversation.

"Oh yes?" says Alex, looking interested.

"It's a community center near where I live. In Catford. It does breakfast clubs, that kind of thing, but it's closing down. Cuts, you know . . ." I pull the leaflet out of my bag and hand it to him. "This is it."

"Good for you," says Alex, scanning the leaflet. "Well, we'll consider it for next year. Or did you want to organize some kind of fundraiser meanwhile? What did you have in mind?"

The lift doors open and we both step in and of course now my mind is totally blank. Fundraiser. Fundraiser. Cupcake sale? No.

"Like, something that's a challenge?" I say, grasping at straws. "So you feel you get something out of it as well as raising money? Like the marathon. But not the marathon," I add hastily.

"Something hard, but not the marathon," says Alex thoughtfully as we exit the lift into the empty, dimly lit lobby. "I'll tell you the hardest thing in the world: that fucking skiing exercise. My personal trainer made me do it last night. Bastard," he adds, so venomously I want to giggle.

"What skiing exercise?" I say, because I've never done any skiing exercises. Or any skiing, for that matter.

"The one where you sit against the wall. Torture. You know the one." He looks at me. "You don't?"

He goes over to a big empty wall, screen-printed with COOPER CLEMMOW in lots of different fonts, and takes up a position sitting against the wall, his thighs parallel to the floor.

"Doesn't look so hard," I say, just to wind him up.

"Are you joking? Have you *tried* it?"

"OK." I grin. "Challenge accepted."

I take up a similar position, a couple of yards away from him, and for a while there's silence. The two of us are concentrating on the task in hand. I have pretty strong thighs—years of riding—but I can already feel them start to burn. Before long they're really quite painful, but I'm not going to give in, I'm *not* going to . . .

"Tough, aren't you?" says Alex, in a kind of gasp.

"Oh, what, this is the *exercise*?" I manage. "This is supposed to be *difficult*? I thought we were just warming up."

"Ha-ha, ha-ha, very funny . . ." Alex is quite pink in the face. "OK, you win. I'm out."

He slithers to the floor, just as my own thighs start feeling like they might spontaneously combust. I force myself to stay put for three more seconds, then collapse.

"*Don't* tell me you could have kept going for another half hour," says Alex.

"I could have kept going for another half hour," I say at once, and Alex laughs. He looks over at me and there's a flicker of . . . something in his eye. The same something I saw before. The you-and-me something.

Neither of us speaks for a moment. It's one of those still little silences that you get when you're adjusting your position in a conversation, maybe striking out in a new direction. . . . But again I'm the one who panics, who brings things back to safety.

"I'm not sure how popular that'll be as a fundraiser," I say, getting to my feet.

"Well, it's easier than a marathon," says Alex.

"You *say* that—" I break off and peer out of the glass doors as a flash of red catches my eye. "Wait a minute. What on earth is that?"

The flash of red has turned into a streak. It's red and white.

A cluster of red and white . . . I stare disbelievingly. Are those *Santa hats*?

"What the hell—" Alex has followed my gaze and breaks into amazed laughter. "What is *that*?"

We give each other a brief look, then simultaneously make for the door. Alex swipes us out with his card and we both hurry into the crisp evening, gasping like kids at the sight before us.

About two hundred Santas on bikes are filling the street. Some are flashing red and white lights, some are tooting horns, and from somewhere is blasting Mariah Carey. It's like a great big traveling Santa party.

"This is insane," says Alex, still laughing.

"Join in!" calls a guy in a Santa hat, seeing us gawping. "Collect a bike and a hat! Join in!" He beckons invitingly. "Don't be scared, be a Santa!" Alex and I stare at him, then at each other again.

"Come on," says Alex, and we dash across the road to where people are collecting bikes from the hire point opposite.

"Twenty pounds to ride, Santa hat included," a girl is shouting, waving a bucket at all the onlookers. "Join in! All for Great Ormond Street Hospital!"

"We have to do this," says Alex. "Why would we *not* put on Santa hats and ride bikes round London? Are you free?" He meets my eyes, and again I feel a little fillip in my stomach.

"Yes, I'm free. Let's do it!" I can't help laughing at the ridiculousness of it. All around us, people are joining the Santa throng and singing along to Mariah. I see a pair of Santas riding a tandem, and one guy has pitched up on a penny-farthing.

This is why I moved to London, I find myself thinking, with a swell of glee. *This is it.*

"I'm paying for both of us," adds Alex firmly. "I haven't done enough for charity recently, and your altruism shames me." He puts a fifty-pound note into the bucket before I can stop him and collects a bike, which he passes to me.

"Here's your Santa hat." The girl with the bucket holds out a hat with a light-up bobble and pops it on my head. I wheel my bike into place and look over at Alex, who's wearing a light-up hat too. Stars are flashing all around the white rim of his, making him look endearingly angelic.

"Thanks," I say, nodding my head at the bucket. "You shouldn't have, but thanks."

"You're very welcome." He smiles disarmingly.

I want to say something else—something witty—but there's no time, because we're moving. It's ages since I've ridden a bike, but my feet find the rhythm instantly, and we're off, down the road, a mass of pedaling Santas, with music and laughter fueling us along our way.

It's one of the most magical nights of my life. We cycle from Chiswick to Hammersmith, then Kensington High Street, still full of shoppers, and past the Albert Hall. Then Knightsbridge, where Harrods is all lit up like fairyland and the shops are full of Christmas displays. We go along Piccadilly and up and down Regent Street, and I crane my neck to look at the dazzling festive lights overhead.

The evening air is rushing against my cheeks as I pedal. There are red-and-white Santa hats everywhere in my vision. I can hear the jingle of bike bells and tooting of car horns acknowledging us and the Santa cyclists roaring familiar Christmas songs over the sound system. I've never felt so invigorated. They're playing that song about it being "Christmas every day"—well, I wish it could be this *moment* every day. Cycling through Piccadilly Circus. Waving at passersby. Feeling like a Londoner. And looking over, every so often, to smile at Alex. There hasn't really been much chance to chat, but he's always within ten yards of me, and I know when I look back I won't remember, "I cycled with the Santas," I'll remember, "*We* cycled with the Santas."

At Leicester Square we stop for hot chocolate provided by a coffee-shop chain. As I'm collecting two cups, Alex comes over, wheeling his bike, a broad grin on his face.

"Hi!" I say, and hand him one. "Isn't it great?"

"Best way to travel," he says emphatically, and takes a sip. "This is the end of the official route, apparently. We all split up and go our different ways; drop our bikes off wherever we like. I'm meeting someone for a drink now, anyway." He glances at his watch. "In fact, I'm late."

"Oh, right," I say, trying not to feel crestfallen. I'd kind of thought . . . hoped we might go on. . . .

But that was stupid. Of *course* he's meeting someone for a drink. He's a successful guy in London with a social life.

"I just need to text . . . them," he says absently, tapping at his phone. "Now, what about you? Where are you headed?"

"I'm going home to Catford. There's a drop-off point at Waterloo." I force myself back into practicality. "I'll head there, then I can catch the train."

"You'll be OK?"

"Fine!" I say brightly. "And thanks again. That was fantastic." I put my hot chocolate down on the stand. (It's lukewarm and not very nice, in fact.) "I'll be off, then. See you in the office."

"Sure." A thought seems to hit Alex. "Oh no. You won't. I'm going to Copenhagen first thing."

"Copenhagen." I wrinkle my brow. "Demeter's going there too. A design conference, isn't it?"

"Exactly." He nods. "But I'll see you around, I'm sure."

"It was amazing, wasn't it?" I can't help saying in a rush.

"Amazing." He nods again, smiling, and we meet eyes. And the appropriate level of eye contact right now seems to be: *full*.

For an instant, neither of us speaks. I'm not even sure I can breathe. Then Alex lifts his hand in a kind of salute and I turn my bike to go. I could probably prolong the conversation a little longer, chitchat about the bikes or whatever . . . but I want to leave while the evening is still perfect.

And then rewind and play it in my head, all the way home.

CHAPTER SEVEN

Life has a dreamy quality at the moment. Good-dreamy and bad-dreamy. The cycling Santas . . . Alex smiling at me as we pedaled along . . . going to Portobello with Flora later today—that's all good-dreamy. The office Christmas party is on Monday night and I keep imagining bumping into Alex in my little black dress. Chatting . . . laughing . . . he puts a careless hand on my arm when no one's looking . . . we go on for a drink . . . back to his place . . .

OK, full disclosure: I keep imagining a *lot* of different scenarios.

So life would pretty much be perfect right now . . . if it weren't for the bad-dreamy stuff. More precisely, the fact that my laptop died on Thursday and I had to buy a new one and it's given me this huge great well of fear, which I'm trying my hardest to ignore.

I still can't believe it broke. The IT people at work couldn't fix it, nor could the guy in the shop. He tried for an hour, then shrugged and said, "That's fucked. Well, you needed an upgrade, anyway," and my stomach went all gnarly with panic.

I need a laptop for all my design projects; I couldn't *not* replace it. But I didn't have that money. I'm on a really tight, planned-out budget; every pound matters—and a broken laptop is like a financial hurricane. It's made a huge hole in my finances, and whenever I contemplate it, I feel cold with terror. I've been so careful with money. *So* careful. And then this comes along. . . . It's just not fair.

Anyway. I won't think about it. I'll have a great day with Flora and browse all the market stalls, and obviously I won't be able to buy anything but that's OK, because that's not what it's about, is it? It's about the atmosphere. The vibe. The friendship.

Flora has suggested we meet at her house, and as I walk along the road, I feel my jaw sagging. If I thought Demeter's house was impressive, it's nothing on these mansions. The steps are twice the size of her steps. They all have front gardens and white stucco like wedding cakes. I find number 32 and survey it cautiously. This can't be Flora's house, surely. Is this . . . her *parents'* house?

"Hi!" The door is flung open and I see Flora framed in the massive doorway, still in her dressing gown. "I saw you walking along. I've *totally* overslept, sorry! D'you want some breakfast?"

She ushers me into a hall filled with marble and lilies and a housekeeper polishing the banisters, then down an underlit glass staircase to an enormous kitchen with concrete work surfaces. Flora's parents are seriously rich, I realize. And seriously cool.

"So . . . this is your parents' house?" I say, to be sure. "It's amazing."

"Oh," says Flora, without interest. "Yes, I suppose. D'you want a smoothie?" She starts throwing fruit into a NutriBullet, followed by chia seeds, organic ginger, and some special seaweed extract which I've seen in health shops and costs about three quid a shot.

"Here!" She hands me a glass and I devour it hungrily. My own breakfast was a cup of tea and oats with milk: total cost about 30p. Then Flora grabs a paper bag full of croissants and ushers me out again. "Come on. Help me get dressed."

Her room is at the top of the house and has its own bathroom and dressing room. The wallpaper is a sheeny silver design of birds, and there are Diptyque candles everywhere and built-in cupboards and an antique desk. Everywhere you look, there's something gorgeous. But Flora doesn't even seem to notice her surroundings—she's pulling jeans out of her wardrobe and cursing because she can't find the ones she wants.

"So you've just lived here since uni?" I ask. "You've never moved out?"

Flora's eyebrows rise in horror. "Move out? God, no. I mean, I could never afford to. Like, the rent and the food and everything . . . Who can do that? *None* of my friends have moved out! We're all going to live at home till we're thirty!"

I feel a tiny swell of some emotion I don't want to admit to, like envy, or possibly even—just for a nanosecond—hatred.

No. Take that back. I don't hate Flora; of course I don't. But she does have everything so *easy*.

"Well, I don't have parents who live in London." I force a cheerful smile. "So. You know. I have to rent."

"Oh, that's right," says Flora. "Aren't you from the Midlands or somewhere? You don't have an accent, though."

"Actuall—" I begin, but Flora has disappeared into her dressing room again. I don't think she's that interested in where I come from, to be honest.

I wait patiently as Flora does her eyeliner about five times, then she grabs her bag and says, "Right! Let's go shopping!" with an infectious beam. She's got her blond hair piled on top of her head, and a boho sheepskin coat, and glittery eye shadow, and if you gave her a caption it would read *Totally Up For Some Fun*. We run down the stairs, both giggling, and a door opens on the second floor.

"Children! You'll disturb Daddy!"

"Mummy, we're not *children,*" pouts Flora, as an elegant woman appears on the landing. She looks just like an older Flora but even skinnier. She's wearing Chanel pumps and tight jeans and smells amazing. "This is Cat."

"Cat!" Flora's mother puts a cool hand in mine, then turns back to Flora. "Are you off to Portobello?"

"Yes, we're Christmas shopping! Only I'm a bit broke." Flora looks wheedlingly at her mother. "And I need to find something for Granny. . . ."

"Sweetheart." Flora's mum rolls her eyes. "All right, look in my bag. Take a hundred. *No* more," she adds sternly. "You're always cleaning me out of cash."

"Thanks, Mummy!" Flora pecks her mother on the cheek and dances down the rest of the stairs. "Come on, Cat!"

My mind is reeling. A hundred quid? Just like that? I haven't asked Dad for money for years. And I never would, even if he did have a load of spare cash, which he doesn't.

I watch as Flora helps herself from her mum's purse, then follow her down the palatial white steps of her house. If

Demeter has steps fit for a princess, these are steps fit for a queen. I want to take a picture, but that would be uncool. Maybe when I've got to know Flora better.

The air is crisp, and as we stride along, I feel buoyant. This is *such* a cool area of London. The rows of pastel houses are adorable, like something from a storybook, and I keep stopping to take pictures for Instagram.

"So, what d'you want to get?" asks Flora as we round the corner to Portobello, slightly battling the crowds of tourists.

"I don't know!" I laugh. "Nothing much. I'll just browse."

My eyes are drinking in the sight of endless market stalls stretching ahead of us, with everything from necklaces to Kashmiri scarves, vintage cameras to antique plates. I've been to Portobello before, but not at Christmas, and it has an extra-fun vibe today. There are decorations up on the lampposts, and a group of guys in hipster hats are singing a cappella carols, while a CD stall blasts out Christmas songs in competition. There are mulled-wine stalls and a mince-pie stall and the delicious scent of freshly made crepes in the air.

I have a sudden flashback to sipping mulled wine with Alex, and find myself thinking, *Ooh, will that be "our drink"?* before I wrench my thoughts away, like a needle off a vinyl record. Get a grip, Katie. Mulled wine? "Our drink"? I might as well say that Santa hats will be "our headwear."

Flora finds a china elephant for her granny and then drags me into a designer shop to buy a sequined dress for the office party. I wasn't intending to get anything, but it turns out that some of the prices aren't *too* scary. I see a woolly hat for Dad, only £8, and then a rack of £1 clothes, which Flora thinks is *hilarious*. Especially when I actually buy a crochet cardigan. At another stall we both try on crazy felt hats and I take loads of photos and I'm exhilarated. This is the quirky London life I always wanted to have.

Flora has been texting throughout the morning, and as we pause by a stall of mirrors she scowls at her phone.

"Something up?" I ask, and she makes a huffing noise.

"No. Yes." She shoves her phone away. *"Men."*

"Oh, *men*," I agree, even though I don't know exactly what she means.

"Anyone in your life at the moment?" she asks, and I feel a flutter in my stomach. I mean, the answer is no. But my mind is roaming back to that moment on the merry-go-round, the feel of Alex's fingers in my hair.

"No. At least, there's this guy . . ."As I meet Flora's eyes I laugh, partly out of relief at having someone to talk to. "I'm sure he isn't interested, but . . ."

"I bet he is! What's he like?"

"Oh, you know. Gorgeous. Dark hair. Tattoo," I add, with a little grin.

There. That's vague enough. It could be anyone.

"A tattoo!" Flora's eyes widen. "Wow. And where did you meet him?"

"Through other people," I say vaguely. "You know. It was a bit random."

"So, has anything happened?" She makes such a comical face that I laugh again.

"Nothing real. Just flirting. Wishing," I add, with sudden honesty. "And what about you?"

"Well, I'm supposed to be seeing this guy called Ant, only

I think he's going off me." She looks disconsolate. "He never replies to my texts. . . ."

"They don't."

"I know, right? What's so hard about sending a text?"

"They think sending a text makes them lose part of their soul," I say, and Flora giggles.

"You're funny," she says, and links her arm in mine. "I'm so glad you've joined the office, Cat."

We walk on for a few seconds, and I take a photo of a stall selling only vintage car horns. Then Flora turns to me, looking thoughtful.

"Listen, Cat, there's something I need to ask you. Did you know we meet for regular drinks at Wednesday lunchtime? Me, Rosa, and Sarah. At the Blue Bear. Every week."

"Oh, right. No, I didn't know."

"Well, we keep it a bit quiet. We don't want Demeter gatecrashing." Flora pulls a face. "Can you *imagine*?"

"Ah." I nod. "I get that."

"So the point is, this isn't an open thing. It's like . . ." She hesitates. "It's like a gang. A club. A special little club."

"Right."

"And I'm asking you to join the club." She squeezes my arm. "What about it? Are you in?"

I feel a joyful little surge inside. A gang. A club. I hadn't realized quite how lonely I was feeling.

"Definitely!" I say with a huge beam. "Count me in!"

I'll have to adjust my budget if I'm going to start buying rounds every Wednesday, but it will so be worth it.

"Cool! We'll start again after Christmas. I'll let you know. Only *don't* tell Demeter."

"OK! I promise!" I'm about to ask where the Blue Bear is, when Flora gives a loud shriek.

"Oh my God!"

"Babe." A tall, dark-haired guy in a trilby has appeared from nowhere and has wrapped his arms round Flora from behind. "Your mum said you were here."

"I've been texting you!" says Flora accusingly. "You should have *texted*."

The guy shrugs, and Flora pushes him and giggles, and I'm wondering whether I should slip away, when Flora grabs my arm and says, "This is Cat. Cat, this is Ant." She pouts charmingly up at him. "And since you've been such a *nightmare*, Ant, lunch is on *you*."

Ant rolls his eyes with good humor, and I hurriedly say, "Actually, I'll be going."

"No, come with us!" Flora links arms with both Ant and me and drags us across the road to the Butterfly Bakery, which I've read about in a zillion blogs. It's all pink and white stripes, and there are paper butterflies hanging everywhere from the ceiling. The customers color them in with felt-tips. It's, like, the gimmick.

We hang up our coats on white wooden hooks by the door, then Flora grabs a floral-printed tray for each of us and bossily starts dumping items on them. "OK, these pumpkin muffins are yummy. And the flapjack hearts are great . . . and we should get a salad each . . . and this ginger cordial is *amazing*. . . ." She loads up each tray, then announces, "Ant, you get in the queue. We're going to nab a table. C'mon, Cat."

She leads me across the room to an alcove where a couple

are just getting up from their lunch and high-fives me as we slide into our seats.

"Result! This place gets sooo crowded." Flora pulls out her sequined dress and looks at it lovingly. "So, what are you wearing to the Christmas party?"

"Little black dress," I say. "Tried and tested."

Flora nods. "Good choice. Last year, Demeter wore such a short dress, you could practically see her Spanx," she adds disparagingly. "Who's she kidding? I mean, just because you have a toyboy, it doesn't mean you're suddenly, like, twenty years younger. She's such a *crone*. Here, I'll show you a picture of what she looked like."

"Toyboy?" I say with interest.

"You know." Flora's busily flicking through photos on her phone. "Alex Astalis."

It takes a moment for the words to imprint on my mind.

"Alex Astalis?" I echo stupidly.

"That guy you met."

"You mean . . ."

"Demeter and Alex? Oh God, yes." Flora nods. "They've been having a totally un-secret affair, like, *forever*."

My throat has clenched up. I can barely speak.

"How . . . how do you know?" I manage at last.

"Everyone does," she says, as though in surprise. "You know Demeter was Alex's boss, years ago? Well, apparently the chemistry between them was *sizzling*. Mark told me. He knew them then. And now Alex is *Demeter's* boss. It's weird, isn't it?"

I nod dumbly. I'm picturing a youthful Demeter . . . a fresh-faced Alex . . . sizzling chemistry. . . .

I think I'm back into bad-dream land.

"Demeter was married, even then," Flora carries on. "But I guess she didn't want to break that up or whatever. . . . Anyway, that's why she came to Cooper Clemmow. Alex went into partnership with Adrian and straightaway he headhunted her. *So* unsubtle. Look, here she is. Doesn't she look vile?"

She hands me her phone, showing a photo of Demeter in a minidress, standing by an ice sculpture, but I can barely see it. I feel a bit cold. And deflated. And above all, incredibly stupid. It's so obvious now. I can see them together. Both lithe. Both intelligent. Both at the top of their game. Of *course* they're lovers.

It suddenly hits me: That's why they're both in Copenhagen. I can see them now, in a Scandi hotel room, having sex in some amazing athletic position that nobody else does except Demeter, because she's the first person on the whole planet to have found out about it.

I'm still holding Flora's phone, staring blindly down, my thoughts scudding around. Demeter really has it all, doesn't she? She bloody has it all. The job, the house, the husband, the children, the fashionable paint shades—*and* Alex. Because obviously when you're Demeter, a devoted husband isn't enough. You need a lover too. A sexy, authentic, organic lover.

But . . . what about me?

My mind keeps torturing me, replaying those little moments I had with Alex. The way he smiled . . . the way he gently fixed my hair . . . glancing over as we pedaled along . . . I didn't make it up. There *was* something; we *did* have a spark. . . .

But what's a spark with me when you've got a sizzling inferno going on with the goddess of sex, or whatever she is? I was just a diversion. I suddenly recall him after the Santa ride, scrutinizing his phone, saying, "I just need to text . . . them."

He didn't want to say "text her." He was being discreet. But that's who he meant.

"Hasn't her husband guessed?" I try to sound like this is all breezy office gossip.

"I doubt it." Flora shrugs. "She's really good at lying. . . . Oh, Ant!"

"Here we go." Ant dumps two trays on the table. One is Flora's, with her muffin, salad, and all the rest of it. The other has a bowl of soup. "Yours is up there." He nods at me. "They've put it aside for you to pay."

Me to pay?

All thoughts of Alex are swept aside and I stare up, feeling a bit hollow. I thought . . .

"Ant, you brute!" Flora pushes him. "You should have paid! Now Cat will have to queue."

"No, she won't," he retorts. "I told them she was coming and they've put it aside. Because I'm thoughtful like that."

"But honestly, Ant." Flora sounds exasperated. "Why didn't you just *get her stuff*?"

"Because I'm *out of cash,* OK?" He glares at her.

Oh God. Now they're going to start fighting about my lunch.

"It's fine!" I say brightly. "No problem! Thanks so much for keeping my place in the queue, Ant!"

But as I head to the checkout, I feel mounting dread. I thought Ant was buying us all lunch. I never would have come in here otherwise. I would have made an excuse and left. I've even got a tuna sandwich in my bag, all wrapped up in cling film.

It might not be that much, I tell myself as I approach the checkout. *Don't overreact. It might be OK.*

The girl at the checkout is waiting for me and beams as she places my tray carefully in front of the till.

"So that's the muffin . . . the salad . . ."

She rings up each item, and I try to look relaxed. Like a cool, rich Notting Hill girl. Not someone who's holding her breath and making frantic calculations as each item is added. It's got to be fifteen . . . eighteen . . . twenty quid, maybe?

"So, your total is thirty-four pounds, eighty-five." She smiles at me and I stare back, dazed. It's far, far worse than I imagined. Thirty-five pounds? For *snacks*? That's a week's supermarket shopping.

I can't.

I just can't do it. I can't spend thirty-five quid on a few little bits. Not after the laptop disaster. I have to leave. I'll text Flora and tell her I suddenly felt ill. She's totally engrossed in Ant, anyway; it won't matter.

"Actually, I've had a change of plan," I say awkwardly. "I can't stay for lunch. Sorry."

"You don't want *any* of this?" The girl looks taken aback.

"Um, no. Sorry. I feel a bit ill, I have to go. . . ."

With shaking legs I head for the exit, take my coat from its hook, and push the door open. I don't look back. If Flora asks, I'll say I didn't want to pass on any germs to her. I mean, it'll sound lame. But lame is better than broke.

The cold air hits me sharply as I step out of the café, and I shove my hands in my pockets. Well, that's it, then. I'd better head home. And just for an instant I want to cry. I want to sit on the pavement and bury my face in my arms. I can't afford this life; I can't be these people. I don't have a mother saying, *Darling, here's a hundred quid*.

Or a mother.

I know I must have sunk very low, because this isn't a thought I let myself have. Much. Tears have actually started shimmering at my eyes, but I blink them back fiercely. *Come on, Katie. Don't be wet.* I've probably just got low blood sugar. I'll eat my sandwich; that'll make me feel better.

I send a quick text to Flora: Not feeling good, had to go, sorry, enjoy lunch xxx Then I find an unobtrusive spot on the pavement, crouch down, and get out my cling-filmed sandwich. It doesn't look as appealing as the pumpkin muffin, but it'll taste better than it looks, and in any case—

"Cat?" My head jerks up so sharply, I nearly crick my neck. Flora is standing three feet away, staring down at me in astonishment, holding a cupcake.

"Flora?" I manage. "Didn't you get my text?"

"What text?" she demands, looking upset. "What happened? Why did you leave? I saw you go. You didn't even say goodbye!"

"Ill," I say, in croaky tones. "Suddenly ill. Sick," I add for good measure, and pull a tissue out of my pocket. I retch into it, turning away as though for politeness's sake.

"Oh my God," says Flora, sounding shocked.

"It's a bug. Don't come near."

"But you were fine a minute ago!" Her eyes are wide. "Should I get you . . . a doctor? A taxi?"

"No!" I cry, sounding like a scalded cat. "No taxis. I

need . . . fresh air. I need to walk. I'll walk. You go back and have lunch."

"Why are you holding a sandwich?" Flora's gaze drops curiously to my hand.

Shit.

"It . . . um . . ." I can feel my face flaming. "Someone gave it to me. Someone thought I looked unwell, so they gave me a sandwich."

"A stranger?" Flora looks perplexed.

"Yes."

"What did they say?"

"They said . . ." My mind scrabbles around. " 'You don't look well. Here's a sandwich.' "

"They just gave you a sandwich?" Flora seems even more flabbergasted. "But *why*?"

"I think it was a . . . a political thing?" I hazard desperately. "Anti-austerity sandwiches or something? I'll have it later, when I'm feeling better—"

"No, you won't!" Flora grabs it out of my hand, looking horrified. "You can't trust some random sandwich from a stranger! Especially if you're ill!" She throws it in a litter bin and I try to hide my dismay. That was my lunch. And now it's in the bin.

"They gave us these freebies." She holds out the cupcake sorrowfully. "But if you're feeling sick, you won't want one, will you?"

I've read rapturous descriptions of Butterfly Bakery cupcakes. This one is an exquisite chocolate creation, with swirly marbled icing. My stomach is growling at the sight.

"You're right," I force myself to say. "Just seeing it makes me feel . . . you know. Ill. Yuck," I add. "Urgh."

"Such a shame." Flora takes a bite. "*God,* that's yummy. Well, you look after yourself. You're sure I can't get you a taxi?"

"No, you go." I make a batting motion. "Go back to Ant. Please. Just go."

"Well, OK. See you on Monday."

Shooting me a last, uncertain look, Flora blows me a kiss, then disappears. When I'm sure she's gone, I slowly rise from my crouched position. I'm gazing fixedly at my sandwich. Yes, it's in a street bin. Which is gross. Unspeakable. But it's still fully wrapped in cling film. So . . . in theory . . .

No, Katie.

I'm not getting my lunch back out of the bin. I'm not sinking that low.

But it's wrapped up. It's fine.

No.

But why shouldn't I?

Without quite meaning to, I'm edging toward the bin. No one's even looking.

"I'll just take a picture of this bin for my blog on food wastage," I say in loud, self-conscious tones. I take a photo of the bin and move still closer. "Wow, an untouched sandwich. So . . . I'll just take a photo of this sandwich for my research about how food wastage is a real problem these days."

Flushing slightly, I pick the sandwich out of the rubbish and take a photo of it. A little girl, aged about five, is watching me, and she pulls at the sleeve of a pale-pink cashmere coat.

"Mummy, that lady gets her food from the bin," she says in high-pitched tones.

"It's for my blog on food wastage," I say hastily.

"She took that sandwich out of the bin," says the girl, ignoring me. "The *bin,* Mummy." She tugs at her mother's arm, looking distressed. "We must give her some money. Mummy, the poor lady needs *money.*" Finally her mother looks up and shoots me a distracted glance.

"There's a hostel a few streets away, you know," she says disapprovingly. "You should get help, not harass people for money."

Seriously?

"I'm not harassing people!" I erupt with indignation. "I don't want your bloody money! And it's my sandwich! I made it, OK? With my own ingredients." Tears have started to my eyes, which is *all* I need. I grab the sandwich and stuff it into my bag with trembling hands. And I'm just starting to stride off when I feel a hand on my arm.

"I'm sorry. Perhaps I was insensitive. You're a nice-looking girl." The pink-cashmere woman runs her eye up and down my shabby Topshop coat. "I don't know why you're on the streets or what your story might be . . . but you should have hope. Everyone deserves hope. So, here. Happy Christmas." She produces a fifty-pound note and offers it to me.

"Oh God," I say in horror. "No. You don't under—"

"Please." The woman suddenly sounds fervent. "Let me do this for you. At Christmastime."

She tucks the note into my hand, and I can see the little girl's eyes shining with pride at her generous mummy. Clearly both of them are carried away with the romance of helping out a homeless stranger.

OK, this is the most excruciating moment of my *life*. There's no point explaining the truth to this woman; it'll be too mortifying for both of us. And, by the way, I know my hair isn't blow-dried or anything and I know my shoes need re-heeling—but do I really look to her like someone who lives on the *streets*? Are my clothes that terrible compared to the average Notting Hill outfit?

(Actually, maybe they are.)

"Well, thanks," I say stiltedly, at last. "You're a good woman. God bless you," I add for good measure. "God bless us, every one."

I walk swiftly away and, as soon as I've turned the corner, approach a Salvation Army officer holding out a tin. And full disclosure: I do feel a slight wrench as I put the money in. I mean, fifty quid is fifty quid. But I couldn't do anything else, could I?

The Salvation Army officer's eyes light up—but as he starts exclaiming at my apparent generosity, I turn away and start walking even faster. What a bloody fiasco. What a bloody *day*.

And now, before I can stop it, my mind miserably fills with a vision of Alex. Alex and Demeter in their hotel room, lying entwined on some Danish designer rug, toasting each other for being so successful and hot and über . . .

No. Enough. There's no point thinking about it. I just need to avoid him at the Christmas party. And then it'll be Christmas and a whole new year and everything will be different. Exactly. It's going to be fine.

CHAPTER EIGHT

Shit. There he is, standing by the bar. *Shit*.

I hastily duck away and reach for a balloon to hide behind. Maybe I can disguise myself with Christmas decorations. Or maybe I should just leave.

The Christmas party has been going for about two hours. We're all in an upstairs room at the Corkscrew, and it's the coolest Christmas party I've ever been to. Which figures.

From the office chat last week, I learned that no one at Cooper Clemmow, at least in our department, does bog-standard Christmas dinner, or "norm-Christmas," as Rosa jokily put it. Demeter and Flora and Rosa are all having goose rather than turkey. (Organic, of *course*.) Mark is having nut roast because his partner is vegan. Liz is doing an Ottolenghi quail recipe. Sarah's doing lobster and is styling her table with a centerpiece made from driftwood that she collected in the summer. (I have *no* idea what that has to do with Christmas.)

Then someone said, "What about you, Cat?" and I had an instant vision of my dad, at our ancient kitchen table, wearing a paper hat from the Cash & Carry, slathering a turkey with some cut-price margarine he got in bulk. You couldn't get more "norm-Christmas." So I just smiled and said, "Not sure yet," and the conversation moved on.

This party is also very much *not* "norm-Christmas." There's a photo booth in the corner, and black and white balloons reading *Naughty* and *Nice* float everywhere. The snacks are themed after the brands on our client list, and the DJ is firmly un-Christmassy—Slade hasn't been played once. And there'd been no sign of Alex all evening. I thought I'd got away with it. I was actually quite enjoying myself.

But now, suddenly, here he is, looking gorgeous in a black-and-white geometric-print shirt. There's a little grin playing at his mouth as he looks around, a glass in his hand. Before he can spot me, I turn around and head to the dance floor. Not that I'm planning to dance, but it's a safe place to hide.

After Portobello, the rest of the weekend passed in a dispiriting nothingness. I watched telly, went on Instagram. Then I came into the office this morning, *finally* finished my surveys, answered Flora's concerned questions about my sudden bug, and wondered whether to pull out of the Christmas party.

But no. That would be pathetic. Anyway, it's a free evening out, and I have been having a good time. I keep remembering Flora's invitation to join the pub gang and feeling a glow of warmth. These guys are my friends. At least . . . they *will* be my friends. Maybe I'll work here for five years, ten years, rise up through the ranks. . . .

My eyes have swiveled back to the bar. I can see Alex talking intently to Demeter and feel a fresh pang at my own stupidity. Look at the pair of them. Their eyes are about five inches apart. They're unaware of anyone else. Of *course* they're sleeping together.

"Hey, Cat!" Flora comes dancing up to me, all glittery in her sequins. "I'm going to go and fess up to my Secret Santa." Her words are slurred and I realize she's got quite pissed. Actually, I think everyone's quite pissed. Free drink will do that to you.

"You can't!" I say. "It's *Secret* Santa. That's the point."

"But I want to get credit for it!" She pouts. "I found such a cool present. I spent much more than the limit," she adds in loud, drunken, confidential tones. "I spent fifty quid."

"Flora!" I laugh in shock. "You're not supposed to do that. And you're not supposed to tell the person who you are either."

"Don't care. Come on!" She grabs my arm, tottering on her heels. "Shit. I should *not* have had those mojitos. . . ." She drags me across the room, and before I can blink, or think, or escape, we're standing in front of Alex Astalis.

My face floods with color and I glance at Demeter, who has briefly turned away to talk to Adrian.

"Hi, Katie-Cat," says Alex easily, and my face gets even hotter. But thankfully Flora doesn't seem to have noticed. She really is very drunk.

"I'm your Secret Santa!" she says in blurred tones. "Did you like it?"

"The Paul Smith hat." He looks a bit taken aback. "That was you?"

"Cool, huh?" Flora sways a little, and I grab her.

"Very cool." He shakes his head with mock disapproval. "But was it under a tenner?"

"A tenner? Are you kidding?" Flora lurches again, and this time Alex grabs her.

"I'm sorry," I say apologetically. "I think she's a bit . . ."

"I'm not drunk!" says Flora emphatically. "I'm not—" She topples and clutches Alex's sleeve. As she does so, it rides up, and his tattoo becomes visible. "Hey!" she says in surprise. "You've got a tat-tat—" She's so drunk she can't say the word. "A tat-tat—"

"I am *not* losing control!" Demeter's voice suddenly fires up in fury, and I start with shock. Is Demeter having a row with Adrian? At the Christmas party? Alex's eyes are tense, and I can tell he's listening to that conversation, not paying attention to us.

"Demeter, that's not what I'm saying." Adrian's voice is calm and soothing. "But you must admit . . . quite concerned . . ." I can't exactly hear what he's saying over the hubbub.

"You've got a tat-too!" Finally Flora manages to articulate the word.

"Yes." Alex nods, looking amused. "I've got a tattoo. Well done."

"But . . ." Her eyes swivel to me. I can see her alcohol-addled mind working. "Hang on." She looks back at Alex. "Dark hair, tattoo . . . and you were *asking* about him."

My heart starts to thud along with the beat of the music. "Flora, let's go," I say quickly, and pull at her arm, but she doesn't move.

"It's him, isn't it?"

"Stop!" I feel a white-hot horror. "Let's go." But Flora can't be shifted.

"This is your man, isn't it?" She looks delighted. "I *knew* it was someone at work. She's in love with you," she tells Alex, poking me drunkenly for emphasis. "You know. Secretly." She puts a finger to her lips.

My insides have collapsed. This can't be happening. Can't I just teleport out of this situation, out of this party, out of my life?

Alex meets my eyes and I can see it all in his expression. Shock . . . pity . . . more pity. And then even more pity.

"I'm not in love with you!" Somehow I muster a shrill laugh. "Honestly! I'm so sorry about my friend. I hardly even know you, so how could I be in love with you?"

"Isn't it him?" Flora claps a hand over her mouth. "Oops. Sorry. It must be another guy with dark hair and a tat-tat—" She stumbles over the word again. "Tattoo," she manages at last.

Both Alex and I glance at his wrist. He looks up and meets my eyes, and I can see he knows: It's him.

I want to *die*.

"So, I'd better go," I say in a miserable, flustered rush. "I need to pack, and . . . um . . . thanks for the party. . . ."

"No problem," says Alex, a curious tone to his voice. "Do you have to go now?"

"Yes!" I say desperately, as Demeter turns to join us again. Her face is pink and she looks rattled, for Demeter.

"So, Cath." She makes a visible effort to put on a pleasant expression. "Are you off tomorrow?"

She's clearly forgotten the fact I'm called Cat. But I can't be bothered to correct her again. "That's right! Absolutely."

"And have you chosen yet? Turkey or goose?"

"Oh, turkey. But with a rather lovely porcini stuffing," I hear myself adding a bit wildly. I shoot an overbright smile around this group of sophisticated Londoners. Everyone so hip and cool, treating Christmas like an ironic event that's all about the styling.

"Porcini." Demeter looks interested.

"Oh yes, from a little place in Tuscany," I hear myself saying. "And . . . truffles from Sardinia . . . and vintage champagne, of *course*. So . . . Happy Christmas, everyone! See you after the break."

I can see Alex opening his mouth, but I don't wait to hear what he says. My face is burning as I head toward the exit, tripping a little in my hurry. I need to get out. Away. Home to my gourmet luxury Christmas. The porcini. The vintage champagne. Oh, and of course the truffles. I can't wait.

CHAPTER NINE

"Come and sample my latest." My dad turns from the kitchen counter and holds out a drink. It's not a glass of vintage champagne or a sophisticated cocktail. It's not even some artisan local organic cider. It's Dad's patented Christmas punch of whatever cut-price bottles of spirits he could get at the market, all mixed together with long-life orange juice, pineapple juice, and lime cordial. "Cheers, m'dear."

It's midday on Christmas Eve, and I'm at home in the country, and London seems a lifetime away. Everything's different here. The air, the sounds, the *expanse*. We live on a farm in a part of Somerset which is so remote, no one's ever heard of it. The papers keep talking about *fashionable* Somerset and *celebrity* Somerset. . . . Well, believe me, we're arse-end-of-nowhere Somerset.

Our house is in a valley, and all you can see from the kitchen window are fields, some sheep dotted around, the rise of the slope to Hexall Hill, and the odd hang glider in the distance. Some cows too, although Dad doesn't go in for cows quite as much as he used to. Not enough money in them, he says.

There are better games to be in. Although he doesn't seem to have found any of those games yet.

Dad lifts his glass and gives me his crinkly, twinkly beam. No one can resist Dad's smile, including me. All my life, I've seen him win people round with his charm, his bottomless optimism. Like that time I was ten and forgot about my holiday project. Dad just turned up at school, twinkled at the teacher, told her several times how certain he was that it wouldn't be a problem . . . and sure enough, it wasn't. Everything was magically OK.

I mean, I'm not stupid. There was a sympathy element there too. I was the girl with no mum. . . .

Anyway, let's not dwell on that. It's Christmas Eve. I step outside the kitchen door, making my way through a cluster of chickens to breathe in the fresh West Country air. I must admit, the air is amazing here. In fact, the whole place is amazing. Dad thinks I've completely rejected Somerset, but I haven't. I've just made a choice about how to live my life—

I close my eyes briefly. Stop it. How many imaginary conversations have I had with Dad about this? And now I'm having them when he's *standing three yards away*?

I take a sip of punch and try to focus on the distant landscape rather than the farmyard, because the closer you get to the actual house, the less picturesque it becomes. Dad's tried a lot of moneymaking wheezes over the years, none of which have worked—and all around the farmyard are the remains and detritus of them, which he's never bothered clearing up. There's the cider press, sitting in its barn, barely used. There's the massage table, from when we were going to have a spa.

(He couldn't find a massage therapist cheap enough.) There's the matching turquoise swirly eighties headboard and bedside tables that he bought off a mate, intending to set up a B&B. They're still wrapped up in their plastic, leaning against a gate. They look terrible.

And there's Colin the alpaca, roaming around in his little paddock, looking like the miserable sod he is. God, the alpacas were a disaster. Dad bought six of them, about three years ago, and he reckoned they were going to make our fortune. They were going to be an attraction, and we were going to set up an alpaca wool factory, and all sorts. He actually charged tickets for some school party to come and visit, but then an alpaca bit one of the kids, and he hadn't done a risk assessment or whatever and it was all a total hassle.

Although that wasn't as bad as his ANSTERS FARM WINTER WONDERLAND! VISIT FATHER CHRISTMAS IN HIS GROTTO! with cotton wool for snow and Poundland tat for presents and me as a fourteen-year-old resentful elf. It was twelve years ago now, but I still shudder at the memory. Those bloody green tights.

"Oh, it's wonderful to have you home, Katie!" Biddy has come out too, holding her glass. She gives me a hug and pats my shoulder. "We miss you, darling!"

Biddy has been Dad's girlfriend for years now. Or partner. Common-law wife, I suppose. After Mum died, for the longest time it was just Dad and me. It worked fine. I thought Dad would be on his own forever. There were a few local women, mostly blond, who came and went, and I didn't really distinguish between them.

But then Biddy arrived, right before I went off to uni. From the start, she was different. She's a quiet, persistent, sensible person, Biddy. She's pretty in her own way—dark, slightly graying hair, deep-brown eyes—but she's not flashy or trendy. There's grit to her too. She used to be a chef at the Fox and Hounds, till the late hours got too much for her. Now she makes jam and sells it at fairs. I've seen her stand there patiently at her stall, six hours at a time, always pleasant, always willing to chat. She'd never overcharge a customer but never undercharge either. She's fair. True and fair. And for some reason—I have *no* idea why—she puts up with Dad.

I'm only joking. Half-joking, maybe. Dad's one of those people—sends you mad with frustration, then comes through just when you weren't expecting it. When I was seventeen, I asked him over and over to teach me to drive. He put it off . . . forgot . . . said I was too young. . . . Then one day, when I'd given up hope, he announced, "Right, Kitty-Kate, it's driving day." We spent all day in the car and he was the most kind, patient teacher you could imagine.

I mean, I still failed. Turns out Dad's got no idea how to teach driving; in fact, the examiner stopped the test halfway because apparently I was "unsafe." (He was particularly unimpressed by Dad's advice: Always accelerate toward changing traffic lights, in case you can nip through.) But, anyway, the thought was there, and I'll always remember that day.

That was Dad's gentler, more serious side. He doesn't always show it, but underneath the swagger and the twinkles and the flirting he's as soft as butter. You just have to watch him at lambing. He looks after all the orphan lambs as tenderly as though they were his real babies. Or take the time I had a bad fever when I was eleven. Dad got so worried, he took my temperature about thirty times in an hour. (At last he asked Rick Farrow, the vet, to stop in and have a look at me. He said he trusted Rick over any doctor, any day. Which was fine until the story got out at school. I mean, the *vet*.)

I still remember Mum. Kind of. I have dim splashes of memory like an unfinished watercolor. I remember arms around me and a soft voice in my ear. Her "going out" shoes—she only had the one pair, in black patent with sensible heels. I remember her leading me around the fields on my pony, clucking fondly to both of us. Brushing my hair after bath time, in front of the telly. I still feel a sad, Mum-shaped hole in my life when I allow myself . . . but that's not often. It would feel disloyal to Dad, somehow. As I've got older, I've realized how hard it must have been for him, all those years, bringing me up alone. But he never let me realize it, not once. Everything was fun, an adventure for the pair of us.

I have a memory of him when I was six, the year after Mum died: Dad sitting at the kitchen table, peering at the Littlewoods catalog, his brow furrowed, trying to pick out clothes for me. Wanting so badly to get it right. He can make you weep, he's so kind. And then he can make you weep because he sold your precious matching bedroom-furniture set with no warning to a guy from Bruton who gave him a really good deal. (I was fifteen. And what I still don't get is, how did the guy from Bruton even *know* about my bedroom furniture?)

Anyway, that's Dad. He's not exactly what he seems. Then, the minute you've worked that out, he *is* exactly what he seems. And I think Biddy understands that. It's why they work as a couple. I used to watch all those other women Dad had, and even when I was a child I could tell they didn't quite *get*

Dad. They could only see charismatic, charming, rogue-ish Mick, with his moneymaking schemes. Standing rounds at the pub, telling funny stories. That's what appealed to them, so he played up that side. But Biddy isn't about charisma; she's about connection. She talks directly. She doesn't mess around or flirt. I sometimes see them talking quietly together, and I can tell that Dad relies on her, more and more.

She's careful and discreet, though, Biddy. She doesn't ever get between me and Dad. She knows how close the two of us were, all those years together, and she's all about standing back. Never venturing an opinion. Never offering unsolicited advice. Nor have I ever asked her for advice.

Maybe I should.

"Crisp, Kitty-Kate?" Dad has followed me outside into the winter sunshine with a bowl of crisps. His graying, curly hair is still rumpled from doing his morning jobs outside, and his skin is as weatherbeaten as ever, his blue eyes shining like sapphire chips.

"I was just saying to Katie, it's lovely to have her home," says Biddy. "Isn't it?"

"Certainly is," replies Dad, and he raises his glass toward me. I raise my own and try to smile—but it doesn't come easily. I can't meet Dad's eye without seeing the little splinters of sadness among the twinkles. So I gulp my drink, waiting for the moment to pass.

If you saw us from the outside, you'd have no idea. You'd think we were a father and daughter reuniting happily on Christmas Eve. You'd never sense the waves of hurt and guilt bouncing invisibly between us.

The internship in Birmingham never caused a problem.

Dad understood that it was all I could get; he knew I didn't want to settle in Birmingham; he didn't worry. The internship in London, he rationalized as well. I was "just starting out" and no wonder I had to get some experience.

But then I took the job at Cooper Clemmow, and something froze. I remember breaking the news to him and Biddy, right here. Oh, he did all the right things—hugged me and said, "Well done." We talked about visits and weekends, and Biddy made a celebratory cake. But all the time I could see the stricken look in his face.

We haven't really been right with each other since then. And certainly not since the last time he came up to London, almost a year ago now, with Biddy. God, it was a disaster. Something went wrong with the tube and we were late for the show I'd booked. A group of young guys jostled Dad, and I think—not that he'd ever admit it—he was scared. He told me in no uncertain terms what he thought of London. I was so tired and disappointed, I burst into tears and said . . . some stuff I didn't mean.

Since then, we've danced warily around each other. Dad hasn't suggested visiting again. I haven't asked him to. We don't talk a lot about my life in London, and when we do, I'm careful to stay upbeat. I never mention my problems. I've never even shown him where I live. I *couldn't* let him see my flat and my tiny room and all my stuff slung in a grotty hammock. He just wouldn't understand.

Because here's the other thing about Dad; here's the flip side of us being so close for so long: He feels everything on my behalf, almost *too* keenly. He can overreact. He can make me feel worse about a situation, not better. He rails at the world when it goes wrong for me, can't let things go.

He never forgave that guy Sean who broke my heart in the sixth form. He still scowls if I mention the saddlery. (I did a summer job there, and I thought they underpaid me. Only by a tiny amount, but that was it as far as Dad was concerned. He's boycotted them ever since.) And I *know* he reacts like that because he loves me. But sometimes it's hard to bear his disappointment at life as well as my own.

The first time I had a run-in with a colleague at work, when I was starting out in Birmingham, I told Dad about it. Well, that did it. He mentioned it *every time we spoke,* for about six months. He told me to complain to HR . . . suggested I wasn't standing up for myself enough. . . . He basically wanted to hear that the colleague had been punished. Even after I'd told him again and again that it was all fixed and I wanted to move on and could we please not discuss it anymore? As I say, I know he was only showing he cared—but still, it was draining.

So the next time I had an issue, I quietly sorted it out for myself and said nothing. Easier for me, easier for Dad. It's easier for him if he doesn't know I've traded his beloved Somerset for a hard, struggling existence, if he believes I'm leading what he calls "the high life in London." It's easier for me if I don't have to expose every detail of my existence to his uncomprehending, anxious gaze.

And, yes, it gives me heartache. We were so close, the Dad-and-Katie team. I never kept anything from him, not my first period, not my first kiss. Now I'm constantly careful. The only way I can rationalize it is that I *will* be honest with him, when I can tell him things that will make him happy. When I'm more secure, less defensive.

Just not yet.

"I was remembering Father Christmas's Grotto," I say, taking a crisp, trying to lighten things. "Remember the fistfight that broke out?"

"Those wretched children." Dad shakes his head indignantly. "There was nothing wrong with those balloons."

"There *was*!" I burst into laughter. "They were duds and you knew it! And as for the Christmas stockings . . ." I turn to Biddy. "You should have seen them. They fell apart in the children's hands."

Dad has the grace to look a bit shamefaced, and I can't help laughing again. This is the territory we do best on, Dad and me. The past.

"So, has Biddy told you?" Dad spreads his arms out, as though to indicate the fields in front of us.

"Told me what?"

"No, I haven't," says Biddy. "I was waiting."

"Waiting for what?" I look from one to the other. "What's up?"

"Glamping," says Dad with a flourish.

"Glamping? What do you mean, glamping?"

"It's where it's at, love. Saw it in the papers. All the celebs are at it. We've got the land, we've got the time. . . ."

"We're serious," says Biddy earnestly. "We want to open a glamping site here. What do you think?"

I don't know what I think. I mean . . . *glamping*?

"Could be a money-spinner," says Dad, and I feel a familiar trickle of alarm. I thought Biddy had calmed him down. I thought the days of Dad's crazy schemes were over. The last I heard, he was going to start getting odd jobs in the neighborhood and build up a handyman business to supplement the farm income. Which is a *sensible* idea.

"Dad, opening a glamping site is a massive deal." I try not to sound as negative as I feel. "It needs investment, knowledge . . . I mean, you don't just wake up one morning and say, *Let's do glamping.* For a start, don't you need permission?"

"Got it!" says Dad triumphantly. "At least, as near as damn it. It's this farm diversification business, isn't it? Bring business to the area. The council's all for it."

"You've spoken to the council?" I'm taken aback. This is more serious than I realized.

"I did," says Biddy. Her dark eyes are shining. "I've had an inheritance, love."

"Oh, wow," I say in surprise. "I didn't know."

"It's not huge, but it's enough. And I really think we could do this, Katie. We've got the land, and it's crying out for some use. I think we'd enjoy it. I don't suppose . . ." She hesitates. "No. Of course not."

"What?"

"Well." Biddy glances at Dad.

"We wondered—do you want to come in on the business with us?" says Dad with an awkward laugh. "Be a partner?"

"*What?*" I goggle at him. "But . . . how can I come in on the business? I'm up in London—"

I break off and look away. I practically can't say "London" around Dad without wincing.

"We know!" says Biddy. "We're so proud of you, love, with your job and your amazing life. *Aren't* we, Mick?"

Biddy is a stalwart supporter of my London life, despite the fact she's about as keen on cities as Dad is. But I wish she wouldn't try to prompt him like that.

"Of course we are," mutters Dad.

"But we thought, if you *did* fancy a change . . ." Biddy continues. "Or in your spare time . . . or weekends? You're so bright and clever, Katie. . . ."

They're serious. They want me to come in on the business with them. Oh God. I love Biddy. I love Dad. But that's a *huge* responsibility.

"I can't be a partner." I shove my hands through my hair, avoiding their eyes. "I'm sorry. Life in London is so busy; I just don't have time. . . ."

I can see Biddy forcing a smile through her disappointment.

"Of course," she says. "Of course you don't. You've done so well, Katie. Have you had your bedroom redecorated yet?"

I feel another massive twinge of guilt and take a sip of punch, playing for time. I came up with the redecorating story when Dad and Biddy came to visit. (That way, we didn't need to go near the flat and I could take them out to Jamie's Italian.) Then I told them it was stalled. Then I told them it was on again.

"It's on the way!" I smile brightly. "Just need to get the color scheme right."

"Color scheme," echoes Dad, with a wry smile at Biddy. "You hear that, Biddy?"

Our farmhouse has never had a color scheme in its life. We've got ancient furniture that's been there for hundreds of years (well, maybe a hundred years) and walls that have been the same mustard or salmon pink since I was a child. What the house really needs, I suppose, is someone to gut it, knock down some walls, come in with a Farrow & Ball chart, and make the most of the view.

Although, actually, the thought of changing a single detail makes me feel all hot and bothered.

"Anyway, it was just a thought," says Biddy brightly.

"Of course you haven't got time, Kitty-Kate," says Dad, his tone a little wistful. "It's understandable."

He's such a familiar sight, standing there in the Somerset sunshine, with his wrinkles and his heavy, stained jersey and his work boots covered in mud. All my life, Dad's been there. Pottering around the house, in the fields, taking me to the pub and feeding me crisps. Trying to make our millions. Not just for him, for me too.

"Look." I exhale. "I didn't mean I can't help. Maybe with the marketing stuff or something?"

"There!" Biddy's face lights up in delight. "I knew Katie would help! Anything you can do, love. You know about these things. Give us some advice."

"OK, so what exactly are you going to do?" I gesture around the land. "Take me through the whole plan."

"Buy some tents," says Dad promptly. "Dave Yarnett's got a good line in them. Gave me the idea in the first place. He'll throw in sleeping bags too."

"No." I shake my head firmly. "Not tents. Yurts."

"You what?" Dad looks baffled.

"Yurts. *Yurts*. Have you never heard of yurts?"

"Sounds like an illness of the you-know-wheres," says Dad, twinkling. "Doctor, Doctor, I've got the yurts." He laughs uproariously at his own joke, and Biddy shoots him a reproving glance.

"*I've* heard of them," she says. "It's Moroccan tents, isn't it?"

"I think they're Mongolian. Anyway, that's what everyone glamps in. Yurts, or retro caravans, or shepherd's huts . . . something different."

"Well, how much are they?" Dad looks unenthusiastic. "Because Dave's doing me a very good deal—"

"Dad!" I cry, exasperated. "No one will come and glamp in cut-price tents from Dave Yarnett! Whereas if you bought some yurts, made them look nice, put up some bunting, cleared up the yard . . ."

I survey the landscape with a new eye. I mean, the view *is* spectacular. The land stretches away from us, green and lush, the grass rippling in the breeze. I can see, in the distance, the sun glinting on our little lake. It's called Fisher's Lake, and we used to row on it. We could buy a new rowing boat. Kids would love it. Maybe a rope swing. We could have fire pits . . . barbecues . . . an outdoor pizza oven, maybe. . . .

I can see the potential. I can actually see the potential.

"Well, I've already told Dave I'm ordering ten tents," says Dad, and I feel a spike of frustration, which somehow I squash down.

"Fine." I down my drink and force a smile. "Do it your way."

It's not till later that afternoon that the subject comes up again. Biddy's preparing potatoes for tomorrow and I'm icing the gingerbread men she made this morning. We'll put them on the Christmas tree later. I'm utterly engrossed, piping tiny smiles and bow ties and buttons, while Christmas hits play through the stereo. The table is Formica-topped, and the chairs are dark green painted wood with dated oak-leaf cushions. Above us is hanging the blue glittery decoration that we've hung up every year since I was ten and saw it for sale in a garage. It couldn't be less *Livingetc,* but I don't care. I feel warm and snug and homey.

"Katie," says Biddy suddenly, in a low voice, and I look up in surprise. "Please, love. You know what your dad's like. He'll buy these wretched tents and open up and it'll be a disaster. . . ." She puts her potato peeler down. "But I want this to work. I think it can work. We've got the money to invest; now's the time. . . ."

Her cheeks are faintly pink and she has a determined look about her that I don't often see.

"I agree." I put down my icing bag. "It's an amazing site, and there's definitely demand. But you need to do it right. And maybe I don't have time to be a partner, but I still want to help. . . ." I shake my head. "But I *really* don't want to see you throw money away on cheap tents."

"I know!" Biddy looks anguished. "I know! We don't know what's right, and your dad can be so obstinate. . . ."

I meet eyes with her sympathetically. This is an understatement. My dad fixes onto a viewpoint—whether it's *the tube is full of terrorists* or *alpacas will make our fortune*—and it's practically impossible to budge him.

Then, to my surprise, I suddenly hear Demeter's voice in my head: *You need a bit of tenacity.*

She's right. What's the point of being the only member of the family with experience in marketing and not speaking out? If I don't at least *try* to talk Dad round, then I'm being feeble.

"OK," I say. "I'll talk to him."

"Who are you going to talk to?" Dad comes in, holding the *Radio Times,* looking merry.

"You," I say briskly. "Dad, you have to listen to me. If you're going to open a glamping business, it has to be cool. It has to be . . ." I search for the right word. "Hip. Authentic. *Not* crappy tents from Dave Yarnett."

"I've told Dave I'm buying them now." Dad looks sulky.

"Well, un-tell him! Dad, if you buy those tents, you're just throwing away money. You need to have the right image, or *no one will come*. I work with successful businesses, OK? I know how they operate."

"You need to listen to Katie!" Biddy cries. "I knew we were getting it wrong! We're buying yurts, Mick, and that's the end of it. Tell us what else we need, Katie."

She pulls out a notebook from the kitchen table drawer, and I see *Glamping* written on it in Biro.

"OK. I think if you're going to do this, you should do it high-end. *Really* high-end. Do food . . . put on activities . . . make this a luxury glamping resort for families."

"A resort?" Dad looks taken aback.

"Why not? You've got the space, you've got the resources, Biddy's had experience in catering. . . ."

"But not in the rest of it, love." Biddy looks worried.

"I'll give you pointers. The more luxury you go, the higher prices you can charge, the more profit you'll make."

"High prices?" Biddy looks even more anxious.

"People love high prices," I say confidently.

"What?" Dad looks skeptical. "I think you're wrong there, love."

"I'm not! It's prestige pricing. They see the prices and they think it *must* be good. If you've got some money to invest, high-end is the way to go. You'll need luxury tents, for a start." I count off on my fingers. "Yurts or tepees or whatever. And proper beds. And . . ." I search around in my mind for things I've seen on Instagram. "High thread count."

My dad and Biddy exchange looks. "What count?"

"Thread count. Sheets."

Biddy still looks baffled. She and my dad use the duvet sets that Biddy brought when she moved in. They're cream and spriggy and date from the 1980s. I have no idea what thread count they are, probably zero.

"Biddy, we'll go online and I'll show you. Thread count is essential." I try to impress this on her. "You need four hundred, at least. And nice soap."

"I've got soap." Dad looks proud of himself. "Job lot from the Factory Shop. Thirty bars."

"No!" I shake my head. "It has to be some kind of local handmade organic soap. Something luxury. Your customers want to have London in the country. Like, rustic, but *urban* rustic."

I can see Biddy writing down *London in the country*.

"You'll need to put some showers in one of the barns," I add.

Dad nods. "We've thought of that."

One of his skills is plumbing, so I'm not too worried about

that—as long as he doesn't choose some terrible knock-off sanitary ware in bilious green.

Another idea hits me. "And maybe you should have an outside shower for summer. That would be amazing."

"An outside shower?" My dad looks appalled. *"Outside?"*

Dad's pride and joy is his Jacuzzi, which he bought secondhand and installed himself when we had some government-rebate windfall. His idea of a top relaxing evening is to sit in his Jacuzzi, drinking one of his homemade cocktails and reading the *Daily Express.* He's not really an outside shower type of guy.

I nod. "Definitely. With wooden screens. Maybe with a wooden pail that drenches you, or something?"

"A *wooden pail*?" Dad looks even more horrified.

"It's what they want." I shrug.

"But you just said they want to be urban! Make up your mind, Katie!"

"They do and they don't." I'm struggling to explain. "They want nice soap, but they want to use it looking at the sky, listening to cows. They want to *feel* rural . . . but not actually *be* rural."

"They sound like bloody lunatics."

"Maybe." I shrug again. "But they're lunatics with money."

The phone rings, and Dad answers. I can see Biddy diligently writing down *thread count, handmade soap, cows*.

"Hello? Oh yes. The scented logs? Of course. Let me just look in the order book. . . ."

"Scented logs?" I say in an undertone to Biddy.

"It's a new thing I'm doing," she replies. "Pine-scented logs for Christmas. We're selling them in bundles. You infuse them with pine oil. It's very easy."

"That's clever!" I say admiringly.

"It's gone quite well." Biddy blushes. "Very popular."

"Well, you can sell them to the glampers. And your jam. And your gingerbread biscuits. And give them your homemade granola for breakfast. . . ."

The more I think about it, the more I think Biddy will be the perfect hostess for a bunch of glampers. She even has apple cheeks, like a proper farmer's wife.

Then Dad's voice impinges on my thoughts.

"No, we don't have a sign. Where are you?" He takes a sip of his drink. "Oh, you can't come *that* way." He chuckles as if it's perfectly obvious. "The satnav always gets it wrong. . . . Oh, that gate? Yes, that gate will be shut. . . . No, I don't know the gate code. . . . Well, you'll have to come round the long way." He listens again. "No, we don't provide bags. Most of our customers bring their own. OK, we'll see you shortly." He puts down the phone and nods at Biddy.

"Customer for your logs." He chuckles again. "She sounded a bit confused, poor love."

"No wonder she was confused!" I erupt. "Dad, do you have *any* idea about customer service?" Dad looks blank, and I clutch my head. "You can't behave like that if you open a glamping site! You need a map! Directions! Bags! You need to hold the client's hand. Hold it *throughout*. Make them feel secure every minute of the process. *Then* you'll have a happy customer."

I suddenly realize I'm channeling Demeter again. In fact, I'm echoing her word for word.

Well, so what? Demeter may be the boss from hell and having torrid sex with the guy I thought I liked, but she's still the most talented person in the office. If I don't try to learn from her, I'm a fool.

I've been reading that book she lent me, *Our Vision,* and making notes on it. Not only that, I've been deciphering all Demeter's scribbled comments in the margins and making notes on those too. And I've only written *stupid cow* once. Which I think is quite controlled of me.

"You see?" Biddy chimes in. "This is why we need Katie's advice. She knows. Now, you listen to her, Mick."

I've never heard Biddy so assertive, and I give an inward cheer.

"So, another question." I look from Biddy to Dad. "Have you thought about marketing? You need a brand. An image." My dad and Biddy look back at me helplessly and I feel a sudden tweak of love for them both. This is something I could do for them. I could create a glamping brand.

My mind is already at work. I'm seeing images. Taglines. Photos of fields, lambs, bunting, campfires . . . Oh God, it could look amazing.

"I'll make you a leaflet," I say. "And a website. I'll create your brand. You just do the practical details. I'll do the image."

"Would you, love?" Biddy claps a hand over her mouth. "That would be wonderful!"

"I want to," I say. "Really, I do."

And it's true. Not only do I want to—I can't wait.

I work at it all Christmas. It consumes me. The sun is out again on Christmas Day, and instead of going to church with Dad and Biddy, I rush round the farm, taking endless pictures of fields, cows, random gateposts, whatever I can find. I download generic pictures of yurts, daffodils, fire pits, lambs, and a close-up of a child splashing in a lake which could easily be Fisher's Lake. I get a shot of Dad's tractor. I build a makeshift den with sticks, decorate it with the only string of bunting I possess, and get a picture of that. I take a close-up of Biddy's jam, cunningly styled on an ancient linen tea towel, with some dried lavender sprigs in the foreground. (Biddy makes lavender bags every year too. And chamomile tea.)

Choosing the font takes a while, but in the end I find one which totally speaks to me. It's cool, retro, a bit rustic but not twee. It's perfect. I filter the pictures, play around with layout, and then start brainstorming copy.

Demeter's voice is in my head yet again as I type:

> **Organic. Authentic. Artisan. Local. Nature. Values. Family. Haven. Space. Simple. Slowdown. Laughter. Freedom. Mud.**

No, scrap *mud*. No mud, no silage, no slaughterhouses, no sheep with gross diseases of the foot. No reality.

> **Earth. Craft. Ancient. Wagon. Campfire. Slow-cooked. Handmade. Pure. Fresh air. Fresh milk. Fresh, authentic, traditional, organic, local, hand-kneaded, homemade bread. (Gluten-free available.)**

By Boxing Day I've finalized the brochure, and though I say it myself, it's mouthwatering. It's fabulous. *I* want to come and stay at Ansters Farm.

"What do you think?" I hand over my printed-out draft layouts and wait for Dad and Biddy to comment.

"Goodness!" Biddy peers at the picture of the farmhouse. "Is that us?"

"I Photoshopped it a tiny bit." I shrug. "It's what you do."

"What's this, www.anstersfarm.com?" queries Dad.

"It's the website I'm going to make for you," I say. "It'll take a bit longer to set up, but it'll have the same vibe."

Both Dad and Biddy are reading the copy, looking a bit perplexed.

"Organic hammocks," reads Biddy. *"Luxe yurts. Freedom for couples, families, lovers. Be who you want to be."*

"With grass underfoot and the wide sky above, children can be children," reads Dad. "Well, what else would they be?"

"We mix traditional values with modern comforts in a haven from modern life," reads Biddy. "Oh, Katie, that does sound good."

"Forget your stresses as you enjoy our program of rural activities. Corn-dolly-making, tractor rides, stick-whittling . . ." Dad looks up. "Stick-whittling? For Pete's sake, love. People don't come on holiday to whittle sticks."

"They do! They think whittling sticks is back to nature!"

"I could bake cakes," volunteers Biddy. "With the children, I mean."

"As long as it's a local, authentic Somerset recipe," I say sternly. "No additives. No chocolate buttons."

"Weekly stargazing barbecues," reads Dad, and looks up again. "Who's doing those?"

"You are," I tell him. "And you're doing tractor rides and cow-milking."

"*All about Esme.*" Biddy has turned to the back page and is reading aloud.

"Who's Esme?" demands Dad.

"One of the chickens. You'll have to name all the animals," I instruct him. "Every chicken, every cow, every sheep."

"Katie, love." Dad looks as though I've gone out of my mind. "I think you're going too far here."

"You have to!" I insist. "The chicken's name is crucial. It's everything, in fact."

"*Esme and her family are part of farm life,*" reads Biddy. "*Visit their henhouse and collect your very own warm eggs. Then scramble them on the fire pit with our locally sourced hemp oil and wild mushrooms.*" She looks up anxiously. "Locally sourced hemp oil?"

"I've already found a supplier," I tell her with satisfaction. "It's totally the new olive oil."

"*Enjoy with our homemade organic bread and range of award-winning jams.*" Biddy flinches. "Award-winning?"

"You've won *loads* of prizes at fairs," I remind her. "Those are awards, aren't they?"

"Well." Biddy turns the printouts over and over, as though digesting them. "It does look wonderful, I must say."

"We can upload fresher pictures on the website," I say. "Once you've got the yurts and everything. But this is like a sneak preview."

"But none of it's true!"

"It is! I mean . . . it will be. It can be. I'm going to get this printed up on special paper," I add.

I already know the paper I want to use. It's a recycled, unfinished paper that we used once at Cooper Clemmow for a cereal brand. I remember Demeter giving the office one of her spontaneous lectures on why *this* paper was the ideal choice, and, I have to admit, I lapped up every word. It'll look perfect.

I could probably spend all day discussing the design, but after a while Dad says he has to check on some sick cow, and he heads out.

"*Ansters Farm Country Retreat.*" Biddy is looking lovingly at the front of the leaflet again. "Doesn't it look beautiful? I don't know how you can leave, darling. Don't you ever think about moving back?" There's a wistful cast to her expression, and I feel a familiar wave of guilt. I think Biddy picks up on it, because she quickly adds, "I mean, I know your life is *very* exciting in London. . . ."

I let her words hang in the air without contradicting them but without nodding either. It's quiet and cozy, sitting here with Biddy, and I almost feel like drawing closer and confiding in her. Asking her about Dad, how hurt he really is. Whether he'll *ever* get over the fact that I've chosen London over him.

But I haven't got the guts to speak. I guess I'm too scared of what I might hear. The prickliness between me and Dad isn't great, but it's tolerable. Whereas to have my worst fears confirmed would just . . . Even the thought makes me flinch. *No. Don't go there.*

Biddy would never volunteer anything without being asked; she's scrupulous like that. She's positioned herself in our family with the utmost tact, and there are places she just doesn't go. So even though I feel as if the subject is dancing around us in the ether, demanding to be discussed, neither of us says a word about it. We sip our tea and it slowly ebbs away again, like these things always do.

After a while, I pull the leaflet toward me. The truth is, I do feel a little tug in my heart as I survey the farm, looking as picturesque as any glossy magazine spread. It gives me such a feeling of . . . what, exactly? Pride? Love? Longing?

"Evening, all." A familiar voice breaks into my thoughts. A familiar, droning, totally unwelcome voice. I look up, trying to mask my dismay—but there he is, Steve Logan, striding into the room with his long, long legs. He's six foot five, Steve. Always has been.

Well, not always, clearly. But since he was about twelve, and everyone at school used to dare him to go into the off-license and buy a can of beer. (Because obviously a super-tall twelve-year-old boy looks *exactly* like an adult.)

"Hi, Steve," I say, trying to sound friendly. "Happy Christmas. How are you?"

Steve works for Dad on the farm, so it makes sense that he's popped in. But I was really hoping he wouldn't.

OK, full disclosure: Steve is the first guy I ever slept with. Although, in my defense, there was *not a lot of choice*.

"Cup of tea, Steve?" says Biddy, and when he nods, she disappears to the kitchen. Steve and I are alone. Great. The thing about Steve and me is, we were together for about five minutes, and I regretted it as soon as we began, and I can't now imagine what I saw in him apart from: 1. He was a boy. 2. He was available. And 3. I was the only one of my friends not to have a boyfriend.

But Steve has behaved ever since as though we're some long-standing divorced couple. He and his mum still refer to me as his "ex." (Hello? We barely dated and we were at *school*.) He makes in-jokes about the time we spent together and shoots me "significant" glances, which I deliberately misunderstand or ignore. Basically, my way of coping with Steve has been: *Avoid him.*

But things should be different now, after what Biddy has told me.

"So, congratulations!" I say brightly. "I heard you got engaged to Kayla. Fantastic news!"

"That's right." He nods. "That's right. Asked her in November. It was her birthday." Steve has this low, intense, monotonous way of talking which is almost mesmerizing. "Put the proposal on Instagram," he adds. "Want to see?"

"Oh. Er . . . of course!"

Steve gets out his phone and hands it to me. Dutifully, I start scrolling through photos of him and Kayla in some plushy restaurant with purple wallpaper.

"Took her out for dinner at Shaw Manor. Three courses . . . everything." He looks up a bit belligerently. "I know how to spoil her."

"Wow," I say politely. "Lovely photos. Gorgeous . . . forks."

There are pictures of every detail of the restaurant. The forks, the napkins, the chairs . . . When the hell did he propose if he was taking all these photos?

"Then I gave her the presents. But the proposal, that was hidden in the last present. In a poem."

"Amazing!" I search for words. "That's just . . . Wow." I'm still scrolling through pictures of place settings, trying to keep my face set to "interested."

"I mean, if it had been you, I'd have done it different." Steve shoots me a look from beneath his brows. "But of course it wasn't you."

"What do you mean, 'if it had been me'?" I feel a stab of alarm.

"I'm just saying. Everyone's different. You'd like different things out of a proposal. You and Kayla, you're different."

OK, this conversation has gone awry. I do *not* want to be talking to Steve Logan about what I might or might not like out of a proposal.

"So, what else is new?" I ask brightly, handing his phone back to him. "Give me the gossip."

"New outlet store's opened in West Warreton," he informs me. "It does Ted Baker, Calvin Klein. . . ."

"Great!"

"I know you have Ted Baker in London, but we've got it here now. I'm just saying." Steve gives me one of his passive–aggressive looks. "You know. Just saying."

"Right—"

"I mean, I know you think you've got everything in London, but—"

"I don't think I've got everything in London," I cut him off. Steve has always been chippy about London, and the trick is not to talk to him about it.

"We've got Ted Baker." He eyes me as though he's proved some massive point. "Discount."

This is torture.

"Biddy!" I call lightly, but she doesn't hear me. "Well, anyway." I summon my most pleasant tones. "Best of luck with the wedding—"

"I could break up with her." He speaks in low tones, leaning toward me.

"What?"

"If you say the word."

"*What?*" I stare at him, aghast. "Steve, if you want to break up with her, you shouldn't be marrying her!"

"I'm not saying I *want* to break up with her. But I would. You know. If you and me . . ." He makes a weird motion with his hands. I don't even want to think about what he's trying to describe.

"No! I mean . . . that's never going to happen. Steve, you're *engaged.*"

"I never gave up on you. Did you give up on me?"

"Yes, I did! I totally gave up on you!" I'm hoping to shock him into reality, but his expression doesn't change.

"Think about it," he says, taps his phone, and winks.

He's insane.

"I'm really happy you're engaged," I say briskly. "I'm sure you'll have a wonderful life together. I must go and help Biddy."

As I leave the room, I want to scream. And Biddy asks me if I want to move back here? She must be bloody *joking*.

CHAPTER TEN

By the beginning of February, Dad and Biddy have bought yurts, feather duvets, fire pits, vintage-style kettles, one hundred meters of bunting, and two hundred labels reading ANSTERS FARM JAM. Dad's midway through converting a barn into a shower-and-loo block, with nice rustic tiles on the floor. (*Not* the vicious bright-blue lino he was going to get cheap from his mate in the trade. Honestly, you can't trust him for a minute.)

Meanwhile, the website for the Ansters Farm Country Retreat is up and running, and it looks amazing! I got Alan to do it for a reduced fee, by saying that if he did, I *wouldn't* phone the landlord to complain about his whey and chicken stock. And so he agreed. The boxes are still all over the flat but I don't care, because the website is *awesome*. There are pages after pages of wonderful country images, with alluring descriptions and a really easy booking form, plus a link to the Pinterest page I've created. There's even a children's page where you run your mouse over pictures of the farm animals and find out what their names are. (I've given all the cows names, like Florence and Mabel and Dulcie. I'll just have to coach Dad.) Alan knows how to bump our site up on search engines too. He's been rather a star.

My brochures are all printed. The final versions arrived yesterday and they're perfect. The paper is just rustic enough, the font is evocative, the pictures are amazing . . . the whole thing works. I'm *so* proud of it. Not only of the farm—but of the brochure. I'm proud of my work.

And as I sit here at my desk, proofreading some endless report on the new brand architecture of Associated Soap, what I keep thinking is: Could I get my brochure to Demeter? Could I get her to look at it properly, really *see* it?

If I leave a brochure on her desk, she won't look at it. If I give it to her at the wrong moment, she won't look at it. Alex's voice keeps running through my head, which makes me cringe, but I have to admit his advice was good. *Pitch her exactly the right idea, exactly when she needs it.* After all, he knows how Demeter works.

(Actually, that's a thought I could do without. Move on.)

I need to make it count. Because I think if she truly focuses on it, she'll love it. I've learned so much from Demeter. I finished that book of hers, *Our Vision,* and at the back I found some old sketches she'd done. Just studying those taught me something. At my most positive, optimistic moments, I even think: Could I become her protégée? If she sees my work and likes it, might she give me a chance? All I have to do is find a moment when she's available and receptive. . . .

But that won't be easy. Demeter has never been less receptive or available. In fact, to be honest, the atmosphere at work has never been weirder.

A lot's gone wrong since Christmas. No one's happy; everyone's tense. And even I, the lowliest of the low, am aware that Demeter's at the eye of the storm. Flora gets the inside track from Rosa, and she's told me all about it. First of all there was The Email. It was sent by Demeter—by mistake—and it insulted one of our clients. He's head of marketing at the Forest Food restaurant chain, and apparently after some stormy meeting Demeter called him *suburban* with *no handle on style* in a draft email to Rosa. And then sent it to him by mistake. Ouch.

So that was a whole big incident, and Demeter walked around for a while with a pale, panicky face. Then, last week, things got worse. Rosa's been working with Mark and some others on a new brief for Sensiquo—one of our beauty clients—and it's been a shambles, with deadlines coming and being missed. Apparently it's not *their* fault—Demeter's been sitting on everything they send to her and not getting back to them. The final straw came last week when Demeter finally set up a meeting with Sensiquo, then had to cancel it. Apparently she didn't seem to know what stage the project was at and it was quite embarrassing.

So the Sensiquo people got furious and complained to Adrian. As a result, Demeter's in a real state. She keeps coming into the room, stopping dead, and looking at us all as though she doesn't know who we are. And the other day, I came across her and Rosa having a furious row in the ladies'. Demeter was talking in a low, frenzied voice, saying: "I should have checked. Rosa, I don't hold this against you. I should have checked the facts for myself. I'm your boss; it's my responsibility."

Whereupon Rosa looked at her with something close to hatred and said evenly, "You knew we weren't ready, Demeter. I told you."

"No, no." Demeter shook her head. "You told me you were ready."

"No, I *didn't*!" Rosa practically screamed, and I hastily backed out of the ladies' altogether. At times like this, you basically want to be invisible. So that's what I'm trying to be. Invisible.

Today, though, everything's pretty quiet, and I wonder if the worst has blown over. I'm just getting up from my desk to make a coffee, when Flora comes bounding up.

"Hey!" she says. "So are you on for a drink at lunchtime? We're starting our Wednesday meetings up again."

"Oh, right." My spirits whoosh straight up. "Great! Yes!"

I've been wondering what happened to the Wednesday thing, only I haven't wanted to ask. To be honest, immediately after the Christmas party I was pretty furious with Flora. But my anger gradually blew over. She was drunk. We all get drunk and say stupid things. And she doesn't even remember it, so at least I can pretend it never happened.

"Everything's been so crazy, we haven't been able to do it. But we're all determined. We need to crack on." She sits on my desk and starts plaiting her hair. "*God*, this place. It's insane. Everyone's imploding."

"So what's the latest?" I lower my voice. I know Flora loves relaying gossip to me—and the truth is, I love hearing it.

"Well." She leans closer. "Apparently Demeter's going to talk to Sensiquo. Like, try to win them back? Because they're worth a *lot*. And if we lose Forest Food too . . ." Flora pulls a face.

"So is the company in trouble?" I feel tendrils of alarm.

"*Demeter's* in trouble. Vile cow. Except Alex will stand up for her, so . . ." Flora shrugs. "If you're shagging one of the partners, you're never in *that* much trouble, right?"

My insides squirm at the image of Demeter shagging Alex. I don't want to think about it.

"Anyway, see you later," says Flora. "Shall we go along together?"

"Great." I beam back. "See you then."

I'm feeling more positive than I have for ages as I head to the kitchen. I'm looking forward to this lunchtime drink so much, it's actually quite uncool. But I'm starved of fun. It'll be so great to kick back, have a drink, and maybe talk about stuff *other* than how the company's imploding and Demeter's a monster.

To my surprise, I can hear Adrian's voice as I get near the kitchen. It's unusual for him to be on our floor, and I suddenly stop dead with a new thought: Shall I give my Ansters Farm brochure to Adrian? I barely know him—he's quite a remote figure—but his smile is always kind. He looks like the sort of guy who might give a junior a chance. I dash back to my desk, grab the brochure, and approach the kitchen again. I feel a bit keyed up, but I'm determined that I won't be coy. I'll just tell him: I want to be noticed and this is my calling card.

It's only as I'm halfway through the door that I actually hear what he's saying. He's speaking in a low voice, his brows knitted.

". . . can't understand what's going on, and, frankly, nor can I. Alex, you told me Demeter was the real deal."

Oh God. It's just Adrian and Alex, having some high-level powwow, and I've stumbled in. Should I back out again?

"She *is* the real deal," Alex retorts. "At least . . . Jesus." He thrusts his hands through his hair. "I'll talk to her."

"You'd better."

Alex draws breath—then notices me standing there, frozen. "Oh." He gives Adrian a warning look, and Adrian turns too.

"Sorry," I stutter. "I didn't hear—I didn't mean to—"

"No, no." Adrian's urbane bonhomie is back. "Go ahead. I'll talk to *you* later." He shoots a meaningful look at Alex and strides out.

So now it's just Alex and me. Alone together. Which is pretty much exactly what I was hoping would never happen again. Trying to ignore him, I head over to the Nespresso machine, shove a pod in, and turn it on.

Alex seems a bit lost for words, which is unlike him.

"So," he says after a lengthy pause. "Hi. Did you have a good Christmas? Porcini stuffing, wasn't it?"

And I know I'm über-prickly at the moment—but even the way he says "Porcini stuffing" seems patronizing. I can sense the pity seeping out of him: through his words, through his sympathetic expression.

My entire body is seething. I don't want his pity. I don't want him to "let me down lightly." What's he thinking right now? *Poor tragic girl, got a crush on the boss; must be kind to her.*

Well, fuck off.

And I know that's not reasonable.

"It was great, thanks," I say stiffly. "Yours?"

"Yes, good." He nods, surveying me with those quick, clever eyes, then takes a deep breath as though he wants to say something awkward.

Immediately, alarm bells ring all over my body. I'm not doing that. I'm not standing here listening to him dole out platitudes while my cheeks burn and my mouth goes to sawdust.

"So," I say shrilly. "Actually, I'm not in the mood for coffee after all."

"Cat—"

"See you later." I walk briskly out of the kitchen, like someone who has a super-brilliant life with lots to get done. As I reach the corridor, a lift is waiting with its doors open, and, without thinking, I get in. The doors close and I utter a tiny scream, my hands clamped over my face, still holding the Ansters Farm brochure.

But then, within ten seconds, I'm pulling myself together. I'm *not* going to lose it. Not over a man. It's fine, I tell myself sternly. Everyone has the odd embarrassing moment in their life and I just need to get this in perspective. What I'll do is: I'll go up to the top and then back down again, and that will give me some breathing space.

The lift travels up to the top floor, where Demeter gets in. I find myself eyeing her curiously—she really looks in a state. Her makeup isn't quite as immaculate as usual, for a start. Her eyes are distant and she keeps muttering something to herself. She doesn't even seem to notice me as she jabs the button for our floor.

And I know this isn't the best time. But something's coming over me, a need to *be* something. I'm still smarting from Alex's pity. So he's sleeping with Demeter—so what? It doesn't mean I'm a tragic nothing. Standing there, watching Demeter scrolling agitatedly through her phone, I have this desperate, overwhelming urge to prove myself.

"Demeter." I rouse her from her reverie. "Can I give you this?" I hold the brochure out and she takes it automatically.

"Cath." She peers at me as if she's only just realized there's another person in the lift.

"Yes! So, let me explain what this is—"

"Cath . . ." Demeter wrinkles her brow as though the sight of me is throwing her into fresh disarray. "Cath . . ." She scrolls back and forth on her phone even more dementedly, frowning at her screen as though it's in Ancient Greek. "I did talk to you. We *did* talk?"

She really seems quite crazy. Flora says the truth is, she's not up to running a department, and to look at her now, I'd have to agree. I mean, what's she on about? Is she worried about not communicating with the junior staff?

I nod reassuringly. "We've talked loads." Then I gesture at the brochure, trying to get her to focus on it. "So, this is a project I've . . . well, masterminded, I suppose. . . ."

Demeter's gaze sweeps over the brochure, but I'm not sure she sees it.

"Because, Cath, what I want to say to you is . . ." Her eyes zoom in on my face as though finally she's found her topic. "What I *really* want to say to you—"

To my shock, she stops the lift, then turns to face me.

"Demeter?" I say uncertainly.

"Cath, I know it's difficult for you to hear this," she says, in those firm, strident tones of hers. "But it will turn out all for the good. In fact, this could be the best thing that ever happened to you." She nods emphatically. "The best thing."

OK, she really has lost it. I don't know *what* she's on about.

"The best thing?" I echo. "I don't quite—"

"You just have to stay positive, OK?" She gives me an encouraging smile. "You're so talented and bright. I know you'll do well in life. I know you'll get there."

There's an angle to this speech that is making me feel . . . not worried, exactly. But—

Worried.

It's almost as if—

"Get where?" I say, more desperately than I meant to. "Positive about what? What are you talking about?"

There's a long, still silence in the lift. Demeter looks at me. She looks at her phone. The wild, starey look has come back to her eyes, a hundredfold.

"Fuck," she says, almost in a whisper.

I have no idea how to respond to this. But there's a new sensation creeping over me. It's gray and clammy. It's foreboding.

"We *haven't* spoken." Demeter knocks a fist to her head. "I didn't *think* we had, but . . ." She peers at her phone and her eyes dim. "I'm going insane."

"Spoken about—" I can't finish the sentence. The words feel like glass marbles, crowding my throat, making me choke.

For thirty seconds, there's silence in the lift. I feel almost light-headed. This can't be happening; this isn't happening. . . . Then, as though breaking the spell, Demeter thumps the lift button and we start to travel again.

"We need a meeting, Cath," she says, in the briskest of businesslike tones. "Why not come to my office straightaway?"

"A meeting about what?" I force myself to say the words, but Demeter doesn't answer.

"Just come along," she says, sweeping out of the lift.

And I follow.

I think there must be a script to these things, and Demeter follows it to the letter. "*Difficult times . . . current financial challenges . . . department contracting . . . budget constraints . . . been such a wonderful addition . . . so deeply and personally sorry . . . wonderful reference . . . anything we can do . . .*"

And I sit and listen, with my hands clamped so tightly in my lap, they ache. My face is immobile. My demeanor is calm. But all the time, my brain is crying out like a child: *There is something you can do. You can let me keep my job. You can let me keep my job. Please, let me keep my job. It's all I want. Please. Please. Please. I can't have no job, I can't, I can't . . .*

No job. The thought is so frightening, so engulfing, it feels like a real physical threat, like a hundred-foot tsunami looming out of nowhere, paralyzing me with its enormity. I can't run, or escape, or beg. It's too late. It's upon me.

I know there are difficult times and current financial challenges. I do read the news. And maybe I should have seen this coming . . . but I didn't. I didn't.

Demeter is now on to the generic stuff: "*Looking for-*

ward . . . any help we can give you . . . proper paperwork . . . " She's started glancing at her screen as she talks. She's mentally moved on. Job done. Tick.

I feel as though I'm in a dream as she suggests I might like to work out my week's notice or I might like to take money in lieu.

"Money," I manage to utter. "I need the money."

There's no point sticking around. If I leave now I can start making applications to other places.

"Fine," says Demeter. "I'll just call talent management. . . ." She makes a quick call that I barely hear, my thoughts are such a whorl of terror. Then she turns back. "In fact, Megan in talent management needs to see you, so she suggested you pop up straightaway. Shall I walk you to the lift?"

And then I've stood up and I'm following her down the hall, and still I feel like I'm in a dream. I'm disembodied. This can't be reality, it can't. . . .

But then we arrive at the lift, and something slices through my dream state. A sharp resentment. I've been *so* good up to now—*such* a model employee-being-fired-and-not-making-a-fuss—that it's as if something in me breaks free in protest.

"So in the lift, you thought you'd already fired me," I say bluntly. I can see I've hit home, from the flinch that passes across Demeter's face.

"I apologize if there was any misunderstanding," she says, and her weasel words make me want to slap her. If? *If?*

"Of course there was a *misunderstanding*." My voice is tart, even to my own ears.

"Cath—"

"No, I get it. It's such a trivial, unimportant detail to you,

you couldn't remember if you'd done it or not. I mean, I understand!" I throw up my hands. "You have a very full, exciting diary. Meetings . . . lunches . . . parties . . . fire your employee. No wonder you can't keep track."

I didn't know I could sound quite so sarcastic. But if I thought I was going to make Demeter chastened, I was wrong.

"Cath," she says calmly. "I appreciate this is an upsetting time for you. But it's a mistake to become bitter. If we stay on good terms, keep the door open, who knows? Perhaps you'll come back and work for us again. Have you read *Grasp the Nettle* by Marilyn D. Schulenberg? It's a very inspiring book for all working women. It's just been published. I read a proof copy, some time ago."

Of course she read a proof copy. Demeter would never wait for a book to be actually available in the shops, like normal people.

"No," I say evenly. "I haven't read it."

"Well, there we are." Demeter looks pleased with herself. "Here's a goal for you. When you leave here, go straight to Waterstones and buy it. You'll find it inspiring. Listen to this quote." She scrolls through her phone, then reads aloud: *"Take your future into your own hands. Make it happen. Life is a coloring book, but* you *have the pens."*

I'm trying to stay polite, but my distress is seething up. Doesn't she understand anything about anything? I can't afford to buy a hardback book telling me to color in my life.

I try not to be envious; I really, really try. But right now all I want to do is yell, *It's all right for you! Your life is already colored in and you didn't even go over the edges!*

The voice in my head is so loud, I feel like she must be able to hear it. But Demeter's still looking at me with that complacent expression. She'll probably boast later about how she gave me lots of marvelous advice and I was really grateful.

And then, just to cap off a perfect day, I spot Alex. He's walking along the corridor toward us with a questioning look. He glances at Demeter, and she makes a quick answering face and my humiliation is complete.

"So," I say stiffly to him. "I'm off. Thanks for the job and everything."

"I thought you knew." I can hear the wince in Alex's voice. "Earlier on. I'm sorry."

I'm aware of Alex and Demeter exchanging expressions in a kind of shorthand. They have a body language I never picked up on before. A kind of easy, close naturalness that you don't get with a professional colleague. I wonder if they shag here at work? Well, of course they do.

Demeter's phone buzzes, and she answers it. "Hello? Oh, Michael. Yes, I did get your email. . . ." She lifts up five fingers at me, which I guess means, "Wait five minutes," and steps into a nearby empty room. And I'm left with Alex. Again.

I glance up at him and see his kind, tactful eyes, and I can't bear it, I can't *bear* it. The horror of my job loss is so devastating, you'd think nothing else would even sting. You'd think I'd be numb to lesser feelings like humiliation and crushed pride. But I'm not. They just smart in a different way.

And suddenly I don't want to keep quiet anymore. Why do we all do that? Why do we all *pretend*? I know what the rules say: Salvage your dignity; walk away; admit nothing. But I'm never going to see this man again in my life. And suddenly the desire to say what I really think is bigger than any other.

"You know what?" I say abruptly. "Let's address what happened at the Christmas party."

"What?" Alex looks so gobsmacked at the idea, I nearly want to laugh.

"Flora said I was in love with you," I press on. "Well, of course I'm not; that's ridiculous."

"Look." Alex seems to be seeking escape. "We really don't have to do this—"

"All I thought was that you and I had . . ." I search for the best way to put it. "A spark. A tiny little spark of . . . I don't know. Connection. Possibility. I liked spending time with you. At the time, I didn't know anything about you and—"

I break off. I'm not going to say "Demeter" out loud in a company corridor. He'll know what I mean.

"So I'm embarrassed now," I resume. "Really embarrassed. Of course I am. But you know something? I'm *owning* my embarrassment. I'm not hiding or playing games." I lift my chin, high and resolute. "Here I am: Katie Brenner, Embarrassed. There are worse things to be."

The wrong name has slipped out, I realize, but I don't care.

Alex looks stupefied by my little speech. Well, *good*. I feel liberated and even kind of exhilarated. So my cheeks are blazing. So my legs are a bit wobbly. So bloody what?

"OK, then," I add. "So that was all I had to say, except goodbye. Tell Demeter I've gone up. Good luck with everything." I jab the lift button and stare fixedly at it, waiting.

"Cat—" Alex begins, then stops. "Katie—" he tries again, but he doesn't seem to know where he wants to go next. And despite the fact that everything about my situation is horrendous—and will seem even more horrendous when I get home—I feel a tiny twinge of satisfaction. At least that patronizing expression has disappeared from his face.

"Cat—" Alex tries a third time. "What are you going to do now?"

"Now?"

"I mean, job-wise."

"Now, I've spoken to Cath." Demeter comes swooping back into the conversation from nowhere. "I've told her to stay positive. She's going to buy *Grasp the Nettle* and take her inspiration from that."

"Oh, great!" says Alex weakly. "Good idea."

"I thought so." Demeter nods, and they both look at me as though: *Phew! We recommended a book. Our consciences can be clear now.*

They have no idea, either of them. Educated people talk about ignorance. Well, how ignorant are these two? Do they know what it's like to live in Catford on a tiny, scraping, heart-juddering budget?

"I'm not going to buy that book, Demeter," I say in a voice which suddenly trembles. "Because it'll be eighteen pounds and I can't afford it. I can't afford anything. Don't you understand? I'm not like you! I'm *not like you*!"

Demeter is peering at me with a blank frown. "Really, Cath, I think if you can afford to eat at Salt Block, you can afford to buy a very inspiring book—"

"I can't afford to eat at Salt Block! How do you think I could ever afford to do that? That was all bullshit! I was trying to *impress* you!" My anguish spills out in a scream. "I don't have a financial cushion. *Or* a famous daddy to give me a career." A dart of shock passes across Alex's face, but I don't care. It's true. "You're so fucking *entitled*. Both of you." I spread my arms wide, encompassing Alex. "Do you know that? Do you have *any* idea, *any* sense of—" I break off and give a little odd-sounding laugh. "Of course you don't. OK. Well, I'm leaving now. So. Enjoy your perfect lives."

The lift doors have opened, and I step inside. I jab the button for the third floor and begin to rise, thankfully without either of them trying to follow me. My eyes are stinging and my heart is miserably pounding. So much for a dignified exit. So much for keeping the door open. But right now . . . I really don't care.

CHAPTER ELEVEN

It's funny how life works like a seesaw: Some things go up while others plunge down. My life is swiftly unraveling while Dad's is finally, it seems, coming together. He's sent me pictures of the constructed yurts, and they look wonderful. The bathroom block is gleaming, the fire pits look picturesque, the bunting is charming, and Biddy has stockpiled homemade jam. Meanwhile, we've sent out the brochures to everyone we can think of. Dad has left piles of them in every trendy café around Somerset, while I've targeted likely places in London. (I left a pile in a café in Wandsworth, and a woman in a Boden mac picked one up while I was *still there*. It was like magic.)

But that's not the half of it. That's not even the 10 percent of it. What's happened to Dad and Biddy this week is like a lottery win, like a freak pot of gold under the rainbow. I still can't quite believe it's happened. *The Guardian* has profiled Ansters Farm Country Retreat in its "Glamping Roundup."

It's nuts! I mean, Ansters Farm isn't even a thing yet! But clearly some journalist was under a deadline and found the website and thought, *This'll do*. It's all in the piece—the yurts, the chickens, even my prose about children being children. They printed a photo of a campfire in front of a yurt and captioned it: *Ansters Farm is the latest family haven for hip glampers,* and I nearly died when I saw it. I mean, *The Guardian*!

And if I'd still been at work, it would have been my greatest-ever triumph. I could have marched into Demeter's office and said, *There's branding for you.*

But I'm not.

It's the last week of February and I don't have a job. I don't have the prospect of a job. I just have aching hands from typing job applications, googling brand agencies, and writing spec letters.

I've written an individual email for each application. I've researched every single possible company in the UK that I might suit. My mind is reeling with product names, campaigns, contacts. I'm exhausted. And panicky. Occasionally I glance in the mirror and see my own stricken face, and it's so *not* the face I want to see that I quickly look away again.

I'm trying to keep the fear at bay by doing stuff. I've reorganized my hammock. I've re-drafted my monthly budget to make it last two months. I'm doing a ton of walking, because, you know, walking's free. Plus it gives you endorphins and will therefore, in theory, cheer me up. Although I can't say that's really working. And I'm still up to date with Instagram. I've posted moody images of London streets at 4:00 A.M. (I couldn't sleep, but I didn't mention that.) I've posted a photo of the new pretzel stand at Victoria. I sound bright and breezy and employed. You'd never know the truth.

Flora's been in touch, quite a bit. She's left phone messages and texts and a long email starting: Oh my GOOOOOOOD. I can't believe the witch FIRED you, that is SO UNFAIR!!!!!!!!

I sent an email back, but I haven't spoken to her. I just feel too vulnerable right now. Sarah's also been in contact—in fact, she sent me a surprisingly long and sympathetic card. Apparently Demeter got rid of Sarah's boyfriend too, before I arrived at Cooper Clemmow. He's called Jake and he's a really good designer, did nothing wrong, but got made redundant. He's still unemployed all these months later, and they're both fairly devastated but trying to be positive. She ended with, *I know how hard this is for you,* and a string of sad faces.

And, you know, I'm sure she had the best of intentions, or whatever, but it didn't *altogether* cheer me up. I never went to that drinks at the Blue Bear either—how could I? I'm not part of the gang anymore. And, anyway, I couldn't afford to pay for my round.

I'm hanging out a lot at home, but even that's stressful, because of our new flatmate. Anita has sublet her room while she's away in Paris. It's totally against the rules, but our landlord never comes round. (I wish he would. He might get rid of the whey.) Our new flatmate is a cheerful blond girl called Irena who has rosy cheeks and wears a floral headscarf a lot of the time, and I had great hopes of her until she invited all her friends round.

I say "friends." That's not exactly what it is. They're a religion. It's the Church of the Something (I didn't quite catch the name and now I don't like to ask). And they all meet in her room and sing and have talks and shout, "Yes!"

I have nothing against the Church of the Something. I'm

sure they're very good people. Only they're also quite noisy. So, what with the singing and the whey boxes and Alan yelling, "Knobhead!" at himself, it's getting quite oppressive in here.

I've come into the kitchen to make my vegetable stew, and I'm crouching on the cardboard boxes, which are now so battered they keep half-collapsing. Maybe I should join the Church of the Something? The thought crosses my mind and I give a wry smile. Maybe *that's* the answer. Only I don't think I have the energy to shout, "Yes!" twenty times a night. I don't have much energy at all, is the truth. I feel drained. Defeated.

I stir my butternut squash and rutabaga stew (cheap and nutritious) and close my eyes with tiredness. And just for a moment, with my guard down, I let my mind roam into places it shouldn't. Places that are cold and scary and full of questions I don't want asked.

What if I don't find a job?

I will.

But what if?

There's a sudden dampness on my cheekbone. A tear is creeping out of one eye, I realize. It's the steam, I tell myself furiously. It's the onions. It's the whey.

"All right, Cat?" Alan appears at the door of the kitchen, leaps up, and starts doing chin-ups from the lintel.

"Fine!" I force a bright smile. "Good!" I shake some dried herbs into my stew and give it a stir.

"Bunch of nutters, aren't they?" He jerks his head toward Irena's room.

"I think we should respect their beliefs," I say, as another "Yesss!" resounds through the flat.

"Nooo!" Alan bellows over his shoulder, and grins at me. "Nutters. You know she wants another room for her friend? Asked if I'd move out. The nerve. They want to turn this place into a commune."

"I'm sure they don't."

"D'you reckon they shag or whatever?"

"*What?*"

"Like, they haven't all taken the pledge, have they?"

"I have no idea," I say frostily.

"I was just wondering." His eyes gleam. "A lot of these cults are into some crazy shit. Some of those girls are pretty hot." He does a few more chin-ups, then adds, "I mean, Irena's hot, come to that. Does she have someone?"

"I don't *know*." I scoop my stew into a bowl and say pointedly, "Excuse me." I clamber down off the whey boxes and past Alan, heading back to my room. *Please don't let Alan hook up with Irena,* I'm thinking. I've heard Alan having sex, and it's like one of his motivational rants but ten times louder.

I sit cross-legged on my bed, start forking stew into my mouth, and try to find something positive to think about. *Come on, Katie. It's not all bad.* I sent off a stack of applications today, so that's good. Maybe I should go onto Instagram now. Post something fun.

But as I scroll through the images on my phone, they seem to be mocking me. Who am I kidding with all this fake, happy stuff? I mean, *who* am I kidding, exactly?

Tears are running openly down my face now, as though they don't care who sees them. All my defenses are crumbling. There's only so long you can tell yourself that a crap situation is good and believe it.

On impulse, I take a picture of my hammock. And then my rutabaga stew. It isn't like any Instagram images of stew I've ever seen—it's an unappealing pile of browny-orange slop, like prison food. Imagine if I posted *that* on Instagram. The crappy truth. *See my cut-price supper. Look at my tights, falling out of their hammock. Look at all my job applications.*

God, I'm losing it now. I'm just tired, I tell myself firmly. Just tired . . .

My phone suddenly rings and I jump, startled, nearly spilling my stew. And for a split second I think, *A job, a job, a job?*

But it's Biddy. Of course it is.

I haven't told Biddy—or Dad—about my job. Not yet. I mean, obviously I *will* tell them. I just don't know when.

OK, full disclosure: I'm hoping desperately that I won't ever have to tell them, ever. I'm hoping that I'll somehow be able to sort things out quietly for myself, get a new job, and tell them *after* the event in a light and easy way: *Yes, I've changed jobs; it's no big deal, it was time to move on.* Let them think it was my choice, a natural progression. Save them all that distress and worry. Save *me* all that distress and worry.

Because if I tell Dad I've been let go from my job at Cooper Clemmow . . . Oh God. Just the thought makes me wince. I won't only be dealing with my own distress, I'll be dealing with his righteous anger too. He'll rail and fume and ask me what went wrong. . . . And right now I don't feel strong enough for that.

Biddy's different, more reasonable. But now isn't the moment to burden her. She's got enough on her plate with the glamping venture—I can already tell she's been overwhelmed. It's been more money and work than she expected, and it's consuming all her energy. I *can't* make her load heavier with my problems.

Nor can I risk her offering me money, which I know she'd do like a shot. That's her inheritance, and it's going on the business, *not* on me. Honestly, I'd rather give up my flat in London than have Biddy subsidizing it.

And I may get a new job tomorrow. I *may*.

"Hi, Biddy!" I wipe my sleeve across my face. "How are you?"

Biddy's been phoning me a lot, ever since Christmas. It's actually been a real upside to this whole glamping thing—I'm talking to her so much more. I've helped her order furniture for the yurts, and we've discussed where to put every fire pit and bench. She's also had a lot of queries for Alan about the website, and, to be fair to him, he's been super-patient. In fact, between us, Alan and I are the total architects of this project.

"I'm not disturbing you, am I, darling? You're not eating? We've just been trying out a new lamb tagine recipe, actually. If we *do* offer dinners, I think it'll be . . . quite good."

Quite good. In the language of Biddy-understatement, that means *utterly delicious*. I have a sudden image of her doling out some fragrant marinated local lamb, sprinkled with herbs from the garden, while Dad pours some of his Cash & Carry red wine.

"Great!" I say. "Well done! So, did you want to talk about menus?"

"No. No, sorry, that wasn't it. Katie, the thing is—" Biddy breaks off. She sounds nervous, I suddenly realize.

"Is everything OK?"

"Yes! Fine! Oh, love . . ." Biddy seems tongue-tied.

"What?" I demand. "Biddy, what?"

"Oh, Katie." She gulps. "People have started booking."

"What?"

"I know!" She sounds dumbfounded. "They're using the website. It's all working. I've taken five inquiries today alone. We've got three families booked in over the Easter weekend and four the week after. Four families, Katie!"

"Oh my God."

Even I feel quite shocked. I mean, I knew people would come, *in principle*. But four families? All at once?

"Well, that's amazing! Biddy, you've done it!"

"But we *haven't*!" she wails. "That's the point! Oh, darling, I'm petrified. We're going to have real customers, and I don't know how we're going to manage them, or entertain them, or . . . what if something goes wrong? And your dad's no help—I mean, he's a good man, but . . ."

She trails off, and I gape at the phone. I've never heard Biddy sound so rattled.

"You'll be great!" I say reassuringly. "I mean, you've got your lovely breakfasts and all the activities. . . ."

"But how do we organize it all? I've asked Denise from the village to help out, but all she does is ask me questions I can't answer."

"Well, put her on to me. Or do you want me to come down at the weekend?"

Even as I say the words, I feel a sickening wrench. A return ticket to Somerset costs a fortune. How on earth can I afford that? But I've offered now.

"Oh, Katie." Biddy seems to dissolve. "Would you? We rely on you so much, you know. When you're around, everything seems to fall into place. We'll pay your ticket, of course. And I know you're busy with your wonderful job in London, and we're *ever* so proud of you, but there was another thing. . . ." She hesitates as though she can't bring herself to continue.

"What?"

There's silence down the line and I wrinkle my brow in puzzlement. Just what can't Biddy bring herself to say?

"Biddy? Biddy, are you still there?"

"Katie, you wouldn't have any holiday, would you?" says Biddy in a rush. "You wouldn't be able to help us out, just at the start? Stay a week or two, maybe? Or as long as you can."

"Biddy . . ." I begin automatically, then break off. I don't know what I want to say. I didn't see this coming.

"I know, I know." Biddy instantly backtracks. "I shouldn't ask. It's not fair. You're making your way in the world, and if you can't do it, we absolutely understand. You've got your career, your life, your flat—how's the redecoration going, by the way?"

"Oh. Yes, it's fine . . . it's . . . argh! Oh God! *Aaaargh!*"

With no warning, the world has turned black. For a terrifying instant I think I'm being attacked. Something's hitting me, banging me, surrounding me. . . . I flail with my arms, panting, panicking . . . then suddenly realize what's happened.

My *bloody* hammock's collapsed.

I fight my way out of a black jersey skirt which has enveloped my head and survey my bed in dismay. The hammock is hanging dismally from one corner. All my crap is everywhere—

clothes, hair products, books, magazines. It'll take forever to sort all this out again. The only plus is that my bowl of stew was on the floor and didn't get knocked over.

Actually, that's not a plus.

"Katie?" Biddy's anxious voice is coming out of the phone. "Katie, what's happened?"

I grab the phone. "I'm fine. Sorry. Just knocked something over. I'm fine. Um . . ." I try to get my thoughts in order. "What were we saying?"

"I realized I never said, darling, we'll pay you!"

"What?" I say blankly.

"If you could come and help out, we'd pay you, of course. You *know* we've been wanting to pay you for everything you've done already, love, and now it looks like we'll have a budget. . . ."

"You'd . . ." I rub my face. "You'd pay me."

It's a job offer. I've had a job offer. I almost want to laugh hysterically—but I don't. I stir my stew, fighting my own thoughts.

An idea has crept into my head, an idea I can barely contemplate. Because it feels like an idea of failure. Of giving up. Of everything collapsing into dust.

I had so many dreams. I used to lie on my bed and study the tube map and imagine becoming one of those fast, confident people I'd seen on day trips to the capital. People in a hurry, with goals, aims, broad horizons. I'd imagined getting on a career ladder that could take me anywhere if I worked hard enough. Working on global brands; meeting fascinating people; living life to the max.

And, yes, I knew it would be hard. But maybe not this hard.

"Katie?"

"Sorry. Just . . . thinking."

It wouldn't be giving up, I tell myself sternly. It would just be . . . what? Regrouping. Because I *can* crack this. But maybe I need some time out first.

"Biddy, hold on," I say abruptly. "There's something I need to check."

I put down the phone, hurry out of my room, and knock on Irena's door. There's no response, but I push my way in, anyway, telling myself that this is urgent and Irena's god will understand.

The room is a sea of bowed, silent heads. Shit. Obviously this is a moment of prayer or something and now I've disturbed it. But I'm not backing away. I *have* to know.

I tiptoe through the cross-legged figures until I reach Irena, who's sitting on the bed, her blond hair shining, her eyes closed, and her rosy face rapt. Alan's right, I find myself thinking; she *is* very hot.

"Irena?" I whisper in her ear. "Irena, sorry to disturb, but is it true you want to sublet a room?"

Irena's eyes pop open and she turns to look at me.

"Yes," she whispers back. "It's for my friend Sonia."

She gestures at Sonia, who is even more blond and hot than Irena. Bloody hell. Alan's going to think he's gone to *heaven*.

"Well, you can have mine."

"Great!" Irena's eyes widen. "When?"

"As soon as we can fix it up. Come and see me when you've finished."

I tiptoe away again, thinking frantically. How exactly am I going to finesse this? I *can't* come clean to Biddy. She's in such a state right now. If she gets hassled by me and my problems too, then that won't help anybody.

So . . . OK. Here's what I'm going to do: 1. Help Biddy and Dad. 2. Not alarm them. 3. Quietly sort out my life. 4. Tell them the details on a need-to-know basis, preferably when everything is safely back on track again.

(5. Even when things are back on track, they will never need to know every painful detail of my life. 6. Especially how Demeter couldn't even remember if she'd fired me or not. 7. Or how I got mistaken for a homeless person.)

The only teeny problem is: What do I actually *say*? Right here and now? What do I *say*?

I pick up my phone and take a deep breath.

"Biddy . . . there *is* a kind of . . . er . . . possibility," I say into the phone. "It's hard to explain . . . kind of complicated. . . . Anyway, the point is, I *can* help you. I'll come down tomorrow."

"You'll come down?" Biddy sounds stunned. "Oh, Katie, love! How long can you stay for?"

"Not sure yet," I say vaguely. "I need to talk to some people . . . make some arrangements . . . probably a couple of weeks. Or a few weeks. Something like that."

"So, is it a sabbatical you're taking?" Biddy hazards. "Like that nice lady a couple of years ago who wanted to learn jam-making, remember? On sabbatical from her job in the city. Six months, she had. Do you think you'll get that long?" I can hear the hope in Biddy's voice. To be honest, I'm not sure what to answer.

Six months. I *have* to find a job in six months, surely.

"I'll stay as long as I can," I say at last, dodging the question. "It'll be lovely to see you! I can't wait!"

"Oh, Katie, nor can I!" Biddy's joy bursts down the line in a torrent. "To have you at home again for a bit! Your dad will be thrilled; *everyone* will be thrilled; oh, love, I really think we can make this glamping into something with your help. . . ."

She talks on and on, and I lean back on my littered, lumpy bed, staring up at my stained ceiling. Her loving, enthusiastic voice is like balm on sore skin. Someone wants me. I'm already looking forward to home-cooked food, a room with an actual wardrobe, the view of the hills.

But at the same time, my resolve is hardening like lacquer. I'm taking time out, but I'm not giving up. I mean, I'm only in my twenties; am I going to let one setback crush my ambition? No. I'm still going to work in branding one day. I'm still going to stride over Waterloo Bridge and think, *This is my city.* It's going to happen.

PART TWO

CHAPTER TWELVE

Three months later

"Right," I say into the phone. "I understand. Thank you."

I put the phone away and stare blankly ahead. Another headhunter with no joy. Another little lecture on how "tricky" the market is at the moment.

"Still that pharmaceutical brand?" Biddy's voice makes me jump, and I swivel round, flustered. I should have learned by now: Never take calls from headhunters in the kitchen. "They do work you hard, love!" Biddy adds, dumping a bunch of beets on the counter. "I thought it was supposed to be your sabbatical."

Guilt is crawling through me and I turn away, avoiding her gaze. You start with one well-intentioned fib. Next thing, you've built up a whole fictitious life.

It all began a week after I'd got home. A headhunter called me back, right in front of Dad and Biddy. I had to think quickly on my feet, and the only story I could come up with was that Cooper Clemmow were consulting me on a project. Now it's become my all-purpose excuse for taking calls and leaving the room. Whenever a headhunter calls me back, it's "Cooper Clemmow." And Dad and Biddy believe me implicitly. Why wouldn't they? They trust me.

I should never have gone along with Biddy's version of events. But it was so easy. *Too* easy. By the time I arrived in Somerset, she'd told Dad I was "on sabbatical," and they both seemed to take it for granted. The thought of unpicking the story was just beyond me.

So I didn't. Everyone believes I've taken a sabbatical, even Fi, because I couldn't risk telling her the truth and it ending up in some Facebook post which Biddy might stumble on. All Fi said was, Wow, UK employers are so *generous*. Then she went straight into some story about going to the Hamptons and drinking pink margaritas and it was so much fun and I *have* to come out. I didn't even know how to reply. Right now, my life could not be further from pink margaritas. Or macchiatos. Or cool pavement cafés in happening areas. When I go on Instagram these days, it's only to promote Ansters Farm.

I told Fi about the glamping, and she asked a few mildly interested questions—but then she wanted to know, So when will you be back in London? and Don't you MISS it? Which touched a sore spot. Of course I do. Then she started telling me about all the celebrities she'd spotted in some hotel bar that weekend.

And I *know* she's still Fi, my mate Fi, down-to-earth Fi . . . but it's getting harder to reconcile this glamorous New York Fi with the friend I could tell anything to. There's less and less about our lives that overlaps. Maybe I *should* go out to New York, forge our friendship again. But how can I afford to do that?

Anyway, it's hardly my most pressing problem. There are jobs to be done. I'm about to help Biddy with the beets when my phone buzzes in my pocket with an email. It's from McWhirter Tonge, the company I've just interviewed for. Oh God . . .

Casually, I open the kitchen door and step outside. The late May sun is warming the fields stretching ahead of me. A spire of smoke is rising from one of the campfires in the yurt village, and I can hear the distant chacking of jackdaws coming from a copse of ash trees in North Field. Not that I'm really listening or admiring the scenery. I only care about this email. Because you never know . . . *please* . . .

As I jab at the screen, I feel sick with hope. I interviewed for them last week. (I told Dad and Biddy I was seeing friends.) It's the only interview I've had, the only crumb of hope I've been given, the only application I've made that's got anywhere. The offices were in Islington, and they were tiny, but the people were cool, and the work seemed really interesting, and—

Dear Cat:

Thanks so much for taking the time to visit us last week. It was good to chat and we enjoyed meeting you, but unfortunately . . .

Just for a moment everything seems to go dark. *Unfortunately*.

I let my phone fall down, blinking away the tears that have started to my eyes. *C'mon, Katie. Pull it together.* I take a few deep breaths and pace a little on the spot. It's one job. One rejection. So what?

But a cold feeling is creeping over me. This was the only chance I had. No one else has even offered me an interview.

Actually, that's not entirely true. When I started out, I had lots of emails offering me positions with *stacks of potential* or *opportunities for development* or *valuable industry experience*. It only took me about three phone calls to work out what those phrases mean: "No money." "No money." "No money."

I can't work for no money. However much experience it gives me. I'm past that stage.

"All right, Katie?" Biddy's voice hails me and I whip round guiltily. She's depositing some peelings on the compost heap and eyes me with curiosity. "What's up, love?"

"Nothing!" I say quickly. "Just . . . you know. Work stuff."

"I don't know *how* you do it." Biddy shakes her head. "What with everything you do here, and all these emails you're always sending . . ."

"Well, you know." I give a weird-sounding laugh. "Keeps me busy."

Biddy and Dad think that when I'm spending hours at the computer, I'm conversing with my London colleagues. Bouncing around ideas. Not desperately sending out application after application.

I force myself to skim the rest of the email from McWhirter Tonge:

> . . . incredibly strong field . . . candidate with significantly more experience . . . keep your name on file . . . interest you in our intern scheme?

The intern scheme. That's all they think I'm fit for.

And I *know* the job market is competitive, and I *know* everyone finds it hard, but I can't help thinking: *What did I do wrong? Was I crap at the interview? Am I crap, full stop? And if so . . . what am I going to do?* A big black chasm is opening up in my mind. A scary dark hole. What if I can't find any paying job, *ever*?

No. Stop. I *mustn't* think like that. I'll send off some more applications tonight, widen the net—

"Oh, Katie, love." Biddy comes over. "I meant to ask you, I had an inquiry earlier, and the lady asked about sustainability. What is it we say again?"

"We talk about our solar panels," I say, glad of the distraction. "And the outdoor shower. And the organic vegetables. And we *don't* mention Dad's Jacuzzi. I'll write you out a crib sheet, if you like."

"You're a star, Katie." Biddy pats my arm, then directs a reproving glance at my phone. "Now, don't let those London bosses get to you, darling. You're on your *sabbatical,* remember!"

"That's right." I smile wanly as she heads back into the kitchen, then sink onto the grass. I feel like I'm two people right now. I'm Cat, trying to make it in London, and I'm Katie, helping to run a glamping site, and it's fairly exhausting being both.

On the plus side, the farm *does* look spectacular today. I'll go around later, take some photos and social-media them. My eye is caught by the glinting solar panels on the shower barn, and I feel a twinge of pride. It was my idea to put in the solar panels. We're not totally green at Ansters Farm—we use a supplementary boiler and we do have proper loos—but we're not totally un-green either. After only a few weeks of the season, I soon realized that some glampers are all about: *Are you sustainable? Because that's really important to us.* Whereas others are all about: *Are there proper hot showers or am I going to die of cold? Because I was never that sure about glamping in the first place; it was Gavin's idea.* So it's great to be able to reassure both camps.

Everyone loves the shower barn, with its reclaimed school lockers and pegs, but they love our open-air roll-top bath even more. It's painted in rainbow stripes—inspired by a Paul Smith design—and has its own mini wicker-fence enclosure, open to the sky, and it's just brilliant. I sent a photo of it to Alan, to upload onto the website. It showed the rainbow bath, with a bottle of champagne in an ice bucket and a cow looking over the wicker fence, and Alan sent back an email: Wow. V cool. I mean, if even Alan appreciates it, it *has* to be good.

The roll-top bath is so popular, we've had to instigate a rota. In fact, *everything* here is popular. I always thought Dad and Biddy would be able to make a go of this. What I didn't realize was how far they'd throw themselves into it or how much effort they'd make.

As for the yurts, they're *beautiful*. There are six of them, in pairs. They're close enough that a couple could put their children in an adjoining one, but far enough away for privacy too. Each one sits on its own little deck and has its own fire pit. Dad knows a guy called Tim who works with wood and owed him a favor. So Tim put together six beds out of local reclaimed timber, and they're spectacular. They're on huge, exaggerated legs, and the headboards have ANSTERS FARM carved into them, and you can even separate them into two single beds, for children. We have extra trundle beds too, because we've found that lots of families like their children in with them, if they're young, and the yurts are plenty big enough. The sheets are 400 thread count—we found a trade supplier—and the cushions are all vintage prints, plus each yurt has a sheepskin on the floor.

Each family gets a little hamper of milk, tea, bread . . . plus homemade organic Ansters Farm soap. Biddy looked around at local organic-soap suppliers and then decided that she could easily do it herself. She makes it in tiny guest-size cakes and scents it with rosemary and stamps AF on the front. And then, if guests want to, they can buy a big bar to take home. Which, usually, they do. She also offers personalized soap with any initials on, which people can order as presents. That was all Biddy's idea. She's incredible.

We've also invested in good Wi-Fi. Not just good-for-the-country, *really* good. It gets beamed straight to us from a mast twenty miles away. It costs a bit and Dad was against it, but I know London people. They *say* they want to get away from it all, but when you tell them there's a Wi-Fi code they nearly collapse in relief. And luckily we have phone signal at the house—although not in the fields or the woods. If they want to call the office from the middle of a hike, too bad.

Meanwhile, Dad's created a bike trail through the fields, and a mini adventure playground, and a gypsy caravan where children can go and play if it rains. At night we light lanterns along the paths of the yurt village, and it honestly looks like fairyland.

"Farmer Mick!" I can hear excited shrieks coming from the path up to the woods. "Farmer Mick!"

This is the biggest revelation of all: Dad.

I thought Dad was going to be the problem. I thought he wasn't going to take it seriously. So I sat him down the week before the first guests arrived, and I said: "Listen, Dad, you have to be *nice* to the glampers. This is serious. It's Biddy's money. It's your future. Everything depends on your being charming and helping the glampers and making life *easy* for them. OK? If they want to climb trees, help them climb trees. If they want to milk the cows, let them. And don't call them townies."

"I wouldn't!" Dad replied defensively.

"Yes, you would. And be especially nice to the children," I added as a parting shot.

Dad was very quiet for the rest of the day. At the time, I worried I'd offended him. But now I realize: He was thinking. He was creating a role for himself. And just as Biddy has blown me away with her ideas, Dad's blown me away with basically turning into a completely different human being.

"Farmer Mick! More tricks!"

Dad appears round the corner of the shower barn, accompanied by the three-year-old triplets who have been staying this week. There are two boys and a girl, and they're supersweet, all dressed in little Scandinavian stripy tops.

Dad, meanwhile, is in his "Farmer Mick" outfit. He's taken to wearing a bright checked shirt with a straw hat, and he practically says "Oo-aarh" every other sentence. He's walking along, juggling three beanbags very badly, but the children don't care.

"Who wants to ride in the pickup?" he asks, and the children all shout excitedly, "Me! Me!"

"Who wants to see Agnes the cow?"

"Me!"

It's not Agnes the cow, it's Agnes the bantam hen, but I'm not going to correct him. I mean, whatever.

"Who's having the best holiday of their life?" He winks at me.

"Meeee!" The children's shouts are deafening.

"Let's sing our song now!" Dad launches into a lusty tune. "Ansters Farm, Ansters Farm, best place to be . . . Ansters Farm, Ansters Farm, never want to leave . . . Who wants a Somerset toffee?"

"Meeeee!"

Honestly, he's like some sort of children's party entertainer. And he's not stupid: Every other minute he tells the children they're having the best holiday of their lives. It's basically brainwashing. All the little ones leave the place actually weeping because they're going to miss Farmer Mick, and we've had a load of re-bookings already.

What with him amusing the children, and Biddy making pots of jam the whole time, plus all the grown-up pursuits too, I do worry they're going to burn out. But every time I say that to Dad or Biddy, they just laugh and come up with some new idea, like offering hay-baling lessons. During the week we've got a whole activity program called Somerset Skills. There's willow-weaving, woodcraft, foraging—and the guests *love* it.

So, basically, the glamping site has started off as a roaring success. But whether they can make an actual *profit* . . .

Sometimes, just the thought of how much money Biddy's thrown into this venture gives me a gnawing feeling inside. She won't tell me exactly how much she's invested—but it's a lot. And that's money that could have been put aside for her old age.

Anyway. There's no point fretting about it. All I can do is help them turn this place into a profitable business. Which means, for starters, that "Farmer Mick" has to stop doling out free Somerset toffees, because: 1. He goes through boxes a day. 2. He eats half of them himself. 3. One of the parents has already complained about her child being given evil sugary treats.

The parents of the triplets appear from their yurt, followed by Steve Logan, who's carrying their luggage for them. Steve helps us out on Saturdays, which are our turnaround days. And although he's incredibly annoying, he's also annoyingly useful. His hands are so huge, he can shift about three holdalls at once, and he always puts on this ridiculous deferential air, in the hope of tips.

"You mind how you go, sir," he's saying now, as he loads their SUV. "You look after yourselves now, sir. You have a safe trip, now. Lovely family. You should be very proud. We'll miss you."

"We'll miss *you*!" exclaims the mum, who is in a stripy top, just like her children, and clutching the lavender cushion she made yesterday. "We'll miss all of you! Farmer Mick, and Biddy, and Katie, you're an angel. . . ." She seizes me in a sudden hug, and I hug her back, because they are a lovely family, and I know she means it.

I'm Katie here, to everyone. Of course I am. I'd never even

try to be Cat. Not only am I Katie, but I'm a version of Katie even I don't quite recognize sometimes. My London accent has gone. No point trying to sound urban here. It was always a bit of a strain, and the glampers don't want to hear London; they want to hear Somerset. Thick, creamy Zummerzet, the way I was brought up.

My bangs have gone too. The hairstyle was so bloody needy, and it never felt like me. It's not even feasible now that I'm not straightening my hair every day. I'm giving it a rest from heat treatments, which means the sleek chignon is gone and I'm back to my trademark Katie Brenner natural curls, tumbling down my back, tousled by the breeze. Nor am I bothering with flicky liquid eyeliner and three coats of mascara these days. And I've put my "city" glasses away in a drawer. You couldn't exactly say I have a "look" anymore, but I'm so busy, I don't care. My face is fuller too—all those delicious dinners—and tanned from the sun. A dusting of freckles has even appeared on my nose. I don't look like me.

Well, maybe I look like a different me.

"What a beautiful family," intones Steve, as the triplets climb into the SUV. "Family of little angels, they are. Little angels from heaven."

I shoot a furious glare at Steve. He's *totally* overdoing it and if he's not careful, they'll think he's mocking them.

But the mum's eyes glow even more, and the dad feels in his pocket.

"Ah. Now . . . here you are. Many thanks." He hands Steve a note and I roll my eyes. It'll only encourage him. Steve practically bows as the doors clunk shut, and we all wave as the car heads off down the drive.

That's the last family of the week. All the yurts are now vacated.

There's a short silence between us all, as though we're contemplating this momentous fact. Then Biddy turns to me, claps her hands together in a businesslike way, and says, "*Right.*"

And it begins.

The thing about turnaround day is, it's fine, as long as you don't stop even for a moment. Biddy and I grab our cleaning things from the pantry and tackle the first two yurts. After half an hour, Denise from the village arrives, and I breathe a sigh of relief. I'm never totally sure that Denise is going to turn up.

While Denise takes over the cleaning, Biddy and I move on to preparing and styling the yurts. Fresh flowers in vases. Fresh supplies in the hamper. Fresh soap, fresh lavender sprigs, fresh WELCOME TO ANSTERS FARM card on the bed, each one handwritten:

To Nick, Susie, Ivo, and Archie.

To James and Rita.

To Chloe and Henry.

Chloe and Henry are James and Rita's children, but they're teenagers, so they're in their own yurt. We don't often get teens, and I hope there's enough for them to do.

To Giles, Cleo, Harrison, Harley, and Hamish, plus Gus the dog!

This week is half term. In fact, last week was half term too—the schools seem to be picking different weeks this year because there's an extra bank holiday this Friday. Which is great for us: double the bookings. So we're crammed full of families, with cots and trundle beds everywhere. As I'm laying out blankets, I quickly check on my phone: Harley's a girl. Right. Some of these trendy names, you really can't be sure.

To Dominic and Poppy.

Divorced dad with his daughter. He mentioned that twice while he was booking over the phone. He said he wanted quality time with his little girl, and his ex keeps her too cooped up, in his opinion, and she needed more outdoor play, and he didn't agree with a lot of his ex's decisions. . . . You could hear his pain. It was sad.

The glampers often do phone up, even though you can do it all online. They'll say it was to check some detail, but I think they want to be sure that the place really does exist and we don't sound like ax murderers, before they put down a deposit. Which, you know. Fair enough.

To Gerald and Nina.

Gerald and Nina are the grandparents of one of the families. I love it when multigenerational families come to stay.

Finally all the yurts are ready. Biddy's laying up tea in the kitchen—we always offer this when the glampers arrive. Good hearty pots of tea, with her own scones and Ansters Farm jam. (Available to buy.)

Our kitchen really isn't up to much—the cupboards are crummy MDF and the counters are Formica. It's not like the "rustic" kitchens you find in London, with their Agas and larders and thickly hewn oak surfaces from Plain English. But we do have original flagstones, and we spread a linen cloth on the table and hang bunting everywhere and . . . Well. It does.

I'm walking back to the kitchen when Dad falls into step beside me.

"All set?" he says.

"Yes, it's looking good," I grin at him and touch the scarf round his neck. "Nice bandanna, Farmer Mick. Oh, and I meant to tell you, the showers got a special mention in one of the feedback forms. It said, *Very good, for a glamping venue.*"

"They're very good for *any* venue," retorts Dad, in a mock-grumbly voice, but I can tell he's pleased. "That reminds me," he adds lightly. "I saw something might interest you. Howells Mill, down in Little Blandon. It's been converted into flats."

I stare at him, puzzled. This seems a total non sequitur.

"Nice bathrooms," clarifies Dad, seeing that I look blank. "Power showers."

OK, I'm still not with him. What do power showers in Little Blandon have to do with me?

"Just in case you were looking," Dad continues. "We could help you with a deposit, maybe. The prices aren't bad."

And then suddenly I get it. He's suggesting I buy a property in Somerset?

"Dad . . ." I barely know how to answer. How can I even begin? "Dad, you *know* I'm heading back to London. . . ."

"Well, I know that's your plan. But plans change, don't they?" He shoots me a sidelong, slightly shifty glance. "Worthwhile knowing what your options are, at least, isn't it?"

"But, Dad . . ." I come to a standstill, the breeze lifting my hair. I don't know how many times I can say, "I want to live in London." I feel like I'm bashing my head against a wall.

There's quiet, except for the distant sound of cows. The sky is light and blue above us, but I feel weighed down with guilt.

"Katie, love . . ." Dad's face crumples with concern. "I feel like we've been getting you back these last months. You're not so thin. Not so anxious. That girl up there . . . that's not you."

I know he means well. But right now his words are pressing all my sore spots. I've been trying to bolster my confidence so desperately all these weeks, telling myself this job loss is only a blip. But maybe Dad's hit the nail on the head: Maybe that girl's *not* me. Maybe I *can't* cut it in London. Maybe I should leave it for other people.

A little voice inside me is already protesting: *Don't give up! It's only been three months*; *you can still do it!* But it's hard. When every recruitment officer and headhunter seems to have the opposite opinion.

"I'd better get on," I say at last. Somehow I manage a half smile—then I turn and head toward the farmhouse.

I'm just double-checking what activities we have lined up for tomorrow, when Denise appears at the kitchen door, holding a large plastic crate. It's what she uses for picking up what she calls "them glampers' crap."

"All done," she says. "Been round the site. All spotless."

"Great; thanks, Denise," I say. "You're a star."

And she is. In a way. She doesn't always turn up—but when she does, she's very thorough. She's ten years older than me and has three daughters and you can see them being marched to school in the mornings, with the tightest plaits I've ever seen.

"The things them people leave behind." She nods at the crate.

"Did they leave a real mess?" I say sympathetically.

It's always a surprise to me, how nice families in tasteful outfits from Boden can be so messy. And inconsiderate. One lot *wouldn't* stop feeding Colin the alpaca all kinds of dumb stuff, however much we told them not to.

"You'll never guess." Denise's eyes are flashing with a kind of dark triumph. "Look at this!" She pulls a Rampant Rabbit out of her crate and I gasp.

"No! *No!*"

"What's that?" Biddy looks round from the cooker. "Is it a toy?"

Damn Denise. I do *not* want to have to explain to my stepmother what a Rampant Rabbit is.

"It's . . . a thing," I say hurriedly. "Denise, put it away. Which yurt was it in?"

"Dunno," she says with an unconcerned shrug.

"Denise!" I clasp my head. "We've been over this. You have to *label* the lost property. Then we can send it on to the guests."

"You sending *that* through the post?" Denise gives a short laugh.

"Well . . ." I hesitate. "Dunno. Maybe not."

"Or this?" She brandishes a tube of cream labeled FOR PERSISTENT GENITAL WARTS.

"Oh God." I make a face. *"Really?"*

"Nice top, though." She plucks a purple T-shirt from the crate and holds it up against herself. "Can I have this?"

"No! Let's have a look." I peer into the crate, and, she's right, it's full. There's a water pistol, a pair of children's wellies, a bundle of papers, a baseball cap. . . . "God, they've been messy this time." My phone rings and I answer, "Ansters Farm, how may I help?"

"Oh, hello!" It's the voluble voice of the mum in the stripy top. "Katie, is that you?"

"Yes! Is this . . . ?"

Shit. What's her name? I've forgotten already.

"Barbara! We're on our way back. About twenty minutes away. We left behind . . ."

Her voice descends into crackles. The signal is so bad on the local roads, I'm amazed she got through at all.

"Barbara?" I raise my voice. "Hello, Barbara, can you hear me?"

". . . very sensitive . . ." Her voice suddenly comes down the line again in a buzz of static. "I'm sure you found it . . . you can *imagine* how I feel . . ."

Oh my God. Did Barbara leave behind the Rampant Rabbit? I clap a hand over my mouth so I don't laugh. Barbara with her clean, makeup-free face and her wholesome triplets?

"Um . . ."

". . . absolutely *mortified* . . . had to come and get it in person . . . see you soon . . ." Her voice disappears. I gape at the silent phone, then look up.

"OK, I think we have the owner coming back."

"Did she fess up?" Denise gives a short laugh. "I'd lie."

"Not exactly. She said it was very sensitive and she was really embarrassed—"

"Could be this." Denise holds up the tube of cream.

"Oh *shit*." The realization hits me. "Yes. It totally could."

I look from the Rampant Rabbit to the genital-warts cream. What a choice.

"You're more likely to come back for a cream, maybe?" offers Denise. "If it's on prescription or whatever?"

"But you could get that replaced."

"The Rampant Rabbit's *worth* more. . . ."

I catch Denise's eye and a wave of sudden hysteria comes over me.

"This is hideous." My voice is shaking. "Which one are we going to offer her?"

"Offer her both."

"We can't say, *Here's a vibrator and some genital-warts cream; take your pick.*" I clutch my stomach, unable to stop laughing.

"Find out which one it is," says Biddy from the stove. "Get her into conversation about it, then when you're sure which it is, go and get the item."

"*Conversation?*" I double up. "What kind of conversation?"

"I'll do it," says Biddy. "Honestly, you girls! And put it in a bag," she adds firmly. "Your dad doesn't want to see that kind of thing lying around. And, yes, I *do* know what it is," she adds, catching my eye with a little spark. "They've changed the designs, that's all."

Wow. This is the thing about Biddy: always full of surprises.

It's only about ten minutes later that the SUV roars back up the drive. They must have been flooring it. We've decided that Biddy will get Barbara into conversation outside, while Denise and I lurk in the kitchen. And the minute we've worked out what the lost property is, we'll come out with it, discreetly wrapped.

"Barbara!" Biddy steps out of the kitchen door. "I'm so sorry you've had to delay your journey."

"Oh, it's my own stupid fault," says Barbara, who has leapt out of the SUV and looks very pink about the cheeks. "But I couldn't relax till I'd retrieved it. A lot of things, you wouldn't bother about. But *that* . . ."

I look at Denise and reach for the Rampant Rabbit with raised eyebrows. It's *sounding* like the sex toy. . . .

"Of course not, dear," says Biddy in that cozy way she has. "Not when it's such a very *personal* item."

"Oh, it's not mine, strictly speaking," says Barbara. "It's my husband's."

What? Denise and I stare at each other with wide eyes, then I take my hand off the Rampant Rabbit and put it on the genital-warts cream. It has to be that. Surely.

"Although he'd say I get more enjoyment out of it than he does," Barbara says with a friendly smile.

Beside me, Denise explodes.

"Stoppit!" I whisper, and reach for the Rampant Rabbit again. I pick up the bag and prepare to head outside, though *how* I'm going to look Barbara in the eye, I have no idea.

"Well, Katie's just fetching it for you," says Biddy. "She'll be out with it any moment."

"That's right." My voice trembles with suppressed hysteria as I appear on the doorstep. "Here it is. Um . . . safe and sound."

I've wrapped the Rampant Rabbit in brown paper and put it in a carrier bag, just so no one gets an untoward glimpse.

"Oh, I'm *so* relieved," says Barbara as she takes the bag from me. "I expect I left it in the bed or somewhere, did I?"

I glance wildly at Biddy, my mouth clamped shut.

"I'm not sure, love," says Biddy, totally unfazed. "But it seems likely, doesn't it?"

"I'm so forgetful," adds Barbara, with a sigh. "And the book hasn't even been bought yet, so you can *imagine* how sensitive it is. As I say, I'm mortified. It's so unprofessional, to leave a manuscript on holiday!"

I've frozen dead. Manuscript? *Book?*

"You've wrapped it up very nicely." Barbara smiles and starts to poke at the brown paper. "I might just double-check it's the right document. . . ."

Shit, *shit* . . .

"Oh!" I try to grab the bag back from her. "Let me just . . . unwrap it for you."

"I'll do it." She starts pulling the brown paper off and my stomach lurches as I see a flash of pink plastic.

"No trouble!" I say shrilly, wrenching the bag out of her hands. Ignoring her cry of surprise, I dash inside. "Papers!" I gasp, dumping the Rampant Rabbit on the floor. "It's the *papers*."

Denise is already one step ahead. She's gathered up all the papers from the crate and shoves them into my hands.

"So, *here* we are." I hurry back outside and thrust the pages toward Barbara, who looks a little taken aback. "I'm afraid they've got a bit muddled. . . ."

"Not to worry." Barbara starts leafing through the pages. "Yes, this is it. Again, I'm *so* embarrassed. It's *such* sensitive material."

"Really," I say weakly. "No need to be."

"We've seen worse," says Denise, stepping out beside me and giving Barbara a bland smile.

"I'm sure." Barbara hesitates, and I peer at her in surprise. Her pink cheeks are turning deeper crimson. "Actually, as well as the book, I did leave another . . . um . . . item. . . . I *think* that might have been it in the bag. . . ."

For a frozen moment no one moves. Then, in an odd, strangled voice, Denise says, "Of course."

She retrieves the Rampant Rabbit and hands it over. I can't look at Barbara. I can't look anywhere.

"Well . . . er . . . enjoy!" I say.

Somehow we all keep it together as Barbara gets back into her SUV and zooms off. Then Biddy catches my eye and starts giggling, and that starts me off. And Denise just shakes her head and says, "Them glampers."

We're all pretty much in hysterics as Dad appears round the corner of the farm and says, "Wake up, you lot! There's a car coming up the drive. The first family's here."

The next few hours are a blur. It's always the same on a Saturday—a crowd of new faces and names and questions, all to be met with a charming smile. *This is Archie . . . this is Poppy . . . this is Hamish, he's allergic to dairy; didn't we write that on the form? Oh, so sorry . . .*

The families all seem nice enough, and I'm especially keen on Gerald and Nina, who are soon sitting out on their deck, mixing gin and tonics and offering them to all the other families. Poppy is already scampering around with her dad, looking at all the animals, while Hamish, Harrison, and Harley are glued to their iPads—but I'm not their parents, what do I care? All that concerns me is that everyone is checked in, greeted, and sorted. Which they all are, except the Wiltons.

I'm walking among the yurts, checking that everything

seems OK, when I notice that Gus the dog has already got into a field of sheep.

"Oh, hi!" I say, heading over to his owners' yurt. "Knock knock? Gus is *such* a gorgeous dog. Only I wonder if you'd mind keeping him this side of the fence? The sheep get a bit freaked."

"Oh, of course," says the dad, who I've remembered is called Giles and comes from Hampstead. He's tall and gangling and is holding a copy of a book called *The Campfire Gourmet*. As he comes out to retrieve Gus, he adds, "We're so looking forward to the willow-weaving workshop tomorrow."

"It should be fun! And if you'd like full English breakfast, just sign up . . . unless you're going to make your own?"

"We're making our own," says Giles resolutely, as he whistles for Gus. "On the fire."

"Good for you!" I say, ruffling Gus's head. "Well, I'll catch you later."

As I head back toward the farmhouse, I feel . . . if not ecstatic exactly, then content. Another turnaround nearly completed. We're getting better at it every week. Denise is catching on to some of our special touches, and Biddy is brimming with ideas, and—

"*So* authentic. *Absolutely* wonderful."

A voice stops me in my tracks. It's a ringing, imperious voice. And it sounds just like—

No.

"*Marvelous* view. Look, Coco. Look at this view. And is everything organic?"

My heart has started to thud. It can't be.

". . . absolutely *adore* to find some proper West Country cuisine; you'll have to recommend a spot . . ."

It *can't* be. But it is. It's Demeter.

Here.

I feel rooted to the spot, between yurts, like a paralyzed gazelle. Whoever she's talking to isn't answering loudly enough to be audible. So all I can hear is Demeter's voice, crashing arrogantly through the quiet, asking typical Demeter questions.

"And is the river organic? . . . And is *all* the produce local? . . . Now, when you say *sustainable* . . ."

I'm still stranded on the grass. I have to move. I have to get a grip. But I can't. My face is prickling and my breaths feel weak. What is she *doing* here?

"Actually, it's Demeter," I hear her saying now, in that smug way she has when she explains her name. "De-meeeeter. It's Ancient Greek."

I suddenly spot Dad coming out of the kitchen. He's holding the master folder, which is where I put all the printouts, guest forms, everything that Dad and Biddy don't want to read on screens.

"Dad," I gasp, and scuttle over to him, keeping well out of sight. "Who are those people? Can I just check . . ." I've already grabbed the folder and am riffling through the paperwork, my hands so shaky that they barely work. "Here we are. The Wiltons."

My mind is racing. I know her as Demeter Farlowe. But maybe that's her maiden name. Is Wilton her married name? *Is* it?

Well, why shouldn't it be?

"James and Rita," I read. *"Rita."*

"I know." Dad chuckles. "Funny name for a woman that age. I thought that when I wrote it down."

"So, you took the booking?" I need every scrap of information. I need to know *how this has happened.*

"She phoned up from her car." Dad nods—then his expression changes. "Now, don't tell me I didn't put the payment through properly. Because I did exactly what you taught me, love—"

"No, it's not that. It's not that. . . ."

My head is spinning. I've just seen the address on the form: Stanford Road. It's definitely her. My chest feels so constricted, I'm not sure I can breathe.

Demeter. Here.

"Love?" Dad peers at me. "Katie?"

"She's not called Rita, OK?" I manage. "I just heard her saying so. She's called Demeter. De-*me*-ter."

"Demeter?" Dad looks highly dubious. "That's not a name."

"It is a bloody name!" I feel like shaking him. If he'd only written it down right in the first place . . . "It's Greek! It means 'goddess of the harvest'!"

"Well. Takes all sorts. De-me-ter." Dad tries the word out again, wrinkling his nose. Then he surveys me again, looking puzzled. "Love, what's the problem? It's just a name. No harm done."

I stare back silently, my thoughts roaring in my head. I don't even know where to start. *No harm done?*

"There's no problem," I say at last. "I just don't like getting things wrong. We'll need to change all the place names and lists and everything. And explain about the note. It doesn't look professional."

Dad strides off toward the shower barn, whistling a merry tune, and I swivel slowly on the spot. I can still hear a conversation going on by Demeter's yurt. It must be Biddy who's checking her in, and they're still at it. Go figure. Demeter is exactly the kind of person to monopolize all the attention.

Slowly I edge my way back toward the yurt. As I get near enough to hear, I stop still and listen with all my might.

"I read about you in the *Guardian* piece, of course," Demeter's saying in her lordly way. "And I had a brochure. Someone gave it to me—I can't remember who now. And so this is a proper, authentic farm?"

"Oh yes," I hear Biddy reply. "The Brenner family have farmed this land for over two hundred years. I'm the newcomer!"

"How fabulous," says Demeter. "I'm a great supporter of authentic rural practices. We can't *wait* to start the activities, can we, Coco?"

Coco. That's the daughter. She was *Chloe* on the form.

"Well, I'll leave you to get settled," says Biddy. "If there's anything you want, please come up to the farmhouse. I'm always there, or Farmer Mick, or Katie. You haven't met her, but she's Farmer Mick's daughter. My stepdaughter."

"Wonderful," says Demeter. "Thank you *so* much. Oh, one last question—are the sheets organic?"

I've heard enough. I back away and sprint into the farmhouse. I don't stop till I get safely into my room. Then I bang the door shut and sit on my bed, staring at the ancient peeling wallpaper, breathing hard. How am I going to survive a week of Demeter? I can't bear it. I have to leave.

But I can't. Dad and Biddy need me. Oh God . . .

I bury my head in my hands. Fucking Demeter. She has to ruin *everything*—

And then a terrifying thought hits me. The minute Demeter recognizes me, it's all going to come out. Dad and Biddy will find out I got let go from my job. That the "sabbatical" was a lie. They'll get all worried . . . it'll be awful. . . .

I'm sitting motionless on my bed, hugging a cushion, my brain working frantically. This is serious. I have to protect myself. Top priority: *Demeter must not realize who I am.*

She only knew me as Cat. If she associates me with anywhere, it's Birmingham. She wouldn't think of me as Katie the farmer's daughter from Somerset. And she's never been great at recognizing people. Could I fool her? Can I?

Slowly I stand up and head over to my battered old wardrobe. There's an oval full-length mirror on it, and I survey myself critically. My curly hair is different. My clothes are different. My name's different. My face isn't that different—but she's not good with faces. My accent's different, I realize. I can play up the Somerset burr even more.

In sudden inspiration, I grab for an eye-shadow palette that Biddy gave me for Christmas a few years ago. I bypass all the neutral shades and head straight for the frosted blue and purple. I daub both colors around my eyes. Then I put on a baseball cap I got years ago from the Bath & West Show and survey myself again.

I look about as unlike Cat as it's possible to look.

"Allo thar," I say to my reflection. "I be Katie Brenner. Farmed this land all my life. Never been to Lunnon town."

There's only one way I'm going to find out whether this disguise works: Try it out.

As I enter the kitchen, Biddy is sitting labeling jam, and she gapes at me in surprise.

"Goodness! Katie! That makeup's . . . very . . ."

"New look," I say briefly, pouring out glasses of lemonade and arranging them on a tray. "Thought I might give the new family some lemonade, since they missed tea."

As I head down over the field, toward Demeter's yurt, I feel sick with jitters. But I force myself to keep going, head down, one foot in front of the other. As I get near, I slow down to a halt and raise my eyes.

There she is. Demeter. In the flesh. I actually feel a shiver as I see her.

She's sitting on the deck, all alone, wearing the perfect, glossy magazine version of country clothes. Slouchy trousers in a slubby gray linen, together with a collarless shirt and some Moroccan-looking leather slippers.

"No, not Babington House this time," she's saying on her mobile. "Ansters Farm. Yes, it's *very* new. Didn't you see the write-up in *The Guardian*?"

She sounds totally smug. Well, of course she does. She's found the Latest New Thing.

"Yes, artisan activities. A real taste of farm life. You know how passionate I am about organic food. . . . Absolutely!

Simple things. Local food, local crafts . . . Oh yes, we all take part. . . ." Demeter listens for a moment. "Mindfulness. That's *exactly* what I said to James. These old-fashioned skills . . . *So* good for the children. . . . I know." She nods vigorously. "Back to the earth. Absolutely. And the people are so quaint. *Absolute* salt of the earth . . ."

Something inside me has started to boil. Quaint? *Quaint?*

"Must go. I have *no* idea where my family have got to. . . ." Demeter gives a bark of laughter. "I know. Absolutely. Well, I'll keep you posted. Ciao!"

She rings off, scrolls through her phone, taps her fingers agitatedly a few times, and thrusts a hand through her hair. She seems a bit hyper. Probably overexcited at being an early adopter yet again. Eventually she puts her phone in her pocket and looks around with a sweeping gaze. "Oh, hello," she says as she notices me.

My chest tightens, but somehow I stay outwardly calm.

"Hello there." I greet her in my broadest West Country accent. "Welcome to Ansters Farm. I'm Katie, the farmer's daughter. Lived here all my life," I add for good measure.

Am I overdoing it? I'm just so desperate to put her off the scent.

"I brought you some lemonade," I add. "It's homemade—organic, of course."

"Oh, lovely," says Demeter, whose eyes lit up at the word "organic." "Can you bring it up here?"

As I step up to the deck, my hands are shaking. Surely she'll recognize me. Surely she'll peer under my cap and say, *Wait a minute . . .*

But she doesn't.

"So, Katie, I have a question—" She breaks off as her phone buzzes. "Sorry, just a sec . . . Hi, Adrian?" She gives a short, resigned laugh. "No, don't worry, what else are Saturdays for? Yes, just got here, and I've seen the email from Rosa. . . ."

I'm prickling all over. It's as if I've whooshed back to the office. Rosa. Adrian. Names I haven't heard in months. If I close my eyes I'm there, sitting at my desk, listening to the office buzz, the tapping of keyboards, the squeak of Sarah's chair on the floor.

And now I'm remembering that last day: Flora telling me Demeter was in trouble. Something about Sensiquo and a deadline. Well, clearly she got herself out of trouble pretty quickly. Flora's voice rings again in my mind: *If you're shagging one of the partners, you're never in that much trouble, right?*

"OK, well, that's good news," Demeter's saying. "Can you tell the team on Monday? God knows they need the morale boost. . . . Yes . . . Yup." She's striding around the deck now, the way she does in the office when she's giving one of her rants. "I know; the cow-welfare concept was brilliant. I can't remember whose idea that was now. . . ."

My eyes open in shock. Cow welfare? That was *my idea*. Doesn't she *remember*?

As I watch her pacing around, completely oblivious to me, a wave of anguish crests over me. That was *my* idea; *my* future; *my* life. OK, it wasn't a Farrow & Ball everything-perfect life. But it was my London life and now it's been shattered. And the worst thing is, it didn't count for anything. She doesn't remember me at all. There I was, worried about being recognized. What a *joke*.

Just for an instant, I want to pour lemonade over her head. But instead I stand perfectly still like a wooden dummy, holding the tray, watching her finish the conversation and put away her phone.

"*Now.*" She turns her attention to me. "Why don't you put that lemonade down here? I want to ask you about these activities." She picks up our activities sheet from the table and jabs at it with a manicured nail. "I have an allergy to willow, and I see that the activity tomorrow is willow-weaving. I'm also mushroom-intolerant, so I can't do the foraging activity on Tuesday either."

I want to laugh, or explode. An allergy to *willow*? Only Demeter.

"I see. Well, all the activities are optional, so . . ."

"Yes, but if I don't weave willow, what will I do?" Demeter fixes me with gimlet eyes. "Are there substitute activities? Obviously I've *paid* for willow-weaving and mushroom-foraging, so I feel there should be some other option available to me. That's what I feel. Something rustic. Or maybe yoga? Do you offer yoga?"

God, she's a pushy cow.

"I'll sort out an alternative for you," I say, in my best customer-service manner. "I'll find you some bespoke activities."

The word "bespoke" works wonders, just as I knew it would.

"Oh, something bespoke would be *wonderful.*" Demeter reaches for a glass of lemonade. "Well," she says, smiling now that she's got everyone running around after her. "It's very beautiful here. Very calm. I'm sure we'll have a wonderful, relaxing time."

As I walk back to the farmhouse, I'm a whorl of conflicting emotion. She didn't recognize me. She looked right at me, but she still didn't recognize me. That's good. I'll be safe. My secret won't come out. It's all good. . . .

Oh, but God, I can't *bear* her. How do I stay polite all week? How do I *do* this? There's a burning sense of injustice inside me that I can't quell.

I could flood her yurt. Easy. Tonight. Go out with a flashlight, drag the hose along . . .

No. No, Katie. Stop it.

With a supreme effort, I shut down the stream of revenge fantasies which has started pouring through my mind. Demeter is probably the most influential guest we've ever had. I *can't* have her going back to London and telling everyone Ansters Farm is crap. We have to give her and her family a good time.

Oh, but . . . but . . .

I sit down on a wooden stump, staring morosely at the picturesque view. I need to get my mood in order before I go inside; otherwise, Biddy will pick up on it. After a while, Steve comes into view, and in spite of myself, I smile.

He has earphones in and is walking along with a rolling gait, doing weird dance moves with his arms. I recognize those moves from the fifth-form dance. Maybe he's practicing his wedding dance.

Oh God, he probably *is*. I clap a hand over my mouth briefly, then regain control.

"Hey, Steve." I wave hard to get his attention, and he comes over, pulling out his earphones. "Listen, I might need some extra help tomorrow. One of the guests wants a bespoke activity."

"Bespoke?" Steve makes a face. "What's that, then?"

"Dunno." I sigh. "I'll have to make something up. She can't do the willow-weaving because she's allergic."

"Which guest?" Steve surveys the yurts.

"She's in Cowslip. Her name's Demeter."

"De-me-ter?" Steve looks as foxed as Dad did.

"I know." I shrug. "It's Ancient Greek. It means 'goddess of the harvest.'"

"Harvest?" Steve thinks for a moment. "Well, she can harvest some strawberries if she wants to."

I consider this. Would Demeter be impressed by a strawberry-picking activity?

"Maybe. It's not very *artisan,* though, is it? She's all about learning farm skills. Or yoga, except we don't do yoga." I squint at him. "What are you up to tomorrow? Could she join in whatever you're doing? You know, some genuine farm activity?"

"I'm muck-spreading." Steve shrugs. "She won't want to do that."

"Muck-spreading?" I can't help a giggle. "Oh, that would be perfect. *Hello, Demeter, welcome to your morning of muck-spreading.*"

"Should've done it yesterday," Steve's saying. "But your dad, he wanted a couple of fences mended." He fixes me with one of his reproachful looks. "Now, I'm not blaming those glampers or nothing. But have you seen the stile into North Field?"

I nod absently, only half-listening. I'm consumed with an image of Demeter on a muck spreader. Demeter falling off. Demeter covered in muck.

"And the litter," Steve's saying. "I mean, I know they like having their picnics and all, but . . ."

Or Demeter rock-picking. Demeter hoeing a field by hand. Demeter *finally* getting some payback . . .

And now an idea is growing inside me. A very bad, wicked idea. An idea that makes me want to hug myself. Because "bespoke" means I'm in charge. It means I can make her do whatever I damn well like.

This is it. At last I'm going to get even. So Demeter wants rural? She wants a "taste of farm life"? She wants "authentic"?

Well, she's bloody well going to get it.

CHAPTER THIRTEEN

The routine at Ansters Farm is that after breakfast, at about ten o'clock, we ring a bell and everyone who wants to do activities assembles in the yard. Today that's all the glampers—and as the families gather, there's a happy hubbub. They look so photogenic, I take a few snaps for the website—and naturally Demeter's family is the most photogenic of all.

Demeter is wearing another rural-chic combo of cropped linen trousers and tank top. Her daughter, Coco, looks like a model, with coltish legs in teeny denim shorts and long, wafty hair. I expect she's been scouted at Topshop already. In fact, she's probably on next month's cover of *Vogue*. The son, Hal, looks cool. He has sticking-up fair hair, an attractive open face, and doesn't even have any zits. Well, of course he doesn't. No doubt Demeter knows some miracle organic zit cure that's only available to people who live in W12.

The husband, James, is lean, with a wry smile and those attractive crow's feet which men of a certain age get. He's talking to the children and they're roaring with laughter, so obviously they all have a brilliant relationship, as well as great looks and clothes and probably talents and hobbies too. He's in cutoffs and a gray marl T-shirt, and he's wearing these limited-edition brown suede sneakers which I saw once in *Style* magazine. He's clearly as much an early adopter as Demeter is. As I watch, Coco pushes him playfully on the chest, then nestles her head on his shoulder, while Hal taps at his iPhone. The latest version, of course.

"Good morning!" Dad greets the crowd. "And welcome to Ansters Farm!"

From nowhere, a cheer materializes. Dad manages to get the glampers to cheer every week, and I have no idea how he does it. I think he must have been a fairground barker in his past life. Or a ringmaster at a circus, perhaps.

"We hope you're looking forward to some fun-packed activities today." Dad twinkles at the crowd. "Kiddies, you'll be doing Farmer Mick's obstacle course, with prizes for everyone!"

Another cheer breaks out, and Dad beams. "Adults, you'll be on the willow-weaving activity with Robin here." He pushes forward Robin, who is very shy and bearded and is our local willow-weaving expert. (He also teaches madrigal-singing, has a small brewery, and keeps ferrets. That's Somerset for you.)

"Teenagers, you'll have to decide: weaving or obstacle course? All I'll say is that the weaving *doesn't* involve homemade fudge. . . ."

I can see Coco and Hal frowning and looking at each other, trying to work out whether the obstacle course is unspeakably uncool or the willow-weaving is even worse. But I can't get distracted by them. I have to start my Demeter campaign. Even though she didn't recognize me yesterday, I'm not leaving anything to chance. So last night I dyed my curly hair with a blue ombre rinse—I always used to do it for festivals. Plus I've put on sunglasses today. From a distance I look like a total stranger.

"Good morrrning!" I adopt my creamiest accent and head over to Demeter. "We met yesterday. I'm Katie, and I'll be leading your special bespoke program. It's a mind–body–spirit program, and it aims to refresh, relax, and restore. Are you ready to start?"

"Absolutely," says Demeter, and waves at her family. "Bye, guys! Have fun!"

"Now, you requested yoga, as I remember," I say as we step away from the hubbub. "Unfortunately, we don't offer yoga at Ansters Farm. Instead, we offer an ancient Druid practice, Vedari. It's not unlike yoga, though a *little* more challenging."

"Vedari," echoes Demeter. "I've never even heard of that."

"Few people have. It's very niche, very ancient, very spiritual. Although I *do* believe Gwyneth Paltrow practices it."

I can see Demeter's eyes light up. I knew mentioning Gwyneth Paltrow would press her buttons.

"So, first of all, we'll be doing a one-to-one Vedari session in one of our open-air spaces. Then we're going to change location and do our special equine de-stress activity. Then lunch." I smile.

"That sounds tremendous," says Demeter, who has been listening intently. "*Absolutely* what I had in mind. The Vedari sounds marvelous. Do I need any equipment?"

"Just yourself." I smile at her beatifically. "Just bring yourself. Are you ready?"

Demeter is tapping at her phone.

"Wait a minute," she says absently. "I want to have a look while we've still got signal. . . ."

I *bet* I know what she's doing. And, sure enough, a moment later she raises her head.

"Vedari! Here it is! *The National Vedari Association . . . Ancient and powerful . . . Suppleness of body and mind . . .* This sounds amazing. Why haven't I heard of it before?"

Because I made it up, I want to reply. *Because that website was invented by me and put up by Alan last night, in about five minutes.*

"Like I say." I smile at her. "It's very niche. Shall we go?"

I lead Demeter off through the fields and spread my arms widely as we walk.

"As you may know, the West Country is a very spiritual area. There are ley lines everywhere, ancient stone circles—"

"Stonehenge," chimes in Demeter alertly, in her I'm-so-clever *University Challenge* way.

"Exactly." I nod. "Stonehenge being the most famous. Now, here at Ansters Farm, we're lucky enough to have an ancient Druid circle. You can't see it anymore, but it's there, and it makes the perfect place for us to practice our Vedari."

We're walking through Elm Field now, and a few cows come wandering toward us. They're tan Jerseys, and they're sweet-natured but very curious. I can see Demeter stiffening as they get near. Is she *scared*?

"Do you have any experience of cows?" I ask politely. I'm remembering Demeter in that meeting at work, lecturing us all on the countryside.

"Not exactly," Demeter says after a pause. "They're quite *big,* aren't they? What are they doing?" she adds in a quivering voice, as a cow comes right up to her, staring with its gorgeous dark eyes. "What do they want?"

She's actually gone pale. Oh my God. After all that guff she said in the office, she's frightened of the cows too! Just like Flora!

"Don't worry," I say kindly. "Just keep walking. That's it. . . ."

We both clamber over a stile, and I lead Demeter into the middle of the six-acre field. It's a totally nondescript field. It's often used for grazing cattle, so there's dried-up cow poo everywhere, and it's got a tiny copse of oak trees. Other than that, it's nothing special. The view isn't even that good.

But as I turn to Demeter, I adopt an expression of reverence.

"This is the Sacred Field," I say. "The Druids lived and worshipped here, and there are powerful ley lines under the ground. If you concentrate, you can still feel them. You have to be spiritually open, though. Not all our guests can pick up the vibrations."

I'm pressing Demeter's buttons again. No *way* is she going to fail at anything, including picking up Druid vibrations.

She closes her eyes, and sure enough after about three seconds she opens them again and says, "There *is* a special aura here, isn't there?"

"You can feel it." I smile. "Excellent. You're going to be a natural. Now, you need to get changed into your Vedari gown. You can go into the little wood."

I reach into my Ansters Farm jute bag and pull out a sack. I customized it with a neckhole and armholes last night. It's the scratchiest, ugliest garment in the world, but as I hold it out to Demeter, I manage to stay straight-faced.

"I won't be wearing the gown," I say, "because I'm the ceremony leader. The disciples wear the gowns."

I can see Demeter's face falter as she takes the sack, and for an awful moment I think she's going to challenge me.

"I think Gwyneth Paltrow might sell them on her website," I add casually. "If you're interested in taking Vedari further."

"Right." Demeter's eyes open wide. "Wow. It's very . . . *authentic,* isn't it?" She strokes the scratchy hessian.

"You can find cheap knockoffs," I say seriously. "But this is the real deal. If you're buying a Vedari gown, it *must* come from the West Country. Now, let's head over to the wood." I nod at the copse. "The first part of the ceremony is called Beauty. That's followed by Truth. And finally Contemplation." I hand her another Ansters Farm jute bag. "You can put your clothes in here. Take off your shoes too."

I want to burst into giggles as Demeter disappears behind a tree. It's amazing how an otherwise intelligent person can become a credulous fool as soon as you mention the words "organic," "authentic," and "Gwyneth Paltrow."

But I don't giggle. I remain in character, gathering mud and twigs from the ground and putting them into a wooden bowl. As Demeter emerges, looking very awkward in the sack, I clamp my lips shut, desperate not to explode.

"Perfect," I manage at last. "Now, as I said, we begin with Beauty. The mud in this wood has a special nourishing quality for the skin. The Druids knew that, and so every ceremony began with applying the mud to the face."

"Mud?" Demeter looks at the bowl, and I can see the dismay in her eyes. "*That* mud?"

"Think of it as a Druid facial. It's *totally* natural and organic, with ancient nutrients." I rub the mud between my palms. "Look at that. Beautiful."

It's not beautiful. It's crappy, smelly mud that I'm sure has a few cowpats mixed into it.

"Right." Demeter is still eyeing the mud warily. "Right. So . . . does Gwyneth Paltrow do this too?"

"I'm sure she does," I say with a serene smile. "And have you seen her complexion? Close your eyes."

I almost think Demeter's going to refuse. But then she closes her eyes, and I start applying mud to her cheeks.

"There!" I say brightly. "Can you feel the natural warming qualities of the mud?" I scoop up more mud and smear it all over her face. I smear it in her hair too and rub it in. "It acts as a hair mask too," I add. "It stimulates growth and prevents hair from turning gray."

God, this feels good. I start slapping Demeter's head as I apply mud to her hair, and that feels ever better. Slap-slap-slap. *That* pays her back for making me do her bloody roots.

"Ow!" says Demeter.

"Just improving your circulation," I say briskly. "And now, the bark exfoliant."

"What?"

Before she can say anything else, I start rubbing twigs across her face.

"Inhale," I instruct her. "Long, deep breaths. Then you'll gain the benefit from the natural bark aromas."

"Ow!" says Demeter again.

"This is doing wonders for your skin," I say. "Now another mud mask . . . this will *really* penetrate. . . ." I slap on another layer of mud, then take a step back and survey Demeter.

She looks a *sight*. The sack is sitting lopsided on her shoulders. Her hair is all matted. Her face is smeared thickly with mud, and as I watch, a small clod falls off.

Another laugh is building inside me, but I *can't* let it out. I *mustn't*.

"Very good." I somehow manage to stay straight-faced. "Now onto the first active part of the ceremony. We call it Truth."

Demeter gingerly touches her face and flinches. "Have you got some water?" she asks. "Can I wash this off?"

"Oh no!" I say, as though in great surprise. "You leave the mud on, then you get the *full* benefit. Come on."

I lead her out of the copse, into the field. I can see Demeter trying to dodge cowpats in her bare feet, and another giggle rises. Oh God. *Don't* laugh.

"So." I come to a halt. "Stand opposite me. Let us be still for a moment." I put my hands in a yoga-type prayer pose, and Demeter does the same. "Now, bend over so your hands are touching the ground."

Promptly, Demeter bends to the ground. She's pretty flexible, actually.

"Very good. Now, raise your right hand to the sky. This pose is Meaning."

Demeter immediately lifts her hand high in the sky. *God,* she's a try-hard. I know she's hoping I'll say, *Wow, you're better than Gwyneth Paltrow,* or something.

"Excellent. Now lift your opposite leg to the sky. This pose is Knowledge."

Demeter's leg rises, a bit more shakily.

"Now lift your other leg too," I say. "This pose is Truth."

"What?" Demeter raises her head. "How can I lift my other leg too?"

"It's the Truth pose," I say with an implacable smile. "It strengthens the limbs and the mind."

"But it's impossible! No one could do that."

"It's an advanced pose," I say with a shrug.

"Show me!"

"I'm not wearing a Vedari gown," I say regretfully. "So I'm afraid I can't. But don't worry; you're a beginner. So don't push yourself. We won't try the Truth pose today."

This is like a red rag to a bull, just like I knew it would be.

"I'm *sure* I can do it," says Demeter. "I'm *sure* I can."

She tries to launch her other leg into the air and falls down, into a cowpat.

"Shit." She sounds totally hassled. "OK, I'm just not doing this right." She tries again and falls once more, into a different cowpat.

"Watch out for the cow manure," I say politely.

Demeter has five more attempts at the pose and each time falls into a cowpat. She's totally smeared with cow shit, her face is red, and she looks furious.

"Enough," I say in a serene voice. "Vedari says one must not exert oneself beyond the limits of one's age."

"Age?" Demeter looks livid. "I'm not old!"

"Let us now move on to Contemplation." I beckon Demeter to a patch of grass free of cowpats. "Lie down and we will use the ancient Druid stones to release your muscles and your mind."

Demeter eyes the ground cautiously, then lies down.

"On your front," I explain. With a look of distaste at the mud visible through the grass, Demeter rolls over.

"Now, this is the Druid version of a hot-stone massage," I say. "It's very similar, except that the stones are not artificially heated. They have only the natural heat of Mother Earth."

I've gathered a few rocks and stones, and I distribute them on Demeter's back.

"Now, relax and contemplate," I tell her. "Feel the energies of the stones penetrate your body. I will leave you to meditate. Free your mind," I add over my shoulder as I walk away. "Feel the ancient aura from the ley lines. The longer you concentrate, the more benefits you will receive."

I walk until I'm out of earshot, then settle down in the grass, leaning against a tree. Despite the sunshine it's a bit breezy, so I pull my Barbour around me. Then I get my iPad out of my own jute bag and fire up an old episode of *Friends*. I watch it, glancing up every so often to check on Demeter. I keep expecting her to get up—but she doesn't. She's sticking it out. She's tougher than I imagined. In fact, I can't help feeling a grudging admiration for her.

Finally *Friends* is over, and I head back to where she's still lying. God only knows how she's feeling, lying in a cold, breezy field full of cowpats.

"I'm now removing the stones." I start taking them all off

her back. "According to ancient lore, your stresses will be removed along with them. How was your meditation?" I add serenely. "Did you commune with a higher power?"

"Oh yes," says Demeter at once. "I could definitely feel an aura. *Definitely*."

As she gets up, I feel a tweak of sympathy for her. Her face is mud-smeared and crumpled from the ground. Her hair is a bird's nest. Her legs and arms are covered in gooseflesh, and her teeth are chattering with cold, I suddenly notice. Shit. I don't want to give her hypothermia.

"Have my jacket," I say in alarm, and proffer my knackered old Barbour. "You look freezing. It *was* a very challenging practice—maybe too challenging."

"No thanks, I'm not cold at all." Demeter gives the jacket a supercilious look. "And I didn't find it too challenging." She lifts her chin in that arrogant way she has. "I actually found it very stimulating. I have a natural aptitude for these things."

At once, any sympathy I was feeling for her vanishes. Why does she have to be such a bloody *show-off*?

"Great!" I say politely. "Glad it worked for you."

I lead Demeter back across the fields, eyeing her gooseflesh as we go. I offer her the jacket twice more, but she refuses it. Crikey, she's stubborn.

"Now," says Demeter bossily as I'm shutting the gate into Elm Field, "I've been meaning to mention something. I liked your homemade granola at breakfast, but I *really* think it should include chia seeds. Just a suggestion. Or goji berries."

"It already contains goji berries," I point out, but Demeter isn't listening.

"Or what's that new seed called?" She wrinkles her brow.

"That new superfood seed. You probably don't get it out here." She gives me a kind, patronizing smile, and I find myself bristling. No, of course not. How would we get the new must-have seed out here in the countryside *where we grow seeds*?

"Probably not." I force a polite smile. "Let's move on to the next activity."

On our way to the stables, I let Demeter get dressed again, and when she thinks I'm not looking, I catch her rubbing the worst of the mud off. Then she insists on stopping to check her emails on her phone.

"I work in something called 'branding,'" she tells me loftily as she swipes through her messages, and I smile back politely. Branding. Yes, I remember branding.

"OK, done." She puts away her phone and turns to me in her bossy way. "Lead on to the stables."

"The stables" sounds grander than it is. There are four dilapidated stalls and a tiny tack room, but only one horse. We've had Carlo forever. He's a great big cob, and Dad keeps threatening to get rid of him, but then he can't quite bring himself to do it, because the truth is, we all love him too much. He's not much trouble, old Carlo. He lives outside most of the year, and he's a good-tempered old beast. Lazy, though. Bloody lazy.

I brought him in last night, especially for this. I also made a sign that reads EQUINE SANCTUARY and put it on the stable-yard gate.

"So!" I say, as we approach. "Now for the equine de-stress activity. Are you a horse lover, Demeter? Here, put this on."

I hand her a riding hat, which probably isn't a perfect fit, but it's only for a bit of grooming. I already know Demeter can't ride, because I heard her mention it at work once. But I'm sure she'll come up with some bullshit or other, and, sure enough, she lifts her chin again.

"Ah. Now. Horses. I've never actually ridden, but I do know a *lot* about horses. They have a special spirit. Very healing."

"Absolutely." I nod. "And that's what we're going to tap into today. This activity is all about communion with horses and carrying on ancient traditions."

"*Wonderful,*" says Demeter emphatically. "These ancient traditions are *marvelous*."

"This horse is particularly mystical." I go over to Carlo and run a hand down his flank. "He gives calmness to people. Calmness and peace."

This is a lie. Carlo is so lazy, the emotion he brings to most people is demented frustration. But I don't bat an eyelid as I continue:

"Carlo is what we call an Empathy horse. We categorize our horses, according to their spiritual qualities, into Energy, Empathy, and Detox."

Even as I'm saying it, I'm sure I've gone too far. A detox *horse*? But Demeter seems to be lapping it all up.

"Amazing," she murmurs.

Carlo gives a whicker, and I beam at Demeter.

"I think he likes you."

"Really?" Demeter looks pink and rather pleased. "Should I get on?"

"No, no." I give a merry laugh. "This isn't a riding activity. It's a *bonding* activity. And we're going to use an implement that was forged in this very farm, generations ago." I reach into my jute bag and adopt an expression of awe. "This," I say in hushed tones, "is an authentic hoof-picker. It's been used on Ansters Farm since medieval times."

Another lie. Or maybe not. Who knows? It's an old cast-iron hoof-pick, which has been knocking around the stable for as long as I can remember. So, actually, you know what? Maybe it *is* medieval.

"We're going to be cleaning out Carlo's hooves, following the traditional, authentic Somerset method."

"Right." Demeter nods intelligently. "So, are there different methods in different counties, then?"

"This is an exercise in trust," I continue, ignoring her question, which was actually quite sensible. "And empathy. And *rapport*. Grasp Carlo's front leg and lift it up. Like this."

I lean against Carlo, move my hands reassuringly down his leg, grab his hoof, and lift it up. Then I replace it.

"Your turn." I beam at Demeter. "You'll feel the power of the horse channeling through your hands."

Looking apprehensive, Demeter takes up the same position, runs her hands down Carlo's leg, and tries to lift up his hoof. Which, of course, he won't let her do. She's far too tentative, and he can be an obstinate old bugger, Carlo.

"Try speaking to him," I suggest. "Try reaching out to his soul. Introduce yourself."

"Right." Demeter clears her throat. "Um. Hi, Carlo. I'm Demeter, and I'm here to clean out your hoof."

She's hauling on his hoof, but she's not getting anywhere. Once Carlo's hoof is planted down, it's as if it's welded to the floor.

"I can't do it," she says.

"Try again," I suggest. "Run your hands gently down his leg. Praise him."

"Carlo." Demeter tries again. "You're a wonderful horse. I feel very connected to you right now."

She yanks desperately, her mud-splattered face puce, but I can tell she's never going to manage it.

"Here, let me," I say, and get Carlo's hoof up. "Now. Grasp the pick, and clear out the mud. Like this." I remove a minuscule amount of mud, then hand the pick back to Demeter.

I feel an inward giggle as I see her aghast expression. I mean, I don't blame her. It's an absolute sod of a job. Carlo's hooves are huge, and the mud has impacted in them like concrete.

Ha.

"Right. Here goes." Demeter starts scraping at the mud. "Wow," she says after a bit. "It's quite . . . difficult."

"It's authentic," I say kindly. "Some things are best done 'old school,' don't you think?"

Like those bloody handwritten surveys, I'm thinking. *They were "old school" too*.

By the time Demeter's done all four hooves, she's breathing hard and sweating.

"Very nice." I smile at her. "Don't you feel a wonderful rapport with Carlo now?"

"Yes." Demeter can hardly talk. "I . . . I think so."

"Good! Now it's time for our mindful cleansing activity."

I lead Carlo out and tie him up. Then I hand Demeter an old bristle broom and say seriously: "This broom has been used by generations. You can *feel* the honest labor in its handle. As you sweep away the manure in the stable, so you sweep away the manure in your own life." I hand her a fork. "This might help. Put all the dirty straw in the wheelbarrow."

"I'm sorry. Wait." Demeter has got the swivelly-eyed look I remember from the office. "I don't understand." She jabs at the broom. "Is this . . . metaphorical?"

"Metaphorical *and* real." I nod. "That's very astute of you, Demeter."

"What is?" Demeter looks more confused.

"In order to sweep away metaphorical rubbish, you must sweep *actual* rubbish. Then the activity becomes mindful and you benefit all the more. Please. Don't wait. Begin." I nod at the manure-strewn straw.

Demeter is motionless for a moment, looking dumbstruck. Then, like some obedient slave, she begins sweeping, so diligently that I feel another tweak of admiration for her.

I mean, good on her. She hasn't complained or bailed out or squealed at the mess, like those children the other week who claimed they wanted to learn "pony skills" and then said it was too smelly and ran off, leaving me to clean up.

"Well done!" I say encouragingly. "Very nice action."

I head out into the sunshine and pull from my bag the flask of coffee I made earlier. I'm just pouring myself a cup when Steve Logan saunters by. Damn. I didn't necessarily want anyone witnessing any of my "bespoke" activities.

"Why's he here?" he says, seeing Carlo tied up. Then he glimpses Demeter in the stable. "What the hell—"

"Shhh!" I grab him quickly and pull him out of earshot. "Don't say anything."

"Is that a glamper?"

"Yes."

"But she's shoveling shit."

"I know." I think quickly. "She . . . um . . . wanted to."

"She *wanted* to?" says Steve in astonishment. "Who wants to shovel shit on their holiday? Is she nuts?"

He looks so fascinated, I feel a spike of alarm. He'll start quizzing Demeter if I'm not careful. Abruptly, I decide to take him into my confidence.

"Look, Steve, actually there's more to it than that. But if I tell you . . ." I drop my voice. "It's a *secret,* OK?"

"Sure." Steve nods significantly.

"I mean it."

"So do I." Steve lowers his voice to a sepulchral whisper. "What is uttered in the stable yard stays in the stable yard."

That is so *not* a thing that I want to roll my eyes at him, but I'm in mid-flow, so I don't bother. Instead, I beckon him farther away, into the tack room, out of sight of Demeter.

"I know this woman," I say in a low voice. "From before. From London. And she's . . ." I think how to put it. "She did me a wrong. So I'm getting even."

I take several sips of coffee while this sinks into Steve's brain.

"Right," he says at last. "I get it. Shoveling shit. Nice." Then he frowns as though he's suddenly realized the flaw in the plan. "But why did she agree to shovel shit?"

"Because I told her it was mindful, I suppose." I shrug. "*I* don't know."

Steve looks so perplexed, I can't help giggling. He helps himself to some coffee and pensively sips it, then says, "I'll tell you a secret now. So we're square."

"Oh," I say warily. "No. Steve, I really don't want to—"

"Kayla doesn't do it for me in bed."

"What?" I stare at him, aghast.

"Not anymore," he elaborates. "Used to, but—"

"Steve!" I clap my hand to my head. "*Don't* tell me things like that."

"Well, it's true," he says with lugubrious triumph. "So. Now you know." He gives me a sidelong look. "Might change things."

"What?" I peer at him. "Change what?"

"Just putting it out there." He regards me with his bulgy eyes. "New information. You can do what you like with it."

Oh God. Does he mean . . . No. I don't want to know what he means.

"I'm not going to do anything with it," I say firmly.

"Think on it, then." He taps his head. "Just think on it."

"No! I won't think on it! Steve, I have to go. See you later."

I hurry out of the tack room, then stop dead in surprise. Demeter isn't sweeping anymore—nor is she on her phone or striding impatiently around. She's standing next to Carlo, her arm over his withers, and he's brought his head round to give her a hug.

I blink in astonishment. It's a trick I taught Carlo years ago, and he hardly *ever* does it spontaneously. But there he is, hugging Demeter in his kind old horsey way. I made up "Empathy horse" as a joke . . . but now I realize it's kind of true. Demeter's eyes are closed and her shoulders are slumped. She looks off guard and exhausted, as though she's been putting on quite an act, even on holiday.

The thing about Demeter, I think as I watch her, is that she doesn't let go. She doesn't switch off. Even when she's "relaxing," she's still ultra-competitive and obsessing over chia seeds. Maybe she should just watch telly and eat Corn Flakes for a weekend and chill.

I gesture to Steve to leave the stable yard quietly; then I sit down on an upturned bucket. Demeter's shoulders are shaking slightly and I peer in fresh shock. Is she *crying*? I mean, I've cried into my ponies' manes often enough over the years, but I never would have thought that Demeter in a million years—

Oh my God. Has my totally fake equine de-stress activity actually *worked*? Have I de-stressed my ex-boss?

That was totally not the intention of this morning. But as I sit and watch her and Carlo in their little twosome, I can't help feeling a kind of warmth inside. Like you do when you see a child asleep or a lamb frisking or even a marathon runner gulping water. You think, *They needed that,* and you feel a kind of satisfaction on their behalf, whoever they are.

And the only thing that puzzles me now is—why? Demeter has the perfect life. Why is she sobbing into Carlo's mane, for crying out loud?

After a little while she looks up, sees me, and gives a startled jump. At once she grabs in her pocket for a tissue and starts patting her face.

"Just . . . taking a moment," she says briskly. "I've finished sweeping. What's next?"

"Nothing," I say, coming forward. "We've finished for the morning. We'll head to the farmhouse now and you can wash your face, have a shower, whatever you'd like, before lunch." I pat Carlo fondly, then turn to Demeter again. "So, did you enjoy the activity?"

"Oh, it was *very* good," says Demeter. "*Very* de-stressing. You should offer this to all the guests. This should be on the brochure. In fact, you should have a separate brochure outlining all the activities."

Her old bossy demeanor is beginning to reassert itself, but I'm more interested in the Demeter I saw just now. The vulnerable, tearful Demeter.

"Demeter," I say hesitantly as we move out of the stable yard. "Are you . . . all right?"

"Of course I'm all right!" she says, without looking me in the eye. "Just a bit tired, that's all. I'm so sorry I lost control. Very embarrassing. It's not like me at all."

She's right. It's not—at least not the Demeter I know. But maybe there's a different Demeter that I don't know about? And all the way back to the farmhouse, I'm thoughtful.

Lunch is served in the barn and is a chance for everyone to chatter about what they got up to that morning. All the adults who did willow-weaving are already there as we approach, and there's a happy hubbub. I glance at Demeter, wondering if she's feeling a bit wrung out, if she'll take a backseat for once.

But oh no.

Already her chin has lifted and her pace has quickened. I can see her eyes flashing with the old Demeter determination.

"Hi!" She interrupts a conversation between Susie and Nick with her usual energy. "How was the willow-weaving?"

"It was great," says Susie. "How was your morning?"

"Oh, it was *marvelous,*" says Demeter. "Absolutely *wonderful*. You know I did a bespoke-activity morning?" she adds airily to Susie. "A special mind-body-spirit program. I can thoroughly recommend it. I mean, it was challenging but absolutely worth it. I feel empowered now. I feel radiant. Oh, is that vegetarian lasagna? Is it wheat-free?"

As the meal progresses, I listen as Demeter regales every single adult with how brilliant her morning was: much better and more authentic than theirs. "This ancient practice Vedari . . . Oh, haven't you heard of it? Yes, very niche . . . I really *sensed* the aura. . . . Well, I am rather a yoga expert. . . ."

Everyone is chattering about their mornings, but Demeter's voice rings out above the hubbub, a constant, show-offy, clarion sound.

"Absolutely empowering experience . . . Gwyneth Paltrow, apparently . . . I could *feel* the natural heat emanating from the stones. . . ."

No, she bloody couldn't! I saw her with my own eyes. She was freezing! But now she's talking as though she's just met the Dalai Lama and he said, *Well done, Demeter, you're the best*.

She hasn't once mentioned Carlo, interestingly. Let alone the fact that he hugged her and she wept. It's as if she's squashed the only real, truthful bit of the morning away where no one can see it.

Then a growing sound of shrieks and laughter heralds the approach of the children. As they all come piling into the barn, hot and excited from their obstacle course, Demeter rises from her seat.

"Coco! Hal! There you are. And James. Were you watching the children? Come over here, I've saved you seats."

As Demeter's family slide into their chairs, I edge closer in fascination. So here they are: the perfect family in their perfect outfits, having the perfect holiday. I expect they'll make intelligent conversation about the environment now. Or that new hip indie band they saw at the weekend, all of them together, because they're such a close family.

But in fact none of them starts talking at all. They all get out their phones, including James.

"I thought we said no phones at mealtimes," says Demeter in a strange, jokey voice I haven't ever heard her use before. "Hey, guys. Guys?" She waves a hand to get the attention of her children, but they totally ignore her.

I'm slightly goggling. I've never seen anyone ignore Demeter before.

"So, how was the obstacle course?" Demeter puts a hand over Hal's phone screen and he glowers at her.

"It was all right," says Coco briefly. "This phone is crap. I need a new one."

"You've got a birthday coming up," says Demeter. "Perfect. Let's go and choose one together."

"My birthday?" Coco fixes Demeter with a malevolent glare. "You want me to wait for my *birthday*?"

"Well, we'll see," says Demeter, and she gives her daughter a smile I've never seen either. It's kind of eager. Craven, almost. It's kind of . . . desperate?

No. I must be seeing things.

"Try the salad." Demeter passes it to Coco. "It's organic. Delicious."

"Granny says organic food is a total con," says Coco, in a pert voice that makes me want to slap her. "Doesn't she, Daddy?"

"Well, it is," says James absently. "It's all bollocks."

I nearly fall over flat. *What?* James isn't into organic food? How can this be? It's Demeter's *religion.*

Coco leans her head on James's shoulder as I saw her do this morning—only now it doesn't look friendly. It looks . . . I don't know. Cliquey. As if she's trying to shut her mother out of the gang or something. I glance at Demeter and I see a flash of pain cross her face. Her brow's furrowed. She's taken her own phone out now, and as she scrolls down, she looks weary.

It's as if the mask has dropped again, and there she is: The other Demeter. The tired, stressed-out Demeter, who needs a hug with a horse.

And suddenly I'm aware of a disconcerting sensation. Do I feel . . . *sorry* for Demeter?

I'm so agog that I don't even notice that someone is tugging at my sleeve.

"Excuse me? Katie?"

"Yes?" I swing round with my professional customer-service smile, to see Susie standing there. She's a slight blond woman with bobbed hair, wearing beige shorts and a white T-shirt with Cath Kidston print sneakers. *Mother of Ivo and Archie,* I quickly remind myself. *Heard about us by picking up a brochure in a Clapham soft-play center.*

"How's it going?" I say warmly. "Are you all enjoying the holiday?"

"Oh yes!" enthuses Susie. "We *loved* the willow-weaving.

And now . . ." She hesitates. "Well, we were talking to Demeter about Vedari, and we—Nick and I—we'd love to try it."

"I'm sorry?" I say blankly.

"Can we do some Vedari?" Susie's face is eager and hopeful. "It sounds amazing!"

I stare at her speechlessly. She wants to do Vedari. Are you *kidding* me?

"Katie?" prompts Susie.

"Right." I come to. "Well . . . Yes! I'm sure we can. I'll look at the schedule. Vedari! Perfect! We'll all do it! Why not?" I'm sounding a bit hysterical, so I add, "Excuse me for a moment," and head out of the barn to the yard, where I give vent to my feelings by kicking a bale of hay. I don't know what I was hoping to achieve this morning—but *none* of it has come out quite right.

CHAPTER FOURTEEN

The next morning I give myself a pep talk. Enough with the obsessing over Demeter. So she's my ex-boss—so what? I've focused on her enough. Time to move on.

Except the trouble with Demeter is, she monopolizes your attention, whatever you do. She's just that kind of person. By nine-thirty, Biddy and I are already frazzled by her breakfast demands. *Almond milk . . . hotter coffee . . . Is there any cornbread? . . . Could my egg be five and a half minutes exactly, please?*

Now the children have finally made it to the breakfast table and I'm eyeing them up as they eat. It's weird: They looked so perfect and charming from a distance. But close up, I'm really not impressed. Coco has a permanently sulky frown, and Hal keeps winding her up.

They're both pretty demanding too, like their mother. They ask for Nutella (not available) and pancakes (not available), and then Coco says, "Don't you do fresh smoothies?" in a really rude way that makes me want to shake her.

As I go round refreshing water glasses, Demeter is scrolling down her phone and she suddenly flinches.

"Oh God." She stares at the screen. "What? No." She scrolls up, then down again. "What?"

"What's up?" asks James, and even I feel curious. Demeter looks properly panicky, the way she did in the lift that time. It must be another of her epic screwups.

"Something at work. This . . . this makes no sense." She peers at her phone, yet again. "I need to call Adrian."

Firmly, I dampen my curiosity. I am not going to focus on Demeter anymore. I'm going to check up on the other glampers. I head outside, and Susie greets me with a smile.

"Hello!" I say. "How are you doing? Just to let you know, I'm not sure we will be able to fit in any more Vedari sessions this week." I make a regretful face. "Maybe another time."

"Oh." Susie's face falls. "It did sound so energizing."

"But how was the willow-weaving?" I try to steer her off the subject.

"It was good! Yes. It was fun. I mean—" Susie breaks off. She's tense, I suddenly detect. Something's up.

"What?" I say in concern. "Is anything wrong?"

"No! It's just . . . well." She clears her throat. "I did feel that some other participants slightly monopolized the teacher—" She breaks off abruptly as another mum, Cleo, approaches us.

Cleo comes from Hampstead and is more earthy than Susie. She's in a drifty dress and wearing an amethyst pendant on a leather thong, her feet incongruously stuffed in desert boots.

"Good morning, Cleo!" I say, trying to ignore the fact that Susie is glaring at Cleo quite openly.

"We've just been cooking eggs and dandelion leaves for

breakfast on our fire pit," Cleo says in her husky voice. "Sprinkled with sumac. Delicious."

"We had Biddy's breakfast in the farmhouse," counters Susie. "Absolutely scrumptious."

"And the willow-weaving yesterday!" exclaims Cleo, as though she's not remotely interested in Susie's breakfast. "I made three baskets. It was marvelous."

"Marvelous for the people who swiped all the best willow," mutters Susie under her breath.

"Oh, and Susie." Cleo turns to her. "I do hope Hamish didn't disturb you with his violin practice this morning. He's gifted, *unfortunately*."

"How difficult for you," says Susie tightly. "I'm sure if you left him alone, he'd settle down to being normal."

OK. There is definitely a vibe between Susie and Cleo. This might need monitoring. I'm wondering whether to warn the pottery teacher, when I see Demeter coming out of the kitchen. Her phone is clenched in her hand and she looks a bit stunned.

"Everything OK?" I say brightly, but Demeter doesn't answer. Can she even see me?

"Demeter?" I try again.

"Right." She comes to. "Sorry. I . . . No. It'll be fine, I'm sure. I just need to . . . James!" She raises her voice as she sees her husband coming out too, and she heads toward him swiftly. I can't hear much of the ensuing conversation, only snippets that make me sizzle with curiosity.

". . . ridiculous!" James is saying. "I mean, if you've got the emails . . ."

". . . can't find them. That's the thing . . ."

". . . makes no sense . . ."

"Exactly! That's what I keep saying! Look!" Demeter shows her phone to James, but his eyes are drifting away, as though he's got other things to think about.

"It'll blow over," he says. "These things always do."

"Right." Demeter seems dissatisfied by this answer—in fact, she still seems pretty stressed—but she visibly pulls herself together and heads off with all the others toward the minibus, which will take them to the pottery class.

And I know it's nothing to do with me anymore. But all morning, as I'm going through the accounts with Dad, I can't help wondering: What's up?

Pottery day is always a good one. First of all, everyone loves pottery, whatever age they are. And second, the pottery teacher, Eve, is very skillful at "helping" people just enough, so that their jug or vase or whatever will actually stand up straight. She'll fire the pots tonight, and all the glampers will get them by Friday, and it's a nice souvenir for them to take home.

So I'm expecting to see a happy group of people piling off the minibus when it returns at lunchtime. But, instead, there's a rather weird procession. Demeter and Eve are together at the front, and Demeter seems to be talking very much *at* Eve. Behind, at a distance, everyone else is following, and I can see a bit of eye-rolling. As Demeter gets into earshot, I think I have an inkling why.

". . . and then we were lucky enough to get a private view of the collection in Ortigia," she's saying smugly. "Have you ever met the curator, Signor Moretti? No? *Charming* man."

I'd forgotten that ceramics was one of Demeter's *things*. I bet she's been ear-bashing poor Eve all morning.

"Welcome back!" I say hastily. "Eve, you must be exhausted; come and have a drink!"

I seat Eve next to Susie and Nick, well away from Demeter, and then it's the usual rush of serving bread and salad and locally made pork pies, while all the guests discuss the morning. Even though I've told myself not to, I can't help hanging around Demeter's table a little more than the others and watching her family.

My opinion hasn't altered: They're dreadful. Coco is outwardly defiant and rude. Hal just ignores his mother. And James, who should be supporting her, is on another planet. If I thought Demeter was distracted, that's nothing on her husband. All he can focus on is his phone. Does he even *realize* he's on holiday?

During pudding, they start talking about some school play that Coco's in, and Demeter gets all show-offy about Shakespeare. She starts going on about a production she saw at the RSC that was "tremendous" and "groundbreaking," while Coco yawns ostentatiously and rolls her eyes.

Demeter really doesn't help herself. Can't she tell that everyone's bored stiff? But at the same time, I can see that she is actually trying to help.

"Honestly, Mum!" Coco erupts at last. "Stop going *on* about it! You probably won't even see me in the bloody play. So."

"Of course I'll see you in it!" Demeter retorts.

"No, you won't. You never come to anything. You know what Granny calls you? Mrs. Invisible." Coco sniggers and catches James's eye. "Doesn't she, Daddy? She says, 'How's Mrs. Invisible today?' "

"Mrs. Invisible?" Demeter sounds calm, but I can see her hand trembling as she takes a sip of water. "What does that mean?"

"The invisible mum," says Hal, glancing up from his phone. "Come on, Mum. You're never there."

"Of course I'm there." Demeter sounds as rattled as I've ever heard her. "I come to all your events, all your parents' evenings—"

"What about my basketball?" Hal gives her a wounded look. "Did you even *know* I was on a basketball team?"

"Basketball?" Demeter has her confused, eye-darty look again. "Basketball? I didn't— When— James, did you know about this?"

"Dad comes to every match," says Hal. "He chants and everything."

"Stop it, Hal," says James sharply. "He's winding you up, Demeter. He doesn't play basketball."

"But why—" Demeter breaks off, bewildered. "Why would you—*James*?" she practically yells, as James starts tapping at his phone again. "Could you please join in this discussion?"

"Hal, cut the attitude," says James. "Say sorry."

"Sorry," mutters Hal.

I wait for James to insist: "Say it *properly,*" like Dad would have done to me, but he doesn't. He's already tuned out again. I don't care how brainy and important he is, he's a *tosser.* Maybe he's one of these men who can't cope with successful women. I have *no* idea what induced Demeter to marry him.

Hal just carries on with his lunch, while Coco shreds a

bread roll into pieces. Demeter is silent and subdued. And all I can feel, right now, is really sorry for her.

After we've served coffee, the two children disappear out of the barn. I should really go and help Biddy with the afternoon's baking activity. But I can't leave. I'm too fascinated by the horror show that is Demeter and her family. I station myself within earshot of them by the old oak dresser, folding and refolding napkins. Not that Demeter and James even notice me. They're engrossed in their own little bubble.

"So your mother calls me Mrs. Invisible." Demeter lifts her coffee cup to her lips, then puts it down again, untouched. "Nice."

James winces. "Look . . . I'm sorry. You shouldn't have heard that. I've told Mum she's out of line."

"But what does she *mean*?" Demeter sounds brittle.

"Oh, come on." James drops his hands onto the table with a thump. "You're out every night. If you're not working late, you're at some awards ceremony—"

"It's my job!" says Demeter, sounding anguished. "You know I have to do this stuff, James—"

"Demeter, they want me in Brussels." James cuts straight across her and she draws in breath sharply. The color drains from her face. There's such a long, breath-holding silence between the pair of them that I think I might keel over.

At last, Demeter says, "Right." She swallows hard, and there's another endless pause. "Right," she repeats. "Wow. Didn't see that one coming."

"I know. Sorry. I've been . . ." He sweeps a hand through his hair. "I've been preoccupied. That's why."

I've frozen beside the dresser. This is clearly a very personal conversation. I should make myself known. But I can't. I can't break the spell. My fingers are clenched around a napkin so hard that they've gone white. Demeter takes breath to speak, and I can sense she's feeling her way.

"I thought we discussed the Brussels thing, James. I thought we decided—"

"I know what we decided. I know what we agreed. I know what I said. . . ." James rubs his eyes with the flat of his hand. Demeter's head is turned away, her chin lowered. The pair look a picture of abject misery.

I can't help flashing back to that photo of them on Demeter's pinboard that I always used to gaze at. The pair of them standing on thc red carpet in black tie, looking like the most successful, glamorous, put-together couple in the world. But look at them now. Tired; wretched; not even making eye contact.

"But?" says Demeter, finally.

"I lied, OK?" James bursts out. "I told you I didn't want Brussels because I thought it was what you wanted. But I *do* want it, and they really want me, and I'm tired of compromising. This opportunity is huge. There won't be another like it."

"Right." I can see Demeter's eyes flicking back and forth nervously. "I see. Yes. Right. So . . . we move to Brussels?"

"No! You have your job . . . the children's schools. . . ." He spreads his hands. "They've talked about a three-year fixed contract. After that, who knows? I hope I can find another great opportunity in London. But for now . . ." James leans forward and waits till she lifts her gaze to meet his. "I *want* this. You wanted Cooper Clemmow . . . I want this."

"Well, then." Her fingers are meshing on the table. "You have to take it. We'll make it work."

"Oh God— You're always so bloody *generous*." He screws up his face, a fist to his forehead. "I'm sorry. I've been a bastard."

"No, no," says Demeter at once. "You haven't. You've been unhappy. I get that now."

"And a bastard."

"A bit of a bastard." Demeter gives a reluctant little smile and he smiles back, with those handsome crow's feet.

For a while there's silence. They're both just looking at each other. I sense they're mentally straightening things out a bit. And now maybe I *can* see why they might have married each other. But bloody hell. What a roller coaster.

"You supported me," says Demeter, spinning her coffee cup slowly on her saucer. "When I moved to Cooper Clemmow. You supported me and you turned down Brussels. And you've been miserable ever since. I can see that now."

"I think . . ." James exhales sharply. "I should have been more honest. I thought I could just *not*-want it. If I tried hard enough."

"You can't make yourself *not*-want things." Demeter gives him a wry smile. "Idiot."

"But this job is big."

"All right, then." She exhales gustily. "We can do big. We'll survive. So what happens next?"

"They want to talk to me." He pauses. "Tomorrow."

"Tomorrow?" Demeter looks at him in horror. "But we're on holiday! When were you going to—"

"I'll nip up to Gatwick this afternoon. I'll be there and back in . . . what? Seventy-two hours."

"Seventy-two hours? Why so long?"

"They want a couple of meetings. . . ." James takes both her hands in his. "Look, I know it's not ideal. But you're busy here. It's fun. The children won't even know I've gone."

"Right." Demeter sags slightly. "I suppose I'd better get used to you being away."

"We'll need to work it out. But it'll be good." James's face has become animated; there's a new, positive energy about him. "So I'll just go and call them, confirm it for definite. I love you."

"I love you," echoes Demeter, shaking her head ruefully, as though she's saying it despite herself.

James leans forward and kisses Demeter with a tenderness which surprises me. Then he leaves the barn without even noticing me. Demeter doesn't move for a while. She seems a bit dumbstruck; her face is wearier than ever.

But at last she rouses herself. She pulls out her phone and starts to text. As she's doing so, the light comes back into her eyes. There's even a little half smile at her lips.

Well, thank God. Because I was getting a bit worried about her there.

She finishes her text, puts down her phone, and leans back in her chair—then notices me.

"Oh, Katie," she says, in her old, imperious manner. "I

wanted to check with you—we will be doing another bespoke activity tomorrow? Because obviously I won't be doing the mushroom-foraging."

I stare back dumbly, not knowing how to respond. I don't even know how to see her anymore.

All I could see before was the nightmare boss with a perfect, glossy life. But now what do I see? Just a person. A person with hang-ups and problems and flaws like the rest of us. Who's basically trying to do her best, even if it comes out badly. I have a sudden memory of her lying on the muddy grass in her Vedari sack and bite my lip. Maybe that was a bit harsh. Maybe it's all been a bit harsh.

"OK," I say. "You're on, Demeter. We'll do a bespoke activity."

A *nice* activity, I decide. Something *fun*. We'll spend the morning together, doing something genuinely enjoyable. I'm kind of—almost—looking forward to it.

A taxi arrives in the yard for James at three o'clock, and from the kitchen window I watch him get into it. Demeter kisses him goodbye, then wanders slowly back. She's scrolling down her emails again, and I hear her exclaim, *"No!"* incredulously, as though yet again the world makes no sense.

Still engrossed, she heads toward the bench and table where her kids are sitting.

"Mum." Coco glares at her. "You forgot to pack my Abercrombie and Fitch hoodie."

"What?" Demeter seems confused. "Hoodie? You're wearing a hoodie."

"My *other* hoodie. This one's all frayed."

"But you packed yourself, darling."

"You said you'd double-check!"

"Coco . . ." Demeter puts a hand to her head. "I can't take care of your packing as well as everything else. Anyway, you've got a hoodie. It's fine."

"Oh, great. So I have to do it all myself, even though I've got to *study*. Which you keep telling me is *important*." Coco practically snarls at her mum. "Mrs. Invisible rules again."

"Don't call me that, please." I can tell Demeter's finding it hard to keep calm. "You have a hoodie."

"I didn't *want* this hoodie." Coco plucks disparagingly at her hoodie, which is from Jack Wills and probably cost, like, sixty quid.

I'm listening in utter disbelief. Who does this girl think she is? And what the *hell* has happened to Demeter? Where's the strong, powerful über-woman I know from work? She seems to fade away as soon as she's with her children, leaving only this anxious, craven person I don't recognize. It's weird. It's *wrong*.

As I'm watching, Demeter's phone rings and she answers it immediately.

"Hi, Adrian," she says, sounding defensive. "Yes, I *am* aware of what's going on. But I just don't understand. There must be some mixed message here. Have you actually *spoken* to Lindsay at Allersons?" She listens again, and her face becomes agitated. "No, that can't be right," she says. "It can't! This is insane!"

She stands up and heads off to talk in private. The two children are still lolling at the picnic table, staring down at their phones as though they're possessed, and something about their attitude makes me boil irrationally.

I know it's none of my business. But bloody hell. If I thought Demeter was entitled, she has *nothing* on her children. On impulse, I open the kitchen door and head out.

"Hi!" I say cheerfully, approaching the table. "How are you two doing? Enjoying the holiday?"

"Yes, thank you," says Coco, without bothering to look up.

"And what have you done to thank your mum?" I say conversationally.

"What?" she says with utter incomprehension. Hal doesn't reply, but he looks equally perplexed.

"Well, you know," I say as though it's obvious. "*She* works really hard to pay for you to go on holiday and buy designer clothes. . . ." I gesture at the Jack Wills hoodie. "So *you* say thank you."

Both children look dumbfounded at this idea.

"She *enjoys* working," Coco says at last, with a dismissive roll of her eyes.

"Well, Biddy enjoys baking," I say with a shrug. "But you still say thank you nicely when she gives you a scone."

"It's not the same," says Coco, sounding cross. "She's our *mum*."

"You don't say thank you for holidays," puts in Hal, as though this is some article from the Geneva Convention which he refuses to deviate from, out of principle.

"Well, I wouldn't know," I say pleasantly. "Because when I was your age, we could never afford holidays. I'd have been really envious of you guys, on holiday all the time."

"We don't go on that many holidays," says Coco, looking

sulky, and I feel an urge to slap her. I've seen photos of her in Demeter's office. Skiing. Standing on a white-sand beach. Laughing on a speedboat in some tropical clime.

"I didn't ever go abroad till I was seventeen," I say pleasantly. "And now I can't afford to go abroad either. And I could *never* afford a Jack Wills hoodie. You're a lucky girl, Coco. I mean, Jack Wills!"

Coco cautiously touches her hoodie, the one she was disparaging a moment ago. Then she looks at my T-shirt—an unbranded Factory Shop special.

"Well," she says, with less of a swagger in her voice. "Yeah. Jack Wills is cool."

"See you," I say lightly, and walk away.

I perch on a nearby wall, pretending to check my activities folder, wondering how this will play out. But if I was hoping that both kids would start discussing how ungrateful they've been and how to make amends, then I was nuts. They both sit there silently, with the same sulky expressions, gazing at their phones, as though we never had a conversation.

As Demeter returns to the table, she looks exhausted and a bit freaked. She sits down, gazing into the middle distance, chewing her lip. For a while, no one says anything. But then Coco lifts her eyes from her phone for a nanosecond and mutters, "Mum, the holiday's really great."

Instantly, Demeter springs into life. The weariness disappears from her face, and she gazes at Coco like someone whose lover just told her he *will* marry her, after all.

"Really?" she says. "Are you enjoying it?"

"Yeah. So, like . . ." Coco hesitates as though making the supreme effort. "You know. Thanks."

"Darling! It's my pleasure!" Demeter looks absolutely radiant, simply because her child gave her a grudging thank-you. It's pitiful. It's *tragic*.

"Yeah," says Hal, and this single syllable seems to make Demeter's day even more perfect.

"Well, it's lovely," she says. "It's lovely just to spend time together."

There's a tremble in her voice, and her eyes give that sudden panicky, darting movement I know so well. What is up with her? What is *up*?

At that moment, Dad comes sauntering up to their table, holding a load of brochures.

"Now," he begins, in his most charming way, "can I say that you are delightful guests. Just delightful. We see a lot of glampers, and *you* . . ." He points with his weather-beaten finger to Demeter, then Coco, then Hal. "*You* come out on top."

"Thank you," says Demeter, with a laugh, and even Coco looks pleased.

"And for that reason," carries on Dad breezily, "we'd like to invite all your friends to come and join us next year. Because we're sure they'll be *just* as delightful as you." He hands Demeter a stack of Ansters Farm brochures from his pile. "Spread the word! Spread the joy! We've got ten percent discounts for all your friends!"

Demeter takes the brochures, and I can tell she's amused by Dad's little riff.

"So we're the best guests here, are we?" she says, her mouth twitching.

"By a *mile*," says Dad emphatically.

"So you're not offering this ten percent discount to anyone else?"

"Ah." Dad twinkles knowingly back at her. "Well, it would be unfair if we didn't let a few of the other guests in on it. But we'll be hoping it's *your* friends who come along."

Demeter laughs. "Of course you will." She turns the brochure over a few times, opens it, and looks at the layout. "This is good," she says suddenly. "I thought that before. Very appealing, great design . . . Who produced it for you?"

"It's good, isn't it?" Dad looks pleased. "That was our Katie did that."

"Katie?" Demeter seems a bit stunned. "Katie as in . . . *Katie*?"

"That's right." Dad catches sight of me. "Katie, Demeter here likes your brochure!"

"Come here!" Demeter beckons me so commandingly, I feel my legs obeying her. I tug my curly blue hair down over my face, pushing my sunglasses firmly up my nose.

I know I'm straying onto dangerous ground here. I should make an excuse and walk away. But I can't. I feel a bit breathless, keyed up with hope. I'm still in thrall to her, I realize. I'm still desperate for her praise.

Demeter's reading my brochure. She's not just reading it, she's studying it closely. She's taking my work seriously. For how long have I dreamed of this happening?

"Who wrote this copy?" She hits the brochure with the back of her fingers.

"I did."

"Who chose the typeface and the paper?"

"I did."

"She designed the website too," says Dad proudly.

"I got a techie friend to help me," I put in.

"But you were in charge of the creative content?" Demeter looks at me with narrowed, thoughtful eyes.

"Well . . . yes."

"It's a good website," says Demeter. "And *this* is outstanding. I should know," she adds to Dad. "This is what I do for a living."

"That's our Katie!" says Dad, and ruffles my hair. "Now if you'll excuse me . . ." Clutching his brochures, he heads off to another group of glampers, where he produces exactly the same shtick he used on Demeter.

"Katie, tell me something," says Demeter, who can't stop studying the brochure. "Do you have *training*?"

"Um." I swallow. "I've . . . I've studied design."

"Well, all your instincts are spot-on," she says emphatically. "I couldn't do a better job myself. Katie, I think you have a rare talent. I only *wish* our juniors were this talented."

I stare back at her, my head prickling. I feel a bit surreal, to be honest.

"I work for a company called Cooper Clemmow," Demeter continues. "Our business is branding. Here's my card." She hands me a Cooper Clemmow card and I hold it dumbly, half-wanting to break into hysterical laughter. "If you ever think about leaving this place, trying to get a job in London—call me. I may be able to give you a job opportunity. Don't look so freaked out," she adds kindly. "We have a very friendly office. I'm sure you'd fit in."

"Thank you," I say, my voice not working properly. "That's very . . . Thank you. I just have to . . ."

On weak legs, I walk away, into the house, through the kitchen, up to my bedroom. I don't look left and I don't look right. I put the business card carefully on my bed and look at it for a second. Then I scream.

"Noooooooo!"

I bang my head against my ancient wallpaper. I clutch my hair. I scream again. I punch my pillows, hard. I can't bear it. I can't believe it.

Finally, finally I've got what I always wanted. Demeter's looked at my work. She's praised it. She wants to give me a chance.

But what bloody good is that now?

At last, panting, I collapse in a chair and consider my options.

1. Go downstairs to Demeter and say, *Guess what? It's me, Cat!* At which point she'll probably freak out, rescind the job offer, reveal to Biddy and Dad that my "sabbatical" story is a lie, and cause all sorts of turmoil. Total nightmare.

2. Take up her job offer under the identity of "Katie" Brenner. Instantly get found out, prosecuted for fraud, and never work again. Total nightmare.

3. I'm not sure there is a three.

My brain circles frenziedly for half an hour. But it doesn't find a solution; it just becomes stiffer and tireder and stupider. And Biddy will be needing help. So I rouse myself, head downstairs, and start peeling potatoes, which is nice and calming.

Or at least it is until Dad comes into the kitchen, whistling cheerily and putting on his "Farmer Mick" hat for the magic show he's doing later. (He *so* can't do magic. But luckily the kids think he's hilarious whatever he does, and the adults are just happy that their children are being amused.)

"That Demeter likes your stuff, doesn't she?" he greets me. "We knew you were talented!"

"What's this?" Biddy looks up with interest from the pie crust she's shaping.

"Demeter. She's an expert on brochures, apparently. I told her, 'Katie did that.' You should have seen her face."

"Oh, Katie!" says Biddy in delight. "That's wonderful! Did you tell her about your job in London, love?" she adds innocently. "Maybe you two should . . . what's-it-called. Network."

I feel an almighty swell of panic.

"No!" I say shrilly. "I mean, it's not appropriate. Not while she's on holiday. I'll keep her card and contact her later."

"Later?" Biddy looks dubious. "Sweetheart, I wouldn't leave it. She may forget about you. Look, if it's awkward for you, I'll bring it up. What's the name of the place you work at again? Cooper Clemmow. That's right, isn't it?"

I feel faint. This cannot happen. Biddy *cannot* start telling Demeter how I've got a top job at this London company called Cooper Clemmow.

"No!" I repeat in desperation. "Look, these London types are really prickly and stressy. They've come here to relax and get away from it all. If you talk work on holiday they hold it against you. They'll . . . they'll put it on TripAdvisor!" I add wildly, and I can see a frisson of fear running through Biddy.

TripAdvisor is terrifying. We've had three entries so far, and they've all been lovely, but we all know how it can go horribly wrong.

"I think she's got a point, love," says Dad to Biddy. "We don't want to look pushy."

"Exactly! It's really, really important." I try to impress this on Biddy. "*Don't* mention work to Demeter. *Don't* ask her where she works. And don't . . ." I feel sick at the very thought. "*Don't* mention Cooper Clemmow."

I resume peeling potatoes, feeling a bit weak. That was close. It still *is* close. It's precarious. Whatever I say to Biddy, she still may take it upon herself to big up my London job to Demeter. With just one wrong word, everything could come out. Oh God . . . I close my eyes, breathing hard. Should I come clean now? Tell Biddy and Dad everything? But they'll be *so* upset, and they've got enough on their plates as it is. . . .

"Katie?" Biddy's voice makes me jump. "Darling, I think you've peeled that potato enough," she says with a laugh, and I look down in a daze. I've been peeling the same potato, round and round, until it's about the size of a marble.

"Right." I muster a smile. "Not concentrating."

"By the way," adds Biddy, "I meant to tell you before. Guess what? We have our first B&B guest arriving tomorrow!"

"Oh, great!" I say, distracted for a moment. "That's brilliant news!"

The B&B room has been Biddy's project. It was her idea to have an "overspill" room in the house for people who don't want to glamp. It's a ground-floor room with its own entrance—it fact, it used to be a sitting room that we hardly ever used. Biddy painted it in Farrow & Ball (my advice), and Dad turned the outhouse loo into a tiny en suite shower, and it's all 400-thread-count sheets, like in the yurts.

"Who is it?" I ask. "Are they staying long?"

"Just a night," says Biddy. "He must want to have a look at the yurts or something. He wanted to stay in one, actually, but I told him they were full."

"Does he want to do any activities?"

"Oh." Biddy looks troubled. "I didn't ask. Well, we'll find out when he arrives. Funny name he's got. Astalis." She peers at her own writing. "Can that be right? Astalis?"

The world has gone black for a moment.

"Astalis?" I repeat, in a voice that doesn't sound like mine.

"Alex Astalis." Biddy wrinkles her brow. "I wonder if he's any relation to that famous Astalis chap. . . . What's he called again . . ."

Alex is coming here. Why's he coming here? And then, in the next instant, I know *exactly* why he's coming here.

"When . . ." I'm trying to keep control of myself. "When exactly did he call?"

"It was earlier on," says Biddy. "About two-thirty."

Two-thirty. About ten minutes after James told Demeter he was going away. I have a sudden image of Demeter sitting there at the lunch table, texting, that half-smile playing on her lips. She didn't hang about, did she? She didn't bloody hang about.

"I hope he finds the bed comfortable," Biddy is fretting. "I found it a little hard myself, but your dad said it was fine. . . ."

"I'm sure it'll be OK," I say numbly.

He won't need the bed, is what I feel like saying. *He won't need the room. He'll be in the yurt all night with Demeter.*

There I was, softening toward her, thinking she had it tough—but look at her. The minute her husband's out of the way, she ships in her lover. She didn't even wait *half an hour* after James had kissed her and told her he loved her. She's a bitch, she's a selfish *bitch*. . . .

And now I'm torturing myself, imagining Alex and Demeter in the yurt. Candles lit. Writhing around athletically on the sheepskin. My breaths are coming in short, angry bursts. I feel like a melting pot of fury and frustration . . . and, OK, envy. Some envy.

Quite a lot of envy.

And then I jolt in panic. Shit. What if Alex recognizes me? He doesn't have Demeter's facial-recognition problem. He's more switched on. I cannot come across him in any shape or form, or everything really *will* implode. . . .

OK. Stop freaking out. It'll be fine. I'll have to pretend to be ill or something. I don't want to see him, anyway; can't think of anything worse.

"What time's he arriving?" I ask, as casually as I can. "This Astalis person?"

"Not till eleven-ish. Plenty of time to make the room nice." Biddy smiles at me. "And what are you going to do with Demeter? She told me you're arranging another bespoke activity. You two are quite a pair!"

I stare back, my brain in overdrive. I'd forgotten about the bespoke activity. I'd forgotten about spending another morning with Demeter. Something "nice," I promised myself.

Something "fun." Well, that was before I knew what a self-centered, conniving, two-faced bitch she really was.

"Do you want to do baking?" suggests Biddy. "I could help you with that." But slowly I shake my head.

"No, don't worry. I'll come up with something else." I give Biddy a bland little smile. "This might be Demeter's last activity with me. I want to think of something absolutely *perfect*."

CHAPTER FIFTEEN

I meet Demeter at ten o'clock the next morning with my brightest, friendliest, "hello, campers" manner. She's wearing a gray tank top teamed with denim shorts just like Coco's, plus Hunter wellies. (I told her to wear something suitable for walking.) She has pretty good legs, actually. Of course she does. She probably thinks she looks like Kate Moss at Glastonbury. She's probably wearing those teeny shorts to look supersexy for Alex.

I feel a surge of hatred that's a bit like bile but manage to suppress it under a smile.

"So!" I greet her. "Demeter! Welcome to our bespoke nature walk. We'll head up into the woods, stretch our legs, and see a huge variety of wildlife. Sound good?"

"Well, all right." Demeter looks a bit unconvinced. "Is there a lot to see in the woods?"

"Oh yes," I say, with a bland smile. "Don't worry. You won't be bored. Do you have sunscreen on?" I add. "It's hot today."

It's not just hot, it's baking. Biddy slathered all the children with sunscreen earlier on, and she's made some ice lollies, which will be ready for lunchtime.

"I'm wearing factor fifty, actually," says Demeter smugly. "I use this *wonderful* brand which I get at Space NK; it has neroli oil and argan milk—"

"Great," I cut her off before she can do my head in with her boasting. "Let's start, then."

I only mentioned sunscreen to sound professional. Where Demeter's going, she won't need sunscreen. Mwah-ha-ha-ha.

I lead the way briskly across the fields, the blood pumping through my veins. I'm a little hyper this morning. I woke at 5:00 A.M., fully alert, my head already full of Demeter.

And Alex. Both, I suppose.

OK, full disclosure: My head was actually full of Alex, with Demeter popping in for the odd cameo. Which is *ridiculous*. This is a guy I met a handful of times. A guy who'll have already forgotten I exist. Why should he have got inside my brain? Why should I feel so . . . what, exactly?

Betrayed. That's what I feel, I realize. I feel betrayed that he should go for someone like Demeter, who's so married, so inappropriate, so *Demeter-ish*. When he could have had—

Well. All right. Before I sound totally tragic, here's the thing. I'm not just saying, *Oh, I wish he'd fallen in love with meeee. . . .* I mean, obviously I do wish that, kind of. But it's bigger than that. It's like: *Are you really a Demeter person, Alex? Because I can't see it. She doesn't have your humor. She doesn't have your flippant airiness, your live-wire irreverence. I can't see the pair of you gelling, I just can't, I can't, I can't . . .*

"Sorry?" says Demeter, and I realize I'm muttering, "I can't," under my breath.

"Just doing a Vedari chant," I say hastily. "Helps me focus. Now, keep your eyes peeled for voles."

"Voles!" exclaims Demeter.

"They're tiny creatures, rather like mice, but much more special." I nod. "And there are stacks of them in this field."

There's no chance that she'll catch sight of a vole, but at least it'll keep her off my case for a bit. Sure enough, we walk on in silence, Demeter determinedly scanning the ground.

"So!" As we arrive at the edge of the woods, I turn like a tour leader. "Welcome to Ansters Woods. In here we'll find a biodiverse world of animals, plants, and even fish, all working together in harmony."

"Fish?" queries Demeter, and I nod.

"There are streams and ponds in the woods which are home to several very rare species."

Which is, you know. Probably true. Whatever.

I've deliberately headed toward the thickest, most tangled part of the wood, and Demeter's eyeing the brambles nervously. Well, what an *idiot* she is, wearing shorts.

"Ow!" Demeter's voice suddenly rings out. "I've been stung by a nettle!"

"Bad luck," I say blandly. As we walk on, I can't help adding, "The trick with nettles is to *grasp* them. Grasp the nettle and everything will be OK. Don't you agree?"

I can't tell if Demeter gets the reference or not. She's staring at the overgrown path ahead and seems unnerved.

"Don't worry," I say reassuringly. "I'll cut us through the undergrowth. Keep close behind me and that way you'll find it easier."

I take a long, whippy stick and start slashing through the

bushes, accidentally on purpose using such a vigorous, wheeling motion that I catch Demeter on the leg too.

"Ow!" she says.

"Oh, *sorry,*" I say in an innocent tone. "I totally didn't mean to do that. Let's carry on. Look around and you'll see birch, ash, and sycamore trees, as well as oaks." I give her about thirty seconds to peer at the trees, then continue: "So, what are you up to tonight, Demeter? It's just you and the kids, isn't it? You must be feeling so sad that your husband's gone. So lonely, all alone in your yurt. Just you, no one else."

As I speak, I feel resentment simmering. *Look* at her, in her denim shorts, catching some sun, revving up for a night of torrid sex.

"I know; it's a shame. Just one of those things," says Demeter with a shrug. She's peering at the trees around us. "So, which is the sycamore?"

"I mean, you came here as a *family*." I smile so hard, my cheeks start to tremble. "With your lovely husband who you made those special vows to. How long have you been married?"

"What?" Demeter looks puzzled. "Um . . . eighteen years. No, nineteen."

"Nineteen years! Congratulations! You must really, *really* love him!"

"Er . . . yes," says Demeter, looking bemused. "I mean, we have our ups and downs. . . ."

"Of course you do. Don't we all?" I give a shrill laugh. All this time, I've managed to keep outwardly calm around Demeter. But today I'm losing it a bit.

"So are there many interesting bird species in the woods?"

asks Demeter, with her "alert and intelligent" expression that *really* rubs me the wrong way.

"Oh yes," I say, breathing hard. "Definitely." As a crow flutters out of a tree, I point upward. "Look! Did you see that?"

"No!" says Demeter, and immediately cranes upward too. "What was it?"

"A very rare bird," I say. "Very rare indeed. The great crested . . . boaster."

I nearly said, *The great crested Demeter.*

"It's related to the warbler but much more rare," I say. "Very predatory. Very toxic, nasty bird."

"Really?" Demeter sounds fascinated.

"Oh yes." I'm on a roll now. "It pushes the younger females out of the way and it won't let them thrive. You wouldn't want to come across it in the wild. It's vicious. Selfish. I mean, it *looks* good. It has very sleek plumage. But it's very crafty. Very pretentious."

"How can a bird be pretentious?" Demeter sounds puzzled.

"It preens itself all the time," I say after a pause. "And then it gouges out the other birds' eyes."

"Oh my *God.*" Demeter looks like she might be sick.

"Because it's got to be top bird. It's got to have everything. It doesn't care if the other birds in the wood are struggling." I pause. "But then, when it's off guard and vulnerable, the other birds take revenge on it."

"How?" Demeter looks utterly gripped.

"They have their means," I say with a bland smile. I wait for Demeter to ask another question, but she doesn't. Instead, she gives me a weird, appraising look.

"I was reading a book about local birds last night," she says slowly. "It didn't mention the great crested boaster."

"Well, like I say, it's very rare. One of our rarest. Shall we?"

I motion for us to carry on, but Demeter doesn't follow. Her eyes are running over me as though for the first time. Oh God, she doesn't suspect something, does she? Was the great crested boaster a step too far?

"Have you always lived in the country?" she asks.

"Oh yes!" I laugh, relieved to be on firmer ground. "I was born in the farmhouse," I add, broadening my burr. "My dad'll show you the marks on the kitchen wall, measuring my height over the years. This is home for me."

"I see." Demeter looks only partially reassured, but she starts following me again.

"You'll want to see the ponds," I tell her over my shoulder. "Beautiful wildlife at the ponds. We'll go there now."

They're always called "the ponds," but it's one pond, really. One quite large, fairly deep pond and one shallower dip, right next to it, which is sometimes a pond and sometimes a swamp. At this time of year, it's swamp. About three foot deep of swampy, froggy mud, all topped off with bright-green weed.

And that's where Demeter's heading, whether she knows it or not. I want her plastered in mud, dripping with weed, screaming with fury, and then—final touch—immortalized in a viral photo, which I'm sure Flora will have *great* pleasure in disseminating to the world. My phone's in my pocket, covered in protective plastic. I'm all set. The only issue is going to be getting her into the swamp. But even if I have to dive in first myself, I'm doing it.

My breaths are coming fast as we walk along. My ears are

buzzing; I'm twitching at every sound from the trees. Every so often, I have a spasm of nerves and think: *Do I really want to do this?*

Shall we just go back to the farmhouse instead?

But then I picture Demeter tapping at her phone with that smug smile, summoning Alex like a take-out order the minute her husband disappeared. Demeter making me do her roots . . . thrusting her Net-A-Porter boxes at me . . . complaining about her tiny journey to work . . . Demeter staring at me in the lift at Cooper Clemmow. She couldn't even *remember* if she'd let me go, because, hey, what does the life of some junior girl sitting in the corner matter?

There I was feeling sorry for her—well, what a joke. *She doesn't need my pity. I mean, look at her.* I glance at her long legs, clad in designer wellies. Her confident, I'm-the-boss stride. If she had a brief moment of vulnerability, it's long passed now, and I was a mug to fall for it. Because Demeter's always been an expert at using other people to sort her life out. Husband disappeared? Order in your lover instead. Deleted a crucial email? Get your assistant to sort it out. Somehow she always manages to come out on top.

Except today.

"Somerset has amazing birds," I say, leading her toward the ponds. "There are loads of rare species around here, so as we walk, you should look up, all the time. Look *up*."

Not down at your feet. Not down at the mud and slippery oil that I may possibly have planted earlier.

As we round a clump of bushes, the ponds come into sight ahead of us. The swamp is a patch of lime-green weed. It couldn't look more glistening and noxious. No one's about.

All the other glampers are miles away, doing their foraging in Warreton Forest, and no one else has access to these woods. The silence around us is eerie and expectant. All I can hear is my own breath and our footsteps on the increasingly muddy ground, sloping downward toward the swamp.

"Look up," I keep exhorting her. "Look up."

Everything becomes boggy around here. And very slippery, even before it's been laced with hemp oil. It's OK, as long as you're careful, don't walk too fast, and don't even *think* about running.

Which is why I'm about to make Demeter run.

"Oh wow!" I whisper as though in sudden excitement. "Can you see the kingfishers? Millions of them! Hurry!" I up my pace to what looks like a run, although I'm careful to plant my feet carefully and stay balanced. "You go first." I turn and make a generous gesture to Demeter. "Go ahead of me. But hurry! Hurry!"

Like a shopper at the Harrods sale, Demeter starts pegging it in a tiptoe run, her eyes fixed upward, gathering momentum. She doesn't see the point at which soggy mud turns to oil slick. She doesn't even notice when she starts to skid—until her feet finally hit the slipperiest bit of the oil slick, and she hasn't got a chance. She slides down toward the swamp, flailing her arms, looking like a really terrible snowboarder.

"Oh my God!" she gasps. "Oh my—oh God!"

"Careful!" I call out cheerfully. "It gets slippery. . . . Oh *no*!"

I'm watching with all my attention, not even letting myself blink. I want to enjoy this fully. I want to see every single moment: Demeter thrashing her arms in panic . . . Demeter sliding off the bank . . . Demeter poised in midair . . . Demeter's horror as she realizes what's about to happen . . .

And Demeter landing in the swamp. With not so much of a splash as a thwump. It's three solid feet of mud, and as she crashes into it, the mud sprays up in great gloopy splatters, landing on her face and hair. There's green weed on her head and down her cheeks, and I can see some sort of bug crawling along her shoulder.

Yes! This could *not* have gone better. Look at her!

She immediately tries to scramble to her feet, but it's not so easy—and she falls several times before she manages to stand up. By this time she's in the middle of the swamp, and if I'd planned the perfect photo op, then this would have been it. Demeter looking drenched, muddy, undignified, and furious.

"Help me out!" She waves an indignant hand at me. "I'm stuck!"

"Oh dear!" I call back, getting my phone out. Trying to hide my euphoria, I take a few photos, then carefully stash my phone back in its bag.

"What are you doing?" shouts Demeter.

"Just coming to help you," I say soothingly. "You know, you should be careful around swamps. You should never hurry."

"But you told me to hurry!" Demeter explodes. "You said, 'Hurry!' "

"Never mind. We'll soon get you back to your yurt. Come on," I beckon.

"I'm stuck," Demeter repeats, giving me an accusing look. "My feet have sunk into the mud."

"Just lift up your leg." I mime pulling a leg out of a swamp, and Demeter copies—but as she wrenches her leg out, her wellie is missing.

"Shit!" she says, flailing her arms again. "My boot! Where's my boot?"

Oh for God's sake.

"I'll get it," I say, feeling like a mother with a three-year-old. I wade into the swamp, reach Demeter, and feel around in the mud for the boot. Demeter is meanwhile standing on one leg, clinging to my arm. "Here." I fish out the missing wellie. "Shall we go?"

I turn toward the bank, but Demeter doesn't turn with me.

"Why did you tell me to hurry?" she asks in even, ominous tones. "Did you *want* me to fall in?"

I feel a tiny spasm of alarm, which I quell. She can't prove anything.

"Of course not! Why would I want that?"

"I don't know," says Demeter in the same ominous way. "But it's weird, isn't it? And you know what else? I feel like I *know* you from somewhere."

She scrutinizes my face and I bow my head hastily under my baseball cap.

"Well, that's ridiculous." I give a hasty laugh. "I'm a Zummerzet girl. Never been to Lunnon town in my life. I don't even know where Chiswick *is*."

"Why did you say 'Chiswick'?" snaps Demeter.

At once I curse myself. Shit. Idiot. I'm losing concentration.

"Didn't you say you work in Chiswick?" I answer as lightly as I can. "Summat like that?"

"No, I never mentioned it." Demeter holds my wrist so tight that it hurts. "Who the hell *are* you?"

"I'm Katie!" I try to wriggle out of her grasp. "Now, let's go and have a nice slap-up cream tea . . . or cake . . . jam tarts. . . ."

"You're hiding something." Demeter gives me an angry wrench and I lose my footing.

"Aargh!" I land in the swamp and feel mud slapping onto my face. Oh my God, this is *gross*. I scramble into a sitting position, wipe my eyes, and glare at Demeter. All my self-control has gone. I feel as if my kite string has snapped; the kite is soaring away.

"Don't you *dare* do that!" I slap swamp mud at her.

"Well, don't *you* fucking dare!" Demeter slaps mud back at me. "I don't know what you're up to, but—"

"I'm not up to anything!"

I crawl to the side of the swamp and dip my head in the fresh water of the adjoining pond, trying to calm my adrenaline rush. OK. Regroup. This was *not* the plan. I have to keep it together. This may be Demeter, but she's a guest too. I cannot be having a mud fight with her. I mean, it really wouldn't sound good on TripAdvisor.

Although—who's to believe her word against mine? You know. If it came to it.

Feeling steadier, I lift my head from the fresh water. My face is clean, all traces of mud gone. My baseball cap's disappeared somewhere, but never mind. I pull my dripping hair back and scrunch it into a knot. Right. Back to my professional tour-leader act.

"OK." I turn to Demeter. "Well. I think we should finish the nature walk there. I do apologize for any—"

"Wait," she says, her voice suddenly quivering. "Wait right there. *Cath.*"

My stomach does a loop the loop of terror.

"No, *Cat.*" Demeter corrects herself, her eyes like gimlets. "*Cat*. Isn't it?"

"Who's Cat?" I manage to keep in control of my voice.

"Don't give me that!" Demeter sounds so incandescent, I almost feel my skin shrivel. "Cat Brenner. It's you, isn't it? I can see it now."

I've wrecked my disguise, I realize with a sickening thud. The hat and the makeup and the curly hair. All gone. How could I have been so *stupid*?

For a few petrified seconds, my mind gallops around my options. Deny . . . run away . . . other . . .

"OK, it's me," I say at last, trying to sound nonchalant. "I changed my nickname. Is that against the law?"

A crow flaps past, cawing, but neither of us moves. We're both standing motionless in the swamp, covered in mud, staring at each other as though life is on pause. My blood is pulsing in terror, but I feel a strange relief too. At least now she'll know. She'll *know*.

Demeter has her swivelly-eyed, has-the-world-gone-mad look. She keeps peering at me, then frowning, then going all distant, as though she's consulting her memory.

Things could go anywhere from here. Anywhere. I feel almost exhilarated.

"OK, I don't understand," says Demeter, and I can tell she's trying to stay calm, with difficulty. "I don't. I'm *trying* to understand, I'm *trying* to get my head round this, but I can't. What the *hell* is going on?"

"Nothing's going on."

"You engineered me into the swamp!" Demeter's starting to sound agitated. "You told me to hurry so I would fall in. Do you have something *against* me?"

She looks so ignorant, so *oblivious,* that I draw breath. Do I have something *against* her? Where do I start?

"And catching me with that stick!" she exclaims, before I can respond. "That was on purpose too. This whole morning has been a vendetta, hasn't it? Has this whole *week* been a vendetta?" I can see her thoughts working, tracking back, analyzing everything, until her eyes snap with suspicion. "Oh my God. Is Vedari a real thing?"

"Of course it's not a real bloody thing!" I explode with pent-up frustration. "Only a totally pretentious early adopter like you would fall for something like that. It's pitiful! I just had to *mention* Gwyneth Paltrow and you were all over it!"

"But the website!"

"I know." I nod with satisfaction. "Good, wasn't it?"

I feel a shaft of triumph as I see her face dropping. *Ha. Gotcha.*

"I see," says Demeter, in the same controlled, even tones. "So you've taken me for a fool. Well, congratulations, Cat, or Katie, or whatever you call yourself. But what I still don't understand is, why? Is this because you lost your job? Are you blaming me for that? Because, one, that was *not* my fault personally, and, two, as I said to you at the time, losing your job is *really* not the end of the world."

She draws herself up tall, despite the swamp, casting herself as the tolerant, put-upon boss figure, and my rage simmers up again into a froth.

"You know something, Demeter?" I say, casting around for my own version of dignity. "When you don't have any funds and you'd rather die than ask your parents for cash, then losing your job pretty much *is* the end of the world."

"Nonsense!" says Demeter with asperity. "You'll find another job."

"I've applied and applied! I've got nothing! At least, nothing that pays. But I'm not like Flora; I can't *afford* to work for no pay. All I ever wanted was to live in London, and that day my dream got squashed, and of course that wasn't your fault. But it *was* your fault that you didn't even remember if you'd let me go or not!" My voice rises in anguish. "That was my life you held in your hands, and you didn't even *remember*! You were like, *Ooh, unimportant junior person whose name I can't recall, have I ruined your life today or not? Please remind me.*"

"All right," says Demeter after a pause. "I accept that. My behavior was . . . unfortunate. Things were very difficult for me at that time—"

"How could they be difficult?" I throw any remaining caution to the winds. "You've got the perfect bloody life! You've got everything!"

"What are you *talking* about?" Demeter stares at me.

"Oh, come on!" I explode. "Don't look at me like that! You have the perfect life! You've got the job, the husband, the lover, the kids, the money, the looks, the trendy clothes, the celebrity friends, the invitations to parties, the haircut, the Farrow and Ball front door, the gorgeous stone steps, the holidays . . ." I run out of breath. "I mean, you've got it all. And you stand there and look at me like *What perfect life?*"

There's another silence. I can hear my own breath coming, short and fast; I have never felt such tension in these woods, never. Then Demeter comes wading through the swamp to me. Her face is still plastered with mud, but I can see the fury simmering in her eyes.

"OK, *Katie,*" she spits. "You want my perfect life? You want to know about my perfect life? I'm tired all the time. *All* the time. My husband and I have a hellish struggle balancing two jobs, but we need the money because, yes, we bought ourselves a big family house with a big, crippling mortgage, and, yes, we redecorated it, which was probably a mistake, but everyone makes mistakes, right? I go to restaurant launches to network for my job. I sit on judging panels, ditto. Parties, ditto. I wear heels that give me backache and I look at my watch every half hour, wishing I could escape."

I stare at her, dumbstruck. I'm remembering the Net-A-Porter boxes, the photos on Instagram, the upbeat tweets. Demeter here, there, and everywhere, being sparkling and brilliant. It never in a million years occurred to me that she might not *enjoy* it.

"I never have time to see my friends," Demeter continues without missing a beat. "Every time I come home late, my children give me a hard time. I've missed so many moments of their lives, I'd weep if I could, but I'm beyond weeping over that particular issue. I'm an aging woman in a young people's game, and one day that's going to lose me my job. My hair is going gray, as you know. And I think I'm getting dementia. So fuck *off* with your 'perfect life.' "

"*Dementia?*" I stare at her.

"Oh, and those steps you mentioned? I hate those fucking steps more than anything in the world." Demeter starts shaking all over. She seems to have reached a whole new level of anger. "Have you ever tried wheeling a pram up a flight of ten steps? Because it's a *nightmare*. Those steps have been the bane of my existence. Do you know what happened the Christmas Eve that my daughter was five? I was bringing in the presents from the car and carrying them up the icy steps when I slipped and fell. I spent the whole of Christmas Day in hospital."

"Oh," I say nervously.

"So *don't* talk to me about my fucking steps."

"OK." I swallow. "Right. Um . . . sorry I mentioned the steps."

I'm a bit shell-shocked, actually. I had such a firm vision of Demeter tripping down her beautiful stone steps in a designer coat, looking all smug and Demeter-ish, living the perfect princess life. But now that's been supplanted by new images. Demeter lugging a pram up the steps. Demeter slipping and falling.

That kind of thing never *occurred* to me.

"It's OK." Demeter seems to calm down a little. "And I'm sorry I let you go insensitively. I truly am. I was in a real state that day, but that should not have stopped me treating you fairly and with respect. I would like to apologize . . . Cat?"

"Katie," I say awkwardly. "Cat never really took."

"Katie, then." She holds out her muddy hand, and after a pause, I take it and we shake.

"Don't tell Dad and Biddy," I say abruptly. "Please."

"Don't tell them what?" Demeter's eyes glitter at me. "That you pushed me into the mud? Don't worry, I wasn't intending to. This is fairly embarrassing for me too."

"No, not that. Don't tell them I got made redundant. They think . . ." I look at the ground. "They think I'm on sabbatical for six months."

"What?"

"They got the wrong end of the stick, and I couldn't tell them the truth. It was too—" I break off. "I just couldn't."

"So—what—they think you've been on sabbatical from Cooper Clemmow all this time?" Demeter seems incredulous.

"Yes."

"And they *believe* that?"

"They think I'm . . . you know. Quite important at the company," I practically whisper.

"I see." Demeter digests this. "So what are you going to do when the six months are up?"

"I'll get a job," I say robustly. "Or if not . . . well, it's my problem. I'll sort it."

"Right." Demeter raises her eyebrows skeptically. "Well, good luck with that." Then something seems to occur to her. "Hey. How do you know about my steps, anyway?"

"Oh. That." I feel myself flushing. "Well, Flora told me where you live, and I . . . I happened to be in the area."

"And you decided to go and look at my house," says Demeter flatly. "And think to yourself, *She lives in that house, she must be a rich bitch.*"

"No! Well . . . maybe a bit . . ." I pause awkwardly. "It's an amazing house. I saw it in *Livingetc.*"

"We hoped doing *Livingetc* might mean we could rent it out for photo shoots," says Demeter, sounding matter-of-fact. "But nobody wanted it."

"It's still fantastic, though."

"I look at it and I see mortgage payments," says Demeter. "The kids love it, though. We could never move."

I never thought about mortgage payments either. I thought Demeter lived such a gilded life, she didn't have to worry about stuff like that.

"You always *behave* like your life is perfect," I say abruptly.

"I put a good face on things," Demeter says after a pause. "Doesn't everyone? I've always thought—wait!" She interrupts herself with an almighty gasp. "Rewind. I *knew* I'd missed something. What was that you said, 'lover'? I haven't got a lover!"

I feel a spasm of anger. Really? She's going to deny it, even now? I feel like we had a little *entente cordiale* going, and now she's smashed it.

"Of course you have," I say shortly. "Everyone knows."

"Everyone knows what?"

"That you're sleeping with Alex Astalis."

"What?" Demeter peers at me. "*What* are you saying to me? *What?*"

For fuck's sake.

"Everyone *knows,*" I reiterate. "That's why he brought you in to Cooper Clemmow. I mean, it's pretty obvious, Demeter. The way you two are with each other . . . always laughing and joking. . . ."

"We're old friends!" expostulates Demeter. "That's all! My God—who told you this?"

"Just . . . people at the office." I'm not going to get Flora into trouble. "But, I mean, it's common knowledge. You haven't hidden it very well."

"There's nothing to hide!" Demeter practically detonates. "This is just a ridiculous rumor! I mean, *Alex*? I love him dearly, but any woman who got involved with Alex Astalis would have to be insane."

I can't believe it. She won't admit it, will she?

"Stop denying it when we all know it's true!" I yell. "What's Alex coming here for if he's not your lover?"

Demeter looks startled. "What do you mean?"

"He wasn't very subtle," I say pointedly. "He didn't exactly book in under the name 'Mr. Smith.' You called him as soon as your husband told you he was off to Brussels, didn't you? Biddy said he rang up at two-thirty. Nice."

"What?" Demeter gives every impression of being horrified. Can't she give it a rest?

"Stop pretending!" I say furiously. "It's really tedious!"

"I'm not pretending!" As Demeter's voice rockets around the wood, she sounds on the edge of panic. "Are you telling me that Alex Astalis is on his way here? Is this true?"

She's so agitated, I pause in my thoughts. Whatever else is true, she seems genuinely shocked at this news.

"Well . . . yes. He's staying in the farmhouse. Arriving this morning." I glance at my watch. "It's nearly eleven. He might even be here by now."

Demeter doesn't reply. For a moment I think she might not have heard. But then, three seconds later, she sinks down into the swamp, as though her legs won't hold her anymore.

"He's firing me," she whispers.

"What?" I'm astounded, almost wanting to laugh at the idea. "No."

"Yes." Her face is ashen and she's staring blindly ahead. "Alex has come here to see me, obviously." She counts off on her fingers, as though working out a logic problem. "If he wanted a meeting, he'd have made contact. He hasn't. So he wants to take me by surprise. There's only one reason for that: He's letting me go. Asking me to resign. However he does it."

"But . . ." I'm so shocked, I find myself sitting down in the swamp too. "But why would they fire you? You're the boss! You're the genius! You're the whole *thing*."

Demeter gives a weird little laugh and turns to face me. "You haven't been in touch with anyone from work, have you?"

"Not really," I say uncomfortably. "I knew things were going a *bit* wrong. . . ."

"Well. They went a lot wrong. And I don't even understand how. I don't understand . . ."

Demeter slowly bends her head to her knees. Her damp hair falls forward, off her neck, and I see her gray roots showing at the base of her skull. The sight makes her seem suddenly vulnerable once more. It's the side she's trying to keep from the world—like that moment with Carlo. And as I watch her, curled up like a hiding animal, I feel a weird, unfamiliar feeling. Like I want to pat her back reassuringly.

"Look," I venture. "It might not be what you think. Maybe he's come here on holiday. He might have seen the brochure on your desk, decided to book himself a little break. . . ."

Demeter raises her head. "Do you really think so?"

I can see hope battling with despair on her mud-splattered

face. "Well, it's possible. After all, the brochure *is* really good. . . ." I risk a little wink at Demeter, and she laughs, her tension briefly lifting.

"It *is* really good. I stand by everything I said before: You've got talent, Katie. The truth is, I should never have let you go. I should have got rid of that good-for-nothing Flora instead. You were always more proactive, more lively—" Her face jolts with realization. "Wait. It was you!" She jabs a finger. "*You* came up with the cow-welfare idea, didn't you? It's the basis of the whole rebrand."

"Oh. Well, yes. It was me."

Hope is flowering in my chest. Maybe Demeter . . . maybe she'll . . .

"I'd love to help you with your career," says Demeter, as though reading my mind. "Especially now I know who you really are. But there won't be much chance of that if I lose my job—" She interrupts herself, her eyes suddenly sharp. "Oh my God, I have it. Katie, you find out for me. *You* find out."

"What?" I gape at her.

"Go and talk to Alex as soon as he arrives. Make conversation. Find out if he's here to let me go. You can do it, I know you can."

"But—"

"Please." She grabs my hands. "*Please*. If I know he's come to fire me, I can put together a defense. I'll have half a chance to save myself. *Please*, Katie, *please* . . ."

And I don't know if it's because finally she's got my name right or if it's the wretched look in her eye, or just that I feel I've been mean enough to her for one holiday, but I find myself slowly nodding.

CHAPTER SIXTEEN

I've never seen someone properly stagger in shock before.

But Alex does. He staggers as soon as he sees me. He's genuinely staggered. (To be fair, he's walking down a grassy bank at the time, which might have something to do with it.)

We're in the only little bit of formal garden we have at the farm—it's just a tiny lawn and some flower beds, with a bank leading down to the field where all the yurts are. It's where we take glampers for their welcome cup of tea. Biddy must have done the same with Alex.

"Jesus." He whips off his sunglasses and squints at me with a hand shielding his brow. "Katie. I mean, Cat. I mean . . . Is that *you*?"

It's midday and a lot has happened since my confrontation with Demeter—most of it involving soap and loofahs. There was a *lot* of mud to clean off.

I discovered as soon as I got back to the farmhouse that Alex had called ahead and was about half an hour away. Demeter's main concern was that Alex shouldn't find her and fire her before she'd had a chance to prepare a defense. So I found her a hiding place in the woodshed, and she thanked me in a humble, grateful way.

I'm feeling like perhaps I didn't know Demeter at all at Cooper Clemmow. Not the *real* Demeter. I want to talk to her again. Peel back the veneer even more. Find out who she is underneath all the success and designer clothes and name-dropping.

But right now that's not the priority. The priority is that I've made her a promise—whether that was wise or not—and I must do my best to keep it. Even though the sight of Alex is throwing me off-balance quite considerably. Even though there's a ticker-tape headline running through my brain: *He's not sleeping with Demeter after all. . . . He's not sleeping with Demeter after all. . . .*

Argh. *Stop* it, brain. So he's not sleeping with Demeter. What does that mean? Nothing. He might be sleeping with someone else. He might be *in love* with someone else. He might not find me remotely attractive. (Most likely. Indeed, even *more* likely, given our last encounter.)

During my shower I rewound and replayed my entire history with Alex, and it made me want to die. Let's face it, the last time I saw him, I was yelling at him that he was "fucking entitled." I was also telling him how I had thought we had a "spark" between us. (Who *does* that? Answer: only me, Katie, the world's least adept traveler on the journey of Finding A Man And Not Fucking It Up.)

So the situation isn't exactly ideal. But I have an agreement to keep, so here I go. And I won't get flustered or anything. . . .

Oh *God*. As I get near him, I'm already flustered.

I'd forgotten how attractive he is. He's as lean as ever, in old jeans and a faded orange polo shirt, his dark hair shining in the sunlight. At once I think: *He's not in a suit! Of course he's not going to fire Demeter.* But then I remember: *Oh. He never wears a suit. This means nothing.*

His gaze is so intense and interested that it seems like he's reading everything in my head: my feelings, Demeter's hiding place, everything. But of course he's not. Get a *grip,* Katie.

I've decided to go for a super-nonchalant approach, although I'm not sure how convincing I'll be.

"Hello there," I say casually.

(Shall I add: *It's Alex, isn't it?* with a frown, as though I can't quite remember who he is?

No. He'll never believe it and he'll know I'm putting it on and I'll look tragic.

Fine. OK.)

"It *is* you!" he exclaims. "Cat."

"Katie," I correct him. "Call me Katie."

"You look different." He wrinkles his brow as though trying to work out what's changed. (Which is such a male response. A girl would instantly have it: *Her hair's blue and curly, she's lost the black eyeliner, gained a couple of pounds, got some freckles, and where are those glasses she used to wear?*)

Now he's heading toward me with a springy, bouncing walk, as though walking's far too slow for him but he doesn't want to run.

"This is insane. What are you doing here?"

"I live here."

"You live here?" Alex peers at me. "Is this your job now?"

"Yes. But it's my home too. Always has been."

"But . . ." He runs a hand through his hair, in that way he does. "Wait. You live in Birmingham, don't you?"

And although I've decided that I'm *not* going to analyze everything he says, I can't help myself. I never mentioned Birmingham to him. Does that mean he's talked about me to someone? Does that mean—

No. Stop. It doesn't mean *anything*.

"I used to work in Birmingham," I say. "Demeter got the wrong end of the stick. But, then, she's not really into details. Or junior staff."

I fold my arms and look at him with a deliberately blank expression. I'm playing a bit of a game here. The more I'm rude about Demeter, the more he might reveal about her. Or at least he'll never suspect I'm having this conversation *on her behalf*.

Will he?

Alex is so sharp, I wouldn't be surprised at anything, but I can do my best.

"You *do* know she's here?" I add. "Are you down here for a meeting, then? Or did you just see the brochure and decide to have a mini-break?"

All my senses are on high alert as I wait for his reply—but Alex doesn't seem to hear the question.

"Have you spoken to her?" he asks slowly. "Demeter, I mean."

"Demeter! Of course not. We've said hello or whatever. . . ." I shrug. "She didn't even recognize me at first. Typical."

"Is it typical?" says Alex, with sudden animation. "*Is* it? You worked for her; you'll know—" He breaks off and rubs his face, looking unexpectedly desolate.

"Know what?"

"Oh, it doesn't matter now. The die is cast."

He lapses into silence, and I can see the lines round his mouth form into little grooves. Anxious grooves.

There's a sinking feeling in my stomach. He doesn't look like someone who saw a brochure and decided to have a holiday. He looks like someone with a mission that he doesn't want to carry out.

Which, actually, is very inconsiderate of him, I find myself thinking. It is not in the Ansters Farm spirit. Being fired is not on our list of relaxing holiday activities.

"So, her whole family are here?" he says after a brooding pause.

"Yes," I reply pointedly. "They're having a really nice time. So, shall I tell Demeter you're here? I'm not sure where she's got to, in fact—"

"No!" he says quickly. "Don't tell her yet. Just give me—" He breaks off. "Look, I had no idea you'd be here, Katie. It's . . . it makes things complicated."

"What's complicated?" I look as puzzled as I possibly can.

"Demeter," he says unguardedly, then winces. "Shit. You know, I was *not* expecting to see you here. You're throwing me off." He gives me an accusing look.

"Well, I don't care what it is," I say, managing to appear supremely uninterested. "Only don't have a row or anything. It'll upset the guests."

" 'Have a row'?" he echoes, with a humorless little laugh. "I'm afraid we might well have a row. If not worse."

I force myself to shrug, then keep quiet for a while. I have a feeling he wants to unburden himself. I can see it in his pained eyes, the way he's twitching his fingers, the way he keeps glancing up at me. . . .

"Look, I think I should tell you something," he says in a sudden rush. "You can be discreet?"

"Of course."

"Things *are* going to get awkward. I have to tell Demeter she's being let go from Cooper Clemmow."

And even though I knew it was coming, I feel a shock wave run through me. I can't imagine Demeter fired. It seems all upside down. Demeter is the creative, inspired one. Demeter is the one who bangs heads together. Demeter leads; others follow. She's the boss. She just *is*.

Belatedly, I realize that I haven't demonstrated any outward surprise at all. Shit.

"I'm so shocked," I say hastily, "that I can't react. I'm numb."

There. Covered myself, I hope.

"I know." Alex winces. "Believe me, it hasn't been an easy decision. I mean, Demeter's brilliant, we all know that. But there have been some issues. . . . Adrian feels—well, *everyone* feels—things have not been going swimmingly, put it like that."

"Right." I wonder if I can get any more out of him. "So, what was, like, the *deciding* factor?"

"Oh God." Alex exhales sharply. "There's been so much. But this latest cock-up with Allersons is unforgivable—" He interrupts himself and looks around to check we're not being overheard. "This is confidential, right?"

"Absolutely," I say gravely. "We have a motto here: What is uttered in the stable yard stays in the stable yard."

I think I maligned Steve before. His stable-yard motto is actually pretty good.

Alex looks confused. "We're not in a stable yard."

"It applies to the whole farm," I reassure him. "You were saying about Allersons?"

"Right. Well, I don't know what you heard, but basically, Demeter went into Allersons a few weeks ago—you know Allersons Holdings?" he adds, and I nod. "They want a three-sixty rebrand of the Flaming Red restaurant chain. *Extremely* big piece of work. And apparently Demeter really impressed them. She had all sorts of ideas about research, workshops, she wanted to set up a 'brand road show'—I mean, she was brilliant in the meeting. Everyone agrees that."

"So?"

"So she never followed it up."

"Was she supposed to?"

"Yes, she was bloody supposed to! But she had some kind of crazy meltdown and got the idea Allersons wanted to stall, for some reason. She gave that message to Rosa and Mark. So no one bothered pursuing it."

"And did Allersons want to stall?"

"No! They were waiting for her! For us! Apparently they kept emailing and she sent reassuring emails back. But clearly they were on one page while she was on the fucking . . . *moon*. So at last they phone up Adrian directly—this is yesterday morning—and he's like, what the hell?"

"So . . . I mean . . ." My mind is working hard. "Have you *told* Demeter about this?"

"Of course! We had a whole series of calls about it yesterday. But—this is the worst bit—she seems totally confused. She maintains she *didn't* make a mistake, that it's Allersons' fault, and when she gets back from holiday she'll show us. But we have the email trail proving the opposite. The whole thing's messed up. Adrian's given up talking to her. Everyone's given up on her. They think she's lost it." Alex looks genuinely miserable.

"And so that's why she's being fired?" I press him. "That one incident?"

"There's been other stuff." He folds his arms around his rangy body, looking harassed. "There was a faux pas where she forwarded an email to the wrong address. I'm sure you heard about that."

I wince. "Yes, I did."

"She had to grovel to Forest Food, big-time. Then there was a big cock-up with Sensiquo. . . ."

"I remember that too." I nod, recalling Rosa screaming at Demeter in the ladies'. "Kind of. I mean, I just overheard stuff," I add hastily.

"She won Sensiquo round, but again, it was a massive, needless drama. And then generally we've had so many complaints about her leadership, her manner with the juniors, her flakiness. . . ." He brings his fists to his forehead in frustration. "I just don't *get* it. I worked for Demeter in my first job and she was fabulous. She was brilliant. She was encouraging. She was *on* it. I mean, yes, she was always a bit impulsive, a bit erratic, but that was Demeter. You put up with it because of the flashes of genius. And she basically kept everything under control. She ran a tight ship. But now . . ." He sighs. "I don't know what's happened to her. I look like a fool, for hiring her, for sticking up for her—"

"You call this sticking up for her?" I can't help sounding incredulous. "Coming to fire her on her *holiday*?"

"I did my best for her, OK?" His eyes become dark and defensive. "And I'd rather do this than have her arrive at work on Monday, get summoned to Adrian, and it's all in front of her team. I *volunteered* to come down here, believe it or not. I'm trying to give her some dignity and space—" He suddenly breaks off. "Anyway, why do you care? I thought you hated her."

"Oh, I do," I say quickly. "She's the one who let me go, remember? Bitch. She deserves all she gets."

"She's not really a bitch," says Alex slowly. "I know everyone thinks she is, but she's not. She gets a bad rap and I'm not sure why."

I want to say: *I know what you mean.* I want to say: *I'm starting to see Demeter in a different light.* But obviously I can't say that. So instead I pick a cornflower and pull all its petals off, which is a bad habit of mine.

"Katie!" Biddy's reproving voice hits my ears. "Leave that poor cornflower alone!"

I give a rueful grin. That is typical Biddy, to catch me out. She's coming into the garden with a laden tray, and I hurry over to help her. The tray has on it a coffee press, cup and saucer, milk jug, two scones with jam and clotted cream, a slice of lemon drizzle cake, and a couple of chocolate chip cookies.

"Oh my *God,* Biddy," I say in a whisper, as I help her arrange it all on our wrought-iron garden table and put up an umbrella against the sun. "Did you give him enough to eat, do you think?"

"I wanted to give him a good welcome!" she whispers back. "He's our first guest! So, Mr. Astalis!" She stands up. "Please come and have a proper West Country morning coffee, and then I'll show you to your room."

As Alex sits down at the table, he looks a bit thunderstruck. But he smiles charmingly at Biddy and compliments everything: "These scones! And the jam—is that homemade?"

Eventually Biddy goes back inside, and Alex puts down the scone. "I *cannot* eat all this," he says. "Sorry. It's just not happening. I had breakfast on the road about, what, an hour ago?"

"Don't worry." I laugh. "Biddy just wanted to make you welcome."

"And 'welcome' would be Somerset slang for 'a coronary patient'?" Alex eyes the dish of clotted cream and I laugh again.

"Seriously, you do have to try her lemon drizzle cake. It's amazing."

"I will." Alex's expression turns sober. "But not now." He wraps up the lemon drizzle cake in a napkin, then puts his hands flat on the table. "Enough procrastinating. I need to do this. Do you know where Demeter is?"

My stomach lurches. *Don't give away anything.*

"Let Biddy show you your room first," I say easily. "Please. It won't take long. She's so excited to have you. Actually . . ." I hesitate. "You're our first B&B guest."

"Really?" Alex looks surprised. "I thought this was an up-and-running business."

"It is. The glamping is. But the B&B's new, and Biddy's quite nervous. . . ."

"Well, I hate to disappoint her." Alex takes a sip of coffee. "But I probably won't even use my room."

"You're not staying the night?" I try not to sound crestfallen. Because obviously I'm not crestfallen.

"I only booked a room in case things took longer than expected. I'll pay, of course," Alex adds quickly. "But staying isn't the plan. I don't want to prolong this any more than I have to."

"Will you still give us a good review on TripAdvisor?" I blurt out before I can stop myself, and Alex laughs.

"Absolutely. Ten stars."

I smile back. "It only goes up to five."

"Five and a half, then." He drains his cup of coffee, then looks at me quizzically, as though greeting me for the first time. "So, Katie Brenner. How have you been?"

"Oh, you know," I say lightly. "Unemployed, mostly." He winces, and I add, "No, it's been fine. Really. It's been good. I've helped my dad start this place up. And Biddy. She's my stepmum," I explain.

"You started this from scratch?" He sweeps his arm around.

"Yes."

"Just the three of you?"

I nod, and Alex picks up the Ansters Farm brochure, which Biddy has helpfully left on the tray. He studies it for a minute, then raises his head. "You know something? I saw this earlier, and I thought: *This looks like a piece of Demeter's work*. You've learned from her, clearly. Congratulations."

I feel an inner whoop but simply reply, "Thanks. Oh, and by the way . . . please can you *not* mention that you know me to Dad or Biddy?"

"Oh?" Alex seems taken aback.

"It's . . . complicated. They don't know that I know Demeter either. It's—" I stop dead. "Anyway."

"Fine," says Alex after a pause. He sounds confused and even a bit offended, but too bad. I *can't* go into it all. Anyway, he probably won't even hang around long enough to talk to Biddy again, let alone Dad.

I pour him another cup of coffee, and he lifts a hand.

"No, I really have to go." But then he takes a pensive sip. (Something I've learned here: Sixty percent of people who say "no thanks" to more coffee then drink two more cups.) For a while there's silence except for the sound of children's laughter drifting over the breeze. I think the kids are with Dad this morning, doing something with scarecrows. After that, they'll go boating on Fisher's Lake. They do have a good time here, you can't argue with that.

I'm feeling a tad awkward and wondering what to say next, when Alex breaks the quiet. "You know, I thought a lot about what you said, your last day at Cooper Clemmow. It got to me. I had a sleepless night or two. I nearly called you up."

He *what*?

I'm utterly taken aback. Playing for time, I look away, fidgeting with a spoon. I want to ask him: *What are you talking about exactly? What did you want to say? Why did you have sleepless nights?* But at the same time, I don't want to go there. It was all too mortifying.

"Right." I make the mistake of raising my eyes, and he's looking right at me with that dark gaze of his.

"Look at you," he says softly, and I feel a fresh lurch in my stomach. What does that mean? And why is he looking at me like that? Oh God . . .

OK, full disclosure: The whole not-getting-flustered strategy has bombed. I don't even know what's doing it. His eyes? His voice? Just . . . him?

"Anyway," I say in a businesslike way. "I'm sorry, but I just have to go and . . . do a thing."

"Of course." Alex seems to come to, and the light in his eyes fades. "You must be very busy. Sorry to have kept you." He puts down his coffee cup. "Well, here goes. Any idea where Demeter is? Your dad thought she was with you."

"Demeter?" I say, with a careless shrug. "Sorry, no idea. But I'm sure she's around somewhere. If I see her, I'll point her in your direction."

"If you *do* see her . . ." He squints at me against the sunlight. "You won't say anything to her, will you? Stable-yard rules."

"*Say* anything to her?" I echo, as though the idea's ludicrous. "Of course I won't. Not a word."

"You're being fired!" I blurt out as soon as I reach the woodshed. "It's all true! Adrian's given up on you, and it's because of Allersons and that Forest Food email and the thing with Sensiquo and your manner with your staff and . . . you know. Everything."

"*Everything?*" Demeter peers at me from the depths of the woodshed, looking like some hostage emerging from a monthlong ordeal. Unlike me, she has *not* visited a shower, because she was too paranoid about bumping into Alex. She has dried mud on her face, dust all over her hair, and wood shavings on her shoulders, looking like monster dandruff. Her expression is stricken, and I realize I was perhaps a bit blunt.

"Well, you know," I amend, trying to sound more diplomatic. "All your mistakes. And . . . well. The stuff with the staff."

"What stuff with the staff?" She gazes at me through the murk, with that myopic, confused, *incredibly* frustrating expression she gets.

"Well." I shrug awkwardly. I'm hardly going to spell it out, am I?

There's silence. Demeter's foot is tapping on the floor in a nervous, repetitive pattern. Her eyes are darting around like a cornered animal's.

"Tell me about the stuff with the staff," she says abruptly. "You were one of them. Tell me."

Oh God. This is excruciating.

"Really," I say at once. "It's nothing."

"It's not nothing!"

"It is! I mean, there were just a *few* tiny things. . . ." I trail off uncomfortably.

"Clearly there were more than a few tiny things," says Demeter evenly. "Katie, I'm asking you as a fellow professional. Give me a review. A full, honest review. No holds barred."

Arrgh. Is she *serious*?

"I can't!" I twist my legs together. "It would be . . . awkward."

"Awkward?" Demeter erupts. "How *awkward* do you think I feel right now, hiding in a woodshed from a man who used to be my junior? Looking at my whole career disappearing down the drain? Feeling I must be going mad?" She clutches her head, and I can see tears suddenly glittering in her eyes. "You

don't know what it's like for me. I don't understand. I *don't understand.*" She bangs her head against her hands, and I gape in shocked dismay. "Nothing makes sense. I really think I may be getting dementia. But I can't admit that to anyone. Anyone. Not even James."

"You haven't got *dementia,*" I say, appalled. "That's ridiculous!"

But Demeter is shaking her head almost savagely, as though she can't hear me.

"Things change. Things . . . they don't make sense. Emails. Messages." Her brow wrinkles as though with the memory. "Every day I get through in a state of, basically . . . panic. Yes. Panic. Trying to keep on top of everything and failing. Quite *clearly* failing, as my imminent dismissal goes to prove." She wipes roughly at her eyes. "I do apologize. This is unlike me."

"Look." I gulp, feeling more and more uneasy. "You're brilliant at what you do. You really inspired me, and you've got amazing ideas—"

"Tell me about the staff." She cuts me off dead. "Where have I messed up? Why do they hate me?"

I'm about to give the pat answer: *They don't hate you.* But something about Demeter's expression stops me fobbing her off. I respect this woman. She deserves better than that.

"Well, take Rosa." I pick a name at random. "She feels . . ." I hesitate, trying to decide how to put it.

She feels you stamp on her fingers with your Miu Miu shoes.

"She feels you don't always encourage her to develop her career," I say carefully. "Like, you wouldn't let her do the mayor's athletics project."

"She's holding *that* against me?" Demeter looks incredulous.

"Well, it would have showcased her talents. . . ."

"Jesus." Demeter closes her eyes. "I don't believe this. Do you want to know the truth? They didn't *want* her at the mayor's project."

"What?" It's my turn to stare.

"I wrote an email recommending her, and we sent off a portfolio, but she didn't make the grade."

"But why didn't you *tell* her?" I exclaim.

"Rosa always seems very sensitive. *Over*sensitive, even." Demeter shrugs. "I thought I'd protect her feelings and say that I needed her. Keep her confidence levels up."

"Oh." I think about this. "Well, maybe you kept her confidence levels up, but . . ."

"Now she hates me," finishes Demeter. "Yes. I can see how that might have happened. Unintended consequences and all that." There's a strange quiver to her face, and I think she's quite upset but trying to mask it. "I won't make *that* mistake again. Who else?"

"OK," I say, feeling worse than ever. "So . . . Mark. He hates you because you stole his thunder with that Drench moisturizer rebrand."

"Really?" Demeter looks astonished. "But that was a massive success. We've won awards. It's boosted his career."

"Well, I know. But he had his own ideas, and you came barging in and took over and embarrassed him. . . ." I bite my lip. "I'm only telling you what people say—" I break off, unnerved at the anger suddenly flashing in Demeter's face.

"I saved him," she says hotly. "I bloody *saved* him. Those

designs he came up with were rushed and substandard. He's talented, Mark, but he does too much freelance work on the side. I *know* that's what he's up to at home. He's greedy; he takes on too much, and it shows." She falls silent and seems to simmer down. "But I could have been more diplomatic," she adds. "When I get a good idea I forget everything else. It's a bad fault of mine."

I don't know what to say to this, so I'm quiet for a while. I can see that Demeter's head is teeming with thoughts, and no wonder.

"So, Rosa hates me and Mark hates me," she says, in an odd voice. "Anyone else?"

"Hate's the wrong word," I say hurriedly, even though it's exactly the right word. "It's just . . . I suppose . . . they don't feel very respected. For example, did you even know that Mark won the Stylesign Award for Innovation?"

Demeter turns her head and surveys me as though I'm mad. "Of course I bloody knew. I put him up for it. I'm on the contributing panel. And I sent him a card afterward." Then her brow creases. "Actually, did I send it? I know I *wrote* it. . . ."

"You *what*?" I gape at her. "Well, did you *tell* him you nominated him?"

"Of course I didn't tell him," she retorts. "It's anonymous."

"So no one at the office has any idea you helped him?"

"*I* don't know," says Demeter impatiently.

"Well, you should!" I practically yell. "You should get some credit! Demeter, you're driving me mad here! You're *so* much nicer than you make out you are. But you've got to help yourself!"

"I don't understand," says Demeter, a little haughtily, and I nearly pop with exasperation.

"*Don't* make people do up your corset dress. *Don't* make people do your roots. *Don't* tell Hannah she's being a drama queen because she's had a panic attack."

"What?" Demeter looks horrified. "I *never* said that. I would *never* say something like that. I've been very supportive of Hannah and her issues—"

"I remember it exactly," I cut her off. "You said to Hannah, 'No one thinks you're a drama queen.' To her that sounded like, *You're a drama queen.*"

"Oh." Demeter sounds chastened. "Oh. I see."

There's a long silence, and I can tell she's mulling. "I think perhaps I don't always communicate what I want to communicate," she says at last.

"We have an expression for it," I say. If I'm going to be honest, I might as well tell her the lot. "We call it 'being Demetered.' "

"Oh my *God*." She looks even more shell-shocked. As well she might.

There's another long silence, and I know some thought or other is bubbling to the top of Demeter's head. Sure enough, a moment later she exclaims, "But the roots! Do you hate me because I asked you to do my roots?"

"Well . . ." I'm not sure how to reply, but luckily Demeter doesn't seem to need an answer.

"Because that I do *not* understand," she continues emphatically. "I thought we were all in the sisterhood. If you asked me to do your roots, Katie, and I had time, then of course I would. Of *course* I would."

She meets my gaze, unblinking, and I realize that I believe her. I think she means it. She'd do my roots in a heartbeat and not be remotely offended.

With every revelation, more of a pattern has started to form. I think in some ways Demeter's the *opposite* of what we all thought. Maybe she's careless—but she's not vindictive. She isn't deliberately stamping everyone with her Miu Miu shoes—she's just not being careful enough about where she places them. She obviously thinks that everyone's like her: focused on having great ideas and making them work and not fussing too much about the details. The trouble is, people—employees—*do* mind about the details.

The more I realize the truth, the more frustrated I'm feeling with her. It could all be so different, if she took more care.

"You know, it *really* doesn't help that you always mix up people's names," I say bluntly. "And the way you look at people as if you can't remember who they are? That's *bad.*"

For the first time in our conversation, Demeter looks truly mortified. "I have a very small visual-recognition issue," she says with dignity. "But it's only a detail. I've masked it successfully all my life. It's never held me back at work."

God, she's perverse. I feel like strangling her.

"You haven't masked it successfully!" I retort. "And it *has* held you back! Because, look, you're about to get fired, and that's a factor. People think you don't care about them. If you just told everyone you had a problem—" I break off as an idea hits me. "Maybe that's why you get confused with stuff. I mean, it's a *thing*. Like being dyslexic. You could get help; you could get support. . . ." I trail off as Demeter shakes her head.

"I wish. It's not that. It's worse than that." She gives me a bleak little smile. "I've googled early-onset dementia. I have all the signs."

"But you're totally with it!" I say, feeling quite distressed at this conversation. "You're sane, you're lucid, you're *young*, for God's sake. . . ."

Demeter shakes her head. "I send emails I don't remember sending. I get confused over dates. I don't remember things I've agreed to. This issue with Allersons. I'm *sure* they told me to stall. They were waiting for some piece of research they'd commissioned." Her face crumples. "But now everyone's telling me they didn't say that. So it must be me. I must be losing my sanity. Luckily I think quickly on my feet, so I've got myself out of a lot of situations. But not all of them."

I have a flashback to Demeter in the office, peering at her phone as though nothing in the world makes sense, turning to Sarah with that confused, helpless expression, deflecting attention with some random loud announcement. And now, of course, it all looks like a coping mechanism.

The thought makes me squirm uncomfortably. I can't believe Demeter is anything other than a powerful, intelligent woman, at the top of her game and just a bit crap at managing people.

She's pacing around the woodshed now, her face tortured. She looks like she's trying to solve some problem involving Pythagoras and string theory, all at once.

"I *know* I saw that email," she suddenly declares. "I printed it out. I *had* it."

"So where is it?"

"God knows. Not on my computer, I've checked enough times. But . . ." Her face jolts. "Wait. Did I put it in my raffia bag?"

She looks transfixed. I don't even dare breathe, in case I disturb her.

"I did. I think I did. I took a bundle of emails home. . . ." Demeter rubs her mud-strewn face. "They're not on my desk. I've checked that too. But could they be in that bag? It's been hanging on my bedroom-door handle for weeks. I never even . . . Is *that* where it went?"

She looks at me urgently, as though expecting an answer. I mean, honestly. What do I know about her raffia bag? On the other hand, leaving a bundle of emails in a bag is a *totally* Demeter thing to do.

"Maybe." I nod. "Absolutely."

"I've got to try, at least." Abruptly, she starts brushing herself down. "I've got to give it a go."

"Give what a go?"

"I'm going to London." She looks directly at me. "It's only midday. I can get up there and back by evening. The children are busy; they won't even know I've gone."

"You're going to the office?" I say, confused.

"No!" She gives a half bark of mirthless laughter. "I can't risk going near the office. No, I'm going home. I need to see what I can salvage from my stuff there. If I've got *any* chance of fighting this, I need ammunition."

"But what about Alex?" I point out. "He's here. He's waiting for you."

"You can tell him what I'm doing when I've gone. Either he'll come chasing after me or, knowing Alex, he probably won't. . . ." Demeter gives me a wry look. "I'll just ask you one more favor, Katie. Give me a head start. OK?"

CHAPTER SEVENTEEN

A head start. How long is a head start?

It's twenty minutes later and Demeter's already gone. I smuggled her into the house, stood sentry while she took a lightning-quick shower, then kept a lookout while she drove away. Now I need to see what Alex is up to.

He isn't in the garden anymore, and when I knock on his bedroom door, I don't get an answer. So I head along to the kitchen and find him sitting at our Formica table, looking at Biddy's array of jams. As I enter, he turns to me with a weird expression of—what, exactly? I can't make it out. Is it amusement? Or disquiet?

Is it *pity*?

I look swiftly at Biddy—what's going on?—but she smiles pleasantly back. Clearly she hasn't picked up anything amiss.

"Hi," I say warily.

"Hi, Katie," says Alex, his voice sounding constrained. "So, I was just talking to your dad and I hear you're on sabbatical from a company called Cooper Clemmow?"

It's like someone drops a set of cymbals inside me. Everything seems to clash and fall, while outwardly I'm perfectly still. All I can do is gaze at him helplessly, thinking: *No. Please no. Nooooo.*

"Not that you're getting any rest, are you, love?" says Dad, with a little laugh. "They call her all the time, wanting advice on this or that. . . ."

"Do they?" says Alex, in the same odd voice. "How inconsiderate of them."

I want to curl up. I want to shrivel.

"Oh, she's always on her laptop or on the phone, talking about these 'brands' they do," chimes in Biddy eagerly. "Everyone wants our Katie."

"These London bosses." Alex shakes his head.

"Too demanding," asserts Dad. "I mean, *is* she on sabbatical or isn't she?"

"Very good question," says Alex, nodding. "I think you've got right to the nub of it, Mick, if I may say so."

"Well." Somehow I manage to speak, even though my lips are trembling. "It's . . . it's not that clear-cut."

"Yes, I'm sensing that." Alex's eyes meet mine, and I can see he's intrigued, he's concerned, and he's not going to give me away to Biddy and Dad. Not right now, anyway. "So, do you know where Demeter is?" he adds.

"She . . . er . . . doesn't seem to be here," I say, looking around the kitchen inanely. Which, to be fair, isn't a lie.

"Why not give Alex a tour of the farm?" suggests Biddy. "You might run into Demeter on the way. Have you been to Somerset before, Alex?"

"Never," says Alex firmly. "I know nothing about the country. It's all a mystery to me. Don't even own a pair of wellies."

"We'll have to put that right!" Biddy pushes open the

kitchen door and ushers Alex out. "Breathe in that air," she instructs. "That'll clear out those city lungs of yours."

A flash of amusement passes across Alex's face and, obediently, he begins breathing in. He's peering around at the view of the hills and fields, as though something has interested him, and suddenly he strides forward, squinting harder.

"I know nothing about the country," he repeats, "and this is just an idea. But if you cut down that bunch of bushes *there* . . . wouldn't you make more of the view?"

He's gesturing at a thicket way over to the east. I guess it is a bit of an eyesore, only we've got used to it.

"Oh," says Dad, sounding taken aback. "Maybe you're right. Yes. I think you're right." He glances at Biddy. "What do you think?"

"I never saw it like that before, but yes." Biddy sounds flummoxed. "My goodness, all these discussions we've had about how to improve the view . . ."

"And he saw it straightaway," chimes in Dad. Both he and Biddy are eyeing Alex in slight awe.

"As I say," says Alex politely, "it's just an idea. The countryside is a mystery to me." He looks at me. "So, are we doing this tour?"

There isn't an official "tour" of Ansters Farm, so I just lead Alex toward the yard. Anything to get him away from Dad and Biddy.

"So, Sabbatical Girl," says Alex as soon as we're out of earshot.

"Stop it." I don't look up or stop walking.

"Why?"

"Because . . . lots of reasons. Well, one mostly. Dad."

"Would he give you a hard time about losing your job?" Alex looks surprised. "He seems like the supportive type."

"He is! It's not that he would give me a hard time. It's . . ."

I screw up my face, trying to separate my mass of feelings into ones I can articulate. I've never spoken about Dad to anyone before. I feel out of my comfort zone.

"I can't bear to let him down," I say at last. "And I can't deal with him being disappointed for me. He's almost *too* supportive, you know? He doesn't cope well when things don't go well for me. He hates London; he hates that I've chosen to be there. . . . If I tell him about my job, it'll be more confirmation to him that London's a terrible place. And the point is, maybe I don't *need* to tell him." I force myself to sound more upbeat. "Maybe I'll get another job in time and I can fudge the truth. He'll never need to know."

Even as I'm saying the words, they sound hopelessly optimistic. But I've got to hope, haven't I? There must be thousands of jobs in London. I only need one of them.

"Isn't this a job?" Alex spreads his arms around. "Running this place?"

"Not the job I want." I bite my lip. "I know it would be a dream come true for a lot of people, but I loved the world of branding. I loved the teamwork and the creativity and the . . . I don't know. The spark. It's *fun*."

"Sometimes it is." Alex meets my eye with a glint, and I suddenly remember the pair of us on the roof of Cooper Clemmow. *That* was fun. I can still remember the exhilaration of the biting winter air on my cheeks. Or was it the exhilaration of being with Alex? Even now my skin is prickling as we walk along together, just the two of us.

I wonder if his skin is prickling too. Probably not. I would glance over at him, to gauge his mood, but everything feels a bit loaded all of a sudden.

"So what are you going to do if the 'sabbatical' ends and you haven't found a job?" Alex breaks the silence. "What will you tell your dad?"

"Don't know. Haven't got that far." I pick up my pace slightly. I don't want to confront that thought. "So, do you want to look at . . ." I pluck something random out of the air. "Sheep? We keep sheep, cows—"

"Wait a minute. What's that?" We've reached the yard, and Alex seems to be peering into the biggest barn, where Dad's stuffed all his crap. "Is that a brewing kit? Can I have a look?"

"Er . . . sure," I say, distracted by the sight of Denise coming out of the farmhouse. "Hey, Denise," I call. "Can I have a quick word? You know Susie's not feeling well today? I wondered if you could pop in and offer her clean bedding if she'd like it, make sure she's OK?"

"Not feeling well?" retorts Denise, with that tight-lipped look of hers. "Have you seen the empty bottles outside her yurt? *I'll* tell you why she's not feeling well—"

"Anyway . . ." I cut Denise off pleasantly. "I'd be very grateful if you could do that for me. Thanks, Denise."

"Prosecco." Denise utters the word with disfavor. "All five bottles. *Prosecco.*"

I've heard Denise's views on prosecco many times before. Not to mention Parma ham.

"Whatever she drinks, she's a *client*. We don't judge our

clients, OK?" I'm about to launch into a small lecture on customer service, when I hear a crash from the barn.

"Shit!" Alex's voice comes from the barn, and I feel a stab of alarm. Don't say he's injured himself, that's all I need. . . .

"Are you OK?" I hurry toward the barn. "You probably shouldn't go in there. . . ."

"This place is insane!" As I enter the barn, Alex turns, a massive grin on his face. He has a scattering of dust and a cobweb on his face, and I instinctively lift a hand to brush it away—then stop dead, in embarrassment. What was I planning to do, stroke his *face*?

Alex darts the briefest of glances at my raised hand, and I can see the same thought process flashing through his eyes. Then he regards me again, square-on. Dust motes are floating between us, and I tell myself that's why I feel breathless. *Not* because I'm slightly falling in . . .

In what? *Lust* sounds wrong, but it's the truth. There's a prickly, tantalizing vibe between us. It was there in London and here it is again. I know I'm not imagining it. Slowly, Alex wipes the cobweb off his own face, and his dark eyes glint at me as though he's acknowledging it too.

"This place is a treasure trove," he says. "Look at this!" He strokes the massive barrel that Dad bought to produce Ansters Farm Original Ale. What a waste of money that was.

I shrug. "My dad used to brew beer."

"And that?" He points to the contraption behind the brewing kit. "Is that a loom?"

"We were going to weave alpaca wool and make our fortune. My dad's what you might call . . ."

"An entrepreneur?" supplies Alex.

"I was going to say 'deluded.' " I laugh. "We've never made any money out of any of this stuff."

"What about that?" He points to the 1950s jukebox.

"Oh, we were going to host rock 'n' roll parties." I can't help giggling at the memory. "Dad styled his hair into a quiff and everything."

"Does it work?"

"I'll see if there's a plug." I edge past him, trying to glimpse the end of the electrical cord, and feel my rib cage brush against Alex's. Because it's a cramped space, here in the barn. (OK, full disclosure: I may have arched my back deliberately toward him as I passed.)

"Sorry," I say.

"No problem," he says, in a voice I can't quite read. "D'you need a hand?"

As he takes my hand, I can't help feeling a frisson. After all those fantasies I had, here I am with my hand firmly clasped in his warm one. Although it's not like we're *holding hands*, I tell myself. We're only holding hands. Temporarily. In very much a practical, necessary movement.

On the other hand, he hasn't let go yet, and neither have I. Which is . . . odd? I glance at him through the dim, dusty air, and his eyes are as unreadable as his voice. Or maybe they *are* readable and I just don't dare believe their message. Because what I'm picking up from his dark gaze is pretty explicit.

"Katie?" Dad's voice penetrates the gloom, and I jump, dropping Alex's hand. "What are you doing in here?" He's peering in from the yard, holding his Farmer Mick hat in his hand.

"Just showing Alex some stuff," I say, reflexively moving away from Alex.

"Oh yes?" Dad's eyes run suspiciously over Alex again. "And what stuff would that be, then?"

His tone is instantly recognizable, as is his expression. It's his *I've caught you up to no good in the barn, haven't I?* expression. Honestly. Just because I'm alone in here with a man?

I mean, to be fair, Dad *has* caught me up to no good in the barn a few times in my life. (The post-exams party; that time after the cider festival; once when I was with Steve—*God,* that was embarrassing.) But, now, hello, I'm a grown woman?

"Mr. Astalis was interested in the brewing kit," I tell him firmly.

"I'm going to pick your brains, Mick," says Alex. "I've always wanted to brew my own beer. In fact . . ." A thought seems to hit him. "Can I buy your brewery off you? I'll put it in my garage."

"Buy it?" Dad's face lights up for a nanosecond; then he instantly adopts what I call his "business" face—i.e., an expression of curmudgeonly suspicion. "Well, now. Thing is, I was planning to go back into brewing. That's valuable kit, that is. I'd have to hear your offer first."

My face is burning with mortification. Dad was *not* planning to go back into brewing, and Alex must surely guess that. But his composure doesn't flicker.

"Quite right," he says seriously. "Well, we'll find a fair price. Do you remember what you paid for it?"

"I'll find out." Dad's eyes gleam. "Give me a few minutes to check my records." He turns with alacrity and practically runs out of the shed.

"Do you really want to go into brewing?" I ask suspiciously.

"Of course I do!" says Alex. "Your dad can set me on the

way." And he gives me a smile so blithe that I can't help suspecting he's done this at least partly out of some other motive. Except I can't think what that motive could be, except simple generosity.

(Unless he's spotted that the brewing kit is worth a fortune. Unlikely.)

"Oh, another thing," he suddenly adds. "I should tell you. Your charity."

"My charity?" I echo, not following.

"Your community center in Catford? We've just decided it's going to be one of next year's official company charities."

"What?" I gape at him.

"I was going to try to let you know somehow. Anyway, here you are." He spreads his hands. "It's official. Next year we'll be raising money for the Church Street Community Center in Catford and for Cancer Research."

I'm almost speechless. He listened. He remembered.

"I went to visit them, in fact," Alex continues, his eyes glowing. "I spoke to the kids. Met the leaders. And you're right. They're awesome."

"You went to Catford?" This is so staggering, I can't quite take it in. "You went to *Catford*?"

For a moment Alex doesn't answer. He's fiddling with the jukebox buttons, his jaw set.

"Like I say, it got to me," he says at last, a little gruffly. "What you said in the office. I don't want to be some entitled bastard who can't see out of his own privileged bubble. I felt pretty chastened, if you must know. There you were, doing something for your local community, forging links, making a difference—"

Oh *God*. Is that what he thinks? My head feels hot with guilt. Me? Forging links with my community?

"Alex." I cut him off. "Listen. I . . . I didn't forge any links. The truth is . . . I never actually went to visit the community center."

"What?" His head jerks up in shock.

"A girl gave me a leaflet and told me about it." I bite my lip in embarrassment. "That's all."

"A *leaflet*?" He stares at me. "I thought you were heavily involved! No wonder they hadn't heard of you. I couldn't understand it."

"Well, I would have been!" I say hastily. "If I hadn't moved away. I mean, I'm sure it's a great project and everything—"

"It is! It's a bloody marvelous project." He stares at me disbelievingly. "Why am I telling *you* about *your* community project?"

"Because . . . er . . . you're a really good person?" I venture, and risk a little smile.

To my relief, Alex's mouth is twitching. I think he can see the funny side.

"Well, do let me give you a tour of your own charity project sometime," he says sardonically.

"Er . . . thanks!" I meet his eye. "I mean it. Thanks."

I've found the plug of the jukebox, and I'm about to ask Alex if he wants to hear it work, when he glances at his watch.

"Shit." He frowns. "I've got distracted. Do you have *any* idea where Demeter might be?"

My stomach flips apprehensively as I glance at my own watch. She's been gone twenty-five minutes now. That's a head start, isn't it?

"Look," I say. "Alex. I have to tell you something." I rub my nose, avoiding his eye. "Demeter's . . . She's . . ."

"What?"

"Well, in actual fact . . . she's . . ."

"What?" demands Alex.

OK, full disclosure: I'm really quite nervous. In the heat of the moment it seemed obvious I should help Demeter. It seemed the right thing to do. But now that I actually have to fess up . . .

"She's . . . gone to London."

"London?" Alex's gaze darkens. "When?"

"Twenty minutes ago or so."

"But what . . . why . . ." His eyes suddenly snap in furious realization. "Wait. You *have* seen her. Did you *tell* her?"

"I gave her some warning, yes," I say, trying to hold my nerve.

"I don't believe this," Alex says evenly. "You mean you ran straight from our conversation and said, 'You're going to get fired!' "

This is so exactly what happened, there's no point denying it.

"She deserved to be told!" I shoot back hotly. "There's more to Demeter than you realize. She's given a lot to Cooper Clemmow; you can't just chuck her out—"

"I don't care what you think of Demeter, it was *not* up to you to warn her." Alex looks absolutely livid. "And if she thinks she can dodge the bullet by running away—"

"She's not! She's looking for a way to save herself! There's some email or something . . . shhh!" I interrupt as I see Dad approaching. "We don't know each other, remember?"

Alex flashes me another incandescent look, then turns to Dad with his charming smile. "So, Mick," he says. "What's the damage?"

"This is what I paid." Dad holds out a scribbled figure. "Shall we say half?"

"Let me think about that." Alex pockets the paper. "I need to get on. Katie, maybe you could show me some more of the farm? I feel we're not quite done with the subject."

There's an ominous tone to his voice, which makes my stomach flip over, but then I remind myself: He's not my boss anymore, is he?

"Sure," I say warily. "What do you want to know?"

"Oh, quite a lot, I'd say," says Alex, flashing me an unsmiling look. He strides purposefully out of the barn, and Dad hurries after him.

"You a man of business then, Alex?" he inquires.

"In a way." Alex smiles at Dad again. "Thanks for your time, Mick, but now I'm very keen for Katie to show me . . ." He turns to me. "The stables, was it?"

"We can look at the stables," I say with a shrug.

"Our Katie will show you whatever you want," puts in Dad eagerly. "Anything you need to know, just ask her."

"Oh, I will," says Alex, in the same ominous tone. "I will."

In silence I swivel and we head toward the stables. Neither of us speaks until we're out of Dad's earshot. Then Alex stops dead. He pulls out his flashing phone and reads the latest messages on it while I wait warily.

"OK, this is a bloody fiasco," he erupts at last. "I drive all this way to spare Demeter's feelings. I've got Adrian here asking, 'Have you dealt with her yet?'" He jabs at his phone. "And you tell me she *was* here but she's scarpered?"

"She hasn't *scarpered*," I retort. "She will face the music, but she just wants to have a chance to make her case. There's some email from Allersons that she thinks might be in her office at home."

"So she's gone home?" His eyes light up with this new information. "To Shepherd's Bush?"

At once I curse myself. I didn't need to give that detail away.

"Look . . . does it matter where she is?" I counter. "You're not exactly going to drive all the way to Shepherd's Bush on the off chance, are you? You're bound to miss her. You should just sit it out here. She'll arrive back here later, and then you can . . ."

I hesitate. I'm *not* going to say, *Then you can fire her.*

"Then you can work things out," I conclude. "Tell Adrian she's gone off on a hike and you can't get through to her. He'll never know the difference."

Alex shoots another glower at me, but I can tell he realizes I have a point. He's not going to go haring off to Shepherd's Bush on a wild-goose chase. He still doesn't look happy, though. In fact, he looks furious.

"You had no right to interfere," he says. "No right. *No* right. You don't work for Cooper Clemmow anymore; you have no idea what the issues are—"

"I know that Demeter deserves a chance!" Somewhere I find an inner robustness. "She isn't nearly as bad as everyone thinks! And taking her off guard like this—it's not fair. She deserves time to gather all the evidence she needs. She deserves a fair trial. Everyone deserves a fair trial."

I stop, breathing hard. I think I'm getting through to Alex. I can see it in his flickering, moody eyes.

"And what's more . . ." I hesitate. Am I going to risk saying this?

"What's more *what*?" he snaps.

"What's more . . . I think you agree with me, if you'll only admit it. There's a risk of a big injustice happening here. You don't want to be part of that. Do you?"

Alex is still silent and glowering. Which I can understand. I've made his life a lot more complicated. People hate that.

"Fine," he says at last, and jabs irritably at his phone. "Demeter can have her fair trial. She can have her time. What do I do meanwhile?"

"Whatever you like." I spread my arms wide. "You're the guest."

Alex looks around the stable yard, still scowling, as though nothing he sees can possibly clear his mood.

"Do you have Wi-Fi?"

"Of course we have Wi-Fi. And I can find you a place to work. Bit of a waste," I add quietly.

"What?" He turns sharply.

"Well, you're here now. You've made it to the countryside. You could enjoy yourself." I pause. "Or maybe firing people *is* how you enjoy yourself?"

I couldn't resist that one, and I can tell it's hit Alex on a sensitive spot. He winces and glares at me.

"Nice. Thanks. I'm clearly a power-crazy despot."

"Well, you said you volunteered for the task. How do I

know this isn't your hobby? Kite-flying, home-brewing, firing people."

I know I'm close to the wire here, but I don't care. I spent so long in London feeling like little Katie. Keeping quiet; in too much awe of everyone to speak out. But now, on home territory, I'm swinging the other way. Which might be reckless or even foolhardy—but I don't care. I *want* to push Alex's buttons. I *want* to get a reaction out of him. And it's a risky game, but my instinct is: I know just how hard to push.

Sure enough, for an instant Alex looks like he wants to explode. But then there's a flash of sunlight, a glimmer of a reluctant smile.

"Is this how you talk to all your B&B guests?" he says at last. "Find their sore points and skewer them?"

"I'm not sure yet," I say with a shrug. "Like I say, you're the first guest. How's it working out for you?"

I'm feeling a secret exhilaration: I judged it right. Alex doesn't say anything for a few moments, just looks at me with that tiny little smile around his lips. My hair is blowing around my face, and probably in London I would be frantically smoothing it down. But here I don't bother.

As though he's psychic, Alex's gaze shifts to my hair.

"Your hair's gone curly," he says. "And *blue*. Is that a Somerset thing?"

"Oh yes," I say. "We have our own micro fashion climate here. I'm the cover girl on Somerset *Vogue,* didn't you know?"

"I'll bet you are," says Alex—and there's something about his expression that makes me warm inside. We're still bantering, right? I swallow hard, the wind still gusting my hair, my eyes fixed on his. Just for a nanosecond, I can't think what to say.

"All right." Alex seems to come to. "Fair enough. I've come all this way. I should appreciate my surroundings. So: the countryside. Fill me in." He swivels around, taking in the panoramic view beyond all the farm buildings.

"Fill you in on 'the countryside'?" I can't help smiling. "What, like it's a new client and you're going to rebrand it?"

"Exactly. What's it all about? There's the greenness, obviously," he says, as though he's standing in front of a whiteboard at Cooper Clemmow. "The views . . . Turner . . . Hardy . . . I can't stand Hardy, as it happens—" Alex stops dead as something attracts his attention. "Wait. What's that?"

"That?" I follow his gaze, past the stables, into the backyard. "It's the Defender."

"It's *spectacular*." Alex is already hastening toward it and runs a hand admiringly over the old Land Rover. It's about twenty years old, all covered in mud, with the windscreen taped up because of the cracks. "I mean, this is a proper off-roader, isn't it?"

"Well, it's not a Chelsea tractor."

Now Alex's eyes are gleaming. "I've never driven off-road before. *Really* off-road."

"You want to drive?" I say, and hold out the keys. "Go on, city boy. Knock yourself out."

Alex wends his way carefully through the yard and out through the back gate, then speeds up as we get into the fields.

"Careful," I keep saying. "Not so fast. *Don't* run over a

sheep," I add, as he drives through the six-acre field. To be fair, he keeps well to the side and goes at a reasonable speed. But the minute we close the gate behind us in the empty far meadow, Alex is like a kid at the dodgems.

The meadow is a massive, bumpy, uncultivated mess—we actually get money from some government scheme for letting it grow wild. Alex drives at speed down one side of the meadow, then reverses at speed, then wheels around like a crazy person. If it wasn't so dry, he'd be skidding by now. He hurtles over a set of rough hillocks at such an angle that I cling on to the handle, then he heads up a steepish bank and careers off the top. He actually whoops as we fly through the air (albeit for a second or two), and I can't help laughing, even though I bumped my shoulder as we took off.

"Bloody *hell*!" I say, as we crash back down. "You're going to—"

I break off. Shit. He's heading toward the ditch. Except he can't see that it's a ditch because it's covered in long grass and reeds.

"Slow down," I say tensely. "Slow down!"

"Slow *down*? Are you nuts? This is the best thing I've done in my l-aaaaaargh!"

The Defender lurches down, and for a terrifying moment I think we might roll. My head has crashed on the ceiling. Alex has bumped himself on the open window frame. He frantically floors it, almost *willing* the Defender upward out of the ditch.

"Go!" I'm screaming. "Go!"

With an almighty whirring of wheels and growling of the engine, we manage to get out of the ditch, career bumpily along for a few hundred meters, then stop. I look at Alex and gasp. There's blood all over his face, dripping down his chin. He turns off the engine, and we stare at each other, both panting.

At last I say: "When I said, 'Knock yourself out,' I didn't literally mean *knock yourself out*."

Alex gives a half smile, then frowns, eyeing my face closely. "I'm fine. But are *you* OK? You got a real bash there. I'm sorry, I had no idea—"

"I'll live." I touch my forehead, which is already sprouting a bruise. "Ouch."

"Oh God, sorry." He looks shamefaced.

"Don't be." I take pity on him. "We've all done it. I learned to drive in this meadow. Got stuck in the ditch. Had to be pulled out with a tractor. Here." I reach in my pocket for a tissue. "You've got blood everywhere."

Alex scrubs the blood off his face, then peers through the windscreen. "Where are we?"

"The meadow. Come on, let's get out."

It's a pretty stunning day. It must be after one o'clock by now, and the sun is high in a cloudless sky. The grass is long and hay-like; the air is still and quiet. All I can hear are the skylarks singing, way, way above us, in their endless streaming ribbons of sound.

I get out the blanket we always keep in the back of the Defender and spread it over the grass. There's a box of cider we keep there too, safely moored under its netting, and I take two cans out.

"If you want to know about Somerset," I say, throwing a can to him, "then you need to drink our local cider. Only, watch ou—"

Too late. He's exploded the can all over himself.

"Sorry." I grin at him. "Meant to warn you. They've had a bit of a shaking."

I open my own can at arm's length and for a few moments we just sit there in the sun, sipping cider. Then Alex gets to his feet.

"OK, I *do* want to know about Somerset," he says, his eyes glinting. "What's that hill over there? And whose house is that on the horizon? And what are these little yellow flowers? Tell me everything."

I can't help laughing at his intensity. He's so *interested* in everything. I can totally imagine him cornering an astrophysicist at a drinks party and asking him to explain the universe.

But I like it too. So I get to my feet and follow him around the meadow, telling him about the landscape and the farm and the flowers and whatever else catches his eye.

At last the sun is getting too hot to keep striding around, and we settle back down on the blanket.

"What are those birds?" asks Alex, as he stretches out his legs, and I feel a tiny satisfaction that he noticed them. He didn't have to.

"Skylarks." I take another swig of cider.

"They don't shut up, do they?"

"No." I laugh. "They're my favorite birds. You get up early and you step outside and . . ." I pause, letting the familiar sound wash over me. "It feels like the sky's singing to you."

We're both silent again, and Alex seems to be listening intently to the birdsong. Maybe he's never heard skylarks before. I have no idea what his upbringing was.

"I called you a city boy before," I say tentatively. "But are you? Where did you grow up?"

"Try 'cities boy.'" He tilts his head as though recalling. "London, New York, Shanghai for a bit, Dubai, San Francisco. L.A. for six months when I was ten. We followed my dad's work."

"Wow."

"I've had thirty-seven addresses in my life. Been to twelve schools."

"Seriously?" I gape at him. Thirty-seven addresses? That's more than one a *year*.

"We lived in Trump Tower for a few months; that was cool. . . ." He catches my expression and winces. "Sorry. I know. I'm a privileged bastard."

"It's not your fault. You shouldn't—" I break off, biting my lip. I need to tackle something that's been bothering me ever since I saw him again. "Listen, I'm sorry for what I said at the office. That your famous daddy gave you your career."

"It's fine." He gives me a wry smile, which tells me he's heard it said a lot of times.

"No." I shake my head. "It's not fine; it was unfair. I don't know anything about how you started out, if you had an advantage—"

"Well, of course I had an advantage," he says calmly. "I watched my dad my whole childhood. I went into the office, the studio . . . I learned from him. So, yes, I had an advantage. But what was he supposed to do? *Not* share his job with me? Is that nepotism?"

"I don't know." I feel confused now. "Maybe not exactly. But it's not . . ." I trail off.

"What?"

"Well," I say awkwardly. "Fair, I suppose."

There's silence. Alex lies back and looks straight up at the endless blue sky, his face unreadable.

"You know the names of birds," he says. "You lived in the same house all your childhood. You have a two-hundred-year-old farming background keeping you stable and grounded. Your dad loves you more than anyone could love anything in the world. You can tell that in thirty seconds." He pauses. "That's not fair either."

"My *dad*?" I say, taken aback. "What do you mean? I'm sure your dad loves you too."

Alex says nothing. I survey his face, sidelong, and it's motionless except for a tiny twitch at his eye. Have I stumbled on ground I shouldn't have? But, then, he's the one who brought it up.

"Doesn't your dad—" I stop dead. I can't say, *Doesn't your dad love you?* "What's your dad like?" I amend.

"Super-talented," says Alex slowly. "Awe-inspiring. And a total shit. He's very driven. Very cold. He treated my mother badly. And, for what it's worth, he *didn't* get me my first job."

"But you had your name," I say before I can stop myself.

"Yes." His face crinkles as though in humor, but he's not smiling. "I had my name. That was half help, half hindrance. My dad's made a lot of enemies along the way."

"What about your mum?" I ask tentatively.

"She has . . . issues. She gets depressed. She withdraws. It's not her fault," he adds at once, and I can see a sudden boyish defensiveness in him.

"I'm sorry," I say, biting my lip. "I didn't realize."

"I spent quite a lot of my childhood being scared." Alex is still staring up at the sky. "I was scared of my dad. And sometimes of my mum. I spent most of my childhood like a fish. Weaving and darting. Trying to avoid . . . stuff."

"But you don't need to weave and dart anymore," I say.

I'm not even sure why I say it. Except that he suddenly looks like someone who's still weaving and darting. And is maybe a bit exhausted by it. Alex turns onto his side, rests his head in his hand, and looks at me with an odd, lopsided smile.

"Once you've got into the habit of weaving and darting, it's hard to stop."

"I suppose," I say slowly. My mind is still reeling at the idea of thirty-seven addresses. It's dizzying just to think about it.

"Whereas *your* dad . . ." Alex interrupts my thoughts, and I roll my eyes.

"Oh God. My dad. If he tries to sell you a bathroom suite, do *not* say yes."

"Your dad's lovable," says Alex, ignoring me. "He's strong. You should tell him the truth about your job, you know. This whole secret thing you've got going . . . it's wrong."

It takes a moment for Alex's words to hit home, and when they do, they make me inhale sharply. "Oh, you think so?"

"How's he going to feel when he realizes you've been keeping such a huge secret from him?"

"He might never have to know. So."

"But if he *does*? If he realizes you felt you couldn't come to him when you were in trouble? He'll be crushed."

"You don't know that!" I can't help lashing out a little. "You don't know anything about my dad."

"I know he brought you up pretty much on his own." Alex's steady tone is relentless. "Biddy told me all about it, earlier."

"*Biddy* told you?"

"I guess I quizzed her a little after I'd realized you lived here. I was interested. She told me how she came into your family and saw the way your dad loved you and thought if she could just get a *fraction* of that love, she'd be happy."

If I know how to press Alex's buttons, he sure as hell knows how to press mine too.

"I know Dad loves me," I say in a muffled voice. "And I love him. But it's not as simple as that. He was *so* betrayed when I left; he'll never accept that I'm a Londoner—"

"*Are* you a Londoner, though?" says Alex, and I feel a fresh stab of dismay. What else from my shaky house-of-cards life is he going to dismantle?

"You think I'm not a Londoner?" I say, in a trembling voice. "You think I can't cut it in the city?"

"It's not that!" says Alex, sounding taken aback. "Of course you can cut it in the city, a beautiful, talented girl like you? That's not the point. It's just . . ." He hesitates. "I think you're more torn than you'll admit."

OK, I've had enough.

"You barely *know* me," I say furiously. "You can't just come here and tell me about my life—"

"Maybe I've got fresh eyes? Perspective?" He cuts me off in reasonable tones, and I suddenly think of him looking at our view and seeing in an instant what was wrong with it. Then I shake my head, dismissing the thought. That was a *view*. I'm *me*.

"All I know," Alex continues, "is that you've got your farmhouse, your family, people who have known you forever—and that's worth something. You know how a rolling stone gathers no moss? Well, that's me." He gestures down at himself. "Not a fucking *speck* of moss. But you? You're a walking, talking mossball."

I look away. "That's irrelevant."

"It's not irrelevant. And, anyway, it's not just your family, it's . . ." He pauses. "I don't know, the way you talk about the land. The skylarks. It's in you. It's your heritage. You're a Somerset girl, Katie. You shouldn't deny that. You shouldn't lose your accent, change your hair. It's you."

I'm silent for a moment, brewing with thoughts, trying to respond calmly.

"You know why I got rid of the accent?" I say at last. "I was in the loos in my first job in Birmingham and I heard two girls talking. Taking the piss out of me. 'Farrrmer Katie' they called me. I wanted to burst out and slap them." I flop onto my back, breathing heavily at the memory.

Alex absorbs this for a few moments, then nods. "I was in the loos at school one day and I heard two sixth-formers talking. I'd just won the design prize. They assumed my dad had done the whole project for me. I wanted to burst out and thump *them*."

"Did you?" I can't help asking.

"No. Did you?"

"No."

Alex sips from his cider and I do the same. The sky is at its bluest and stillest at this time of day. There isn't a sound except the incessant skylarks.

"You don't have to choose, London or Somerset," says Alex at length. "You can be both, surely."

"My dad makes me feel I *have* to choose." A familiar strain comes over me. "He makes it this either-or situation. . . ."

"So you need to talk to him even *more,* surely. Not less."

"Will you stop being right?" The words burst out of me before I know I'm going to say them. Abruptly, breathing fast, I get to my feet and set off on a circle of the meadow. My thoughts are teeming; my ears are buzzing. I can't listen to Alex and his voice of reason anymore. But at the same time I'm craving some of his words again. The ones I think I might have misheard.

A beautiful, talented girl like you. Beautiful.

As I turn the corner, I see that he's stood up from the blanket too. It's so boiling hot, I can feel sweat trickling down my arms, and impulsively I peel off my shirt, leaving only a strappy, skimpy tank top underneath. I can see Alex blink at the sight; I can see him size up my body with barefaced desire. Ha. So I did read him right in the barn. And now I know for sure: There *was* a spark between us in London. I didn't need to apologize or feel embarrassed or any of it.

As I get near to Alex, my own lust levels are rocketing too. Only it's not as simple as that. I don't just want him; I want control. To jettison insecure, defensive little Katie with all her hang-ups and humiliations. I want to feel empowered. I've never particularly been a first-move kind of girl, but right now I can really see the point.

I head to the Defender, reach for two more cans of cider, and hold one out to him.

"Hot day," I say. "D'you mind if I sunbathe?" And before I can get cold feet, I peel off my tank top.

There. How's *that* for a first move? I've never done anything so bold in my life, and I feel a slight inner breathlessness.

It's a good bra I've got on—a black lace balconette one, very flattering—and Alex stares frankly at my tits as though he's in some kind of torture heaven. As I crack open my cider, he starts, then, without speaking, takes his own can and opens it.

The atmosphere is unbearably charged. My head feels muzzy and I can barely breathe. All I can think is, *I'm standing here in my bra* and *I'd better not have misread this* and *What happens now?*

"Maybe I'll sunbathe too," Alex says at length, and strips off his shirt. His torso is leaner than I expected, almost boyish, with a strip of dark hair running downward from his navel. I can't quite tear my eyes away from it. "Plenty of time before Demeter'll get back," he adds. His eyes are running over me too, and I feel my breath coarsening in response. There I was, obsessing about the "sizzling chemistry" he had with Demeter. Well, this is pretty sizzling.

"Loads of time," I manage, my voice sounding blurry to my own ears. "And nobody will disturb us here. We can sunbathe all afternoon," I add for good measure. "As long as we like."

"Luckily, I've got sunbathing protection on me," says Alex slowly. His eyes meet mine and I know exactly what he means, and I almost want to laugh, except I'm so desperate.

"So, what factor are you?" I step forward and run a hand down his chest. "Because it's pretty hot out here."

In answer, he cups my waist and presses his chest to mine, his hands swiftly roaming below my jeans waistband. As I inhale his scent—part sweat, part soap, part Alex—I feel a fresh, sharp flare of hunger. *God,* I need this.

Sex has not been on my agenda for a long time, and I can feel my body waking up, like a dragon after hibernation. Every nerve ending. Every pulsing bit of me.

"You know, I wanted to sunbathe with you the moment I met you," says Alex into my neck, and his lips brush along my skin, making me whimper.

"Me too," I murmur back, unbuttoning his jeans, trying to move things along.

"But I was your boss. It would have been fucked up. . . ." He hesitates and draws back, his brow crumpled. "Hey, wait. You *are* OK with this? I mean, you're not . . ." He hesitates. "This is a yes?"

When I was at senior school, I studied judo for three years. Without thinking twice, I wrap my foot round Alex's leg, unbalance him, and pin him on the ground, ignoring his startled cry.

I straddle him, looking down at him, feeling more in charge of my life right now than I have done in a long time. I lean down, cup his face, and find his mouth for a long, sweet kiss, and for the first time I think, *You. There you are.* Men's mouths are like their personalities, I find. (Which is why I never really took to kissing Steve.) Then I sit up, unhook my bra, and toss it aside, relishing Alex's instant, unmistakable reaction.

"It's a yes," I say, and lean down to kiss him again. "Don't you worry. It's a yes."

CHAPTER EIGHTEEN

We wake up in the early evening, a breeze cooling our skin. Alex glances at me and I see a sleepy smile come to his eyes. Then reality sets in.

"Shit." He scrambles to his feet. "What time is it? Have we been *asleep*?"

"It's the country air," I say. "Knocks everyone out."

"It's six." I can see him doing calculations in his head. "Demeter might be back."

"Maybe." I feel my rosy glow dim a little. I don't want the bubble to burst. But Alex is already out of the bubble, his face alert, his fingers moving quickly as they do up his buttons.

"OK. We need to get back. I need to—" He breaks off and I finish the sentence in my head. *Fire Demeter*.

Already, he looks beleaguered and stressed out by the thought. Maybe some bosses get a kick out of sacking people and throwing their weight around—but it really doesn't suit Alex.

I take the wheel this time, and as we bump back to the farmhouse, I can't resist speaking my mind.

"You're not enjoying this prospect, are you?"

"What, having to fire my friend and mentor?" he replies evenly. "Funnily enough, no. And I know she's going to try to wriggle out of it, which will make it even harder."

"But even if she wasn't your friend and mentor?"

Alex is silent, his face taut, as we bump over a hillocky patch of ground. Then he sighs. "OK. You got me. I'm not cut out to be a boss."

"I didn't say that!" I say, dismayed. "That's not what I meant—"

"It's true, though," he interrupts. "This management stuff—I hate it. It's not *me*. I should never have taken on the role."

I drive on, feeling a bit speechless. The famous Alex Astalis feels insecure about his job?

"Have you ever shaken up a compass and seen the arrow whirling around, trying to find a place to settle?" says Alex abruptly. "Well, that's my brain. It's all over the place."

"Demeter's like that," I volunteer. "Totally scattershot."

"If you think Demeter's bad, I'm ten times worse." Alex gives me a wry grin. "But bosses aren't like that. They're focused. They can compartmentalize. They like process. And long tedious meetings." He shudders. "Everything I hate, bosses love. Yet here I am, a boss."

"No one likes long, tedious meetings," I protest. "Even bosses."

"OK, maybe not all bosses do," he allows. "But a lot of manager types do. Biscuit people do."

"*Biscuit* people?" I snort with laughter.

"That's what I call them. They come into the meeting room and sit down and take a biscuit and plop back with this air of contentment, like *Well, life can't get any better than this, can it?* It's as though they're settling in for a long-haul flight and they're pretty chuffed to get the legroom and who cares what else goes on?"

I grin. "So you're not a biscuit person."

"I never even sit down at meetings." Alex looks abashed. "It drives everyone mad. And I can't deal with conflict. I can't manage people. It bores me. It gets in the way of ideas. And *that's* why I shouldn't be a boss." He sighs, gazing out of the window at the passing landscape. "Every promotion requires you to do less of the thing you originally wanted to do. Don't you find?"

"No," I say bluntly. "If I got a promotion I'd do *more* of the thing I want to do. But, then, I'm at the opposite end from you."

Alex winces. "That makes me sound ancient."

"You are ancient. In prodigy years."

"Prodigy years?" Alex starts to laugh. "Is that like dog years? Anyway, who says I'm a prodigy?"

"You came up with Whenty when you were twenty-one," I remind him.

"Oh yeah," he says, as though he'd half-forgotten. "Well, that was just . . . you know. Luck." He comes to. "Shall I get that gate?"

I watch as he unhooks the gate, then drive through and wait for him to close it and hop back in. The engine's still running, but for a moment I don't move. We're in a kind of limbo-land here, and I want to broach something with Alex, while I have the chance.

"Was it really luck?" I say tentatively. "Or do you think maybe you were trying to impress your father?"

I want to add: *Is that why you can't stand conflict?* But let's not turn into Freud.

Alex is silent for a few minutes, and I can see thoughts buzzing round his eyes.

"Probably," he says at last. "Probably still am." Then he turns to me, with a wry acknowledging smile. "Will you stop being right?"

I grin back—*touché*—and start driving on again. I sense that Alex might carry on unburdening himself, and, sure enough, after a few moments he draws breath.

"Sometimes I worry my ideas might dry up," he says, an odd tone to his voice. "I'm not sure who I'd be without them. Sometimes I think I'm really just an empty vessel floating about, downloading ideas and not much else."

"You're a funny, gorgeous, sexy guy," I say at once, and he smiles at me as though I'm joking. I can tell he's not pretending: He really feels this. I can't believe *I* need to bolster Alex Astalis.

"What would you do," I say impulsively, "if you weren't rushing round the world, creating award-winning branding concepts?"

"Good question." Alex's face lights up. "Live on a farm. Drive the Defender. That was the best fun I've had in *years*. Eat Biddy's scones." We come to a halt in the yard, and Alex twines his fingers around mine on the steering wheel. "Kiss a beautiful girl every day."

"You'd have to find a farm with a beautiful girl on it," I point out.

"Don't they all come with beautiful girls?" His dark eyes glow at me. "This one does."

Beautiful. That word again. I want to take it away in my hands and keep it in a jar forever. But instead I smile easily back, as if perhaps I didn't even hear him, and say, "Not all of them, no."

"I'd put it in the search engine, then. En suite bathroom, fields of sheep, beautiful girl with freckles like stardust." He touches my nose. "Actually, I think there *is* only one of those."

He leans over to kiss me—and there he is again. The sweet, gentle Alex that's been such a surprise. The truth is, I'm falling for this guy, and I can't find a single reason in my brain not to, except for Demeter's voice running through my mind: *Any woman who got involved with Alex Astalis would have to be insane*.

Why insane? I need to talk to her.

"Maybe you shouldn't be a boss anymore," I say as we finally draw apart, my head buzzing a little. "I'm not sure it's making you happy."

"Maybe you're right." He nods, his eyes absent—then suddenly focuses on me. "Whereas you, Katie, *should* be a boss. You will be, one day. I know it. You'll be a big boss."

"What?" I stare at him in disbelief.

"Oh yes." He nods matter-of-factly. "You've got what it takes. Stuff I haven't got. You've got a way with people. I watched you just now, managing your cleaner. You know what you want and you make it happen and nothing gets broken. There's a skill in that."

I gaze back at Alex, feeling a bit overcome. No one's ever said anything like that to me before, and my insecure, defensive hackles can't help rising: Is he just being kind? But he doesn't look like he's trying to do me a favor. There's not one patronizing note in his voice—he sounds like he's saying it as he sees it.

"Come on." He opens the door. "I can't put off the evil moment anymore. Let's see if Demeter's back."

I'm half-hoping Demeter will be at the farmhouse already, will greet us with her old Demeter panache and stride around on her long legs with some story about how she's fixed everything and spoken to Adrian and it's all *marvelous* now. But there's no sign of her.

The afternoon's golden glow has ebbed away, and Dad's already got a campfire going at the center of the yurt village. On Tuesday nights we always have a campfire, sausages, toasted marshmallows, and a singsong. Everyone loves a fire and a singsong after a few beers—even though the actual songs we sing depend on who the glampers are. (One time we had a guy staying who'd been a backing singer for Sting. That was amazing. But last week we had the I-know-all-of-Queen's-repertoire-listen-to-me! dad. That was *bad*.)

Biddy is walking along the path, lighting lanterns as she goes, and she looks up with a smile as I approach.

"Hi," I say breathlessly. "Have you seen Demeter?"

"*Demeter*? No, love. I thought she'd gone to London."

"She did. But I thought she might be back. . . ." I sigh anxiously, then glance at Alex. He's standing on the edge of the yurt village, already scowling miserably at his phone. He must be picking up his emails.

"Look, there's nothing you can do for now," I say, tapping his shoulder. "Why not come and sit by the campfire and . . . you know. Relax?"

The campfire usually brings out the inner child in people, and I'm hoping it might appeal to the quirky, playful side of Alex that I love. As we sit down on the grass, the flames cast an orange flickering light on his face. The familiar crackle-and-spit sound of the fire instantly calms my nerves, and the smell is like every bonfire night I've ever known. I turn to see if he's enjoying it too—but his face is still tense and preoccupied. Bearing in mind the situation, I can't really blame him.

On the plus side, everyone else seems to be having fun. All the glampers are toasting marshmallows, leaning forward with their toasting irons. Occasionally Giles throws a firelighter onto the fire to get an extra-large flame, and I lean politely over to him.

"Actually . . . that's a bit dangerous for the children?"

"Only a bit of fun," he says, but stops and swigs his beer and I breathe out. The last thing we need is some monster flame singeing someone's eyebrows. I mean, we do have enormous buckets of water placed at strategic points, but even so.

On the other side of the fire there seems to be a bit of jostling and dispute going on.

"Stop it!" exclaims Susie suddenly, and I realize a full-scale row is breaking out. "No one else can get a look in!" she's saying heatedly to Cleo. "Your children have pinched all the best places, all the toasting irons. . . ."

"For heaven's sake," says Cleo in her drawling way. "It's a campfire. Relax."

"I'll relax when my children can toast marshmallows as well as yours—"

"Here we go! Here we go now!" Dad's cheerful voice penetrates the atmosphere, and we all look up to see him skipping into view with a jingle-jingle sound. He's wearing white trousers, a waistcoat, jingle bells attached to his legs, and sticks in his hands. Accordion music is playing from a CD player plonked on the grass. "La-la-la . . ." He starts singing some random line or other. "La-la-la . . . And-a-one-and-a-two . . ."

"Farmer Mick!" shriek the children as though he's a celebrity. "Farmer Mick!"

I clap a hand over my mouth, trying not to laugh. Dad's been talking about Morris dancing, but I didn't think he'd actually *do* it. I mean, what the hell does he know about Morris dancing?

He's still humming an indistinct tune and skipping about, and every so often he bangs his sticks. You couldn't call it dancing. More . . . capering. The grown-ups are watching as if they're not sure if it's a joke or not, but the children are all whooping and cheering.

"Who's going to be my assistant?" Dad whips a bell-covered stick from his waistcoat and proffers it at the children. "Who wants to join the dance?"

"Me!" they all shout, grabbing for the bell stick. "Meeeeee!"

I can see Poppy standing up eagerly. She's the little girl who's here with her single dad, and she seems really sweet. But Cleo at once pushes Harley forward.

"Harley, you dance, darling. Harley does ballet and jazz dance and Stagecoach every Saturday—"

"For God's sake, give it a *rest*!" Susie explodes. "Poppy, why don't you dance, sweetheart?"

"Give what a rest?" demands Cleo, sounding offended. "I'm simply pointing out that my child is a trained dancer. . . ."

I catch Dad's eye and he gets my drift at once.

"Everybody dance!" he bellows. "All the kiddies up! And-a-one-and-a-two-and-a—"

"Katie." A voice in my ear makes me turn, and I see Demeter's son, Hal, at my side.

"Hi, Hal!" I greet him. "Have you toasted a marshmallow yet?" Then I look more closely at him. He's pale and blinking hard. "Hal," I say urgently. "What's happened? What's up?"

"It's Coco." He looks a bit desperate. "She's . . . she's drunk."

Thankfully she made it out of the yurt in time. I find her retching into a nearby patch of grass and put a comforting arm around her whilst simultaneously averting my eyes and thinking, *Urgh. Gross. Hurry up.*

When she seems a bit better, I lead her over to the outdoor shower. I'm not going to drench her—even though it's tempting—but instead I dampen a sponge and clean her up a bit, then get her back to the yurt.

I mean, it could be worse. She could be comatose. As it is, she's able to walk and talk, and there's already a bit of color returning to her cheeks. She'll live.

"Sorry," she keeps saying in a mumbly voice. "I'm so sorry."

As we get into the yurt, I flinch at the sight. So this is what happens when two teenagers are left to their own devices for a day. There are plates and crumbs *everywhere*—they must have been raiding Biddy's larder—plus sweet wrappers, phones, an iPad, magazines, makeup . . . and, sitting in the middle of it all, a half-empty bottle of vodka. Nice.

I put Coco into bed, prop her up against a mound of pillows, then sit on the bed. I gesture at the vodka bottle and sigh. *"Why?"*

"Dunno," says Coco, with a defensive, sulky shrug. "I was bored."

Bored. I look at the magazines and the iPad. I think about the campfire and the marshmallows and Dad capering like a mad thing, just to entertain everyone. I think about Demeter, working her socks off to pay for Jack Wills hoodies.

I should have taken bloody *Coco* to muck out the stable, that's what I should have done.

"Where did you get it?"

"Brought it. Are you going to tell Mum?" Coco's voice quickens with worry.

"I don't know." I give her a stern look. "You know, your mum really loves you. She works super-hard to pay for all your cool stuff. And you're not that nice to her."

"We said thank you for the holiday," says Coco in a defensive way.

"What, so that's it, you say 'thank you' once and you're quits? And what's this 'Mrs. Invisible' crap I keep hearing? If there's one thing your mum's not, it's invisible. And you know what? It's hurtful. Really hurtful."

I can see Coco and Hal exchanging guilty looks. I think

they're actually quite nice kids; they've just got into a bad habit of being down on their mum. And their dad hasn't been helping. But he's not here right now.

And then a new thought hits me. If Demeter's managed to hide all her best qualities from her own staff, she's probably done the same with her kids too.

"Listen," I say. "Do you even *know* what your mum does at work?"

"Branding," says Coco, so tonelessly that I know it's just a word to her.

"OK. And do you know how awesome she is at it? Do you know how clever and bright and brilliant she is?"

Both Coco and Hal look vacant. Clearly this thought has never passed through their brains.

"How do you know about my mum's work?" queries Hal.

"I used to work in the same area. And, believe me, your mum is a legend. A *legend*."

I pat the bed, and after a moment Hal comes to sit down. I feel like I'm telling the pair of them a bedtime story. *Once upon a time there was a scary monster called Demeter, only she wasn't really scary after all. Or a monster.*

"Your mum's full of ideas," I tell them. "She's bursting with them. She sees a packaging design and she instantly knows what's wrong or right with it."

"Yeah," says Coco, rolling her eyes. "We know. You go round the supermarket and she's got an opinion on, like, every single box."

"Right. So, did you know she's won a stack of awards for those opinions? Did you know that she can inspire big teams of people to do amazing work? She can take a whole bunch of ideas and distill them into a concept, and as soon as she says it you think, *Yes.*"

I glance up, and they're both listening intently.

"Your mum can bring a room to life," I continue. "She makes people think. You can't be lazy when she's around. She's original, she's inspiring . . . she's inspired *me*. I wouldn't be who I am without her."

I said that more for effect than anything else—but as the words hit the air, I realize I mean them. If it weren't for Demeter, I wouldn't have learned everything that I have. I wouldn't have created the Ansters Farm brochure and website in the same way. We might not have taken off.

"You're very lucky to have her as your mum," I conclude. "And I know, because I don't have a mum."

"Isn't Biddy your mum?" Coco looks puzzled.

"She's my stepmum. And she wasn't around when I was younger. I grew up with no mum, so I was *especially* observant. I looked at everyone else's mums. And yours is one of the best. She's having a really tough time at work right now, did you know that?" I add.

Coco and Hal look at me dumbly. Of course they didn't know. Another trouble with Demeter, I'm realizing, is her instinct to protect others. Protect Rosa from knowing she was rejected. Protect her kids from knowing she's stressed. Keep up the charmed, life-is-perfect myth.

Well, enough. These kids aren't toddlers; they can bloody well support her.

"Maybe she hasn't told you." I shrug. "But take it from me,

things are difficult. And the way you can help is to be charming and appreciative and keep this yurt tidy and *not* ask for stuff or complain or get pissed on vodka."

I eye Coco, and she looks away.

"I won't," she mumbles, so indistinctly I can barely hear her.

"I'll tidy up the yurt," volunteers Hal, who seems eager to make amends.

"Great." I stand up to leave. "And, Hal, keep an eye on Coco. Do *not* leave her. Any problems, you come and get me or the nearest grown-up. I'll be back in half an hour to check on you. OK?"

Hal nods vigorously. "OK."

"Are you going to tell Mum?" Coco's plaintive voice comes from the bed. "Please?"

Her face is pale and she's lost that annoying, sulky chin-jut she often has. She actually looks about ten years old. But I'm not letting her off the hook that easily.

"Depends," I say, and push my way out of the yurt.

As I'm walking across the field, I come upon Dad, sitting alone on a bench, sipping a can of beer. His Farmer Mick hat is off, his bells are lying silent by his side, and he looks exhausted.

"Hi, Dad." I sit down beside him.

"Hi, love." He turns to look at me, his eyes crinkling in affection. "Where did you go rushing off to just now?"

"Coco." I roll my eyes. "Drank too much. I had to sort her out."

"*Drank* too much?" Dad's eyes open wide, then he gives a wry shrug. "They all do it. I remember you coming home once from a party in a terrible state. About her age, you were."

"I remember that too." I grimace. I'd had too many black velvets, as I recall. *Not* one of my finest moments.

"I was that worried. Sat up all night with you, dozy fool that I was." He grins merrily. "You woke up as right as rain, ate a plateful of eggs and bacon!"

I'd forgotten Dad sat up all night with me. He must have been really stressed out. And just him; no one to share it with.

"Sorry." I give him an impulsive hug.

"You don't need to say sorry. What else are dads for?" He sips his beer, and as he moves, the bells jingle at his side.

"I like the Morris dancing," I say. "It's funny."

"Well, it keeps them entertained, doesn't it?" Dad flashes me another smile, but I can still see a cast of weariness in his face.

"Listen, Dad . . . don't overdo it, will you? You and Biddy. You're putting so much energy into this."

"Paying off, though, isn't it?" He spreads an arm toward the campfire; the contented hubbub of the glampers; the shadowy yurts. "Finally got something right, Katie, love. *You* got it right."

"We *all* got it right," I correct him. "I think 'Farmer Mick' is about fifty percent of our success."

"Ha!" Dad gives a pleased laugh. "Keeps me young." He sips his beer again, and for a while we're silent. Then he adds, in slightly wary tones, "You need to be careful about overdoing it too, love."

"*Me?*"

"I saw you at the computer the other day. Stressed out, you looked. They shouldn't be working you like that. You've got enough on your plate here."

He pats my shoulder and my stomach clenches so hard, I have to shut my eyes briefly. I feel a bit winded by the sudden realization that Alex is right. This situation is bad. I can't keep lying to Dad about my job, I *can't*.

"Actually . . . Dad . . ." I begin, feeling sick. How am I going to put this? Where do I start? What if he flips out?

"Yes, love?" replies Dad absently. He's peering through the dusk at some distant approaching figure. Probably just a glamper wandering around.

"Dad, I need to talk to you about something." I swallow hard. "It's about me . . . and . . . and my job in London. . . ."

"Oh yes?" Dad's face closes up slightly. He's clearly not very keen on hearing about my job in London. If only he knew what I was about to tell him.

"Well. The thing is . . ." I rub my nose, feeling even sicker. "It's . . . What's happened is—"

"Dave!" Dad's exclamation drowns me out. "Dave Yarnett! What are you doing here, you old rogue?"

Dave Yarnett? My eyes focus in disbelief on the familiar figure of Dave, in his trademark black leather jacket. His paunch is snugly clad in a knockoff Calvin Klein T-shirt, his graying beard neatly trimmed and his eyes sparkling as he approaches.

"Mick!" He slaps Dad on the back. "Can't stay long. Just wanted you to have first look at my latest lot. You interested in rugs? Persian rugs?"

"We don't need any rugs," I say at once, and Dave shoots me a look of gentle reproach.

"Now, Katie, I'm offering your dad a retail opportunity here. All these glampers of yours—they've got houses to furnish, haven't they? I got this job lot of rugs from a bloke in Yeovil. Proper Persian antiques. Bit of furniture too. Take a look, anyway."

"Sorry, Katie." Dad pats me on the shoulder again. "I'll just have a quick look. Be back in a minute."

I know Dad. He can never resist a poke around Dave Yarnett's van.

"OK, no problem." I shrug, feeling a guilty relief wash over me. I'll tell him later, when it's a better time. When I've worked out a script. And maybe had a vodka or two. "Hey, *don't* buy any rugs," I call after Dad, as he disappears off with Dave. "Not without discussing it. We're a partnership now!"

I sit there awhile longer, watching the sky change tone gradually, from intense mid-blue to a softer indigo. Dave's van disappears back down the drive and I see Dad making his way over to the campfire again. I just hope he isn't making plans to turn us into the Ansters Farm Glamping and Rug Emporium.

I decide to head back over to the fire myself, toast a marshmallow, and get myself a sugar hit. But as I'm walking in that direction, I see a familiar car wending its way up the drive. Oh my God. Demeter.

I increase my pace to a run and arrive in the farmyard as she's getting out. She looks white and exhausted. Her eyebrows are drawn in a frown and there's a piece of paper in her hand, which she keeps glancing at.

I'm about to greet her when another voice gets in first: "Hello, Demeter."

It's Alex, stepping out of the kitchen door. He's holding his phone and staring grimly at Demeter. Like an assassin.

"I'd like to see you for a meeting," he says. "Biddy says we can use the sitting room."

I feel a dart of shock. *That's* what he's been doing. Setting up the execution chamber.

"*Now?*" Demeter seems a little stunned. "Alex, I've only just got back. I need some time, I need a chance . . ."

"You've had plenty of time. Plenty of chances." His voice is strained, and I can tell he's been psyching himself up to do this. "Things have been getting worse for months. Now they've tipped over the edge. Demeter, you *know* that. Things are a shambles. And that's why we need to talk."

"I need to work some things out first." Demeter closes her car door, then comes toward him on trembling legs, her eyes like shadows in her pale face. "Please, Alex. Give me till tomorrow."

"Demeter." He steps toward her, his face tight, avoiding her eye. "I don't want to be doing this, you *know* I don't, but I have to. Things have got out of hand and they can't carry on. We'll put together a story for the press; you'll get a good package—" He stops. "We should go to the meeting room."

"I'm not going to any meeting room." Demeter shakes her head adamantly. "Alex, there's another side to this. There's stuff that doesn't make sense. I need to show it to you."

But Alex isn't listening.

"All we think is, you took on a big job," he presses on doggedly, as though reading lines. "It was too much, but it's not your fault—"

"Stop the spiel, Alex!" Demeter yells. "Just listen to what I have to say! OK, so I went home today. I looked through some old emails, trying to . . . I don't know. Work out what the hell has been going on." She gestures to a massive bin bag I hadn't noticed before, stuffed full of email printouts.

"What the *hell*?" says Alex incredulously, as some of the printouts start to flutter on the evening breeze.

"They were in my attic. I print out a lot of emails," says Demeter defensively. "I know it's old-fashioned, but . . . Anyway, so I found this." She holds out the paper and Alex glances at it without interest.

"It's an email."

"Look at it!" Demeter exclaims, shaking it at him. "Actually *look* at it!"

Alex puts both fists to his face. "You will *kill* me," he says in a muffled voice. He looks up. "OK, *what*?" He takes the paper, reads it, then raises his head again blankly. "It's an email from Lindsay at Allersons. Forwarded to you from Sarah, two weeks ago. So what?"

"Read it aloud."

For a moment, Alex looks as though he might spontaneously combust. But he starts to read: *"Dear Demeter, thanks for that, and I must say, we appreciate your ongoing patience—"*

"Stop there." Demeter lifts a hand. "My *ongoing patience.* Do you see? My *ongoing patience.*"

Alex frowns blankly. "What about it?"

"Why would Allersons 'appreciate my ongoing patience'? They say they were waiting for us to get a move on. So why would I have needed to be patient?"

"Who knows?" Alex brushes it off. "It's a turn of phrase."

"It's not! It's crucial! This email fits with *my* version of things, where they told me to halt on everything until further notice. I remember reading it. I replied to it! Do you realize I thought I was going mad?" She jabs at the paper. "Well, I'm not!"

"Jesus, Demeter." Alex sounds exasperated. "We've been through this. Sarah's shown us the email correspondence; *none* of it accords with what you're saying—"

"Well, that's my point!" She cuts him off, trembling.

"What? What's your point?"

"I don't know exactly. At least . . ." She sounds suddenly hesitant and less Demeter-ish. "I know it sounds far-fetched, but maybe someone hacked into my computer and . . . I don't know. Messed with my emails."

"Oh Jesus." Alex looks as though this is all he needs.

"Alex, I *know* I received an email from Lindsay, telling me that Allersons wanted to pause. It said they were waiting for some research to come in." Demeter's voice shoots up in agitation. "I read it! I *saw* it!"

"OK, so show me now. Is it on your laptop?"

"No." Demeter looks beleaguered. "It . . . it disappeared. I went up to London to find the printout, and I couldn't, but I found this one instead. This email isn't on my computer either. I know, I *know* it sounds crazy . . . but look. This is proof. Look!" She thrusts the paper at him and he reluctantly takes it. "If you give me time to go through all my old printouts . . . I'm sure I've been hacked, or *something*. . . ."

"Stop saying that!" Alex looks properly upset. "Demeter, I'm an old friend and I'm telling you: *Don't* go around saying things like that. You sound—" He breaks off. "Who would do it, anyway? And why?"

"I don't *know*." Demeter sounds desperate. "But it doesn't make sense, nothing makes sense—"

"Hey," I chip in. I've been gazing at the email over Alex's shoulder and something's caught my attention. "Look at the email address. It should be Demeter-dot-Farlowe at Cooper Clemmow-dot-com. But this has been sent to Demeter-*underscore*-Farlowe at Cooper Clemmow-dot-com. It's a totally different email account."

Even Alex is silenced. He peers closely at the email address, his brow furrowed.

"Oh my God." Demeter grabs the paper from him. "I never even *noticed* that."

"There are lots of possible explanations," begins Alex. "It could be . . . I don't know. An IT-department experiment. Or maybe you started a new email account yourself and forgot—"

"Me, start an email account?" retorts Demeter derisively. "Are you joking? I wouldn't know where to start! Sarah does all that stuff. She organizes my emails, she forwards things, she's the only one who ever—" Demeter breaks off and we meet eyes. And I feel a huge lurch.

Sarah.

It's like a curtain has fallen down. I can suddenly see. *Sarah*. Oh my *God*.

Demeter's face has turned ashen. I can see her mind is turning over this idea as quickly as I am. Sarah. *Sarah*.

It all makes sense. Emails changing . . . messages disappearing . . . Sarah and her hostile, exaggerated patience . . . Demeter standing in the office, peering at her phone as though she thinks she's going mad . . .

"*Sarah?*" I say at last.

"Sarah," echoes Demeter, looking a bit ill. "Oh God."

"What?" Alex is looking from Demeter to me and back again. "Who's Sarah?"

Demeter seems speechless. So I draw breath, trying to organize my racing thoughts.

"She's Demeter's PA. You know, with the ponytail? She basically runs Demeter's life. She writes emails in Demeter's voice; she *is* Demeter, often. And she's always forwarding Demeter's emails back to her when they get deleted. So she could easily . . . well . . ." I breathe out. "Fake one."

"*Why?*" Alex looks bewildered. "Why would anyone do that?"

Again, Demeter and I exchange looks. It's hard to convey an office atmosphere to someone who hasn't lived in it forty hours a week.

"To screw with me," says Demeter, her voice bleak. "At least, I would imagine."

"Again—*why*?"

"My relationship with her hasn't been . . . perfect." Demeter is wringing her thin hands.

"She's never forgiven you for making her boyfriend redundant," I venture. "She wrote me this whole letter about it. She sounded pretty bitter. And if she's been holding that against you all this time, if she wanted to get revenge—"

"OK, let's stop right here." Alex interrupts, looking alarmed. "These are *very* serious accusations—"

"Think about it, Demeter," I continue, ignoring Alex. "She ran your in-box. She could enable different accounts. Control which emails you saw and didn't see, write replies in your name, send things and delete them—I mean, she could conduct an entire fake correspondence if she wanted to."

I'm recalling how Sarah would boast about how many emails she used to send out in Demeter's voice. "I've been Demeter *all afternoon,*" she used to say, in that long-suffering way. And who checked them? I bet Demeter never did.

"Enough!" snaps Alex. "There's no evidence for this."

"This is evidence!" Demeter shakes the page at him. "This is! It doesn't make any sense! And there were other emails like this; I *saw* them."

"But you say you *replied* to them too," objects Alex.

"Yes." Demeter's face falls. "I did." She puts her fingers to her brow, looking desperate. "Oh God, nothing makes sense—"

"Did you ever check the email address you were replying to?" I ask. "Lindsay's address?"

"What?" Demeter stares at me. "Of course not. It just popped up in my email contacts."

"Well, then." I shrug. "I'm guessing your replies never made it to Lindsay. And we can *prove* it," I add in sudden inspiration. "Ask Lindsay if she ever sent Demeter this email." I gesture at the paper. "And if she says she didn't—"

"Contact Allersons?" echoes Alex incredulously. "Allersons never want to speak to any of us again!"

"Then commandeer Sarah's computer. They can trace all this stuff. . . ."

"Are you mad?" He glares at me. "Do you *know* what a state our staff morale is in right now? You think I'm going to go blundering in with these fantasyland tales? Demeter, you're an old friend and I respect you very deeply, but this is over. *Over*."

"You're not still getting rid of Demeter?" I say in disbelief. "Not after this?"

"There is no 'this'!" he explodes. "Demeter, when you said 'evidence,' I thought you meant *evidence*. Something *solid*. Not one email and a far-fetched theory. I'm sorry. You've had your chance, but now it's the end of the line."

And the way he says it, my heart starts to thud.

"Alex, leave it till tomorrow," says Demeter, sounding desperate. "Sleep on it."

"I have people on my back. I need to get this done." He rubs his face, looking thoroughly miserable. "So if you're really refusing to come to the meeting room, refusing to do this properly—"

"Stop!" My voice rockets up in panic. "Stop! Don't fire!"

"You're fired." Alex's voice is like a bullet. "End of."

"You can't do that!" I cry, outraged. "Un-fire her!"

But Alex is already stalking out of the yard, back toward the yurt village. The fire is still in full blaze, and some of the glampers are singing along to a guitar. Steve Logan has joined the throng, and I can see him swaying along to "Brown Eyed Girl."

"You can't do that!" I shout again as I leg it after Alex. "That wasn't even a proper firing! It was against EU regulations!"

I have no idea if that's true, but it probably is.

"*Please,* Alex," says Demeter, hurrying beside me. "This email is proof that something weird's been going on. And if you can't even—"

She stops abruptly as Dad looms out of the darkness, jingling his Morris-dancing bells at her.

"La-la-la . . . and-a-one-and-a-two . . ." He bangs his sticks together cheerily at Demeter and she flinches, dropping the email printout.

"Shit!" I shout, as the paper gusts away on the breeze.

"Get the email!" shouts Demeter, chasing it desperately. "Get it!"

We're both running frantically after the floating paper, toward the fire, stumbling over children's feet in the darkness, causing a trail of shrieks and "ow"s but not caring. We *have* to get that email.

"Excuse me . . . let me through . . ." I edge past Cleo and Giles, who are lying full length in front of the campfire as Nick strums his guitar.

"Well, really," says Cleo, affronted. "There's room for everyone, you know. . . ."

"Oh God," gasps Demeter, swiping for the paper but missing.

"Get it!"

"I'm trying to—"

"*No!*" I scream in sudden dread as I see Giles reaching for another firelighter to throw on the flames. "No, don't, *don't*—"

But it's too late; he's thrown it. The fire flares up with a fresh burst of energy and catches the paper midair. Within twenty seconds it's burned away to nothing except a few specks of ash.

It's gone.

I'm so stunned, I can't move for about thirty seconds. Then I turn to Demeter and she looks like a ghost.

"Demeter, it'll be OK," I say desperately. "*I* believe you; something strange has *definitely* been going on—shit!" I gasp as I see a spark coming from her trousers. "Your leg! Fire! *FIRE!*"

To my horror, Demeter's slouchy linen trousers have started to smolder at the edges. She must have caught a flame when she was trying to get the email.

"No," she says, as though this is the last straw, and starts stamping her foot, trying to quench the flames.

"Buckets!" cries Dad, dropping his jingle-bell stick and running. "Fire! Get the buckets!"

"Coming through, coming through, coming through, everyone—" Steve's strident, intoning voice cuts through the hubbub. The next thing I know, there are screams and cries of surprise, Demeter is drenched in freezing water, head to foot, and Steve is standing there with an empty bucket and a look of grim satisfaction.

I cannot believe he just did that.

"Well . . . thanks," says Demeter, shivering and pushing her dripping hair off her face. "I suppose. Although did you need to throw it *all* over me?"

"Health and safety," he says. "Plus you deserve it. Don't she, Katie?" He gives me a great big wink, and I glare back, livid.

"Steve, you *moron.*" I'm almost too angry to speak. "You total *moron.*"

"Just acting on your behalf," he says unrepentantly. "She did you a wrong, so. Therefore. Ergo. You don't mess around with Katie," he adds ominously to Demeter. "Not unless you don't want *me* not to hear about it."

"That doesn't even make sense!" I say, feeling an urge to hit Steve. "What are you even trying to *say*?"

"I'm saying it like it is, Katie." Steve gives me his bulgy-eyed look. "Saying it like it is."

"You got him to do that to me?" says Demeter in disbelief.

"No!" I say in alarm, but I'm not sure Demeter even hears me. She seems at the end of her tether, unaware of everyone around.

"Haven't you done enough?" She shakes her head. "Haven't you punished me enough? What else are you going to do, tie me up and set the dogs on me? I mean, Jesus, Katie. I *know* I let you go insensitively, I *know* you think I ruined your life, but it's what I had to do, OK? It was my job!" She's practically shouting by now. "I *had* to let you go. And I know it was difficult, but sometimes you just have to get over things! You have to—"

"Let you go?" Dad interrupts. "What's she talking about, love?"

I jump like a scalded cat and turn to see Dad peering at Demeter with a bright-eyed, inquiring expression.

"Shit," says Demeter, and brings a hand to her head. "Katie, I didn't mean to say that."

"Does she know you from London?" Dad looks still more puzzled. "Katie, who *is* this?"

"She works for Cooper Clemmow," Steve tells him with lugubrious importance. "Googled her, didn't I? 'Demeter Farlowe' she calls herself there. *And* he works there." Steve jerks a finger toward Alex, who has been standing on the sidelines. "They're Katie's bosses, come down from London. *That's* who they are."

Dad is looking from Demeter to Alex, a muscle working in his jaw.

"Why didn't you let on who you were?" he says shortly, addressing them both. "What's the big secret?"

"Well." Demeter glances at me. "It's . . . delicate. . . ."

"Have you come here to fire Katie?" he says, in sudden wrath. "Because that's not on. That's *not on*!" he practically bellows. "She's been a good employee, has our Katie." He turns on Alex, who gives a startled jump. "She's on the computer all the time, taking calls, working all hours . . . even during her so-called *sabbatical*. . . . I mean, what kind of bosses are you, anyway? It's exploitation! That's what it is!"

"Dad, stop!" I lift up a hand in desperation. "You've got it wrong. They haven't come to fire me. The truth is . . ." I gulp hard, feeling unsteady on my feet. "I was trying to tell you earlier. . . ."

Tears are edging down my cheeks. I'm aware of all the glampers staring at me in shock, and Demeter standing there, still dripping, and Alex . . . Alex, gazing at me with the kindest, saddest expression I've ever seen. . . .

"Dad, I need to talk to you," I manage. "You and Biddy. Right now."

—

The "what" is easy. It's the "why."

After I've explained exactly what happened, what exactly the reasons for my redundancy were, and how I've attempted to rejoin the job market, I still haven't told them anything, really. Dad and Biddy are sitting on our old, faded pink chintz sofa in the sitting room—this felt like a sitting-room thing—and they're both silenced.

"But, Katie . . ." says Dad at last, and he doesn't need to say any more. He looks profoundly shocked, as though the world isn't as he thought it was. And it's my fault.

"Dad—" I break off, my cheeks taut with the effort of not crying. "I didn't want to worry you. I thought, if I quickly got myself a new job . . ."

"So *that's* what you've been up to," says Biddy gently.

"I've applied for so many jobs. *So* many jobs . . ." The memory of how many jobs I've applied for feels exhausting. "I thought you'd never need to know." I bite my lip and close my eyes, wishing it were three months ago and I had the chance to do everything differently. "I'm sorry." At last I open my eyes. "I'm so sorry, Dad. . . ."

"Katie, don't be *sorry,*" he says at once, his voice rough with some emotion I can't read. "Love, there's nothing for you to be sorry about. You've had a hard time of it, and I just wish we'd known . . . I wish we could have helped . . . but there it is." He leans forward and takes my hands tightly in his big ones. "Katie, all we care about is your happiness. *Sod* the lot of them. *Sod* them. You come back here. You run Ansters Farm for us. You're a brilliant, brilliant girl, and if they can't see it, well, we can. Right, Biddy?"

I don't know how to respond. I glance over at Biddy, and

she's shaking her head, a little frown notched between her brows.

"But, Mick," she says in those quiet, measured tones of hers, "I don't think it's quite as simple as that. I don't think Katie *wants* to make her life and career here. Do you, darling? Or am I wrong?"

I've never felt such tension in this room; it's like the air is viscous with it. I need to speak; I need to tell the truth. But without hurting my dad.

"Dad . . ." My voice trembles so much, I can hardly utter the words. "I want to live in London. I still want to give it a go. I know you'll never understand it, but it's my dream." I rub my face hard, feeling desperate. "But I don't want to break your heart. If I go to London I know I will. And so I'm stuck. I don't know what to do. I don't . . . I can't . . ."

My words are all mixed up and incoherent in my head. Tears are running down my face again. I dart a glance at Dad and he appears stricken.

"Katie!" he says, and exhales. "Love. What gave you the idea I don't want you to live in London?"

Is he serious?

"Well . . . you know," I gulp. "Like, saying London's overpriced and dangerous and dirty . . . telling me to buy a flat in Howells Mill . . ."

"Mick!" exclaims Biddy. "Why did you tell Katie to buy a flat in Howells Mill?"

"I only *suggested* it," says Dad, looking caught out.

"I feel guilty all the time. *All* the time." As I say the words out loud, I feel a massive relief. And dread. I'm venturing into places I would never have dared to tread before. But maybe they need venturing into.

"You know what? *I* want to say something." Biddy's voice makes me start. As I turn to her in surprise, I can see that her cheeks are pink. She looks nervous but resolute. "I always try to stand back when it's the two of you at odds. I try not to put my oar in when it's not wanted. But I think right now it's *needed*. Because I can see two people I love—I love the pair of you, you know that, don't you?" Biddy adds, her cheeks flaming even darker pink. "I can see two people who are hurting each other, and I won't stand it anymore. Mick, can't you see what pressure it puts on Katie, telling her to buy a flat in Howells Mill, for Pete's sake? Why would she do that? And you *know* what I thought about our last trip to London. . . ." Biddy turns to me and adds, "I told your dad he should apologize to you, some of the ridiculous things he said." She lifts a hand as Dad opens his mouth to protest. "I *know* you worry about Katie, Mick. But eight million people live in London safely enough, don't they? They haven't *all* been gunned down or mugged, have they?"

Dad is looking a bit shamefaced. Meanwhile, I'm so gobsmacked by Biddy's sudden eloquence, I can't find a response.

"But there's something else, Katie." She turns back to me. "You know, we're not stupid. We know life in London is tough and expensive and all the rest of it. We see the headlines; we watch the news reports. You always sound so positive, as though everything's a dream come true . . . but it can't be that easy *all* the time? Is it?"

There's a huge pause. I'm feeling slightly as though I want to throw myself to Biddy's knees and hug her.

"No," I admit at last. "It's not. It's not at all."

"No one's life has to be perfect." Biddy leans over and puts an arm round me, tight. "Don't put so much pressure on yourself, love. Whoever started the rumor that life has to be perfect is a very wicked person, if you ask me. Of course it's not! And none of this nonsense about breaking your dad's heart," she adds. "How could you ever break his heart?"

Slowly, almost not daring to, I raise my eyes to meet Dad's. Dad's eyes. They've been my benchmark all my life, my North Pole. I gaze into their blue depths, allowing myself to see his love, burning amid the twinkles. And just a few splinters, still.

I think Biddy hasn't got it quite right. I think maybe I did break Dad's heart a little. But maybe I did that just by growing up.

"Love . . ." Dad exhales slowly. "I'm sorry. I know what it must look like to you. And I'll be honest: I'm not the greatest fan of London. But if you like it, maybe I'll come to like it." He glances at Biddy and hastily amends: "I *will* come to like it."

"Well, you may not need to." I make an attempt at a lighthearted laugh. "If I stay unemployed."

"Those *bastards* . . ." Dad instinctively clenches a fist, and Biddy puts a soothing hand on his arm.

"Mick," she says. "Katie's a grown-up. She'll find her way. Let her do that. And now we'd better all get on, don't you think?" As she stands up, she winks at me, and I can't help smiling back.

CHAPTER NINETEEN

I'm not quite up to rejoining the merry singsong round the campfire. So I wander along to the kitchen, thinking I'll have some tea—to find Demeter sitting at the table, dressed in dry clothes with a towel turban round her head.

"Oh." I stop dead. "Hi."

"I just bumped into Biddy," says Demeter. "She told me I might find you here. Katie, I need to apologize. I didn't mean to betray your confidence."

"Don't worry, it's fine." I shrug awkwardly. "I was planning to tell my dad, anyway. It just forced my hand a bit."

"Even so. I shouldn't have, and I'm truly sorry." Demeter fiddles with her sleeve for a few seconds, her face drawn. "I gather I owe you thanks too," she adds, darting me a glance. "I hear you were very helpful with Coco. Hal told me."

"Right." I nod. I can understand that. Poor Hal seemed a bit freaked out by the whole thing. He probably saw his mum and couldn't help blabbing the whole story.

"And I don't know *what* you said to them, Katie, but Hal had put a bouquet of flowers on my bed. He'd gathered them from the garden, so I'll have to apologize to Biddy," she adds with a short laugh. "And Coco was—" She breaks off, her eyes wide. "I've never heard Coco so conciliatory. So *mature*."

"Well, I guess she's started looking at the world from your point of view a bit more. Demeter . . ." I hesitate. How on earth do I put this? "I think you could be a bit tougher on your kids," I say at last. "I think they take you for granted."

There's a long pause. Demeter is still twiddling at her sleeve. She's going to wear it away to a shred if she doesn't stop.

"I know." She breathes out. "But it's not easy. I barely ever see them. I feel so guilty. So when they ask for things I just want to please them."

"You're a totally different person with your kids from how you are at the office." I try to impress this on her. "*Totally* different. And not in a good way."

"I know." She looks a bit bleak. "But when we have such a short time together, the last thing I want is to cause a row. . . ."

"It can't be easy," I say. "With your husband away and everything . . . I overheard your conversation in the barn," I add bluntly. "Sorry."

"No. Don't worry. We weren't exactly discreet." Demeter exhales strongly. "That situation is definitely a work-in-progress."

"I'm sorry," I say again. "I mean . . . I'm sorry you're having such a hard time."

"It's fine." She leans back in her chair, her eyes closed as though she's tired, and I see the fine lines round her eyes. "No, it's not fine, it's difficult. Getting the balance between two careers and children . . ." She exhales, sitting back up again.

"James has been trying desperately *not* to want this big job, because of the pressure it would place on me. Meanwhile, I've been so preoccupied by work, I haven't even noticed. But we'll get there. Maybe rethink everything—" She cuts herself off. "Anyway. What am I saying? It won't be a problem anymore, will it? From now on I'll be around at home all the time." She gives me a bleak smile. "One advantage of losing my job."

"What?" I say in horror. "Don't say that. It's not going to happen."

"Oh, Katie, you're very sweet, but I can't dodge the bullet anymore. Alex and I have agreed to leave the subject for this evening, but tomorrow . . ." She shrugs. "He wants a meeting at ten A.M. to go over some of the official stuff. The package, waivers . . . that kind of thing. There's a process when someone leaves a job," she adds wryly. "As you know."

"So you have another chance!" I say eagerly. "He can *un*-fire you. No one heard him tonight, there weren't any official witnesses, nothing's been signed . . . I mean, have you actually legally been fired?"

"It's irrelevant." Demeter shakes her head. "I will be."

"Only if you accept it. Only if you don't fight your corner. Didn't you look at the other emails in the bag?"

"Yes. But they're mostly very old. I hadn't realized. So." She lets her hands drop. "I have nothing."

"Listen, Demeter." I flip on the electric kettle, feeling my energy return. "I reckon Sarah's been seriously messing with you. Not just your emails, but your calendar . . . your messages . . . everything. She's been *trying* to make you doubt yourself."

I'm remembering Sarah saying in that calm way, "It was Tuesday, Demeter. Always *Tuesday*." And Demeter staring back with that panicky, swivelly-eyed look.

"I've wondered about that myself," Demeter says after a long pause. "It all makes sense. I didn't realize because it was so gradual. It was just a few tiny slips at first. Emails going astray . . . documents deleted . . . calendar mix-ups . . . I would think I'd given Sarah an instruction and she would insist, point-blank, to my face, that I hadn't. But then the errors got bigger. Worse. Mortifying." Anguish flickers over her face. "I didn't dare draw attention to my blunders. I really thought I had . . . something. I googled dementia every week."

"That's wicked!" I say furiously. "She needs to lose her job!"

"But who would believe it?" Demeter sounds desperate. "I barely believe it myself. I mean, I *know* I'm genuinely absent-minded, especially when I'm stressed. I forget to send emails, I forget to tell James things. . . . And the way I treated you, Katie . . ." She puts her hands to her cheeks. "Again, I'm so sorry. I was *so* pressured that day. I felt as though the whole world was going mad, including me."

"It's fine," I say, really meaning it.

"I looked back in my diary for that day, you know," Demeter adds, a little bleakly. "Sarah had put a check mark against *Talk to Cat,* as if I'd done it. And I doubted myself *so* much, I thought . . . I honestly thought . . ." She looks suddenly agonized again. "*How* could I have doubted myself so much?"

"But don't you see?" I say fervently. "*That's* what she played on. You're naturally scatty and you're insecure about it, and she knew it. She's evil and we need to catch her."

"There's no proof." Demeter shakes her head. "A lot of it would be her word against mine. And I'm sure she's been very clever and covered her tracks."

"No one's *that* clever," I retort at once. "We could get a computer forensics person—"

"You think anyone's going to allow a computer forensics person in the building?" Demeter gives a stark laugh. "You saw Alex's reaction, and he's supposed to be on *my* side. Everyone else at Cooper Clemmow will want me gone with minimal fuss. I'm just a middle-aged, embarrassing problem. They'll give me a nice package. . . ." She trails off.

She sounds so defeated. This isn't Demeter. This crushed, acquiescent woman can't be Demeter. I won't *let* it be.

"Demeter, you need to fight! When they expect you to give up, *that's* when you should put your foot down and double your speed."

"That sounds familiar." Demeter frowns faintly. "Is that a quote?"

"It's from *Grasp the Nettle,*" I admit, a bit sheepishly. "I bought a copy after all. Discounted."

"Oh!" Demeter's face lights up. "It's good, isn't it?"

"Yes, it is. Especially the chapter on *Don't let your bitch assistant win, because you're not just letting her win, you're letting the axis of evil win.*"

Demeter gives a little laugh, but I don't smile back. I'm deadly serious.

"If you won't fight this battle, then I will. Whatever it takes." I come over to the table, trying to imbue her with some spirit. "But you *can't* let them sling you out with the rubbish. You're the *boss,* Demeter."

"Thank you." Demeter puts out a hand and squeezes mine. "I appreciate that."

"Have you told your husband?" I say, as the thought suddenly occurs to me.

"I've filled him in." Demeter sighs. "But he can't really comprehend it. His first reaction was, 'We'll sue them.' That's very James." A little smile comes to her lips. "But there's not a lot he can do to help in Brussels, to be honest."

"OK." I nod. "So, here's what we do. We plan all night and have a meeting tomorrow morning, early."

Demeter shakes her head disbelievingly. "You really think we can win round Alex?"

"We *have* to win him round." I force myself to let a pause elapse before I add, as casually as I can, "Do you know where he is?"

"Right now, you mean? Don't know." Demeter scrutinizes me. "I've been wondering something. Are you two . . ."

"No." I feel the color rush to my cheeks. "I mean, we . . . we . . ." I clear my throat and get up to make my cup of tea.

"Oh God," says Demeter, watching me. "You *are*. I thought so. Oh Christ. You're not smitten, are you?"

"No!" My voice leaps up like a fish. "Of course not. Don't be ridiculous—"

"Katie, listen. Don't get smitten." She sounds almost urgent. "Protect yourself. Don't let him into your heart."

"Why not?" I try to ask as nonchalantly as possible.

"Because you'll get hurt. Alex is—" Demeter breaks off, wrinkling her brow. "He's adorable. But he's incapable of commitment. What he loves is novelty. New cities, new ideas, boom-boom-boom. Right now you're the latest novelty, but before long . . ."

I remember Alex on the office roof, darting about, enthusing about virtual experiences as if they were the real thing. Then I thrust that thought from my mind. Because it's irrelevant.

"Look, Demeter, it's fine," I say, as robustly as I can. "It isn't *serious*. I don't expect it to *go* anywhere, it's just a bit of . . . you know. Fun."

"Well, as long as that's all it is." Demeter eyes me doubtfully. "But I've known a lot of his girlfriends and I've seen a lot of broken hearts. You know his nickname? It's 'One-Way Alex.' Because once he's off, he doesn't come back. He's like a one-way ticket round the world; never touches the same ground twice. I've seen bright, intelligent girls, waiting and hoping . . ." She shakes her head. "They know deep down he'll never come back."

"So why do they hope?" I can't help asking.

"Because it's human nature to hope for impossible things." She eyes me shrewdly. "You're in marketing. You know that."

"Well, don't worry." I tear my gaze away from hers. "I have no expectations or hopes or anything. Like I say, it's just a bit of fun. *Fun*."

"OK." She nods once, then looks at her watch. "I'd better get back to Hal and Coco. See you in the morning. Thanks, Katie." She stands up, then comes over and kisses me on the cheek. As she does, there's a knock on the kitchen door.

"Hi," says Alex, coming in. "Oh, hi, Demeter."

"Hello, Alex." She shoots him a mistrustful look. "What do you want?"

"Came to see Katie."

His eyes meet mine and the intent in them is so visceral, I catch my breath. I have an immediate flashback to the meadow. For a moment I can't quite speak for lust.

"Hi," I manage.

"Are you OK?"

"Fine."

My whole body is quivering, wanting a whole, delicious, uninterrupted night with this man who turns me to jelly. I want his touch. But I want his voice too. His thoughts and his jokes . . . his worries and sadnesses . . . his theories and wonderings. All the secret parts of him that I never guessed existed.

"Well, I'll let you get on with it," says Demeter, standing up. "Whatever you're up to." And she shoots such a reproving glance at Alex, I almost want to giggle.

"Demeter, it's fine," I say as she reaches the door. "Really. What you said just now . . ." I gesture surreptitiously at my heart. "I *won't*."

But Demeter shakes her head wryly. "You think you won't."

CHAPTER TWENTY

At about six o'clock in the morning, I nudge Alex's bare calf with my foot. "Hey, you," I say. "City boy."

We haven't really slept all night. We've just dozed and laughed and devoured each other in a bubble of him and me and nothing else. But now the birds are chattering and sun is filtering past my curtains and real life begins again.

"Hmm," he murmurs, only half-waking up.

"You need to go and sleep in your bed."

"What?" Alex turns a rumpled face to me. "Are you chucking me out?"

"Biddy will be really upset if you don't. You're her first customer. Go and try it out, at least. And, anyway, you don't want to use my shower. It's, like, a dribble."

"In a minute," says Alex, sucking the bare skin of my shoulder, pulling me toward him, and I succumb because I can't not; he's like some magnetic force that just drags me in.

But then, a while later, when we're both sated, and I'm wondering belatedly if we were a bit noisy, I give him a firmer kick.

"Go on. Be a good B&B customer. I'll see you at breakfast."

"All right." He rolls his eyes and pushes back the duvet. I think it was the description of my shower as a "dribble" that tipped the balance. He strikes me as a guy who might have quite uncompromising shower standards.

"See you at breakfast, then," he says, heading to the door in boxer shorts. Which isn't very discreet, but if he bumps into Biddy, he can always say—

Oh, whatever. He can say what he likes. She's not stupid.

I wait until I'm sure he's gone before I move. Then I leap out of bed and take my puny shower. I yank on some jeans and a top and creep out of the house in the other direction. I hurry over the dew-laden grass to Demeter's yurt, say, "Knock, knock!" and let myself in.

Demeter is sitting up in her wooden Ansters Farm bed, wearing pale-gray marl pajamas and one of our alpaca blankets round her shoulders. She's sipping from a water bottle and tapping feverishly at her laptop.

"OK," she says, as though we're seamlessly continuing the conversation from last night. "I've remembered something. There's a whole stack of email printouts in my office."

"In your office?" I think doubtfully back to the piles of paper on Demeter's floor. "But won't Sarah have gone through those and thrown out anything incriminating?"

"Not the ones in the cupboard." Demeter looks up with a glint. "The ones she doesn't know about."

"Doesn't *know* about?" I echo in blank astonishment. There's something in Demeter's life that Sarah doesn't know about?

"She got so cross at me for printing out emails that I used to do it secretly. And then I put them all in that big cupboard. There must be hundreds in there. The cupboard's locked." She pauses. "And I've got the key. Here on my key ring."

"Hundreds?" I stare at her. "Why did you keep hundreds of email printouts?"

"Don't you start!" says Demeter defensively. "I suppose I thought I might need them one day."

"Well," I say after a pause. "You did."

"Yes," says Demeter dryly. "Turns out I did."

She meets my eye and I feel a sudden rise of confidence. A conviction. She's bloody well going to win this. Demeter taps again at her computer and I can see her eyes teeming with ideas again. Ideas and anger.

"You seem different this morning," I say tentatively. "You seem like . . . you want it."

"Oh, I want it," says Demeter, and there's a steeliness to her that makes me want to cheer. The strong, determined woman I know is back! "I don't know what got into me last night. But I woke up today and I thought . . . *what*?"

"Exactly!" I nod. "*What?*"

"I am *not* being fucked over by my own fucking assistant."

"Hear, hear!"

"The only thing which *has* come to me . . ." She pauses and rubs her brow. "I think Sarah must have teamed up with someone else. Some of that information she played around with came from meetings she didn't attend."

"Right," I say after a pause. My mind is already working round the possibilities. "So who do you think . . ."

"Rosa," says Demeter flatly. "Has to be."

"Or Mark," I say.

"Right." Demeter winces. "Or Mark. Equally likely. Any other contenders?"

I'm not being very tactful here, I suddenly realize. It can't be much fun to think there are so many people out to get you.

"Look, don't think about that," I say hastily. "Whoever it was . . . we'll find out. But now we need to work out a plan."

Demeter and I march into breakfast half an hour later, side by side. We have a strategy worked out and now we just need to find Alex. Which isn't hard to do, as he's sitting at the kitchen table, looking a bit shell-shocked while Biddy piles mushrooms onto his plate. A plate which already holds three sausages, four rashers of bacon, two fried eggs, two tomatoes, and some of Biddy's famous fried bread, which, honestly, is *heaven*. (If heaven had four hundred calories a slice.)

"That's wonderful." Alex gulps. "That's plenty. No!" he almost yelps as Biddy advances with the other frying pan. "No more bacon, thanks."

"So, as I say, Alex," Dad seems to be concluding a conversation, "it's a one-off opportunity, which an astute businessman like yourself will be quick to spot. Anyway . . ." He darts a shifty look at me and crunches a piece of toast. "We'll leave that subject for now. HP Sauce, Alex?"

"What opportunity?" I say warily.

"Nothing!" says Dad with a guileless smile. "Just chinwagging with Alex here. Passing the time of day."

"Are you trying to sell him something?" I glare at him. "Because *don't*."

"Your dad was interesting me in a wigwam venture," says Alex with a straight face.

"*Wigwam venture?*" I echo, thunderstruck. "Dad, what are you *on*?"

"Trying to expand the franchise!" says Dad defensively. "If you stand still you go backward, love. There's a site over by Old Elmford; Dave Yarnett can get us some wigwams. . . ."

I shake my head in despair. "I thought I'd weaned you *off* buying tents from Dave Yarnett."

"I could be Big Chief Mick!" Dad makes a Native American–type sign. "The kiddies would love it!"

"Dad, stop right there! We're *not* buying wigwams and you're *not* dressing up as a Native American. . . ." I wonder whether to launch into a lecture about political correctness, but decide against it. Not the right time. "For *so* many reasons," I conclude. "And, anyway, we need to talk to Alex. So could you possibly . . ." I gesture at him to move, and Dad shifts along the table. "Can you stop the other glampers coming in?" I add to Biddy. "We just need five minutes."

"Morning, Alex," says Demeter, and takes a seat opposite him.

She's got a crisp white shirt on today, and her hair is glossy (she blow-dried it in my room), and she looks calm and focused and on it.

"Morning." Alex doesn't seem particularly keen to have her sitting opposite him. "Look, Demeter, there's no rush, we can do this later—"

"I need another day," Demeter cuts him off. "Give me one day."

"Oh, bloody hell." Alex looks balefully at her and then me. "I *knew* you were hatching something."

"One day." I back her up. "That's all. It's nothing."

"I can't give you one day," he snaps. "I've already told Adrian that I've broken the news to you."

"We haven't had a meeting," shoots back Demeter. "You haven't explained my employment rights. Nothing's official. You can give me one more day. You *have* to."

"Yes, you have to," I affirm. "Or else."

Alex darts a suspicious glance at me. "Or else what?"

"Or else you'll be a wanker. Sorry, Dad," I add.

"You go for it, Katie my love!" Dad waves his toast cheerily. "Give him all you've got!"

"This is my livelihood," says Demeter evenly. "And it's not going to be finished off like this. After all the chances I gave you, Alex, all the support I gave you, you owe me more than that. And you know it." She sounds scathing, almost contemptuous.

For a moment no one breathes. I can tell from Alex's flickering eyes that she's got to him. He's thinking . . . thinking . . . Then, breaking the spell, he sighs.

"OK. Suppose you had one more day." He shrugs as though to say: *What then?*

"There are more email printouts in the office. Hundreds of them, stashed away in my cupboard." Demeter places her hands on the table like a politician. "Let me look through them."

Alex shakes his head. "Demeter, you won't be able to step into that office without Adrian being all over you. He'll march you into talent management on the spot, and you'll be out before you can draw breath."

"We've thought of that," I say. "I'll do it. I'll pretend I came back for something. No one will suspect me."

"I'll give her the key to the cupboard." Demeter produces her key ring and dangles it. "I'll write some letter allowing her in. Predate it. I mean, who's going to stop Katie going in?"

"That might work," Alex allows.

"It *will* work."

"Muffins?" Biddy comes bustling over to the table, holding a basket of muffins. "I've got bran . . . apple . . . blueberry . . . Alex!" She looks in disappointment at his plate. "You're not eating!"

"I am," Alex says hastily, and shovels a load of food into his mouth. He sits back, chewing, then shakes his head. "Here's the other thing. Adrian's expecting to hear from me that I've finished the process this morning. Done everything properly. Case closed."

"Well, fob him off," says Demeter impatiently.

"How?"

"Be out of signal."

"All *day*?"

"Or send him an email. Give him some excuse."

"What excuse?"

"I don't know!" snaps Demeter. "Be inventive! Isn't that your strong suit?"

"Excuse me overhearing," says Biddy with a beam. "But would you like some help?"

Both Demeter and Alex stare up at Biddy as though the teapot has suddenly begun to speak.

"Well," says Demeter politely, "I'm not sure how you could help, Biddy. Obviously if you *could* keep my boss off my back for a day, then I'd be very grateful." She gives a short laugh.

Alex nods. "So would I."

"Easy," says Biddy. "Do you have his number?"

Alex darts a startled glance at Demeter—then a wicked smile spreads over his face and he holds out his phone to Biddy. "Here's his mobile number. But he'll still be at home."

"Even better." Biddy twinkles at him. "We'll catch him off guard. Oh," she adds to Demeter. "He knows your married name is Wilton, doesn't he?"

"Yes." Demeter looks intrigued.

"Good!"

We all watch, agog, as Biddy dials the number and draws breath. "Hello?" she says. "Is that Adrian? It's Biddy here, the farmer's wife from Ansters Farm in Somerset." She's making her vowels creamier than usual, I realize, just like I did. "I'm very sorry to say, sir, both Mrs. Wilton and Mr. Astalis are terrible ill. *Terrible* ill."

I can hear some sort of exclamation coming from the other end of the line, to which Biddy listens peaceably.

"Terrible poorly," she reiterates. "Yes, it's been quite a night here, sir, with both of them suffering, like. Poor loves. So they asked me to let you know."

There's another outburst at the other end, and Biddy winks at us.

"Oh no, sir," she says calmly. "There's no chance of them coming to the phone. Although," she adds brightly, "I've a message for you. Mr. Astalis asked me to pass on that what with him being so poorly and all, he hasn't *quite* finished the job that he came here to do." She listens placidly to another eruption from Adrian. "That's right. Not quite finished, but he'll get to it as soon as he can. Whatever it is," she adds innocently.

I glance at Alex. He's slowly shaking his head, looking both outraged and on the verge of laughter.

"Such a shame," Biddy continues. "And on their holiday too. Anyway, they're best off in bed and I'm calling the doctor later. Shall I send them both your best regards? Any flowers at all, sir? A Somerset bouquet for each of them?"

She listens again and then rings off.

"He sends his love," she says with a twinkle, and hands the phone back to Alex.

"Biddy, you're incredible," says Alex, lifting his hand to high-five her, and I feel a glow of pride. Then he turns to Demeter and gives her a wry shrug. "OK. Well, there it is. You've got your day."

CHAPTER TWENTY-ONE

I'd forgotten the smell of London, the busyness, the crowds. I'd forgotten about coming up out of the tube steps into the hot, concentrated city sunshine, surrounded by people of all descriptions, and thinking, *I could do anything, go anywhere, be anyone*.

Ansters Farm is like a circle. It is what it is. And you basically go round and round in a peaceful way, never digressing. But London's like a spiderweb. There's a million possibilities, a million directions, a million endgames. I'd forgotten that feeling of . . . of what? Being on the brink of something.

And right now I could not feel more brinksman-like. It's all down to me. Katie Brenner. As I turn my steps toward the Cooper Clemmow offices, nerves are gnawing at my stomach, but I firmly tell them to pipe down.

Demeter and Alex aren't with me. They've stationed themselves at a café, two tube stops away, because the last thing they wanted was to run into Adrian. But they're on the phone. We're all in contact, constantly. As though reading my mind, Demeter texts me:

There yet? x

I pause and send back a reply:

Nearly. All good. x

As I push my way through the big glass doors, Jade on reception looks up in surprise.

"Oh, hi," she says. "It's Cat, innit? Didn't you . . ."

"Leave? Yes." I nod. "But I've got to pop upstairs, if that's OK? I left some stuff at the office and I never picked it up. So, you know, I thought I'd pop by. . . ." Oh God. I'm starting to gabble with nerves.

Jade nods. "Fine."

"I've got a letter from Demeter, giving me permission," I blurt out before I can stop myself.

"I said it's fine." Jade gives me an odd look, scribbles a visitor pass, and presses the button to open the barrier.

OK. First hurdle over. As I get into the lift, I'm prickling with apprehension, but there's no one else in it, and I make it to our floor safely.

As I walk along the familiar corridor, I feel a bit surreal. It's all the same as it was. The same black shiny floor; the same crack in the wall as you pass the men's; the same distinct smell of coffee and floor cleaner and Fresh 'n Breezy home scent diffusers. (They used to keep sending us freebies, which Sarah would put out. Guess they still do.)

And then there I am, in our office space. It's just as it ever was, with the distressed-brick wall and white desks and the naked-man coat stand—although there's a new red coffee machine in the corner, with a stack of Coffeewite sachets on top. I glance over at my desk—but it isn't there anymore. They've moved them all around. There's no trace that I ever sat there.

The office is pretty empty. There's no Rosa, no Flora, no Mark, no Liz—and Sarah isn't at her desk either. Thank God. I timed my arrival carefully for 1:15 P.M., as I know she's usually at lunch then, but it's still a major relief.

Hannah is sitting at her desk and looks up as I enter.

"Oh, hi." She blinks at me through her glasses. "Wow. Cat. How are you?"

"Fine." I nod. "How are you?"

"Oh, fine, all good . . ." She looks around. "A lot of people are out at lunch, I'm afraid. You've missed them."

"Not to worry." I hesitate, then add nonchalantly, "Actually, I just need to pick some stuff up from Demeter's office. I left it and she held on to it for me."

"Oh, right." Hannah nods, totally accepting this story. "Well, I'll say hi from you, shall I?"

"Yes, do."

"OK. It must be weird for you, being back here," she adds, as though the thought has just occurred to her.

"Yes." I force a smile. "It is."

It's more than weird; it's freaking me out a bit. I'm unnerved by my own reaction. I thought I'd be fine, coming back; I thought I'd got past it. But now, standing here, it's as if the last few months have concertinaed into nothing, and the hurt is as fresh as ever.

As I survey the empty office, it suddenly hits me: It's Wednesday. Flora, Rosa, and Sarah will be at their drinks at the Blue Bear. The fun, cool-gang drinks I would have gone to if I'd stayed. It seems like a lifetime ago now.

"So, have you got another job?" Hannah's voice breaks into my thoughts.

"No."

"Oh. D'you still live in Catford?"

"No. I had to move home."

"Oh. Bummer," says Hannah, looking awkward. "I'm really sorry. I mean, I'm sure you'll get another job. . . . Have you applied for any?"

This is such an inane question, I think even Hannah realizes it, and she blushes.

"I'll get my stuff," I say, letting her off the hook. "Nice to see you."

As I head into Demeter's office, I check back, and Hannah is already engrossed in her work again. She's obviously not remotely curious about what I'm up to, and neither is Jon, who's sitting way over in the corner. I never really got to know him.

Trying to look natural, I head to the cupboard. This should take thirty seconds, tops. Pile the email printouts into a bag, don't bother checking them out, just get them and go. I unfold the big laundry bag I brought and place it on the floor. I take out Demeter's key ring, quietly unlock the door, and swing it open, ready to scoop piles of paper out.

The cupboard's empty.

For a moment I can't actually compute what I'm seeing. I had such a strong vision of what I was going to find: piles and piles of messy printouts, in a typical Demeter-ish shambles. Not this.

I shut the cupboard door and open it again, as though I might be able to perform a magic spell. But it's still clean and white and empty. Then I glance around the rest of Demeter's office with a looming feeling of dread.

It's tidy. It's really tidy. There aren't any piles of anything, anywhere. What's happened?

I lean my head out of the door and give Hannah an easy smile. "It's really tidy in here! What's happened?"

"Oh, that was Sarah," says Hannah, still focused on her screen. "You know what she's like. Demeter went on holiday, so she was like, 'At last! I can clear out her office!' "

"But the cupboard's empty." I try to say the words calmly. "That's where I left my stuff, but it's all gone." I'm counting on Hannah not being curious enough to question why I left my stuff in Demeter's cupboard and, sure enough, she doesn't.

"Oh." She pulls a face and shrugs. "Sorry. No idea."

"So, does Sarah have a key to the cupboard?"

"Er . . . yes," says Hannah vaguely. "She must do, because I saw her sorting it out yesterday. She chucked out a huge load of papers." Hannah looks up and I see her brain finally kicking in. "Oh God. Was that your stuff?"

I stare back dumbly. *A huge load of papers.* Chucked away. All the emails, all the evidence, gone. My throat is tight; I'm not sure I can breathe. What am I going to tell Demeter?

"Look, I'll tell Sarah you were here and maybe she can sort it out."

"It's OK," I say hastily. "Don't bother Sarah."

"It's no bother. Or I could speak to Demeter. . . ." Hannah lowers her voice. "Actually, there's a rumor that Demeter's getting the chop."

"Wow." Somehow I'm managing to speak. "Well, I'll just have another quick search in Demeter's office, just in case. . . ."

But after ten minutes, I know. There's nothing here. No physical scraps of anything. Sarah must have been through it like a whirlwind.

I can't stay here forever. I have to leave; I have to think. . . . My chest feels compressed by panic as I walk out, down the stairs, out into the open air. A flashing from my phone catches my eye, and I see it's a new text from Demeter:

How r u getting on? x

I emit a tiny whimper. My legs are moving on autopilot. I'm her only hope right now. I *can't* tell her the plan is wrecked. I have to come up with something else. Go to the recycling bin and search? But it all gets taken away on Tuesday night. Get into Sarah's computer and find some evidence there? But how can I do that in front of Hannah? And how would I guess her password?

Come on, Katie. Think. Think . . .

And then it hits me. The Blue Bear. Sarah will be there right now. She might say something off guard. If I can just get her to chat, if I can just get her to relax and trust me . . .

Gathering up all my resolve, I take out my phone and send a text to Demeter:

Going a bit off-piste. x

Not that I have ever skied in my life—how could I afford to ski?—but she'll get the reference.

Immediately she sends back a reply:

What???

But I thrust my phone away and ignore it. I can't get into conversation now. I have to concentrate.

As I enter the beery, noisy atmosphere of the Blue Bear, I see Rosa and Sarah standing at the bar, and my stomach swoops with nerves.

"Cat?" Sarah notices me at once. "Cat! Oh my *God*!"

After all my conversations with Demeter, I'd started to imagine Sarah almost as a demon. But of course she's not. She's the same pretty Sarah, red hair tied back, blue eyes neatly lined, and white teeth flashing in a broad smile.

"Look, Rosa, it's Cat!" she's saying. She holds out her arms wide and so does Rosa, and the next minute we're all hugging like the oldest of friends.

"How *are* you?" Sarah keeps saying. "We've missed you!"

I feel a bit overwhelmed at their welcome. I thought everyone would have forgotten about me. But here they are, genuinely interested in me and my life, and it's . . . well. It's nice.

Even though *Cat* feels like an alien word now.

"What are you doing here?" Rosa wants to know, and I shrug carelessly.

"I was in the area and I remembered you always have drinks on a Wednesday."

"You never came to that, did you?" Sarah gives me a sharp look. "But we asked you."

"So, where are you working now?" Rosa demands, and I feel a trickle of humiliation.

"I'm not. At least, not in branding, not at the moment. I'm actually . . . I'm working in Somerset, on a farm."

The aghast expressions on their faces would make me laugh if I didn't feel so mortified. I hadn't thought it would affect me so badly: me standing here with no job, while they still luxuriated in theirs. But it's not a great feeling. In fact, to be honest, if it weren't for Demeter I'd probably make an excuse right now and leave.

"Cat." Rosa looks genuinely upset. "That's terrible. You're really talented."

"Which *Demeter* never noticed," says Sarah, and squeezes my arm. "Bitch."

"How is Demeter?" I ask, trying to sound casual.

"Oh my God, you don't know." A flicker of triumph runs over Sarah's face. "She's been fired!"

"No!" I clap a hand over my mouth with a gasp—and, actually, I am a bit shocked. Because of course she *hasn't* been fired, not properly, not yet. But obviously the story is that she's gone.

"I know!" Sarah flashes her little white teeth again. "Isn't it great? Everything's going to change. *Rosa's* going to run the department, like she should have done in the first place." She puts an arm round Rosa and gives her a hug.

"Well." Rosa gives a modest shrug. "We don't know that. I'll be running it while they decide what to do."

"And then they'll give it to you!" insists Sarah. "You should always have got that job. There'll be a completely different atmosphere in the department. No more bloody *drama*."

"So, why was Demeter fired?" I ask warily.

"Try *everything*." Sarah rolls her eyes. "You know what she's like. Finally Adrian was like, *OK, I get it. She's a demented cow. She has to go.*"

"Hey." Rosa has been quiet, thinking hard. "Cat. Did you know that Flora's leaving?"

"Really?" I say in surprise. "No, I had no idea. We kind of lost touch. Where's she going?"

"Traveling. She's leaving in a month. So . . ." She looks expectantly at me.

"So?"

"So, how do you feel about applying for her job?"

I feel a bolt of disbelief. Apply for Flora's job?

"Oh yes!" Sarah exclaims in delight. "Perfect idea! What a good thing you walked in here, Cat!"

"It would be a better salary than you had before," says Rosa. "I know you're up to it, Cat. I've seen your work. And I'll tell you something: I'm not like Demeter. I want to *help* people develop. You have a great future, you know that?"

There's a weird kind of humming in my head. Nothing feels quite real. *A job. A better salary. A great future.* I mean, if Demeter *didn't* get her job back . . . if Rosa *did* want me to work for her . . . I have to give myself the best chance in life, don't I?

I'm squirming inside. I feel like an octopus tied up in knots, being pulled in different directions.

The barman has placed three glasses and a bottle of champagne on the bar, and Rosa pays for it, then turns to me.

"Come on," she says. "Have a drink with us. We always go in that little back room. Flora's there already."

"We don't always have champagne on Wednesdays," adds Sarah, with a twinkle. "But, ding-dong, the witch is dead!"

In my pocket, my phone begins to buzz. It feels as if Demeter is nudging me, and instantly my brain snaps into place with a tweak of guilt. What have I been *thinking*? There aren't two options here, there's only one: *Do the right thing.* I blink at Sarah and Rosa, trying to get my ideas straight, trying to find a way into the conversation.

"You must have found it so difficult, working for Demeter!" I say to Sarah. "Did you ever feel like . . . I don't know . . . getting revenge in any tiny way?"

Sarah gives me a clear blue look. "What do you mean?"

My stomach flips at her expression. Has she guessed? No. She couldn't have done. But I need to prove I'm on her side, quick.

"Well, you'll never believe it . . ." I try to sound natural and chatty. "But Demeter turned up at my family's farm on holiday. And I got my own back on her for everything! Look!"

I wince inwardly as I reach for my phone. Demeter would *really* not be happy if she knew I was sharing a photo of her, all spread-eagled and muddy in the swamp. But, on the other hand, I can't think of a better way of gaining Sarah's trust.

"No!" exclaims Sarah as she sees it. "That's priceless! We have to hear all about it! Will you send that picture to me?"

"Of course I will!" I answer lightly. *Never in a million years.*

"You're quite something, Cat!" says Sarah, as Rosa grabs the phone to have a look. "We could have done with your help." She puts an arm around me and gives me a swift hug.

"Let's go," says Rosa, and motions to me to pick up the glasses. "Grab another one of those. Flora will be waiting."

It's one of those pubs with little rooms and passages and steps everywhere. We head down a shabby corridor painted dark red, with old prints of London views lining the walls. Then at the end Rosa opens a door into a small bare-boarded room with squashy sofas and bookshelves holding old paperbacks.

"Wooo!" Flora greets Rosa with a whoop and a fist pump. "Champagne! About bloody right!"

"And look who we found in the bar?" says Sarah, gesturing at me.

"Cat!" Flora squeals, and zooms over to wrap me in a hug. "I've missed you! This is so cool!"

"Ding-dong, the witch is dead!" exclaims Sarah again, popping open the bottle of champagne. "At last!"

"Here's to that," says Flora fervently.

"And look what Cat has been getting up to!" Sarah grabs my phone and shows Flora the picture of Demeter in the mud. "You didn't tell me you'd recruited a country branch of DA!"

"Oh my God." Flora's eyes widen, and she bursts into peals of laughter. "Oh my *God*! Cat, you're a genius!"

"DA?" I echo lightly. "What's that?"

"DA," says Sarah, sounding puzzled. "*You* know."

"Cat never knew," says Flora, handing me a champagne glass.

"You never knew?" Sarah looks astonished. "But Flora said you were in."

"Of course Cat was in!" says Flora impatiently. "She was totally in. Only I never told her *exactly* what was going on."

She turns to me. "And then you got the push. That evil *cow*. Have you been OK? You haven't replied to my texts!"

"I've been fine, really. So . . . what exactly has been going on? What's DA?"

I meet Sarah's eyes and I can see her guard has dropped with me.

"Demeter Anonymous, of course," she says with a laugh. "We share our terrible Demeter stories and help one another."

"What did you *think* we were doing every Wednesday?" Flora gulps her champagne. "Honestly, we've needed this; otherwise we'd go insane."

"The worst time was when she made Sarah cook those gross Chinese herbs." Rosa screws up her nose. "D'you remember? The *smell*. I think that was before your time, Cat."

"No!" Flora bats the air, her mouth full of champagne, then swallows and turns to me. "Dyeing the roots!"

"Oh my God, the roots." Sarah claps a hand over her mouth.

"The roots!" Rosa explodes. "I'd forgotten about the roots. Cat, you win! Worst Demeter story *ever*." She clinks her glass against mine and I grin back as widely as I can, even though my mind is working frenetically. While Rosa is refreshing glasses, I take out my phone as though to check for texts, press RECORD, and slip the phone back into my pocket.

"So what happened?" I say innocently. "How did Demeter get herself fired?"

All three of them exchange conspiratorial, triumphant looks.

"Go on," says Flora to Sarah. "Tell her. Sarah's *brilliant*," she adds to me. "*She* got Demeter fired." Flora clinks her glass against Sarah's. "Sarah's the star."

"It was all of us," rejoins Sarah modestly. "It was teamwork. And it's been a long time coming. Hasn't it, Rosa?"

"*Too* long," says Rosa wryly.

"Wow!" I open my eyes wide. "But how on earth could you . . . I mean, what happened? I think I heard about some muddle with Allersons. . . ."

"Sarah's so clever," says Flora proudly. "She sent Demeter all this wrong information so she wouldn't pursue the project. And then she made sure the Allersons people never got to speak to Demeter on the phone; otherwise it would have come out. See? Brilliant."

"I sent them the wrong mobile number." Sarah gives me an angelic smile. "And I always answer Demeter's phone in the office, so. It was easy."

"But the way you juggled all the emails," says Rosa. "I still don't know *how* you did that."

"Oh, Demeter's such a technological shambles," says Sarah. "It's pathetically easy to fool her." There's such a contemptuous flick to her voice that I'm quite shocked.

"Sending The Email to Forest Food, though," says Flora. "That was genius."

"Well, it *was* in her drafts folder," says Sarah, with a wicked little grin. "I just helped it along."

"D'you remember that, Cat?" Flora turns to me. "The Email?"

"Just about!" I force a grin back. "So what actually happened?"

"Well, Demeter typed out this furious email—you know, letting off steam—and put it in 'Drafts.' So Sarah went to her computer and pressed SEND." Flora collapses into giggles. "It took, like, ten seconds. Demeter never even *questioned* whether she'd sent it or not."

"Always know what's in your boss's drafts folder," says Sarah, with that one-cornered smile I remember.

I try to smile back—but I'm remembering Demeter's face at the time of The Email. Her white, panicky desperation. And here they all are, assuming that she doesn't have any feelings at all, toasting her misery in champagne.

They've turned her into a monster. I think they have *literally* forgotten that she's a human being.

"And did you mess with her calendar?" I say, forcing another bright smile. "Because she used to get *so* confused. . . ."

"Oh, all the time!" Sarah picks up her phone and imitates Demeter, right down to the swivelly-eyed look. *"Shit. Shit. I know that meeting was on Friday . . . how has this happened? How has this happened?"*

She's so accurate, everyone bursts into laughter. But I'm feeling a kind of burning fury that I'm afraid is going to burst out any minute. *How* could they be so cruel?

"But what if you got caught?"

"No chance," says Sarah smugly. "I'd just deny it. There's no evidence, not one shred. I deleted all the fake emails off everything, as soon as she'd seen them."

I have a sudden memory of Sarah grabbing Demeter's phone out of her hand and jabbing at it. Managing everything. Controlling everything.

"As for the calendar stuff . . ." Sarah shrugs. "Her word against mine. Everyone *knows* she's hopeless. Who would believe Demeter?"

"You could write a book!" says Flora to Sarah. "*How to Get Back at Your Bully Boss*. You are brilliant, you know."

"Everyone's been brilliant," says Sarah firmly. "Rosa, you were great with the Sensiquo deadline. You totally landed her in it. And, Flora, you've been feeding me information the whole time. . . ."

"You have no idea, Cat," says Flora. "It's been this team effort. It's been epic."

"I can see that!" Somehow I'm managing to sound pleasant. "So I suppose the only thing I don't get is . . . why?"

"Why?" Flora echoes blankly. "What do you mean, why? We *had* to get her fired. I mean, it's a health thing, right?" She looks at the others for affirmation. "I mean, we need *therapy* after having her as our boss!"

"Demeter is definitely bad for the health," says Sarah. "She's a nightmare. Management just couldn't see it."

"I know what we did was a bit extreme." Rosa seems to be the only one to have the slightest qualms. "But it was going to happen anyway. I mean, Demeter can't run a department. She's so scatty! She's all over the place!"

"We only accelerated what was inevitable," says Sarah crisply. "It always should have been Rosa in that job."

"But what about Demeter?" I keep the same easy, unthreatening tone. "What if you really messed her up? What if she thought she was getting dementia?"

There's a slight silence. I can tell this thought has not crossed anyone's mind.

"Oh for God's sake," says Flora at last. "This is *Demeter* we're talking about." As though Demeter counts for nothing, has no rights, no viewpoint, is just some kind of subspecies. I stare at her, feeling chilled.

Don't say anything, I tell myself, *don't provoke them, just leave. . . .* But I already know I can't do that.

"You called Demeter a bully," I say lightly. "But actually I never saw her bully anyone."

"Yes, she did!" Rosa gives a short laugh. "You saw her; she was a nightmare!"

"No, she didn't. She used to assert herself, yes. And she was tactless, yes. But she didn't *bully* anyone." I draw breath, trying to stay calm. "Yet here you are, rounding up on her like some lynch mob."

"Lynch mob?" Sarah sounds offended.

"Isn't that what you are?"

"For God's *sake,* Cat," says Flora, glaring at me. "I thought you were signed up."

"Signed up to what? Drumming someone out of a job by messing with their mind? Destroying someone's sanity? Well, sorry if I'm boring, but no thanks."

"Look, Cat," snaps Rosa defensively. "With all due respect, you *left* Cooper Clemmow, you *weren't* there, you *don't* know what Demeter's like—"

"I do," I say curtly. "And I'd take her as a boss over you any day." I stride to the door, my heart pumping, desperate to get away. But as I open it, I turn back and survey the aggressive, defensive faces. "You know the really sad thing? I admired you all so much. I wanted to *be* you, more than anything. But now I realize . . . you're just a big bunch of bullies."

"*What?*" rejoins Flora, sounding outraged.

"You heard me. Bullies."

I let the word sit in the air for a few seconds, then close the door.

And now it's nearly an hour later. It didn't take long for Demeter and Alex to arrive in Chiswick. Nor for them to join me in a little café, listen to my playback, and realize the truth. As the recording ended, none of us said a word. I felt quietly vindicated. Alex looked chastened. But Demeter . . . Demeter looked properly shocked.

In a way, it should have been a sweet victory for her. We should have been whooping. But how can you whoop when you've just learned that so many people are out to get you?

At last Alex drew breath and said, "OK. Let's take this to Adrian."

"Yes," said Demeter, her tone strangely flat. "Let's."

And I didn't say anything, just got up with them from the table.

That's where they are now: in with Adrian at the Cooper Clemmow offices. I'm sitting outside Adrian's room, in his private reception area, waiting for them. Adrian's assistant, Marie, is at her desk nearby, typing away. She looked pretty surprised as we all marched in, but she hasn't asked me a single question about it. She's discreet like that, Marie. I have no idea what's going on in there, but I can only imagine. And then, as I've almost drifted away into a trance, I hear my name being called.

"Cat?"

"It's Cat!"

It's them. Rosa, Flora, and Sarah. They must have caught sight of me as they were on their way back in from lunch, and now they're all coming toward me, their expressions wary and hostile.

"What are you doing here?" demands Flora accusingly as I get up from the sofa. "Are you waiting for Adrian?"

"Are you talking to Adrian about Flora's job?" Rosa shakes her head. "Because that's not on. You shouldn't go over my head."

I give her a withering look. "You're not running the department. So it's nothing to do with you."

"She will be," says Sarah loyally.

"I doubt it," I retort, and Rosa draws breath in anger.

"God, Cat," says Flora, shooting me a look of dislike. "What is your *problem*?"

"What is *my* problem?"

And as if on cue, Adrian's door opens. As he steps out, with Alex and Demeter, he looks profoundly shocked and upset. His iron-gray hair is rumpled and his face is craggy and he's saying, "It beggars belief. It fucking beggars belief—"

He breaks off as he sees Rosa, Sarah, and Flora, all standing there before him, and his face becomes even craggier. His eyebrows draw together and for an instant I think he's going to bellow. But instead he looks levelly at each of them in turn and says, "We're going to talk. Don't go back to your desks, any of you. Stay here." He gestures to the seats in the reception area, then turns to Marie. "Clear the rest of my day."

"Of course," she says, in that unflappable way she has, and picks up the phone.

Rosa is staring at me in sudden, startled comprehension. Her face has gone a bit green and I almost feel sorry for her. *Almost*. Flora is gaping at Demeter as though she's come back from the dead. Sarah is still baring her teeth in that defiant way she has, but I can see a twitch at her eye, and her hands have started to clasp and unclasp. I have no idea what she's thinking right now. . . . And you know what? I don't care.

I turn away from the little group to Demeter, who's looking a bit shell-shocked and sheeny-eyed after her meeting.

"Are you OK?" I murmur.

"I'm fine. Or, at least, I *will* be fine." She closes her eyes briefly. "Katie, I don't know what to say. You're amazing. If it weren't for you . . . I mean . . . Come here." Demeter pulls me into an impassioned hug. "Thank you," she says into my ear. "Thank you a million times over."

As we draw apart, I can see Flora staring at the pair of us, flabbergasted. Unlike the other two, she doesn't look properly scared yet. I don't think it's quite dawned on her fully what's happening.

"I don't get it," she blurts out. "Are you two *friends*? Have you been friends all this time?"

"Well . . . not exactly *friends*," I say, just as Demeter says, "We've had our ups and downs."

I have a flashback to Demeter groveling around the swamp, covered with gloop and nettle stings. I glance at her—and I can tell she's having a similar memory.

"I think our shared love of yoga *really* bonded us," Demeter adds, deadpan. "If you can call it yoga." She raises her eyebrows at me, and I don't *want* to start laughing but I just can't help it. The more I think about what I put Demeter through—the sack, the stones, sweeping out the stable—the more my stomach heaves.

"I'm sorry," I gasp. "I'm so sorry, Demeter. I can't *believe* I did all that."

"Nor can I," says Demeter, and she suddenly erupts as well. As I catch sight of Flora, she looks even more gobsmacked than before.

"Demeter and I have to talk," Alex says, coming over. "But then we both want to buy you the biggest drink you can consume without *actually* being poisoned. Meet you back here in an hour?"

"Great!" I nod, trying to ignore the gazes of Flora, Rosa, and Sarah. "See you then."

"And again, thanks, Katie." Demeter grabs my hands for a final squeeze. "Thank you *so* much."

"You *still* can't get her bloody name right, can you?" says Sarah, and I wheel round in surprise. Sarah is gazing at Demeter, trembling with contempt and defiance, even now. "It's *Cat*."

"No it's not, Sarah." I flick her the most cutting look I can muster. "It's *Katie*."

I step past the lot of them, my head high, and feel a lightness take hold of me as soon as I get out of their toxic atmosphere. As I reach the glass doors, it's as if a delayed reaction hits me. It's all good! We've done it! Demeter's vindicated!

I practically skip down the steps to the street, a huge smile licking across my face. I'm wondering how to fill the hour till I see Demeter and Alex again, and already looking forward to our drink, when my phone buzzes with some new message or other. As I pull it out I wonder—half-hope—if Demeter's already summoning me back to the office.

But it's not from Demeter. It's from a digital branding agency called Broth, which I applied to weeks ago. My breath catches as I fumble to open the email and skim the words:

> Dear Ms. Brenner . . . recent application for the post of junior associate . . . impressed by your application and would like to discuss this further . . . please call to arrange an interview . . .

And I stand transfixed, clutching my phone, my blood dancing in my veins. An interview. An actual interview. Oh my God!

CHAPTER TWENTY-TWO

I start next month. The salary's pretty much what I was on before and the offices are in Marylebone, and I'm thinking about living somewhere west this time. I've been looking in Hanwell, which is quite cheap.

They were really friendly, the two women who interviewed me. They loved my portfolio and said I *had* to join their pub quiz team. It's a great place to work—I can tell that already. And they phoned to offer me the job while I was on the train back home. They really want me! I've got everything I ever wanted. So I don't know why I don't feel more euphoric.

OK. Full disclosure: I know exactly why I don't feel more euphoric.

First of all, two weeks have passed, but I haven't seen Alex since we were in London together. After that extraordinary, heady day, I ended up staying the night at his place, and it was so *exactly* what I'd always dreamed of that I felt like I must have taken some mind-altering drug. He lives in this big, light flat in Battersea, with a balcony and a view of the river (if you lean over the balustrade to look), and we had sex all night with all of London's lights twinkling along as accompaniment. And then we had the perfect morning-after breakfast of croissants and more sex. And then he said he'd call, but—

OK. Stop.

I am *not* going to be that person. Nor am I going to tot up how many times I've texted Alex. (Five.) Or how many times he's texted me in return. (Once.)

And, anyway, this isn't all about him. The honest truth is that it's not just Alex who's left me feeling a little bit small and disappointed. It's Demeter. She, unlike Alex, has been good at keeping in touch. We've spoken on the phone nearly every day, in fact. But her reactions have been a bit weird.

I thought when I told her about my new job, she'd be delighted for me. But she's been all prickly. She even said at first I shouldn't take the job, as she was sure I could do better. (What? Is she nuts?) Then she backtracked and said, "No, you have to take it." Then she fired a whole load of questions at me about the job and exactly what my deal was—then seemed to lose interest. We haven't really talked about it, the last few days.

And all the time there's this big, unanswered question which, every time I think about it, makes me feel a bit hollow: Why didn't *she* offer me a job?

She could have done. I mean, they need new staff. It's been carnage at Cooper Clemmow since it all came out. Sarah's been fired. Rosa's been fired. Flora was leaving to travel, anyway, so she wasn't fired, but she won't get a reference. None of them will get references, in fact. Which means they'll find it very, very hard to find work now.

Although that's better than prosecution, which is what it could have been. *Should* have been. They deserve it, especially Sarah, and I've told Demeter so loads of times. Sometimes I think I'm more angry about what happened than she is. I'd *love* to see Sarah standing in the dock, weeping into her retro-print hankie, mascara smeared everywhere. . . .

But Demeter's decided that she's not going to press charges. Her point of view is that sometimes you have to be pragmatic. She doesn't want the whole story coming out in the press; she doesn't want to testify in court; she doesn't want to become known as the woman whose staff stitched her up. She wants to move on. And Adrian is willing to support her, whatever she decides. So. Case closed.

Demeter did take the rest of the department out to lunch, though, and explain a few things. She told Mark that *she'd* nominated him for the Stylesign Award. She explained that Rosa never had been selected for the mayor's project. She apologized for being scatty and tactless. Then she explained exactly why the other three had been fired. Apparently there was stunned silence for a full three minutes. I *wish* I'd been there.

So the department is up and running again—apparently much more happily than before. But it has some holes in it now, obviously. And I don't know what they're doing about it. Nor can I bring myself to ask.

Anyway, who cares? I *have* a job. A fab job. There's no point feeling hurt by Demeter. Or Alex. I have more important things to do, like training up Denise to take my place here.

"OK, let's try again." I adopt a wide-eyed glamper's expression. "Hello! We've just arrived! Is this Ansters Farm?"

I'm in the kitchen, doing some role play with Denise, who needs a bit of work on the charm side of things.

"'Course it's Ansters Farm," Denise responds flatly. "Says so on the sign."

"No, don't say that. Just say, 'Yes, it is! Well done!' "

" 'Well done' for coming on holiday?" says Denise sardonically, but I ignore her.

"OK, now, smile. Say something like, 'What a lovely dog!' "

"Them ones with dogs are the worst," counters Denise. "Bloody pain, they are."

"Well, they pay your wages. So smile and pat the dog. Got it?"

"Fine!" explodes Denise. "What a beautiful dog," she says in syrupy tones, an unnerving smile on her face. "We can't wait to welcome your wonderful dog. In fact, we love him already, on account of him being so marvelous. See, I can do it," she adds with a sniff. "*Now* can I get on with my cleaning?"

I give an inward grin. I think she'll rise to the challenge.

"How's it going?" Biddy comes into the kitchen, holding a bundle of carrots from the garden, and I feel a familiar wave of guilt run through me. It happens every time I see Dad or Biddy—i.e., about a hundred times a day.

Not that I let on. Biddy won't allow me to feel guilty for a moment. Not a *sliver* of a moment. The minute I started saying how bad I felt at leaving them, she got quite cross.

"We are so, so proud of you," she said, clutching my hands. "You've given us so much, Katie. Without you, we'd have none of this, *none* of it. You've done your bit, my love. Now you go and follow your dreams. You deserve it."

And I know she means it. But it's another reason I don't feel as euphoric as I expected. I love this place. Maybe I'm allowing myself to love it more now. I'm proud of the business, of Dad in his Farmer Mick outfit, of the yurts all lit up by lanterns at night. Ansters Farm has turned into such a *thing*. It's going to be hard to leave.

"Do you need help with those?" I say to Biddy, nodding at the carrots. And I'm just rolling up my sleeves when I hear a voice behind me that makes me think I'm hallucinating.

"Hi, Katie."

Is that . . . *Alex*?

"Katie! Oh, good, you're here." Another voice greets me, and I blink. *Demeter?*

I whip round—and I'm not hallucinating. They're both here in Somerset. Standing in the kitchen doorway. Demeter's wearing one of her edgy London outfits, and Alex has had a haircut, I dimly notice. I'm so flummoxed, I can barely speak.

"What—" I look from face to face. "What are you *doing* here?"

Alex grins. "As ever, you get straight to the point. It was Demeter's idea, so blame her. We could have just got on the phone. . . ."

"Katie deserves more than a phone call," says Demeter.

"You wanted an excuse to come down here again and eat Biddy's scones." Alex prods Demeter on the shoulder. "Admit it. We both did."

"Maybe," says Demeter, starting to laugh.

"But what are you *doing* here?" I try again.

"Right," says Demeter. "Let me do this *properly,*" she says mock-reprovingly to Alex. "No interruptions." Then she turns back to me. "Katie, I've been talking to Adrian about you. And we would very much like it if you would come to Cooper Clemmow for an interview."

My mouth falls open. I try to frame some sensible words, but they're not coming out properly.

" 'Please.' " Alex nudges Demeter. "You didn't say 'please.' No manners."

"I've got a job already," I manage.

"With Broth." Alex nods. "Don't worry, those guys owe me one. We'll sort it out if need be. You haven't signed anything yet?"

"No, not yet—"

"Great!" says Demeter crisply. "As you know, we have some gaps to fill at Cooper Clemmow, and we're hoping to lure you into one of them. Subject to your impressing Adrian, which you most certainly will. Please?" she adds, and gives me one of her sudden radiant smiles.

"You're fighting them off!" exclaims Dad, coming into the kitchen. "You go, Katie girl!"

"Mick!" Alex greets him in delight. "Mick, I've missed you. How are the wigwams?"

"Not so good." Dad's mood dims. "That Dave Yarnett's a lying scoundrel. Wigwams for kiddies, weren't they? No bloody good for us." He shakes his head dismally—then brightens. "So, are you offering Katie a job?"

"It's only an *interview,*" I put in quickly.

"If you can spare her for an afternoon," says Demeter, eyeing my ensemble of jeans and Factory Shop T-shirt. "Have you got an outfit?"

"You mean . . . now?" The truth dawns on me. "We're going *now*?"

"After lunch," says Alex firmly. "Biddy, put us both down for the full Somerset farmhouse blowout."

"But my clothes." I'm trying to think what I've got that's clean and ironed. Then I put my hands to my head. "My *hair*."

"Nothing a quick blow-dry won't sort out. Although . . ." Demeter peers more closely. "Katie, what's going on with your color?"

"Oh, that." I chew my lip. "Well, I wanted to get rid of the blue, so I went for a chestnut rinse. Only . . ." I can hardly bear to admit the truth. "It was a knockoff pack of dye from Dave Yarnett."

"No!" says Alex in mock horror.

"I know! What was I thinking? But he was round here, and he had the boxes in his car, so . . . And there wasn't enough stuff in the packet to cover all my hair. Is it *really* bad?"

"Not *really* bad, but . . ." Demeter hesitates diplomatically. "Maybe you should touch it up." Then she gives me an odd little smile. "I'll do it, if you like."

It's a pretty intimate thing, doing someone's hair. It's certainly an icebreaker. As Demeter brushes the dye onto my hair, we chat like old, close friends.

I tell her about the evening I spent with Dad last week, looking over old photos. There were pictures of Mum that I'd never seen, images of my childhood I'd completely forgotten. Biddy hovered by the stove for a while, busying herself with pans, as though she was too diffident to join in—but then I summoned her to look at a picture of me on a donkey at the seaside and patted the chair beside me. We spent the rest of the evening, all three of us, leafing through the photographs, listening to Dad reminisce, and I felt more like we were a proper family than I ever had before.

Then Demeter tells me all about James starting his big job in Brussels.

"The first night, I was really lonely," she says with a grimace. "We have a *very* large bed, you know—custom-made French oak, actually—and when only one of us is in it . . . Well." She exhales. "It's a big old empty bed."

"I bet," I say, biting my lip at the custom-made French oak bed. I almost want to ask, *Is the oak organic?* But I hold my tongue. Demeter's unbending to me here, and it's nice.

"So the next night, I did it differently," Demeter continues. "I piled a whole lot of cushions on the bed and I let our new puppy sleep there too. He's not supposed to go upstairs. And it was fine."

"What's James going to say about the puppy?" I can't help asking.

"He'll be furious." She gives me a sparky grin in the mirror. "Well, he shouldn't have gone to Brussels."

She seems far lighter in spirits than usual. Her brow is less drawn; she hasn't looked swivelly-eyed once. Her life seems manageable and enjoyable, even with James away. She seems like a different Demeter.

And I find myself thinking: Maybe the Demeter I got to know wasn't ever the real her. It was the stressed-out, beleaguered, victim-of-bullying version of Demeter. Maybe *this* confident, happy woman is the real Demeter. *This* is who Alex headhunted; *this* is who she was meant to be, all the time.

When the dye has done its magic and been rinsed out, we

set up a blow-drying station in front of my dressing-table mirror. Demeter wields the hairdryer and sprays products randomly into my hair, while I tell her about my life in London. My *real* life in London. The flat in Catford, the hammock, and Alan's boxes of whey. Shopping with Flora and panicking about money and being mistaken for a homeless person. We both end up in fits of laughter, and I remember thinking, all that time ago: *Can Demeter laugh?* Well, yes, she can. When there's something to laugh about.

But then she becomes more thoughtful. "I looked at your old Instagram feed," she says, and I feel the color rush to my face. I haven't posted anything on my personal Instagram page for months. "You projected quite a different image there."

"Well." I shrug. "You know. That's Instagram for you."

"Fair enough." She nods. "Everything's hype and spin. But you can't *believe* it all. Not of yourself . . . and not of other people." Her eyes flick to me and away again.

I know what she means. She means: *Why did you believe my hype when you knew your own hype was all fiction?* And it's a fair point.

I've had time to reflect about this—and I think I believed it because I *wanted* to believe it so badly. I *wanted* London to be full of perfect princesses like Demeter, living their perfect-princess lives.

"So, this interview," I say, meeting her eyes in the mirror. "What do I say?"

"Just be yourself," says Demeter at once. "Nothing to worry about. Alex and I know you're brilliant already. We just need Adrian to see it for himself, which he will."

"That's easy for you to say."

I'm actually quite nervous about it.

OK, full disclosure: I'm petrified.

"I'll tell you something, Katie," says Demeter, playing with the hairdryer cord. "I got back to work and I missed you. I wanted to consult you about stuff. I wanted you to *be* there."

"I missed you too," I admit.

And it's true. I missed her voice. Her opinionated, annoying, dynamic voice. No one attacks life quite like Demeter.

"OK. Serum." Demeter starts squirting the serum onto her fingers. "Now, the *trick* to serum is the touch," she adds, in her usual show-offy way.

"Demeter." I roll my eyes. "What do you know about hairdressing?"

"Nothing," she says without blinking. She flicks at my hair a few times. "There. Brilliant, no?"

I can't help smiling back. "It's perfect, thank you. Let's go." And it's only as we reach the door that I ask the question that's been humming round my brain but I haven't quite dared ask: "So . . . am I being interviewed for my old job?"

"Everything's changed," says Demeter after a slight pause. "So not exactly."

I feel a sudden plunge in spirits, which I try to conceal. She's not going to offer me some crappy unpaid internship, is she? She wouldn't do that. She *wouldn't*.

"It's pretty much the same level, though?" Somehow I manage to sound light and nonchalant.

But Demeter is searching for something in her bag and doesn't seem to hear the question. "Come on," she says, raising her head. "Time's ticking. Let's go."

We don't talk about the job at all, throughout lunch, farewells to Dad and Biddy, and the journey up to London. Alex tells outrageous stories about his childhood, and Demeter takes several work calls on the car speakerphone, and then both of them want to know how the glamping business is going.

By four o'clock, we're in W6. By half past four I'm sitting outside Adrian's office, trying to remember all the branding jargon I ever knew. By five o'clock, I'm sitting *in* Adrian's office, my nerves shredded, as he and Demeter leaf through my portfolio. Adrian has this calm, unhurried demeanor about him, and he's examining everything carefully.

"I like this," he says occasionally, pointing to a page, and Demeter nods, and I open my mouth, then close it again. I'm actually quite glad of the respite.

My last interview wasn't anything like this. It wasn't nearly so *intense*. Adrian's already grilled me on a million different topics, some really technical, and I feel a bit battered. I keep rerunning my answers, thinking: *Did I tackle the logo question right? Should I have voiced more views on the Fresh 'n Breezy rebrand? Am I using the phrase "design DNA" too much? (Is that possible?)*

And now there's this ominous silence as they both pass judgment on my work. I feel as though I might be sick from nerves, from anticipation, from hope. . . .

"So." Adrian suddenly looks up, making me jump. "Demeter tells me that in the time since you left us, you've set up a business from scratch." He pulls out the brochure from where it's got hidden underneath my portfolio. "I've seen this. It's good." He nods. "And you can pitch?"

"Katie can bullshit like no one else," says Demeter. "I was *convinced* you'd been to every top restaurant in London." She winks at me. "And I've seen her think on her feet. She's like lightning."

"As you know, we're rebuilding our staff levels right now," continues Adrian. "But we're not there yet. It's going to be hard work meanwhile. You up for that?"

"Absolutely," I say, trying not to gabble. "Of course."

"And you can manage a team?" He regards me intently, as though this is the most important question of all.

Through my head flashes: *Why is he asking that?* But I don't let it distract me; I just answer as professionally as I can.

"Yes." I nod. "I've managed and trained the staff at the farm. I've managed vacationers. I'm good with people."

"Believe me," says Demeter, with feeling, "she can make people do things they don't want to do. This girl can manage a team."

"Well, then." Adrian surveys my portfolio again, then looks up at me, his craggy face easing into a smile. "It's a yes. Welcome back, Katie. We'll sort out a package that I think you'll like."

Package. That means . . . An almighty relief crashes over me. It's paid. It's a paid job! This entire interview, I haven't liked to ask—but it's paid! Thank God, thank God—

"It's a yes." Demeter looks at him alertly. "But is it a *yes* yes?"

Clearly she's using some code that only Adrian will understand.

"It's a *yes* yes." Adrian nods at her. "No doubt about that."

Demeter looks ecstatic. "*Good* decision," she says. Then she leans over to hug me, so tightly that I gasp. "Well done, Katie." Her voice is strangely constricted, as if some emotion is spilling out. "I'm *so* proud."

"Thanks!" As she releases me, I rub my nose, still feeling puzzled. "But I don't get . . . Why did you ask about managing a team? A research associate doesn't manage a team."

"No," says Demeter, and she looks at me fondly. "But a creative director does."

I'm in shock. Creative director. *Creative director.*

I'm sitting in Demeter's office, holding a cup of tea but not daring to drink from it in case I drop it.

Creative director. Me. Katie Brenner.

"You have no idea how hard I've been pushing for this," says Demeter, who's striding around her office and seems almost more pumped than I am. "I *knew* you had the potential, but I had to work on Adrian." She shakes her head dismissively. "Men. So narrow-minded. I told him, '*This* is the girl we should have kept! We should have fired all the others!' Well, we did fire all the others," she adds, as though in an afterthought.

"I still can't believe it," I say. "Are you sure . . . I mean, can I do this?"

"Of course you can," says Demeter airily. "You'll report straight to me and I'll teach you everything. You're quick. And you have the right instincts—that's the main thing. That's what *can't* be taught. It'll go perfectly, the pair of us working in tandem. I know it will. You'll be a second me."

I can't help laughing. "Demeter, *no one* could be a second you."

"I'm going to train you up." She shoots me a glinting look. "Then *you* can start going to a few industry events on my behalf. And *I'll* stay at home with Coco and Hal."

"Sounds good." I try to conceal my totally uncool excitement. Industry events!

"I think I need a bit of space in my life for . . . other stuff," says Demeter. "Family. My children."

I wander over to her pinboard and gaze at the familiar collage of Demeter images. Career success, family success, general coolness . . . Then I notice a new set of photos, which make me blink. It's the whole family at Ansters Farm. There's Demeter and James by their yurt, holding champagne glasses as bunting flutters behind them in the breeze. There's Coco sitting on a hay bale, looking like a catalog ad with her endless tanned legs. There's Hal, lolling against a gate, grinning at a curious cow. You'd look at those pictures and you'd think: *Well, there's a family with not a care in the world.*

At least, other people might think that. But not me. Not anymore.

"Hey." A voice at the door makes us both turn, and it's Alex, beaming at me. "I've been pacing the floor," he complains to Demeter. "You could have *told* me the news. Well done, Katie. Welcome back to Cooper Clemmow."

"Thanks! Oh God." I have a sudden thought. "I'll have to tell Broth I can't take their job."

"In your *face,* Broth," says Alex emphatically, making me laugh again. "Don't worry," he adds, as he sees my guilty expression. "Just think, some other lucky person will get that job now. It's a win–win."

I can't help picturing some desperate job-seeking person like me, sitting on their bed with their hammock strung above, feeling desolate . . . then getting a call and hearing the wonderful news. Alex is right: It's a win–win.

"So." He glances meaningfully at Demeter. "Give us a minute?"

"This is *my* office," says Demeter, rolling her eyes. "One minute." She heads past him, through the door. Alex closes it, and we're alone.

"Good day." His eyes spark at me.

"*Really* good day."

"Well, you deserve it, Katie Brenner. Of all people. Come here."

He envelops me in a hug. Within about ten seconds we're kissing, and I'm lost. I'm jelly.

No. I *cannot* be jelly in the office.

"Stop!" I pull away, my voice blurry. "I'll get fired before I begin!"

"You're delicious, you know that?" He strokes my hair.

"So are you."

His hand is touching mine, playing with my fingers, and I can't stop smiling up at him, and I think I've never felt as blissful as I do right now.

"You've done a lot for me, Katie," Alex says, breaking the quiet. "Do you know that?"

"Same goes!"

"No." He shakes his head. "You don't understand. You got to me. You made me think about stuff."

"Oh, right. What stuff?"

"What you have in Somerset. Your setup. Your moss."

"My moss?" I give a little laugh.

"Biddy. Your dad. The farm." He spreads his arms. "Moss, moss, moss. *I* want moss." As he looks at me, I realize he's not joking. He's deadly serious. "I had the shittiest upbringing for moss." A tiny spasm runs across his face, as though he's trying to dodge the memory. "But it's not too late, is it?"

"No, of course it isn't. You just have to . . ." I pause, feeling as if I'm treading on eggshells. "Decide to stay. To commit. To reach out to people and *be* with them and . . . well . . . let them turn into your moss."

There's silence. Alex is gazing at my face, his brow furrowed, as though he's trying to learn something very difficult and impenetrable from me.

"You're right," he says abruptly. "I run. I always fucking run. Well, I'm not running anymore. I want stability. I want love," he adds, and I feel a tiny frisson as he says the word. "You know? Long-term proper love. I mean, that's what it's all about, isn't it?"

"Well, I think so." I feel a kind of spreading joy inside me. "I think you'll be happy that way. And so . . ." I hesitate. "So will the people you love."

There's a taut silence between us. His dark eyes are still searching my face; he's never seemed so intense.

"I agree," he says softly. "I have a whole new outlook. I'm committing. This is it." He bangs his fist in the other hand as though inspired. "I'm going to New York."

What?

Did I hear that right?

"I'm going to find my dad," he says with sudden passion. "Because I've ignored him. I've hated him. And that's all wrong. Isn't it? I mean, we're in the same field. Maybe we should try working together."

"You're going to *live* in New York?" I'm so crestfallen, my voice breaks.

"Not sure yet. All I know is, I want the same relationship as you have with your dad. Maybe we *are* both tricksy sods, but shouldn't we at least try?"

"But . . ." I'm still struggling to take in this hammer blow. "What about your job?"

"Oh, Cooper Clemmow need me back in New York next week," he says as though this is some minor consideration. "American Electrics want me back on their rebrand—*not* in the role I'm in at the moment," he adds firmly. "Forget that. I've realized I'm not cut out to be a manager. But what I can do is create. And I want to create a whole new life. A *family*-based life. Stable. Forever."

He falls silent. Somehow I manage an encouraging smile, even though there's a hot, looming sadness in my head. I thought . . .

No. Stop. It doesn't matter what I thought.

"Wow. New York. I mean, that's—" I break off, my voice not quite steady. "It's a great idea."

"It is, right?" Alex nods eagerly. "And it was *you* who gave me that idea."

"Great!" I say shrilly. "I'm so pleased."

The more brightly I talk, the tighter my throat feels and the harder I have to blink. I'm in shock. I hadn't realized. I did let him into my heart. I did. I didn't even know I was doing it, but somehow there he is, wrapped up with everything that I love.

Suddenly I notice Demeter watching us from the open doorway. She must have arrived back a while ago, because I can tell from her expression that she's heard. And although she says nothing, I can hear her voice in my head, clear as a bell. *One-Way Alex . . . never touches the same ground twice . . . a lot of broken hearts . . . don't get smitten . . . protect yourself.*

Protect myself. I can feel my mental armies springing into action. I can feel every self-defensive instinct waking up. Because here's the thing I need to remember: Life is good at the moment. And I'm *not* about to blight it by pining after a man. I'm *not* about to hope for impossible things. However well we seemed to work together.

"Actually, Demeter?" I say, in the most nonchalant tone I can manage. "Could you give us another moment?"

Demeter turns away with one last, sympathetic look at me. I turn to Alex and draw breath, my heart hammering.

"So, I don't know how you saw things working out between us, but . . . you know." I force a bright, carefree smile. "We'll both probably find . . . different paths from now on. So. No hard feelings. It was fun, wasn't it?"

"Oh." Alex seems a bit discomfited. "I see. Got it."

"I mean, New York's a long way away!" I give a breezy laugh. "You'll be busy . . . I'll be busy. . . ."

"Yes. I mean, I *had* thought . . ." He trails off and shakes his head, as though dispelling an uncomfortable thought. "But . . . OK. Right. Understood."

"So." I clear my throat. "That's . . . good. Sorted."

There's an awkward silence in the office. I breathe out a few times, my gaze distant, trying to keep my cool. I feel a bit like giving myself a high five, for sorting my life so efficiently, and a bit like bursting into tears.

"I'm not going for a week or two," says Alex eventually, in wary tones. "I was actually going to ask if you wanted to come round to my flat tonight?"

"Right." I swallow, trying to maintain my indifferent demeanor and *not* give away how much I want him.

It's not only the sex or the way he makes me laugh or his sudden, random, always-entertaining ideas. It's the sharing, the confiding, the peeling away the layers of him. Which is, I guess, how I ended up letting him into my heart. And so, really, I should say, *No, let's end it here*. But I'm not quite that strong.

"Well, OK," I say at last. "That might be fun. Just fun," I add for emphasis. *"Fun."*

"Absolutely. Just fun." Alex seems about to say something else when his phone rings. As he pulls it out of his pocket, he winces at the display. "Sorry. Do you mind if I—"

"Of course! Go ahead!"

The interruption is exactly what I need to get my thoughts in order and stiffen my inner resolve. I walk over to the window, my chin set, talking firmly to myself.

OK. This is what it is. It's fun. It's an interlude. And I'm going to enjoy it simply as that. Repeat: Life is good at the moment. No, it's brilliant. And when Alex disappears out of the picture again, it *will not throw me*. Because the thing about letting people into your heart is, you can just push them out again. Easy.

CHAPTER TWENTY-THREE

I've called it @mynotsoperfectlife and I've already got 267 followers! I post utterly unvarnished, unposed, un-Instagrammy photos with captions, and it's turned into one of the most fun hobbies I've ever had.

A photo of bad-tempered crowds on a tube platform: *My not-so-perfect commute*. A picture of the revolting blister on my heel: *My not-so-perfect new shoes*. A photo of my hair, drenched: *The not-so-perfect London weather.*

The amazing thing is how many other people have joined in. Mark from work posted a picture of himself eating a doughnut, captioned *My not-so-perfect eat-clean regime*. Biddy posted a picture of some ripped trousers, which she'd obviously caught on some barbed wire, entitled *My not-so-perfect rural existence*, which made me laugh.

Even Steve's fiancée, Kayla, has posted a picture of a receipt for the deposit on a tent (£3,500). She called it *My not-so-perfect wedding* and I'm *really* hoping that Steve knows all about it and sees the joke too.

Fi has deluged my page with photos from New York, and to be honest, it's totally changed the way I see her and her life.

For a start, I hadn't quite realized how small her apartment was. She's posted lots of pictures of her shower—which I have to admit is really unappealing—all captioned *My not-so-perfect New York rental*. Then she posted a photo of a text message that some guy sent her, dumping her as she arrived for their date. She could actually see him at the bar, chatting up another girl. She called that one *My not-so-perfect New York date*, and got about thirty responses from people with even worse stories.

After Fi had posted about six times, I called her up and we had a bit of a heart to heart. In fact, it lasted all evening. I hadn't realized how much I'd missed her voice. Words on a screen just aren't the same.

And it's not as if she said, *Guess what, my fabulous life was all made up, I haven't really got quirky friends, nor do I drink pink margaritas in the Hamptons*. Because she has got quirky friends, and she did drink pink margaritas in the Hamptons. At least once. But there's other stuff in her life too. Stuff that balances out the bright-and-shiny. Just like there is for all of us. Bright-and-shiny on the one side; the crappy truth on the other.

I think I've finally worked out how to feel good about life. Every time you see someone's bright-and-shiny, remember: They have their own crappy truths too. Of course they do. And every time you see your own crappy truth and feel despair and think, *Is this my life*, remember: It's not. Everyone's got a bright-and-shiny, even if it's hard to find sometimes.

"Katie?"

I raise my head and smile. There's my bright-and-shiny, right in front of me—at least, two big chunks of it. Dad and

Biddy have come into the kitchen, dressed up in their visiting-London outfits. They're both wearing stiff blue jeans (Dave Yarnett) and gleaming white sneakers (Dave Yarnett). Dad has a new I ♥ LONDON T-shirt, which he bought yesterday at the Tower of London, while Biddy's wearing a sweatshirt with Big Ben on it. Dad's holding the tube map and Biddy's clutching a flask of water. They're going to Kew Gardens today, and I think they'll love it.

They promised me they'd come to stay after I'd had "time to settle in," and I thought they meant in the autumn, after the season was over. But I'm only six weeks into my new job and here they are, leaving Steve and Denise in charge of the glampers for a couple of days. It must have meant heroic amounts of organization, and I'm truly appreciative.

The only snag is, I haven't been able to take time off work—but they insist that they don't mind. This way they can "enjoy London," as they keep putting it. Dad has told me about five times how he's been finding London "extremely enjoyable" this visit and how he "never really looked at it the right way before."

I smile at them. "All ready?"

Biddy nods. "All set! Goodness, you do have an early start, darling—" Then she stops herself, flushes, and glances at Dad.

I think Biddy and Dad must have made a joint vow on this visit: *We will not utter one single even slightly negative opinion.* I can tell they think my new bedroom is a little small (they should have seen the last one) and they think my commute is a bit long (I think it's a picnic). But all they've done since they arrived is shower me with positive comments about

London, Londoners, jobs in offices, and basically everything about my life.

"Handy window," comments Dad now, looking at my nondescript little kitchen window. "Makes the kitchen very light."

"Very nice!" chimes in Biddy eagerly. "And I noticed you have a Japanese restaurant at the end of the road. Very exotic! Very glamorous! Isn't it, Mick? That's what you get in London. The restaurants."

I want to give Biddy a hug. My little road in Hanwell is not exotic. Nor glamorous. It's well priced and the commute is half what I had before, and there's room for a sofa bed. Those are the main attractions of my flat, as well as not having to share with weirdo flatmates. But if Biddy's going to call it exotic and glamorous, then I can too.

The truth is, Biddy and Dad will never see or feel or understand the London-ness that gives me a spring in my step, every single day. It's intangible. It's not about being glossy and it's not about trying to live up to an image; it's about who I am. I love Ansters Farm, and I always will—and who knows? Maybe one day I'll end up back there. But something about this life I'm leading now makes me feel super-alive. The people, the buzz, the horizons, the connections . . . Like, for example, I'm having a meeting with some people at Disney this afternoon. Disney!

OK, full disclosure: It's not really my meeting. Demeter and Adrian are having the meeting, but they said I could come along. Still, I'll be meeting the Disney people, won't I? I'll be learning, won't I?

I check my reflection in the mirror and run a last-minute dollop of serum through my curls. I'm doing London differently this time. More confidently. I'm not trying to be a girl with straight, tortured, unfamiliar hair. I'm being me.

"So, let's go." I pick up my bag and usher Dad and Biddy out of my flat, through the little communal hall, out of the main front door . . . and to the top of the steps.

Yes! I have steps!

They aren't quite as grand as Demeter's steps. And she's right: They are a pain to lug shopping up. But they're gray stone and kind-of-almost elegant, and every time I open the front door in the morning, they give me a spark of joy.

"Nice . . . um . . . bus stop!" says Dad, gesturing ahead. "Very handy, love." He looks up, as though to check I'm listening, and I feel a tweak of love for him. He's praised everything in this street, from the houses to the scrubby trees to the bench outside the newsagent's. Now he's reduced to admiring the bus stop?

"It's useful," I agree. "Cuts my traveling time down." (Let's not mention the bus fumes or the crowds of schoolchildren who use it.)

As the bus draws up, it's a bit of a scrum, and by the time we're all inside, I've ended up separated from Dad and Biddy. I gesture reassuringly at them and take the opportunity to check a text which just beeped in my phone.

Hi Katie, how's it going? Jeff

I blink at it for a moment. Jeff is this guy that I've dated, like, twice. We met at a conference. And he's . . . polite. Nice-looking. Nondescript.

No, *not* nondescript. Quickly I steer my own thoughts onto a strictly positive, upbeat path: *Wow. Jeff texted. We've only dated a couple of times, so this is a sweet gesture of his, to check in like that. It's nice of him. Really, really nice. Considerate. He's a really considerate guy, in fact. It's a really good quality of his, being considerate.*

This is my new guiding principle: Find a man of *quality*. Not a man who excites me but one who *values* me. Not a man who takes me to the moon and then vanishes off to New York but one who takes me to . . . Bracknell, maybe. (Jeff is from Bracknell and keeps telling me how great it is.)

Well, OK. Obviously the moon would be even better than Bracknell. But maybe Jeff *will* take me to the moon. I just need to get to know him. I text a reply:

Hi Jeff! How are you?

As I'm typing I have a sudden flashback to a memory which I must *not* keep having. It was just before I moved in here and Alex left for New York, and I texted him from a very dull residents' meeting in my upstairs neighbor's flat:

Help! I'm surrounded by biscuit people!

He started sending me photos of all sorts of biscuits. Then he started Photoshopping them with faces. And I got the giggles and I felt that glow, that warmth, that you-and-me feeling he gives me.

But the you-and-me feeling is a mirage, I tell myself sternly, a *mirage*. Let's look at the facts. Alex is in New York on his one-way lifelong spree around the world. I haven't heard a word from him. Whereas Jeff is here, in Bracknell, actually being interested in my life.

To be fair to Alex, he didn't break off contact; I did. More self-preservation. Really, I should have broken off the whole affair that day in Demeter's office, when he first told me about New York. But I was weak. I couldn't resist a night in his flat, and then another night . . . and another . . .

So we had these golden, heady few days: spending time with each other and being in the moment. I didn't dare to peer into the future. I didn't dare think too hard about things. We cast the whole thing as "fun." We both used that word, a lot, until it started sounding hollow. Where other people might tentatively have talked about love or connection or a relationship, we resolutely pitched the word "fun" at each other. *I've been having so much fun. You're so much fun. That evening was just . . . fun!*

A couple of times, I caught him looking at me uncertainly, as though he sensed the element of charade. Catching my hand; taking it to his lips. A couple of times I couldn't resist sweet, small murmurings into his neck, which sounded closer to love than fun.

But the word "love," even uttered in my mind, made me jolt in alarm. *No, no, no, DON'T fall. . . . Protect yourself. . . . He'll be off; he'll leave you. . . .*

And he was, and he did.

"Look, Katie, you don't *mind* me going, do you?" Alex said once as we lay together, as though the thought was slowly dawning on him. "I mean . . . this has been fun. This is fun. But . . ."

"Mind?" And I laughed, an incredulous, bubbling, carefree laugh; I could have got an Oscar for it.

Oh, just jogging along.

The beep of Jeff's text brings me out of my thoughts. *This* is reality, I remind myself. Jeff is reality. Alex is gone. A memory. A myth.

I try to think of some witty response to *jogging along,* but the very phrase seems to dull my fingers. *Jogging along.* Oh God. Very slowly, I begin to type.

Sounds . . .

I have literally no idea what to say next. Sounds what? Sounds super-fun? Sounds like my idea of hell?

And now, despite myself, I'm remembering another painful–magical Alex moment. It was a night that we had martinis, and Alex suddenly announced, only a little drunkenly, "I do admire you, Katie Brenner. I do so admire you."

"*Admire* me?" I felt my jaw sag. No one had ever admired me before. "What on earth—"

"You're tough. And you're . . ." He seemed to search for the word. "You're straight. You fought for Demeter because you thought it was right. You didn't have to fight for her; in fact, you had every reason *not* to—but you did."

"Actually, I was a mercenary," I replied with a shrug. "Did

I never tell you that? Made five grand. Result." And Alex laughed and laughed, until martini came out of his nose. I could always manage to tickle him; I'm not even sure how.

I remember that we lapsed into silence then, and I gazed at him, while jazz played in the background and soft lights danced on his face. And although I knew full well in one part of my head that he was planning to leave, right at that moment it seemed impossible that he wouldn't always be there with me. Entertaining me with his random comments and impulsive plans and infectious smile. I just couldn't compute the idea of him gone.

Head over head, I guess.

Thankfully we've arrived at the bus stop where we need to change, so I'm able to quit this train of thought. Shake my head clear of old memories and hopes and whatever else rubbish is in there. I put my phone away and shepherd Dad and Biddy through the whole fight-your-way-through-the-schoolkids process. (I can see it from their point of view; it *is* a bit stressy. Although I will say: They're both getting very good at tapping their Oyster cards.)

The second bus whizzes along straight to Chiswick (well, as much as you can whiz in London), and there's summer sunlight glinting in through the window and Biddy even gets a seat. It really could be worse. At Turnham Green, I put Dad and Biddy on a tube to Kew, tell them I can't wait to hear all about it later, and then walk briskly the rest of the way to Cooper Clemmow.

"Morning, Katie," Jade greets me from reception as I walk in.

That's another change I've made. I'm Katie these days, and I don't know why I ever tried being anyone else.

"Morning, Jade." I smile back. "Is Demeter in?"

"Not yet," says Jade. And I'm about to head to the lift when she clears her throat and motions toward someone sitting in the reception area. I turn and blink a few times as I see the figure, feeling a sudden rush of emotions. It's me. OK, it's not me. But it's like looking at myself.

Sitting there, fiddling with her handbag strap, is our new research associate, Carly. She's wearing cheap black trousers and her hair in a plastic clasp and an anxious expression. As she sees me, she leaps up, practically knocking over her glass of water.

"Hi," she says breathlessly. "Hi, Katie, isn't it? We met at my interview? I wanted to get here early on my first day, so . . . Hi."

She looks so apprehensive, I want to give her a hug. Except that would probably freak her out.

"Hi." I shake her hand warmly. "Welcome to Cooper Clemmow. You're going to love it here. Demeter's not here yet, but I'll get you settled in. . . . How was your commute?" I add, as we head toward the lift. "Miserable?"

"Not too bad," says Carly robustly. "I mean, I'm in Wembley, so . . . but it's not too bad."

"I know what it's like." I catch her eye. "Truly."

She nods. "Yes, I know. I've seen your Instagram page. *My not-so-perfect commute.*" She gives a sudden nervous half giggle. "And all the other photos. They're brilliant. They're really . . . *real.*"

"Well, yes." I smile. "That's the idea."

As we head into the airy office space, I can see Carly looking around wide-eyed at the distressed bricks, the naked-man coat stand, the amazing giant plastic flowers that have just arrived from Sensiquo.

"It's so *cool,*" she breathes.

"I know." I can't help catching her enthusiasm. "It's pretty good, isn't it?"

We had some kids over from the Catford community center last week—we set up an outreach day to complement our fundraising efforts. And they were fairly impressed by the office too. Even Sadiqua was, though she tried not to show it and asked everyone she met, "Can you get me on reality TV? 'Cause I want to be a presenter."

That girl is going to go far. I have no idea in which direction—but she'll go far.

"So," I add, as we reach Carly's desk, "I can't remember, sorry—where are you from originally?"

"The Midlands," she says, a touch defensively. "A place near Corby; you wouldn't have heard of it. . . ." She eyes up my print shift dress, which I bought when I got my first month's salary. "So, are you a Londoner? You don't *sound* like a Londoner. Are you . . ." She wrinkles her brow. "West Country?"

I haven't tried to lose my accent this time round. I'm proud of it. My accent's part of me, like Dad and Mum. And the farm. And the fresh country milk that's made my hair so strong and curly. (That's what Dad always said, anyway, to get me to drink up. It was probably bollocks.)

I am what I am. I'm just sorry it took me so long to realize it.

"I'm a Somerset girl through and through." I smile at Carly. "But I live in London now, so . . . I guess I'm both."

Demeter's out at meetings all morning, so I keep an eye on Carly. She *looks* OK, but I know what it's like to be that new girl, putting a brave face on. So at lunchtime I head to her desk.

"Come for a drink," I say. "We're all going to the Blue Bear. Give you a chance to get to know everyone."

I can read her emotions like a book. A flash of delight—then hesitation. She glances at the homemade sandwich in her bag and instantly I know: She's worried about money.

"On the company," I say at once. "All on the company. It's a thing we do."

We'll sort it later. Demeter and Liz and me. I'm quite friendly with Liz these days, now that the axis of evil has left.

On the way to the pub I text Demeter, telling her about our plans. She says she's on her way, then texts back a picture of a vintage typeface she's just seen: What do you think? I send back an enthusiastic reply, and we ping back and forth a few times.

We talk a lot by text message, Demeter and I. In fact, we talk a lot, full stop. Most evenings the pair of us will be the only ones left in the office, making herbal teas, talking over some issue or other. Once we even ordered Chinese food, just like in my old fantasy. We crack stuff. We work out solutions. (To be fairer, it's often Demeter working out the solution and me listening avidly, thinking, *Oh my God, I get it.*)

I was always trying to learn from Demeter, but I only had scraps to work with. Now I'm exposed to the full Demeter creative mindset, and it's great. No, it's *amazing*. Don't get me wrong—Demeter still has her flaws. She's tricksy and unpredictable and the most disorganized woman on the planet . . . but, bloody hell, am I picking up a lot.

Then sometimes, when I'm in her office, we'll relax a little and move on to family stuff. I'll tell her the news from Ansters Farm and hear the latest gossip from the Wilton household. James's job in Brussels is working out well, and they're loads happier, apparently. In fact, seeing him only once a week has its advantages, Demeter added. (She didn't spell out what the advantages are, but I can imagine.)

Coco has a boyfriend, and Hal wants to take up cage fighting, which Demeter is fiercely opposing. ("Cage fighting? I mean, *cage fighting*, Katie? What's wrong with fencing?")

I even went to supper with the family one midweek evening, in their amazing house in Shepherd's Bush. It was lovely. Both Coco and Hal were on best behavior, and they'd made a lemon pudding as a joint effort. We sat round a reclaimed-oak table with Diptyque candles scenting the air, and the cutlery was some special French kind, and even the loo was like something out of a magazine (hand-printed wallpaper and a vintage basin). And I might have started sinking back into the belief that Demeter's life was perfect, if Coco hadn't shrieked, "Urrrrgh!" from the kitchen and we hadn't all rushed in and seen that the puppy had been ill all over the floor.

(Coco wanted to win Best Not-So-Perfect Life for the photo of the mess, which she posted on my Instagram page. Mmm, nice.)

As we approach the Blue Bear, I see Demeter coming from

the opposite direction, wearing her new leather jacket and looking very impressive as she taps on her phone.

"Hi, Demeter!" I greet her. "You remember Carly, our new research associate?"

"Hello! Welcome!" Demeter shakes Carly's hand and flashes her that slightly intimidating smile, and I can see Carly gulp. Demeter *is* quite a daunting prospect if you don't know her. (Although not so much if you've seen her facedown in the mud, wearing a sack.)

In the Blue Bear we order three bottles of wine and hand out glasses, congregating around a couple of high bar tables. And I'm just wondering whether Demeter should make a little welcoming speech to Carly, or whether she'll feel too conspicuous, when the door to the street opens and there's a bit of a gasp and I hear someone saying, "Alex?"

Alex?

Alex?

My throat constricts and, very slowly, I turn.

It's him. It's Alex. He's wearing a slightly crumpled linen jacket and his hair is disheveled and he hasn't shaved. He fixes his gaze instantly on me, and I feel something lurch inside me.

"I know you said it was just fun," he says without preamble. "I know that. But . . ."

He shakes his head as though trying to sort his troublesome thoughts. Then he looks up again, his eyes dark, frank, without any playful spark—and as they meet mine, everything stops. I feel as though I've divined everything he wants to say at once, in that one look. But I can't believe it, can't let myself believe it.

As we're staring wordlessly at each other, Alex sways slightly and grabs a barstool for balance.

"Are you OK?" I take a step forward in alarm.

"Haven't slept for a few days," he says. "I've been thinking. I didn't sleep on the flight either. Katie, I got things wrong. So wrong. Everything wrong."

He rubs his forehead and I wait silently. He looks a little devastated, a little desperate.

"I'm tired of darting and weaving," he says suddenly. "Spinning. Constantly spinning. Never being still, never being grounded . . ."

"I thought your dad was going to ground you," I say tentatively. "I thought your dad was your moss."

"Wrong moss," he says, and his eyes delve into mine as though they never want to leave. "Wrong moss." He seems to become aware of the gaping Cooper Clemmow staff members all around. "Can we go somewhere quieter?"

There isn't really anywhere quieter, but we edge a few feet away from the rest of the crowd. My heart is pounding; I feel almost light-headed. Where do we go with this? What *is* this? Has he flown back . . . for me?

"So you didn't get on with your dad?" I say carefully.

"Fuck him and all who fuck him," says Alex with a flippant gesture. "But that's another story." He shoots me a charming half grin, but I can see pain in his face too. I wonder just what's been going on in New York these last few weeks. And I feel an unwarranted, irrational spike of fury toward Alex's dad. If he's hurt him, even a little bit . . .

"Katie, I've finally realized. I don't want what you and your dad have. I want—" Alex breaks off, locking his eyes on to mine. "You."

At once I feel my throat thickening. I thought I was on top of the situation, but I'm really not feeling on top of it right now. I'm feeling like I might dissolve.

"All I've been thinking about is you," he presses on. "All the time, you. No one else is funny like you. Or wise like you. You're very wise, you know that? As well as having incredibly tough thighs," he adds, glancing at my legs. "I mean, they're superhuman."

I open my mouth and close it. I don't know what to say. "Alex—"

"No, wait." He lifts a hand. "I haven't finished. That's what I want, and I was an idiot to leave, and I should have realized—" He interrupts himself. "Anyway. But I don't know if I can have you. And that's why I'm here. To ask you. If you say no, then I'll go away, but that's why I'm here. To ask you. I'm repeating myself, aren't I?" he adds matter-of-factly. "I'm nervous. This isn't my style. It's really not my style. Coming back."

"I know," I say, my voice barely above a whisper. "I . . . I heard."

"So, yes, I'm nervous, and, yes, I'm embarrassed right now, but you know what? I'm *owning* my embarrassment."

He finishes speaking into utter silence. Clearly everyone in the entire bar has surreptitiously stopped talking to eavesdrop on us. I glance up and catch sight of Demeter listening. Her hand is to her mouth as though in disbelief, and her eyes are a little sheeny.

"I'm owning my embarrassment," Alex repeats, apparently oblivious to the audience. "Here I am, Alex Astalis, in love with you. Owning that too."

I'm tingling in shock. Did he just say he was *in love* with me?

"But of course there are many, *many* reasons why this might not be a good idea," he continues before I can reply, "and I wrote most of them down on the plane, just to torture myself." He produces an airline sick bag with scrawled writing all over it. "And the one I kept coming back to was: All you ever wanted was fun. You told me. That's what you wanted. And me turning up here like this, it's not fun. Is it?" He takes a step toward me, his expression so agonized, so questioning, so quintessentially *Alex,* that I have to fight the urge to throw myself at him. "Is it?" he repeats. "Fun? This?"

"No." Tears are shimmering in my eyes as I eventually manage to speak. "It's not fun. It's . . . us. It's whatever we are. And that's all I ever really wanted too. Not fun. Us."

"Us." Alex takes another step toward me. "That sounds good to me." His voice is a little husky and hesitant. "That sounds . . . like what I want."

"Me too." I honestly can't speak anymore. My throat is clogged and my nose is prickling. I never did push him out of my heart. How do you push Alex out of your heart?

And I'm frantically telling myself: *We're in a public place, behave with dignity* . . . but then his face is a foot away . . . six inches away . . . and I inhale his scent and feel his strong arms around me . . . and, oh God, I'm lost.

I'm pretty sure that kissing your boss in full public is against protocol. Although . . . is he my boss right now?

Finally we draw apart, and *everyone's* blatantly been watching us. Don't they have lives? As the hubbub starts up again, I glance over at Demeter and she clasps her hands tightly, blows us both a kiss, then puts a tissue to her eyes, as though she's my fairy godmother.

"Katie Brenner." Alex cups my face as though drinking me in. "Katie Brenner. Why did I go to New York when I had you right here?"

"I can't *believe* you left me," I say, nestling into his jacket.

"I can't *believe* you didn't stop me." He kisses me again, long and deep, and I find myself calculating whether I can take the afternoon off. Special circumstances.

Alex passes me a wineglass and I clink with his and lean against his chest again. And something in me unwinds, something I didn't even realize was tense. I feel like: At last. At last. At *last*.

"Katie Brenner," says Alex again, as though just saying my name makes him happy. "So, let me take you out to dinner tonight. I never take you out to dinner." He frowns, as though we're an old married couple. "Where would you like to go?"

"I've got Dad and Biddy staying with me at the moment," I say, a little regretfully, but his face lights up.

"Even better. Family reunion. You *do* realize I'm only after you for Biddy's cooking?"

"Oh, I know." I laugh. "I'm not stupid."

"So, family supper, then back to mine and . . . see how it goes? Let's go somewhere really special." His eyes are sparking with enthusiasm; I can feel the happiness emanating from him.

"Somewhere *really* special?" I eye him carefully. "You mean that?"

"Absolutely." He nods. "Somewhere really, truly, extraordinarily special. Is there anywhere you'd like to go?"

Is there anywhere I'd like to go?

"Hang on." I scrabble in my bag. Right at the bottom is my ancient handwritten list of restaurants, the one I've been carrying around all this time.

"Any of those." I point. "That. Or that. Or this one. Or that. Maybe there? Not there. And this one . . . hmm, not sure . . ."

Alex is staring at the list, a bit stunned, and I suddenly realize this is probably not how most girls react when they're asked out to dinner.

"Or anywhere," I amend hastily, crumpling the list. "I mean, really . . . you choose. I'm sure you've got loads of good ideas—"

"Bollocks I do." He grins. "You're the expert; you choose."

"Oh," I say, discomfited. "But don't you want to—I mean, shouldn't the man—"

"Own it, Katie." He cuts me off. "Enjoy it. *You're* choosing, OK? Over to you, my gorgeous Somerset girl." He kisses my fingertips and pulls me close again, his voice soft in my ear. "You're the boss."

ACKNOWLEDGMENTS

No one's life is perfect. But mine was made a lot more perfect by the brilliant people who helped me create this book.

Jenny Bond and Sarah Frampton offered me insight and ideas on city life and country life alike. I'm especially grateful to Jenny for her expert help on the corporate world of advertising, marketing, and brands.

Meanwhile, I am constantly in awe of the amazing work of "Team Kinsella" in the UK, the U.S., and around the world. Thank you to everyone who works so hard on my books—and a special thank-you to my agents and publishers in the UK and U.S.:

At LAW: Araminta Whitley, Peta Nightingale, Jennifer Hunt

At Inkwell: Kim Witherspoon, David Forrer

At ILA: Nicki Kennedy, Sam Edenborough, Jenny Robson, Katherine West, Simone Smith

At Transworld: Francesca Best, Bill Scott-Kerr, Larry Finlay, Claire Evans, Nicola Wright, Alice Murphy-Pyle, Becky Short, Tom Chicken and his team, Giulia Giordano, Matt

Watterson and his team, Richard Ogle, Kate Samano, Judith Welsh, Jo Williamson, Bradley "Bradmobile" Rose

At Penguin Random House U.S.: Gina Centrello, Susan Kamil, Kara Cesare, Avideh Bashirrad, Debbie Aroff, Jess Bonet, Sanyu Dillon, Sharon Propson, Sally Marvin, Theresa Zoro, Loren Noveck

May your lives always live up to your Instagram posts. . . .

PHOTO: © JOHN SWANNELL

SOPHIE KINSELLA is the author of the bestselling Shopaholic series, as well as the novels *Can You Keep a Secret?*, *The Undomestic Goddess*, *Remember Me?*, *Twenties Girl*, *I've Got Your Number*, *Wedding Night*, and *Finding Audrey*. She lives in London.

sophiekinsella.com
Facebook.com/SophieKinsellaOfficial
Twitter: @KinsellaSophie
Instagram: @sophiekinsellawriter

About the Type

This book was set in Sabon, a typeface designed by the well-known German typographer Jan Tschichold (1902–74). Sabon's design is based upon the original letter forms of sixteenth-century French type designer Claude Garamond and was created specifically to be used for three sources: foundry type for hand composition, Linotype, and Monotype. Tschichold named his typeface for the famous Frankfurt typefounder Jacques Sabon (c. 1520–80).